Touch
the Sky

SCEPTRE

Touch
the Sky

ZITA ADAMSON

SCEPTRE

First published in 1998 by Hodder and Stoughton
A division of Hodder Headline PLC
A Sceptre Book

10 9 8 7 6 5 4 3 2 1

British Library Cataloguing in Publication Data

Adamson, Zita
  Touch the sky
  1. English fiction – 20th century
  I. Title
  823.9'14 [F]

  ISBN 0 340 68943 9

Typeset by Palimpsest Book Production Limited,
Polmont, Stirlingshire
Printed and bound in Great Britain by
Mackays of Chatham PLC

Hodder and Stoughton
A division of Hodder Headline PLC
338 Euston Road
London NW1 3BH

To Mama who told me 'Hitch your wagon to a star'. And Papa who will never give up trying to touch the sky.

I would like to thank Simon for encouraging me and pointing out factual inaccuracies. Also Steve for all his support. And Mike Smith of Bristol Flying Centre for helping me find the 'big picture'.

'We are all in the gutter, but some of us are looking at the stars.'

Oscar Wilde,
Lady Windermere's Fan

'I quicken in the excitement of being
And knowing that I am being –
This pulse of breath and thought,
The world a balloon outside a house
Announcing a party that will not end.'

1

Una sat up and looked around, down to where the green of the grass ran into the gold of the corn and beyond that, the blue of the sky, as if there was nothing else in the world except green and gold and blue. Those three colours.

'You know, I think this is my favourite place in the world. All it needs is a tree to give some shade.'

'And make love under,' added Rob.

'Yes, I suppose so,' she agreed, frowning and then smiling. 'Trust you to think of that.'

He wanted to say that it was difficult not to think of it with her bare arms stretched out, up above her head, her hair spread around her, tangled with grass and seed, a glorious mass of gold and red, her skin warm, and her mouth, that mouth, that mouth he would recognise anywhere, opening now, parting, smiling at him.

'Whose turn is it?' she asked.

'I don't know. Mine, I think. Yes, you've just done "k". Don't you remember. Kipper and kite.'

'Oh yes. Go on then. No, wait a minute. Give me the stop watch. I don't trust you. You probably only start it halfway through. No wonder you got so many "j"s.'

He handed the watch over, protesting his innocence.

'Ready?' she asked.

He nodded.

'Go!'

'Lick, lettuce, lollop, lobster, lawless, licentious, listen, leaden, lid, Lichfield, lottery, lost, lose, losing . . ..'

'They're all the same. Remember, we said only one part of a verb counts,' interrupted Una.

'OK, OK.'

He went on, breathless, waving his hands as if to conjure the words out of the air.

'Listless, libel, liturgy, lobe, litter, lilac, lilt, li . . . li . . . li.'

'Out!' shouted Una triumphantly.

'Lilliputian, liver . . .'

'No, you're out. You hesitated. Nineteen words in ten seconds. So I win. I got twenty-four "k"s.'

He rolled over again, this time on top of her, burrowing his face in her neck.

'It's difficult to concentrate,' he said. 'With you lying there, looking up at me. All I want to do is kiss you.'

'Go on, then,' she said gently.

They kissed and he slid one hand under her dress round to the back where the zip was, pulling it down.

'You're not wearing a bra!'

'I know.'

'Why not?'

'I don't always, you know. There's no law about it,' she said, amused by his surprise.

For some reason, the discovery that her breasts were bare, that they had been all the time, excited him even more and he pulled the dress down further.

'Don't, Rob. Someone might come. They might see us.'

'They won't, they won't,' he said, stopping her mouth with his, pressing her legs open.

But she wriggled away, pulled the dress up.

'I don't want to. Not now. Not here.'

For a moment, he lay sulking. Then she stretched out a hand, stroked his arm.

'I'm sorry. It's just that, well, I'm not like you. I feel exposed in the open.'

He turned away, looked up at the sky.

'Just think,' she said, laying her head on his shoulder. 'In two weeks' time we'll be in Bali, lying on the beach, the waves lapping at our toes.'

'Umm,' he said.

'You don't sound very enthusiastic. You do still want to go, don't you? Rob?'

'Yes, it's just that I worry it will all be a bit aimless, drifting around, moving from one country to the next, going to the same places thousands of other students have been to. I mean, why are we doing it exactly?'

She stared, amazed he could ask such a question.

'Because if we don't do it now, we'll never do it. We won't be able to. We'll have jobs, flats, mortgages maybe, responsibilities, things we won't be able to leave at the drop of a hat.'

'Sometimes you talk as if life ends when you get a job,' said Rob irritably. He still hadn't forgiven her for moving away. 'As if you can never do anything exciting or interesting again. As if overnight you become a different person.'

'Well, don't you?' said Una. 'Look at Dad. Look at your father before he died. Look at everyone we know who has a job. Are they the same people they once were?'

'My father was different. He didn't want to be a builder. He wanted to be at sea. That's where his heart was. But he couldn't because that would have taken him away from Mum.'

'Well, look at my father then. Look at Martin even.'

'All I mean is it doesn't have to be like that. One can do work one enjoys, work that matters, that changes things, that has an effect on other people's lives.'

'Like what?'

'Well, like finding a cure for AIDS.'

'But you're not going to be a scientist. You didn't even pass your physics GCSE.'

'I know. It's just an example.'

He looked down, saw the look in her eyes, the doubt his words had inspired.

'Don't worry. I do still want to go. It's going to be fantastic. A real adventure. Something we'll always remember.'

'You're sure?' she asked, trying to hide the hurt.

'Yes. Come on. We'd better be going. I promised Mum I'd help her with the washing up.'

He stood up, held out his hands.

'Is it one of her cream tea days?'

'Yes, and with this weather she'll be doing a roaring trade. There'll be tea-cups stacked up to the ceiling.'

He zipped up her dress, holding her hair out of the way

so that it wouldn't get caught, then turned her round gently.

'Would you do it in the dark? Would you do it in the dark here?'

'Honestly, Rob. What's got into you today?'

'No, but would you?'

'Maybe. I don't know. Yes. Perhaps. Why?'

'Nothing. Just a thought. I just wondered.'

He took her hand and they walked away together, down to where the green met the gold, and below that, hidden from sight, the city of Bath, bathed in sunshine.

2

'Mind how you go. I tripped over here, earlier.'

'What do you mean, "earlier"?' asked Una. 'You mean you've already been up here?'

'Yes, I brought some blankets before picking you up from the station. I know what you're like.'

He paused and held a branch back so that it didn't hit her in the face.

'What do you mean? What am I like?'

'Spoilt, pampered, a much-loved only daughter brought up from an early age to think she's absolutely wonderful – which you are, of course, you are,' he added as Una swung her bag at him.

They came out from the wood into the field, laughing, stumbling, twigs in their hair and clothes.

'There. Over there,' said Rob, pointing. Una followed his finger and made out a dim shape at the spot where they had lain down that afternoon. As they came closer, she saw that it was two blankets. A large red tartan one and a smaller green and purple striped one which she had seen often on his bed. There were cushions too and at the bottom of the blankets a wooden table, more of a stool really, on which stood two glasses and a vase of flowers – dog rose, daisies, soapwort, maiden pink, and yellow celandine.

'Champagne,' announced Rob, producing a bottle from one of the bags he was carrying. 'Or would Madam prefer something non-alcoholic to start the evening.'

She flung her arms round him and they kissed, still holding their bags, swaying backwards and forwards until finally they overbalanced, and collapsed, giggling, in a heap.

'Oh no, look! You've squashed the bread,' said Rob, pulling a flattened French stick from under Una's leg and tapping her lightly on the head. She grabbed it, tore off a piece, put it in his mouth, then tore off a piece for herself.

'When did you do all this?' she mumbled, her mouth still half-full.

'I told you. Just now. Before I picked you up.'

'It's lovely. Thank you,' said Una, bending down over the vase. 'You've even got water in the flowers.'

'Well, I didn't want them to wilt.'

'Whatever would someone have thought if they'd come across all this after you'd gone?'

'Probably that some strange ceremony was going on. In fact, at this very moment, there's probably someone on the phone to Bath police station. "Yes, officer, and there was a table and two glasses and a vase of flowers. And no one in sight. Not a soul. I waited but no one came."'

He opened the champagne, holding the bottle up high so that the cork flew up towards the sky, landing in the grass behind them with a soft thud.

'Here you are. Here's to us. And the future. And picnics. And making love outside . . .'

'And travel and talk and feeling alive. Seeing things fresh. Not becoming tired and jaded and narrow-minded,' said Una.

'What's this? Why are we drinking out of this?' she added, holding up a small squat bottle with a cherry embossed on the glass.

'It's the bottle,' said Rob. 'The bottle my mother found.'

Rob's father had been a sailor. Once, when he was bored, he had written a message – not a long one, just his name, address, and a cheery 'Let's be hearing from you!' He had put it in a bottle, sealed it, and thrown the bottle into the sea. A year later, exactly a year, Rob's mother had found the bottle washed up on a beach. And written back. And met him. And fallen in love. Una had heard the story many times, and seen the bottle. It stood in pride of place in the centre of the mantelpiece in the sitting room of Rob's house. The message lay inside, the writing still just visible.

'I wanted us to drink from it,' said Rob. 'I thought it would be appropriate, symbolic. You know.'

He sounded embarrassed as if caught doing something childish, something he should have grown out of long ago.

'We'd better not break it,' said Una, turning the bottle round gently in her hands. 'Did you ask your mother if you could borrow it?'

'No, but we won't break it. We'll put it down now. Look. There.'

He placed it next to the vase of flowers.

'I just wanted us to drink from it. That's all.'

Una looked at it, seeing it rise and fall on the waves, bringing two people together, changing their lives. The storybook miracle of it. The casual chance. It had been a nice idea to bring it, she told herself, not convinced. That was their story, she thought, Rob's parents. It was in the past. Over. Their story, hers and Rob's, was now, ahead. It had nothing to do with the sea or messages in bottles.

'Come on,' said Rob, sensing he had made a mistake. 'Let's have something to eat.'

'What have you got?' asked Una, starting to take things out and unwrap them. 'Have you got olives? Did you find any?'

'What haven't we got?' said Rob, his good humour returned. 'We've got olives, pâté, ham, Gruyère, oatcakes, Dolce latte cheese, French bread – if you haven't eaten it all – and for pudding, strawberry tartlets. Here you are.'

He prised the lid off a tub of black olives in oil and garlic and passed it to Una. She took one, rolling it round the inside of her mouth, biting the stone free, then spitting it out, listening for the sound as it fell.

They ate with their backs to the woods, looking out towards the horizon where the dark was rolling up to the light, stifling it, snuffing it out, blue by blue. He cut her thin slices of cheese topped with ham or olives, swilled down with red wine.

'What will you do afterwards? When we've finished travelling? When we come back?' he said finally, breaking a long silence.

'I don't know. I haven't really thought about it. There doesn't seem much point when we're going to be away for so long.

Everything could have changed then. We could be in the middle of another world recession. There could be no jobs to apply for . . .'

'There are hardly any now,' he interrupted.

'All I know,' she continued, 'is what I don't want to do.'

'And what's that?'

'I don't want to be like Dad. I don't want to do a job I don't like. Not ever. Not even for a single day. It's not worth it. Not even as a means to an end.'

'You're so idealistic,' he sighed. 'So starry-eyed.'

Una sat up sharply.

'That's what you always say. But if you don't start out with ideals, you might as well give up now – throw away your rucksack, start studying share prices. I may not get where I want to, I may not find the job I'm looking for but at least I'll have tried. At least I won't be one of those people who reach the age of fifty and start saying, "If only I'd done that, if only I'd taken my courage in my hands and tried, then, when I was young and I could. It's too late now. Too late." At least I won't be saying that.'

Rob sat up too.

'I didn't mean you shouldn't have ideals. That you shouldn't aim high. I just meant that it isn't always easy. That sometimes responsibilities, circumstances, things you have no control over, force you to compromise. My mother, for instance. She never wanted to run a bakery. But when Dad died and left her with me to bring up, she had no choice. It was the only thing she knew. The only thing she had any experience of. She didn't have the luxury of choice. She had to have money coming in. Money to pay bills. She couldn't afford to dilly-dally finding a job she wanted to do.'

Una knew that he was right. Knew that, compared to her, he was experienced, worldly-wise, pragmatic. But then he had had to be. His father had died of asbestosis when he was twelve, leaving his mother to work a fourteen-hour shift. He had had to make his own meals, wash his own clothes, write his own sick notes even. She knew all this and the knowledge irritated her. It wasn't her fault her father worked in a bank. That they lived in a nice house. Had no money problems.

Were tame and middle-class. One couldn't buy experience in a shop.

'It was supposed to be a compliment,' said Rob soothingly. 'It's one of the things I like best about you. That you're so unspoilt, so untouched. You don't even acknowledge the possibility of failure.'

'Just now you said I was spoilt,' said Una, still ruffled, wary of being patronised.

'You are and you aren't. You're like spilt oil. You look different in different lights. One can't get a hold of you.'

She leant back again against the cushions, mollified. It pleased her to know he thought her fluid, changeable, her opinions unfixed by habit or prejudice. That was one of the things she feared most – becoming set, set in her ways and thoughts, reacting automatically.

'How about you?' she asked after a while. 'Have you heard from the paper? The one that was advertising for a trainee reporter? The *Post*, wasn't it?'

'No, not even a letter saying "thanks but no thanks". There's been nothing.'

They were silent again.

'You're shivering. Here. Take this.'

He handed her a blanket, a red one, and wrapped it round her shoulders. Then he draped another blanket over her legs.

'A firefly. Look! A firefly.'

He stared but could see nothing.

'No,' he said, shaking his head. 'There are no fireflies in England. Not at this time of year, anyhow. Not in July. Later maybe. In August.'

'It was,' she insisted. 'It was. Honestly. You can't see it because you don't think you will. Close your eyes and tell yourself that when you open them you will see one. Then you will.'

He closed his eyes obediently, disbelieving. But she was right. When he opened them, there it was. And then another and another and another. The whole air was dancing with flame, flickering with tiny yellow sparks. It was like a private fireworks display. A celebration. A party just for them.

I could die now, thought Una, looking up at the stars, murmuring their names. I could die now and be happy. As she gazed heavenwards, it seemed to her that the sky was her future, rich, infinite, glittering with opportunity. She could do anything. Be anyone. She was adazzle with possibility. All she had to do was reach out and touch the sky.

3

'There. There's a car. Maybe that's her now.'

Philip jumped up from the edge of the sofa and ran to the window.

'No. It's going on. It's not stopping.'

He walked back slowly and sat down, this time on a chair.

'Tell me again. What did she say exactly?'

Helen hid her face in her hands.

'I don't know. She said they were going on a picnic . . .'

'In the dark?'

'Yes. Why not?' She lifted her face defiantly. 'They're young, they're in love. They probably thought it would be romantic.'

'And? What else did she say? About getting back? Didn't you ask her?'

'I don't know. I've told you. I think she said Rob would drive her back. That he was going to borrow his mother's car. Look, there's no point going over and over it. She knows she's not to walk back late on her own. She's probably just . . . well . . . they're probably just having a good time.'

'Maybe I should ring his mother. Maybe they've gone back there.'

He jumped up again and began to walk towards the hall.

'You can't. Philip, you can't! It's one o'clock in the morning. Besides, she won't hear it. You know how deaf she is.'

He turned and walked to the window again then came and sat next to her on the sofa, drumming his fingers on the arm rest.

Suddenly, they both heard a noise, the sound of a key turning in the back door.

They leapt up and rushed into the kitchen.

'Where's Rob? Where's his car?' said Philip, opening the door wide.

'Darling, are you OK? Are you all right? We've been so worried.'

Una blinked, clearly surprised.

'Yes, of course. I'm fine. The car broke down. That's why I'm so late. We had to walk to the station. I was only just in time to catch the last train back.'

'Where's the taxi then? The taxi you caught from the station?'

'I decided to walk instead,' said Una, taking a mug down and filling it with cold water at the sink, turning her back to them. 'It's such a lovely night. So clear. I thought it would be nice to walk home under the stars. I would have been back earlier only I met this man who thought he knew me. A tramp. Quite old. He called me Marjorie and said he hadn't meant to let the plants die. He kept going on and on about them. How he'd been sick. How they'd never have died if it hadn't been so hot. It was the heat that had killed them, he said. They'd have been OK if it hadn't been so hot. I handed him over to a policeman in the end.'

Helen glanced nervously at Philip.

'What do you mean "you walked"!' he shouted, thumping the kitchen table with his fist. 'We've told you and told you and told you. You must never walk home alone in the dark.'

Una turned round, startled.

'Yes, I know but . . .'

'But nothing! We've told you. Haven't we told you? And you promised. You said you wouldn't. There are madmen out there. Addicts, rapists, lunatics of every sort. This is a city, a big city. It's not a village.'

He was trembling, Una saw, pacing the room like a caged animal. She glanced inquiringly at her mother who frowned and shook her head slightly.

'You could have been killed, stabbed. Somebody could have come after you in the dark. Followed you down a road. Somebody you'd never met before or only met once, somebody . . .'

'She's OK,' interrupted Helen, taking hold of him by the arm, preventing him moving. 'Nothing's happened. She's OK. Come on, now. She's OK.'

She raised her eyebrows at Una, jerking her head towards the door as if to signal that she should leave them alone.

'I'm sorry, Dad. I won't do it again. I didn't mean to upset you,' said Una.

Then, after another nod from Helen, she left the room.

'Come on. Shall I make you a drink? Something hot. A cup of hot chocolate perhaps.'

He allowed her to lead him to the kitchen table, sit him down, make him a drink, and afterwards, when he had drunk it, lead him upstairs to their room. The curtains were undrawn and he moved to the window and looked up at the sky. Una was right, he thought. It was a lovely night.

But it had been a lovely night then. He had been standing outside, looking at the stars just as he was doing now, the air sweet and heavy with the scent of roses. They had walked past. The girl first. Then, some way behind, the man. He had thought they were lovers, that they had had a tiff, and had felt jealous. That was why he had stared after them. It would be nice to have someone to have a tiff with, he had thought. Then the man had started to run, the girl running too, one shoe coming off, flying up into the air, like Cinderella. The man had grabbed her, pulled her down and she had screamed. He had been paralysed for a moment. He remembered that. Standing there, rooted to the spot, thinking 'This isn't happening, it can't be happening.' Then he too had started to run. There had been a fight, the blade of a knife. It had gone through the girl's dress, hit something, a bone, her hip maybe, slid sideways. They had wrestled for control, rolling away from the girl onto the road. Then they had heard voices, footsteps running. He had edged away. Someone was coming, coming to help. They would take him then, overpower him, together they would do it. He would wait until then. But the man, as if reading his thoughts, had started to shout.

'She walked out. She just went. She didn't even say she was going. She shouldn't have done that. She shouldn't have done it.'

He had stared, puzzled, and in that instant, the man had plunged, the knife going in deep, turning like a corkscrew. He had screamed, pressing both hands against the rip, his knees drawn up tight, hearing the man run off down the road.

Then he had heard a different voice, another man's voice, and felt someone touch him on the arm.

'Are you OK? Can you hear me?'

It had felt as if it were on fire. As if it were red and raw, scraped out, a jellied mess.

He had heard his own voice then. Had known it was his voice but had not understood the words.

'What's he saying?' asked a woman's voice.

'I don't know. Sounds like Latin. Something about the stars.'

Then the light had gone out and the dark had come in.

Remembering this, the dark especially, the sense of sinking, of being swallowed up by monstrous jaws, he drew the curtains and turned round to face the room. Helen sat on the bed, rubbing cream into her hands.

'Don't you think we should tell them, Philip?' she said after a long silence. 'Don't you think they should know. I don't want them to find out. For someone else to tell them.'

'How could they find out?' he said, moving to her dressing table, picking up a hairbrush. 'Everyone else who knows is either dead or not speaking to us. There's only your sister now. How could they find out?'

'I don't know. I just worry that they might. Besides, I think we should tell them. That they ought to know. Especially Martin. It's not right to let him go on thinking that . . .'

Philip put the brush down suddenly.

'Helen?'

'What?'

'Hello.'

'Hello,' she said softly.

He came over and put an arm round her.

'I'm sorry about just now. About shouting like that. It just brought it all back. I saw it happening as if it were yesterday. Him grabbing you by the arm and you screaming – screaming and screaming and screaming . . .'

'I know. I know. It's OK. I know.'

He let her take him in her arms and rock him, stroking his hair as if he were a child. But he thought: 'You don't know. You can't know. No one can.' And he felt in the dark for the hole where his eye had been.

4

Una walked round the gallery once more. No, Rob wasn't there. He obviously hadn't arrived yet. She wondered again why he had asked her to meet him at an exhibition of black and white photographs of – she looked more closely at one of the pictures hanging on the wall – what looked like rock formations.

Maybe he was going to . . . no, why here, in a photographic gallery? He would have chosen somewhere more romantic. And yet it was important, whatever it was he wanted to tell her. She knew that. She had heard it in the urgency of his voice on the phone.

She glanced at her watch, noticing irritably that he was late. Her feet had swollen in the heat and her sandals were pinching now, threatening blisters. Also, her left buttock hurt where she had had an injection that morning for tetanus. She felt the spot covertly now as she walked around looking at the pictures – the strange lunar landscapes, the plants with bulbous, prehensile tendrils, the streets ripped in two by an earthquake. The other visitors were more interesting, she thought. The young mother with dyed red hair and a child who kept running off to slide on the floor. Two old ladies, sisters maybe, with white hair in buns, and a Pekingese in a basket which they kept passing between them like a shared treat. A tall balding man with freckles, sunburnt where his hair failed to cover his scalp.

The door opened and Rob came in. He was wearing a faded turquoise T-shirt and green shorts with paint stains. His hair, just washed, flopped over his face. He looked happy, she saw, happy but nervous at the same time.

They kissed, but quickly, perfunctorily. She wanted to know

what he had to say, why it could not wait until the evening when they had been going to meet anyway.

'The car's still in the garage. Sorry. The train was late. I ran all the way from the station.'

They sat down on some black and chrome chairs, Una leaning to the right so that she would not put weight on her left buttock.

'Well?'

He ran his fingers through his hair, smiled, looked away.

'What it is, what it is . . .'

She knew then, knew as soon as he looked away, that he was not coming, that they would not be lying on a beach in Bali together in a week's time. All that remained was the reason, the excuse.

'Yes?' she said, her voice hard.

'I got a phone call on Monday from the editor of the *Post*. The *Evening Post*.'

'Yes?'

She would not help him. She would not make it easy. He could do his own dirty work. Break the news himself.

'He asked me to go for an interview yesterday. They weren't going to take on a trainee, he said, even though they'd advertised, but then they changed their minds, decided they would after all . . .'

He paused, glanced at her, then looked away again quickly.

'So I went for the interview and today, this morning . . .' he took a deep breath, 'he phoned me up and offered me the job.'

'And what did you say?'

He looked up, met her eyes, looked away again.

'Una, I couldn't . . .'

'What did you say?'

'I said yes.'

She saw her rucksack standing in her room, the passport and tickets laid out on her desk, the lists she had made of places to visit, the red hard-backed notebook she had bought to use as a travel diary.

He turned to face her and this time it was she who looked away.

'I couldn't say no, Una. Surely you understand. It's what I want to do. I might not get another chance like this. I asked if I could put the offer on hold, if I could start in two or three months' time, but he said no. He said they needed to send me on a course and that the course started in two weeks' time. He said if I didn't want to take it, they would offer it to someone else. So I had to say yes. I had to.'

He paused, as if to allow her to make some conciliatory gesture, some remark suggesting forgiveness. When she said nothing, he went on.

'I'm sorry. I really am. I didn't want it to happen like this. I'll pay you back. For the ticket. The money you spent on visas and things.'

'I don't want your money.'

She spoke slowly, enunciating each word, her lips taut.

'And anyhow, what makes you think that just because you're not going, I'm not going either?'

He looked down.

'And don't think I don't know why you asked me to come here. You were worried I'd make a scene, weren't you? You thought I wouldn't be able to here because I'd feel too embarrassed. Well, I'm not. Do you hear?'

Rob blushed.

'You never really wanted to go anyway, whatever you say,' she went on. 'Why else did you apply for the job when we already had the tickets and everything?'

'That's not true. I did want to go. I did. I just . . .'

'I don't care. I don't want to know. You're not going. That's all that matters.'

She rose, glared at the attendant and stalked towards the door. Rob jumped up.

'Una . . . Una . . . come back . . . don't . . .'

But she was already gone, swallowed up by a party of Japanese tourists, leaving Rob standing outside on the pavement feeling foolish and cowardly.

He would go after her, he thought. Later. When she had cooled down a bit. He would catch a train into Bristol. Go round to her house. She would come round. He knew she would.

5

Una rolled out another red snake, added eyes and a tongue, and added it to those she had already made. Maybe she could work with children, she thought. She wouldn't be in an office and it would be fulfilling to nurture young minds, to watch them develop emotionally and intellectually. Yes, it was worth considering. She liked playing with Matty. And she was quite good at it. Even Teresa said so.

'So what will you do?' asked Teresa, swiftly removing a lump of Plasticine from the onion she had just chopped and handing Matty a wooden spoon in place of the sharp knife she had been about to grab. 'What will you do now?'

'I don't know,' said Una, rolling out yellow eggs for a bird's nest. 'I did think about going on my own but I decided not to.'

'Isn't there a friend you could ask? Sinead, for instance. Wouldn't she be interested?'

'She hasn't got any money. Besides, that's not the point. It's not that I don't want to go on my own. I don't want to go at all. All the magic's gone out of it. I couldn't go now. Not with anyone. Not even if Rob turned round and said it had all been a mistake, he didn't want the job at the paper after all. I've no longer got the heart for it.'

Teresa nodded sympathetically.

'So you're going to look for a job then?'

'Yes. Only goodness knows what. Every time I see Dad he asks if I've been to the job centre as if it's a simple matter of just turning up and saying, "Here I am." I keep telling him that I can't look for a job until I know what I'm looking for, what sort of thing I want to do. But he doesn't seem to understand. I don't think he cares what I do as long as I'm doing something, as long as I'm not on the dole. That's all he's bothered about – having a daughter on the dole.'

Teresa smiled. She got on well with her father-in-law, a cause of some irritation to Martin, who had about as many points of reference to his father as a cactus to a jelly.

'Have you seen Rob since he told you?' she asked, pouring out Ribena with one hand while stirring the Bolognese sauce with the other.

'No. He came round once in the middle of the day when Mum and Dad were out. I pretended I wasn't there.'

'Una! You can't do that.'

'Why not? I don't want to speak to him.'

Matty grabbed the beaker of Ribena, spilling half of it down her dress.

'But you still like him, don't you? You get on so well. It would be silly to fall out over something like this.'

'What do you mean "something like this"? We're taking a year off to travel. We've bought the tickets, had the injections, got the Visas, and then, suddenly, a week before we're due to leave, he turns round and says he's not going, that he's found a job.'

'I'm not condoning what's he done. Or the way he did it or how he told you or anything. But you know how much he wanted to get into journalism. And it's a good paper. Well, an evening paper, at least. He must have been up against hundreds of other candidates. They must have really liked him.'

'But that still doesn't make it right. He could have waited. The world of journalism isn't going to disappear in a year.'

'I'm not saying it makes it right. I'm just saying that one can see his point of view. That he might never get another opportunity like this. It's very competitive, you know, journalism. Martin teaches one of the media courses at college – goodness knows why, he knows nothing about it – anyhow, he has students ringing him up at home trying to get on the course. It's always over-subscribed.'

Matty, frustrated by the lack of attention she was receiving, began to bang the table with her wooden spoon. Una quickly presented her with the completed bird's nest, relieved at the opportunity not to answer Teresa. She would make it up with

Rob. Of course she would. Later. But in the meantime, she was rather enjoying playing the hurt, aggrieved role. There was no need to hurry.

'There. I can leave it to simmer now,' said Teresa, putting the lid on the saucepan and turning the heat low. She scooped Matty up from the floor where she was sticking Plasticine on the chair legs and lifted her high above her shoulders.

'Who's my beautiful girl?'

'Me!' said Una quickly, teasing.

'No, me!' said Matty, alarmed by the prospect of a rival.

Teresa smiled.

'Who's my laughing girl?'

'Me!' said Matty, quicker this time, looking anxiously at Una.

'Who's my singing, dancing, jumping girl?'

'Me!' said Matty, smiling now.

'Who's my sticky, dirty, tired, snake-making girl?'

'Me! But I'm not tired.'

Una and Teresa both laughed and Matty burst into tears. Una watched as Teresa coaxed back a smile then looked around for her handbag, finding it finally in Matty's toy pram, covered with a blanket. As she went out to buy a bottle of wine, she heard Matty crying again and Teresa, her patience finally snapped, shouting.

Martin was there when she got back, crouched on the floor, making a house out of Duplo.

'Oh good, you've got one,' he said, seeing the bottle of wine. 'I was just about to go out myself.'

He put the last brick in the roof and leant back on his knees.

'Look, there's a sweet inside. See.'

He lifted the house up so that she could see through the windows.

'I like to surprise her,' he said, taking the bottle of wine and unwrapping it.

Teresa came in.

'She'd like you to read her a story,' she said to Una, adding that if Martin cleared away the toys and laid the table, she would put on the water for the spaghetti.

Una read Matty four stories, two more than she had intended. When she came down, Martin was on the phone.

'Tell him if he doesn't play, the game's off. I'm not running round like a headless chicken trying to find someone to take his place,' she overheard him say. The toys, she saw, were untouched.

'She wants a cuddle and kiss from you both,' she said, going into the kitchen where Teresa was slapping cutlery on the table. 'Shall I pour out the wine?'

'Yes. Do. Only not much for me. There are some serviettes in there if you can find them. Underneath the dusters, I think,' said Teresa, pointing at a drawer before going upstairs.

The phone rang again just as they were about to sit down to eat.

'Tell them to ring back later,' shouted Teresa as Martin went to answer it.

She turned to Una.

'Honestly, this is what always happens. I wish he wouldn't give students his home number.'

'Una, it's for you,' said Martin, coming back into the room. 'It's Rob. He wants to talk to you.'

'Well, I don't want to talk to him. I've got nothing to say. Tell him that.'

'Can't you tell him yourself?'

'No. I didn't ask him to ring up,' said Una, sitting down firmly and unfolding her serviette.

They talked of Matty at supper, of the funny things she had said and done that day. Also, of Una and Martin's parents.

'How's Dad?' asked Martin. 'Still complaining about work?'

'Yes, Mum says it's really getting to him at the moment. Apparently the new man above him is making his life very difficult . . .'

'Honestly. Dad and the bank,' interrupted Martin. 'He complains about it but he'd be lost without it. He wouldn't know what to do.'

'Well, neither would most of us. We all want to matter, to feel needed,' said Teresa.

Martin picked up the bottle of wine, waving it in their direction.

'More wine?' he said. Una and Teresa both shook their heads, then watched as he refilled his own glass to overflowing.

Una woke up in the night feeling thirsty and went downstairs to fetch a glass of water. She was surprised to see a light on in the kitchen and the sound of voices.

'Oh, it's you. What on earth are you doing?'

Teresa was sitting at the kitchen table, papers spread out before her, the radio turned on low.

'Working. I've got a deadline to meet tomorrow. A new leaflet for the leisure department.'

Teresa was a freelance graphic artist.

'But it's one in the morning.'

'I know but I didn't manage to finish it earlier.'

'But Matty will be up again in about five hours.'

Teresa smiled.

'It's OK. I'll collapse later when she has a nap. I'm used to it. I often work at this time. Besides, some of the best World Service programmes are on now. You hear all sorts of things. I've just been learning about quartz crystals – why they help watches to stay accurate.'

Una shook her head disbelievingly. Upstairs, on her way back to her room, she paused at Matty's door then went in. Matty was lying like flung dough, her arms outstretched, the covers falling off, her favourite cuddly squashed under one arm. Una listened to her breathing, resisting the temptation to bend down and kiss her.

Yes, she thought. She would enjoy working with children. She would find out about courses tomorrow. Ask what qualifications she needed. Her father would be pleased.

6

Philip hung his jacket on the wooden hanger provided. Upstairs, on the fourth floor, in the executive suite, there were wardrobes. Also fridges, drinks cabinets, leather sofas, and glass coffee tables that had once been the height of fashion. The rooms were larger too. Not just the offices but the lavatories too. This had always amused Philip. As if directors needed more room to shit, he thought.

As usual it was stuffy and as usual Philip went to the window and opened it. At least the windows opened, he reflected. Downstairs, on the first and second floors, where the junior and middle managers worked, one was at the mercy of the air conditioning system which invariably meant shirtsleeves, even when there was frost outside.

A wasp flew in and, instinctively, he felt for his anti-histamine tablets. He had five minutes to live after being stung by a wasp or bee, according to his doctor. The last time he had fainted, sitting on a park bench near a bin where a child had discarded a half-eaten iced bun, people had thought he was a tramp who had fallen asleep. If it hadn't been for a colleague, looking for somewhere to eat his lunchtime sandwiches, he would have died. As it was, they had had to airlift him to hospital.

The door connecting his office to that of his secretary opened and Joanne came in with the post.

'Mark phoned,' she said, dumping the letters on his desk and waving the wasp out of the window. Mark was his new boss, the fourth he had had in three years. It was rumoured he had ordered a new wooden coffee table to replace the glass one but Philip did not know if this was true. So far, their meetings had taken place either in Philip's office or on more neutral ground, in a meeting room.

'Did you see the note? He said it was urgent.'

She pointed at a piece of yellow paper stuck to the front of his computer.

'Yes. I mean "No". I've only just got in. There was an accident. A blow-out on a roundabout.'

'He said he'd ring you back. He said not to ring him unless you got in before nine because he'd have someone with him.'

Philip wondered if the 'someone' was an applicant for the new post they had been advertising, a post which he had been assured would not, in any way, change or diminish his own responsibilities.

'Would you like a drink? I've just put the kettle on.'

'Yes. A tea would be nice.'

Alone again, Philip stayed by the window, looking out at the sky. An aeroplane passed overhead. It was a light aircraft, he saw. Possibly a private plane. It was too high up to recognise even if he had been able to, which maybe he wouldn't, not now, after so long.

He had not flown for years. In the summer, when they had gone to France on holiday, they had taken the ferry. Once, they had driven to Spain, even though it had cost twice as much in petrol as it would have done in air fares. The children thought he was scared, a belief he had encouraged.

He had flown again three years ago when he and Helen had gone on holiday alone for the first time since having the children. It had been a jumbo jet with two aisles, much larger than anything he had ever flown, and he had been able to persuade himself that he was on a boat or a train, had sat in the middle as far away from the windows as possible.

He looked down, down at the ground where the tourists were strolling along the waterfront, admiring the transformation of what had, until five years ago, been an industrial wasteland, the docks all silted up, choked with rubbish and weeds. And as he looked, it occurred to him to walk out as it had occurred to him so many times before. He would put on his jacket, pick up his briefcase and walk outside to the lift. Press the button, go down to the ground floor, get out, and leave the building.

Leave it for ever, without explaining, without a party, without the humiliation of listening to a speech in which a colleague struggled to find something of interest in a career uniformly dull and predictable.

They had said in his appraisal, in the report they had sent him last week, that he lacked ambition, that he was not sufficiently determined. He had smiled bitterly when he had read this. It had taken him three years to find a job, three years to find an employer willing to take on a one-eyed man. And that had just been the start. There had been years of fighting after that, years of struggling to prove that the accident had not left him deficient in his mind as well as his sight. Yet they said he lacked determination, had suggested that this was a weakness, that perhaps he could take action to improve it, could borrow a video from the company learning centre. He had ripped the report into small pieces and thrown them out of the window. It had been a windy day and the paper, instead of falling, had blown up instead, some of it blowing back into the building through the windows open on the fourth floor, one of them belonging to Philip's boss, Mark. He had picked up the paper, two or three pieces, had recognised his signature on one, and wondered how it had come to be blowing around in the wind. Philip, had he known this, had he seen the puzzled expression on his boss' face, would have been even more comforted.

Joanne came in with his cup of tea and asked what he would like for lunch. This was another benefit enjoyed by senior management. They did not have to queue in the canteen. Their secretaries did it for them. Philip had refused to take advantage of this perk at first but had been told by the managing director that it would be advisable for him to do so. 'You'll make it difficult for everyone else if you don't,' he had said.

Philip walked over to the noticeboard where the canteen menu was pinned.

'Beef salad, I think, with English mustard,' he said. 'And a piece of fruit. A pear, if they have any. Otherwise, an apple.'

The phone rang. It was Mark. Joanne left, after doffing an imaginary cap with exaggerated deference in the direction of the receiver.

'Have you seen *The Times*?' Mark asked accusingly.

'No. Not yet.'

'They've run a story on the branch closures. I don't know where they got their information from. It's totally wrong. Completely unbalanced. They say we're going to make three thousand staff redundant.'

Philip hesitated.

'Well, we are, aren't we?' he said finally.

'Well yes, but they don't say anything about the new jobs we're creating. Telephone banking, for instance, they don't even mention that.'

Philip wondered whether to point out that the pilot telephone banking project employed only twenty-five people but decided not to.

'You'll see what I mean when you read it. Have you got today's cuttings?'

Philip drew the pile of letters brought in by Joanne towards him.

'Yes, yes, they're right in front of me. I just haven't had a chance to . . .'

'I want you to phone the editor. We can't take this sort of thing lying down. Ask if we can have a correction. Point out how inaccurate the article is. That kind of thing. Let me know how you go on.'

Philip wondered whether to point out that it was not in the bank's best interests to go running to editors every time there was negative media coverage of its activities, that a correction would probably draw far more attention to the proposed redundancies and branch closures than the original story had and that a better plan might be to exert a bit of pressure on the journalist who had written the story and persuade him or her to write a new, different story about the pilot telephone banking project. Again, he decided not to, which was just as well because Mark had already put the phone down.

It had been better when he had been a branch manager, he thought ruefully, replacing his own receiver and starting to read his post. At least he had had some degree of autonomy then. Too much, according to his superiors, especially after the marble incident.

A man had approached him for a loan to start up his own

business as a monumental mason. He was a pleasant man – quiet, thoughtful, intelligent. Philip had asked for a business plan and the man had given him one. He had done the sums, worked everything out. He had more than fifteen years' experience in the masonry trade. He was of good character. And so Philip had met his request, virtually without a second thought, confident that the venture would succeed.

A week after the loan came through, the man wrote out an order for white marble. He made a mistake in the order, ordering thirty times as much as he wanted. He realised his mistake when the marble arrived but thought nothing of it. He would send it back, he thought. The day after the marble arrived, his mother died. And in the ten days that elapsed while he saw to the funeral arrangements, the market for marble crashed. The company which had sold him the marble refused to buy it back, at least at the same price. He was ruined. And the bill went to the bank.

Philip went to visit the man once, after he had been pulled back to head office. He found him in his back garden, sitting on the white marble. It was piled six foot high on either side of a narrow flowerbed planted with marigolds. He remembered that, the yellow of the flowers running through the white of the marble like a crack, a cheerful fault line.

They had drunk a cup of tea sitting on the marble side by side, looking down on the neighbouring gardens. The man had been philosophical.

'At least I won't have to fork out for a headstone,' he said. 'That's one thing.'

Philip smiled as he remembered this, then picked up the phone. He would have to do as Mark wanted, even though it meant acting against his better judgement.

As expected, the editor declined to speak to him in person but suggested, through his secretary, that he should complain in writing to the person responsible for dealing with complaints. Philip did so and asked Joanne to copy the letter to Mark. At eleven he attended a meeting on a new savings product. At one, he ate lunch at his desk, reading a briefing paper at the same time. Afterwards, he dictated letters to Joanne, chatted briefly about her forthcoming holiday in Crete and attended another meeting.

At six, he tidied his desk, clicked his briefcase shut and checked his reflection in the small mirror on the back of the door.

'Sheep,' he muttered crossly, unlocking the top right-hand drawer of his desk and removing a hardbound book. He crossed another day off on the calendar he had made. There were now one thousand and ninety-five days left until he retired, until he could be a tiger again, if there was any tiger still in him, which he doubted sometimes, increasingly often.

He found himself saying things he did not mean. That morning, for instance. Why had he asked Una again about what she was going to do? As if there was a hurry? As if he was anxious to see her earning money immediately? He had said it because it was the sort of thing a senior bank manager ought to say, the sort of thing his father would have said. This distressed him. The feeling that the noose of his genetic inheritance was tightening daily round his neck. He thought he was still acting, that he was playing a part, that the other 'him', the real 'him' was inside, waiting to come out. Maybe he had become the part, he thought, unlocking the door to his company car. Maybe, after thirty years, he now was a bank manager. Even if he didn't play golf.

7 ∫

Rob pushed his bike slowly up the hill. When he had enough money, he would buy a proper bike, a bike with gears, he told himself. He reached the brow of the hill and paused to catch his breath, delighted as always with the view that opened before him – the road dipping sharply and then rising equally sharply, terraced painted houses tottering on each side, their bright red roofs colliding with the sky. Four girls walked by – giggling, lipsticked, expectant. Further on, he passed a group of boys, strutting, hands in pockets, necks stuck out. He turned and watched as the boys caught up with the girls – jostling, clumsy, laughing loudly to cover their uncertainty. The girls – now acting cool and assured – ignored them. Rob smiled but more in sympathy than in mockery. He had been like the boys. He still was sometimes.

It was the third time he had been to see Una. The first time, Una had been in but had refused to come to the door. The second time, the house had been empty. This was the last time he would be able to come – he was off to Hastings the next day to start his six-month course in journalism – and he was determined to see her.

He checked to see that the flowers – the roses he had picked from the front garden – were not getting crushed. They were yellow rather than red. There had been red roses but he had decided against them. Too obvious, he had thought. Besides, yellow was Una's colour. Cheerful, sunny, trusting. How she was.

He remounted his bike and began to pedal, slowly at first then faster as he gathered speed and confidence. He would invite her down the following weekend, take her out for a meal, show her the sights – the pier, the Old Town, the spot where the Battle of Hastings was supposed to have been fought. Later, on another weekend perhaps, they could catch the train to Brighton, go to a gig, find a good pub, eat fish and chips on the beach, barefoot, salt in their hair and clothes. By the time he reached her house, he had almost forgotten that they were not speaking, that she had refused to talk to him on the twelve, or perhaps more, occasions when he had phoned.

He propped his bike against the hedge surrounding the back garden and pushed the gate open, briskly so that it did not squeak. There were no lights on but that didn't mean anything. It was only half past nine, still light enough to see. He walked up to the back door then stopped. He would walk round to the front first. See if there were any lights on there in case she turned them off when she heard the doorbell. No, there were none there either. No sign of activity, no flicker from the television screen. Still, she might be listening to music. She might be having a bath. He walked round to the back again. Listened. No, nothing. He rang the bell. Waited. Rang it again. Rang it a third time, this time for much longer. Still nothing. He went round to the front. Rang the doorbell there. No, not a sound. They were all out. Still, he reassured himself, they would come back. They had to come back unless they had gone away for the weekend. No, Una wouldn't have done that. She knew he would come.

He laid his bike down flat behind a flower bed where it could not easily be seen. He put the roses on the ground too, feeling it warm against his hand with the last of the sun. Then he checked to see that the other presents – an engraved locket with a lock of his hair, a joke because she was always badgering him to have it cut; the *Faber Book of Love Poems*; two Belgian chocolates, one each; and two bottles of Somerset beer, also one each – were still in his rucksack. Finally, satisfied all was in order, he sat down and closed his eyes.

It was a beautiful evening, still, calm, and surprisingly warm considering that it was now – he opened his eyes and glanced at his watch – almost ten o'clock. There was a blackbird singing close by or possibly a thrush – he could not tell one from the other – and behind him, in the hedge, rustling, twittering, hopping from one branch to another, other birds putting themselves to bed. In the distance, there was the noise of a lawnmower, the cries of children playing, the laughter of friends round a barbecue – all the usual sounds of an affluent suburb on a summer evening.

He closed his eyes again and lay down on the grass, thinking of Una. He knew she would forgive him. She understood. She knew how important it was to him, how much he wanted to be a journalist. She knew him.

Elsewhere, on the other side of the city, Una's parents finished their interval drinks and went back to listen to the second half of the concert Philip's bank was sponsoring as part of its corporate hospitality programme. At about the same time, just after her parents had taken their seats and made polite small talk with their neighbours, the finance director of a sausage factory on one side, the managing partner of a local law firm on the other, Una tried to jump on to a bus that was already moving, missed, and fell. A swimming teacher on her way home from an evening coaching session drove her to the nearest hospital where, after a wait of more than two hours, the doctor on duty in casualty pronounced her ankle sprained but otherwise undamaged and asked the nurse to order her a taxi.

The wail of a police siren woke Rob. He stumbled to his feet, unsure where he was, his body hunched in self-defence. Then he remembered. He glanced at his watch. Half past twelve. Perhaps it was the chill of the night or the dull ache in his left leg where he had been lying awkwardly but something in him hardened. He wrenched off the bottle tops and poured the beer over the lawn. She knew I'd come, he thought. If she'd wanted to see me, she'd have been here. And he ground the roses into the grass with the heel of his shoe.

He rode back to the train station with no lights on, swaying dangerously, hurling the chocolates and poetry into a skip at the side of the road.

Ten minutes later, Una pressed the 'Play' button again on the answerphone in case she'd made a mistake the first time. No. There was just one message, from one of her mother's friends on the Talking Newspaper committee. She hobbled to the front door in case there was a letter on the mat. No, just a circular from a local DIY superstore offering cut-price patio furniture.

She walked back, puzzled. She'd stayed in all day in case he came, had not even left the house to eat her lunch outside in the garden. Finally, at seven o'clock, she'd gone to see her friend Sinead, but only because she'd sounded so depressed on the phone the night before, only for half an hour or at least it would have been half an hour if she hadn't fallen, if she hadn't miscalculated the speed at which the bus was moving.

Maybe he would come tomorrow. Maybe his course didn't start yet. Maybe she'd misunderstood. She knew he would come, that he would know she wanted to make up. He understood her. He knew her.

8

Una's father found the beer bottles and crushed roses the following morning. He picked them up triumphantly. He knew it. He'd said so to Helen only last night. The neighbourhood was going down.

Inside, Helen sat at the kitchen table studying a brochure advertising evening classes at the local college. Weaving maybe, she thought. She'd always fancied making a rug. No, maybe something a bit more practical. Computer skills perhaps. An introduction to word processing. No, there was no point. She didn't use a computer at work and she didn't want to change her job; she enjoyed it too much. She had joined the estate agent's where she worked five years ago as a maternity-leave replacement and remained there after the woman on leave failed to return. She now worked three afternoons a week, mainly showing round prospective buyers.

She poured herself another cup of tea and flicked through the brochure again. German, maybe. No, she'd never been much good at German at school. Besides, she didn't particularly want to go to Germany. Italian then. Yes, that was a possibility. She loved Italy. She'd gone to Rome once and had always wanted to return.

The door opened and Una came in, frowsy with sleep.

'What's the matter with your leg? Why are you limping like that?'

'I've sprained my ankle,' said Una, hobbling to the fridge and filling a glass with orange juice.

'When? How? Why didn't you say?'

'Last night. Jumping on to a bus and missing. You weren't

here,' said Una, answering each question in turn with exaggerated care. Why did parents always ask so many questions? It started when one went to school and never stopped. Did you have a nice day? What did you do? Did you paint a picture? Did you eat all your lunch? Who did you play with at breaktime? Sometimes she had felt like hanging a little notice round her neck. 'No, I didn't have a nice day. Sophie wouldn't sit next to me and said I wasn't her friend any more and Jack spilt water all over my painting and ruined it. So now you know. OK?'

Helen opened her mouth to ask another question but then shut it. She could see that Una was feeling uncommunicative.

'Has Rob phoned?'

'No. Not today. Not so far as I'm aware. I'll say you're not in, shall I, if he does phone, like last time?'

'What do you mean "last time"? When did he phone? Why didn't you tell me?'

'But I did. You said to say you weren't in. Don't you remember? It was on Friday, no, Thursday night.'

'He hasn't phoned since then?'

'No, darling. I'd have said.'

'Well, if he does phone, I'm in now. I mean, I do want to speak to him.'

'Fine. Fine,' said Helen, puzzled, examining her daughter covertly. First, she didn't want to speak to him. Now she did.

'Would you like some breakfast? I can do you some bacon.'

'No thanks. I'm not very hungry.'

'A poached egg perhaps.'

'I'm not hungry.'

She had spoken more aggressively than she had intended, startling even herself.

Helen picked up the brochure again. Honestly, sometimes! She could be so prickly, so irritable.

'I'd love a cup of tea,' Una said, gently this time, as if conferring a favour. 'Only not too strong. Not like Dad makes it.'

Helen stood up and filled the kettle at the sink.

'Those are for you,' she said, pointing at a pile of ironed clothes on top of the washing machine. 'Take them upstairs with you when you go, will you?'

Una nodded, not looking.

'What's this?' she asked, holding up the brochure Helen had been reading.

'It's from Brunel College. I'm going to do an evening class in Italian.'

'Why? What for?'

'No reason,' said Helen, amused by the suspicion in her daughter's voice. 'I just felt like doing something this winter instead of staying in all the time. Besides, we might go there on holiday again. It would be nice to be able to make myself understood, to know what I was ordering in restaurants.'

Una grunted something unintelligible.

The back door opened suddenly and Philip came in.

'Look!' he said, dumping the beer bottles on the table. 'Look what I found outside. The cheek of it.'

Una picked up one of the bottles and turned it round in her hands. It was the beer she liked. She and Rob. Their favourite. Still, it was a common enough brand, she reflected. No doubt lots of other people liked it as well.

'Did you ask that security firm for a quote?' asked Philip. 'I really think we ought to consider having an alarm installed.'

'Not yet,' said Helen calmly, pouring boiling water into the teapot. 'We only discussed it this morning.'

Philip looked disconcerted.

'So we did. Sorry. I thought it was yesterday,' he said.

Of course, she knew where she got it from – her prickliness, her irascibility. Her father. They were very alike. Warm, charismatic, passionate, but tetchy too, particularly when tired.

Una stood up and limped to the fridge to refill the milk jug.

'What's the matter? Why are you walking like that?' asked Philip.

'She's sprained her ankle,' said Helen swiftly. 'Jumping on to a bus and missing.'

'What were you doing jumping on to a bus?'

Una sighed, as if faced by two very wearing toddlers.

'I know it's dangerous, that one shouldn't ever jump on to a moving vehicle, that you've always told me not to, but I thought I'd make it, that it wasn't moving very fast, that I could just do it.'

'I thought they were supposed to shut the doors when they pulled out.'

'He did,' said Una.

'Then why did you jump?'

'The door was open when I started to jump but closed by the time I finished.'

She banged the jug down on the table so that milk slurped out of the spout.

Helen and Philip exchanged glances.

'Una's in by the way if Rob phones,' said Helen brightly.

'Right,' said Philip, waiting for an explanation but soon realising none would be forthcoming.

He poured himself a cup of tea then poured it back when he saw how weak it was.

'I think we'd better go to that cricket match after lunch, if you don't mind,' he said. 'Just to show our faces. We don't have to stay long. Only Mark said he was going.'

Helen nodded. The concert last night. The charity fair last weekend. And now a cricket match. They had to 'show their faces' an awful lot nowadays, far more than they used to, she thought.

'Would you like to come, darling?' she said, turning to Una. 'It might be rather pleasant.'

Una drew back her chair.

'No. I don't want to walk anywhere. My foot's hurting.'

'What's got into her?' asked Philip after she had left the room, forgetting to take the ironed clothes with her.

'Oh, just Rob, I think. I'll be glad when they've made it up. It's getting a bit much this. You never know what to say. Whether to talk about him or not.'

She picked up the beer bottle Una had been toying with.

Odd, she thought, picking off the yellow petals that still clung to the mouth, sticky with beer. We don't have any yellow roses. We never have done.

Una saw Rob's mother in Bath the following Saturday looking in the window of the South American shop opposite the Pump Room.

'Mrs Perry, Mrs Perry!' she called, trying to push her way

through the crowd gawping at the stilt-walking juggler. She trod on someone's foot and bumped into a man with a video camera. A beggar demanded money.

'Mrs Perry, Mrs Perry!' she called again, almost shouting this time, conscious that Rob's mother had very poor hearing.

A crowd of French teenagers, dressed identically in jeans, trainers and T-shirts, surged past, temporarily obscuring Rob's mother. Another beggar, this time accompanied by a mangy dog, accosted her. Someone touched her on the arm.

'It's Una, isn't it? I thought it was. What a coincidence! Do you know, you're the third person from school I've bumped into this morning.'

It was Julie, an old schoolfriend. Una had not seen her for years and did not particularly want to now. She smiled unenthusiastically then looked around, worried she would lose sight of Mrs Perry.

'It's busy, isn't it? I'd forgotten how crowded it gets on Saturdays. All the tourists, I suppose.'

Another group of teenagers poured past, Spanish this time.

'I suppose you've just left college. Durham, wasn't it? Or am I getting you muddled up with someone else?'

'Exeter actually,' corrected Una, anxious now. Where was Mrs Perry? She couldn't have vanished.

'That's right, Exeter. You did History, didn't you. History and Politics.'

'English,' said Una, increasingly distracted, standing on tip-toe.

'And what are you doing now? Have you got a job?'

'No, not yet,' said Una, forced to stop looking around for a moment in order not to appear rude. 'I was going to spend a year travelling but something came up. I'm not now. How about you? What are you doing?'

Julie gratefully seized the opportunity to talk about herself.

'I'm working for GA. General Accident. I got a place on their management trainee scheme last year. I'm based in Bristol although I usually spend at least one day a week in Swindon. I live in Keynsham. It's quite handy because it's halfway between Bristol and Bath and it's on the railway line. Chris works here, you see. I don't think you've met him? Have you?'

Una shook her head. There was no sign of Mrs Perry any-where.

Julie leant closer and placed a confiding arm on Una's.

'Actually, we've just got engaged.'

She giggled. Una tried to look pleased or at least surprised.

'That's why I'm here. I'm looking at rings. Chris is playing cricket and anyway he's not very good in shops so he told me to choose something I liked.'

How unromantic. Rob wouldn't do that, thought Una. Then she remembered. Rob had not phoned. That was why she needed to talk to Mrs Perry. Why it was so important.

'I'm sorry. I don't want to be rude but I was just on my way to meet someone. I'll have to go . . .'

'Oh. OK. Sorry,' said Julie, clearly put out. She fumbled in her handbag.

'Here. Here's my card. You're still in Bristol, are you?'

'Yes,' said Una, taking the card and moving away.

'I'll send you an invitation. To the wedding,' Julie called after her.

'Thanks. That would be nice. I'd love to come.'

There. At last. She was free. She struggled against a tide of tourists, middle-aged this time, mostly Japanese, fighting her way to a small flight of steps leading to a gift shop. She surveyed the square carefully from the top of the steps. It was clearer now, mainly because the stilt-walking juggler was having a break. Was that her, over there, by the arches? No. She wasn't there. She had gone. Damn Julie!

Mrs Perry told her version of this encounter to Rob when he phoned her later, as he did every evening, mindful that she was on her own, that he was her only child.

'I went over to her but then she bumped into someone else, a girlfriend by the looks of it, and she cut me dead. Didn't even say hello. I was standing right behind her, waiting for her to break off and introduce me, but she just went on talking. After a bit, I felt embarrassed and just went. I must say I was surprised. It was so unlike Una. Nothing's happened, has it? Only . . .'

Rob said no very quickly, adding that Una probably hadn't even seen her. Then he asked about the goats and cream-tea business and allowed her to extract some information of a strictly factual nature about his activities before ringing off. There was an envelope on his desk, addressed and sealed but unstamped. He picked it up, looked at it for a while, then tore it in four and put the pieces in the bin.

There were plenty more fishes in the sea, he thought later, walking along the beach in the dark. That was what they said. And plenty out of it as well, he added shortly afterwards, stubbing his toe against the washed-up carcass of a flounder.

Una waited to hear from Rob all that week. The following week she began to doubt that he would phone but still waited in. By the third week, she had lost hope and on the Thursday she put away the photo of him on her dressing table.

Her mother picked up a copy of the *Post* that night on her way home from work. She wanted to check an advertisement on behalf of one of her clients.

'I wonder how Rob's doing?' she said absent-mindedly, opening the paper out, looking for the property section. 'Isn't he going to work for the *Post* once he's finished that course he's on?'

'I don't care,' said Una.

Helen looked up.

'I don't want to talk about him. I don't want to hear his name again. Not ever. So can you tell Dad? Because I'm fed up with you asking. Both of you. Going on and on and on.'

And she ran from the room, banging the door behind her.

Helen let her breath out slowly. What did she mean 'going on and on'? She hadn't mentioned Rob's name for weeks, not until just now. She wondered whether to phone Rob's mother – to have a word with her, mother to mother. No, best not to perhaps. They would sort it out between themselves. Sooner or later. They always had done before.

9

What was she to do? She needed a job. No, that was not quite right. She did not 'need' a job. She felt she needed one. That was what one did. One left school, went to university, got a job, bought a house, had children, brought them up, went to evening classes, died. It was the next stage, the next rung on the ladder of life.

She decapitated another daisy and added the flower to the pile in front of her. The thing was, she didn't want just a job, a 'job' job, a job for the sake of a job. 'It pays the bills,' people said when describing a dull job, a job they didn't like, had never liked, still didn't like, as though somehow that made it all right. 'Oh, hello, St Peter, yes, I spent my whole life doing something tedious but I did pay my gas bill on time.'

Shouldn't one aim a little higher if one could – if one had the time, the opportunity, the space? Shouldn't one try to find a job one liked, that was fulfilling, satisfying, demanding even? No, maybe not. Why was it so important to like a job, to feel one was doing something that mattered, that was important? Surely, when it came down to it, all jobs were just jobs, a way of filling in time, giving one something to do between birth and death?

Yes, she knew she was privileged. That it was a luxury to be able to deliberate, to ponder, to choose between this and that. She knew that thousands, millions, had no choice, no freedom, no friendly careers officer down the road. But that was like telling a child: 'Eat up your greens. There are children starving in Africa.' It was all relative. Besides, it didn't feel like a luxury – this doubt, this worry, this endless, circular questioning. She would be quite happy, yes, very happy, if someone were to knock at the door that night and say, 'You start work tomorrow at Beeson's Bun factory. Nine o'clock. Hair tied back, please. Fifteen minutes' break in the morning and another in the afternoon. Four weeks' holiday a year. Plus the statutory bank holidays, of course.'

No you wouldn't, she told herself. Not really. You know you wouldn't. You'd be horrified. The grass is always greener.

If only she had a talent, a vocation, something she'd always wanted to do. If only she was like Sinead. Even at school, even at primary school, that was all Sinead had cared about – drawing, painting, making things out of clay. A green-glazed ash tray. A girl dancing, one arm slightly longer than the other. A man's head, frowning, wriggly worms for hair. But she had nothing like that. Nothing she excelled in. She was academic but not very academic. Good with her hands but not very good. An average sort of person.

But she had to find something. She had to. They hadn't said anything, even her father. They had not said they wanted her to go, that they wanted their house back, that they wanted to be by themselves. But she knew they did. It was their time now, their time for 'rediscovering' one another, taking up new interests, finding themselves again.

She glanced at her watch. Six o'clock. Damn! She'd promised Mum she'd put the casserole in the oven at four. She'd have to get something out of the freezer instead. A pizza perhaps. Or some of that breaded cod Dad liked. She stood up abruptly and went into the house, leaving the rug on the lawn, the tea pot on its side, a fly drowning in the spout.

10

Una's mother looked at her watch. Five o'clock. He was late. She lay back against the headrest and surveyed the house she was to show someone over. It was a bungalow, 1950s or maybe slightly later, ugly but comfortable, well maintained. An old lady had lived in it until her death five weeks ago. Now her son wanted to sell it.

Outside, on the small gravel driveway, stood a dressing table, probably discarded by the firm employed by the son to clear the house. Someone had removed the mirror and one of the drawers was open, the clothes inside just visible – scarves and handkerchiefs, unwanted, pathetic, like a kite seen snagged in a tree on a windless day, a reminder of what had been. A house full of light and noise. Children squabbling over whose turn it was to play the piano. The day one of them, perhaps a little girl called Alice, had cut her head on the sideboard running to meet the postman on her birthday. All the scraps that constitute a life, the life gone now, snapped like a sapless twig.

Helen climbed out of the car and shut the drawer so that she could no longer see the clothes inside. There. That was better. Now she could pretend it was empty.

Back in the car, she lowered her seat, feeling drowsy, the street outside still and heavy with heat. There. Was that him? No, too old. The man on the phone had sounded the same age as her, maybe slightly older, just retired. She watched as an elderly man walked slowly by and disappeared round the corner.

Philip had been worried when she had first joined the estate agent's. Had said he didn't want her showing people over houses, people she didn't know, who might be anybody, do anything.

She had assured him that there were rigorous safety procedures which she followed strictly. There was a book in the office which had to be filled in before every appointment. Where one was going, who one was meeting, their name, address, and, if they had one, their place of work. Afterwards, when the prospective buyer had left and the house or flat had been locked up, one had to ring in on a mobile phone. Even at the weekend or in the evening, one always phoned in. If one didn't, an alarm was automatically triggered and the police alerted. She had forgotten to phone in once. It was the end of the day and she had called in to see a friend who lived near by the flat she had been showing people round. Afterwards, she had done some late-night shopping. When she finally got home she had found a police car outside and Philip, white-faced, sitting at the kitchen table trying to remember what she had been wearing that morning.

She looked at her watch again. Ten past. Another five minutes. She hoped Una had remembered to put the casserole in the oven.

She had worked as a secretary for the first few months after their marriage until her pregnancy had become impossible to conceal and her boss, the manager of a carpet showroom, had begun to make leading comments. Things had been tight then, very tight. Philip could not find a job and there had been no help from relatives, not even when Martin was born. She had taken in ironing and typing, looked after a neighbour's child three mornings a week, collected two other children from school, scoured jumble sales for baby clothes. Then, when Philip found a job, when Martin had been old enough to send to nursery, she had not gone back to work because she had wanted other children, at least two more. She had waited three years and finally, after referral to a specialist, had been told that she would not be able to conceive again, that Martin's birth had damaged her, changed her irreversibly. I know that, she had thought. You don't need to tell me that. It's damaged everyone. The whole family.

Una had been born three years later, a little miracle, her head covered with red curls, exclaimed over by the nurses. She had not cried for a week and only then when the Sister had undressed her to inspect her umbilical cord. They had called her Una after the heroine in Spenser's 'Faerie Queene', knowing that she would be the only one, that there would be no more.

After the birth, she had not worked until both the children were at secondary school, Martin aged seventeen, Una aged eleven, her hair still curly but less red, more golden. She had worked as a temporary secretary at first, two days here, three days there, the first to be blamed when things went wrong. Next she had worked as a receptionist in a doctor's surgery. She had enjoyed that even though the patients had been trying at times but had lost her job when the practice had been merged with another. That was when she had started working for the estate agent's.

She liked this job best of all. True, it was not important. It did not change anything, would not entitle her to an obituary in *The Times*. But it was, in its small way, interesting. She loved looking round houses, spotting their potential, imagining what she would do if it was her house, how she would arrange things, where she would put the sofa. She liked watching the people too, wondering if they were genuinely interested or just curious, deciding if they were right for the house and the house for them, a good match.

She became aware of a man standing at the end of the driveway, fumbling in his pocket, looking around. Was that him? Yes. Almost certainly. She scrambled out of the car.

The man apologised for being late. A friend had phoned just as he was leaving, he said. And then the bus journey had taken longer than he had anticipated.

Helen smiled. She was right. He was older than her but not by much. Five or six years perhaps. She wondered what he did. A teacher perhaps or a lecturer. He didn't look like someone who worked in an office.

'This is the kitchen,' she said, showing him in. 'That's the airing cupboard over there and that's the larder, plenty of shelf space.'

Mr Pope obediently opened the door to the larder and admired the quantity of shelves. He was not much of a cook, he admitted. More of a tin-opener if she knew what he meant. Helen wondered if he was married. Maybe not, by the sound of it.

As if reading her thoughts, he said: 'My wife died six months ago. She'd been ill a long time. That's why I'm looking for somewhere new. The house where I live now it's . . . well, it's too big for one person. Besides, it's got . . . you know, memories, associations.'

Helen nodded vigorously. She was a firm believer in atmosphere, could sense as soon as she walked into a house whether it was happy or sad. She led him out of the kitchen and into the master bedroom where she pointed out the double glazing and the heated towel rail and told him which way the room faced. They looked at the guest bedroom next, then the bathroom and the sitting room. Then they walked out of the French windows into the garden where they inspected the ornamental pond in the middle.

'Dangerous, of course, if you've got grandchildren,' said Helen, pointing at the pond. 'I had a neighbour once who had a friend whose child drowned in a pond like this. Only four inches of water there was at the time and the mother only yards away. They panic, apparently, and breathe in. Their lungs fill with water.'

'No, there are no grandchildren,' said the man. 'We didn't have any children. My wife, my late wife . . . she . . . there was a problem. She couldn't have children.'

Back in the kitchen, she closed the door to the larder.

'Well? What do you think?'

He wrinkled his nose.

'It's very nice, very comfortable but . . . well . . .' He laughed. 'It's a bit flat, isn't it?'

She laughed with him.

'I thought a bungalow would be a good idea,' he explained. 'That it would be sensible. You know. But walking round . . . well, I feel that something's missing. Like a car with no wheels.'

She nodded.

'Yes, I'm afraid I'm like that too. I like to have stairs. They give a house shape.'

He laughed again, shook her hand and apologised for wasting her time. She saw him out, waved goodbye, and phoned the office. He was nice, she thought, as she got back into the car. Very charming. Good company probably.

On the way home she stopped at a late-night corner store. She would buy some ice cream, she decided. Strawberry because that was Una's favourite. Maybe it would cheer her up. She had been so miserable lately. So wrapped up in herself.

She was spoilt, of course, terribly spoilt, she thought, as she opened the lid to the deep freezer. Philip was right. It would do her good to stand on her own two feet for a bit. It would make her less selfish, more thoughtful, more understanding. She could be so hard sometimes. And yet she didn't want her to leave home. Didn't want her to live in a squalid bedsit above a fish-and-chip shop. Didn't want her to be cold at night. She wanted, as a mother, to protect her from all this and yet she knew she needed a bit of hardship, a bit of suffering even, failure, struggle – that she would be a better, wholer, happier person because of it. And yet how could one wish suffering on one's own child, she thought, handing over the money for the ice cream, the most expensive in the shop. One couldn't, she thought, driving away. It was impossible.

Behind, back in the shop, the teenage assistant picked up the book she had been reading, a biology textbook, and began to study the function of the heart again. She was to be a doctor. That was what her parents had decided.

11

Philip rearranged his desk again. There. That was better. That was the most sensible, efficient use of space. Then he put his head in his hands. This couldn't go on. It was ten thirty in the morning and he had nothing to do. No meetings to attend, no papers to read, no letters to dictate – all had been taken out of his hands by the person recruited by Mark, ostensibly to help him – a thirty-something woman of androgynous appearance and a name to go with it – Robyn. It had all happened with a speed and subtlety that had impressed as well as surprised him. Nothing had been said. Nothing had been done even. It was more a question of what had not been said.

He would have to say something. And yet how could he? He would be talking himself out of a job. That was probably what they wanted, of course. For him to admit that he no longer had a role, a place, a contribution to make.

He opened his diary. Nothing until Friday. And then only one short meeting. That left him with three blank days. Three days in which to do nothing except pretend he was busy. This was worse, he thought. Far worse than taking orders from an incompetent boss. It was a refined form of torture. Thank God Joanne was on holiday. Even so, it was embarrassing trying to find jobs for the temporary secretary. She had already sorted through two filing cabinets. Now there was only one cabinet left and she was already halfway through that. His own desk was immaculate, the pens lined up like soldiers, even the paper clips tidy.

Mark phoned at eleven and asked him to come up to his office for what he described as a 'little chat'. Philip saw with interest that the coffee table *was* made of wood, not glass. So the rumours had been right, he thought, sitting down in the chair indicated and accepting a cup of coffee.

They talked of Robyn first. About how she was settling down. The changes she had suggested. Then they talked about the corporate hospitality programme. It had been a good concert, that last one, hadn't it, said Mark. Philip nodded and helped himself to a chocolate biscuit, wondering if Mark knew that he avoided eye contact, that he looked in the opposite direction of the person to whom he was speaking. It was quite funny really, this uncomfortable preamble – like a form of courtship, he thought.

Mark offered him another cup of coffee. Uncrossed his legs. Looked out of the window. Then he said what Philip knew he had been going to say. They wanted to offer him early retirement. As he knew, they had been asked to make savings by their American parent company. Told to make a specified number of redundancies at a specified level.

'It's not that we don't value your contribution. We do. You're an important member of the team with a wealth of experience. But we have to find five redundancies at your level . . .'

Level, thought Philip. That's what it comes down to. A life-time's service reduced to numbers, counters, beads on an abacus flicked from side to side by someone the other side of the world. Two here, three there. There, that's better, trimmer, leaner, never mind if we're asking fewer people to do more work. That's how it is today, how you've got to be if you want to survive in the tough, new global marketplace.

'Naturally, we thought of you first because you're the closest to retirement age. There was no other reason. None at all. It was thought you might welcome it, see it as an opportunity, a new start. People do, you know. It's impossible to know until one asks . . .'

No other reason, thought Philip. No, of course not. No other reason at all. You don't like me. That's the reason. I don't know why but you don't. You haven't from the day you started. My face doesn't fit. I'm too old and I don't have a postgraduate degree in business management. I don't watch enough videos on time management and interpersonal skills. I look at my watch instead, smile, try not to interrupt, look people in the eye. 'No other reason.' That's a good one. I like that. Very funny. Ho, ho, ho!

'Personnel have worked out the terms . . . what you would get if you were to accept . . . if you were interested. It's all written down. Here you are . . .'

He handed Philip a small white envelope with his name typed on the front – Philip Dart.

'I think you'll find it's quite a good deal, that you're not losing very much – off your pension I mean, what you would get if you were to stay, to work until you were sixty, until the normal retirement age here.'

Philip took the envelope and looked down at his name. It looked so small and insignificant surrounded by all that white – like a fishing boat out at sea.

'There's no hurry. No tremendous urgency. But if you could just give me some indication of how you feel, say by Thursday, that would be a great help.'

They shook hands and talked about the current test match – two grown men pretending that nothing had happened, hiding their feelings behind silly mid-on.

Downstairs, Philip told the temporary secretary to take the rest of the day off.

'You can finish that filing cabinet tomorrow,' he said. 'It's OK. You'll still get paid.'

He made a pot of tea in the staff kitchen, took it back to his office and reopened the window the secretary had just closed. Mark was right, he thought, reading the letter for the fourth time, his tea growing cold in front of him, a pale scum on its surface. The deal was quite good. But did he want to retire, he thought, torn between elation and fear? Did he really want to leave? OK, yes, so he was bored. But one could be bored at home too. Lonely as well. At least he saw people here. He had a place, an identity, a sense of belonging. He was someone.

He walked over to the window. Did he really want to be one of them, one of those black dots down there, faceless, anonymous? He was safe here, protected. And yet . . . and yet . . . He glanced back at his desk, at the top drawer where one-thousand-and-sixty-five days lay waiting to be ticked off. He wanted to live as a tiger again. That's what he'd promised himself all these years.

That one day, even if it was only for one day, he would live as a tiger rather than a sheep. He looked back out of the window, then back towards his desk, wavering, unsure.

The letter he wrote to Mark was brief and to the point. It was silly to beat about the bush. He dropped it in the internal mail box and left the office, taking the stairs instead of the lift, walking slowly and carefully, one step at a time, wondering whether he'd made the right decision.

12 ∫

'What do you think? Do you like it?' asked Philip.

'Well, yes,' said Helen doubtfully. 'But what are we going to use it for?'

'It's got its own fridge. And a place to put your coffee cup while you're driving along,' called Una from inside.

Philip had bought a purple camper van from a man he'd met that afternoon in the off-licence. He'd been buying French wine to celebrate the start of his new life, the man beer to celebrate the birth of his daughter, Sashka.

The man played the double bass in a London orchestra. That's why he'd bought the van, he said. To get around more easily. But his wife found it difficult to park and had told him to sell it.

'I'm not going to hospital in that thing,' she had said shortly before giving birth. 'You'll have to ring for a taxi.'

The man had protested that a taxi was a waste of good money. But his wife had insisted.

'So it's got to go, you see,' the man said to Philip, dangling a pack of four cans from his right index finger. 'It's very reliable. Always starts first time. Doesn't like going much above sixty but apart from that it's fine.'

They had talked terms in the pub round the corner, Philip giving the man his business card, the man giving Philip his address.

'Why Sashka?' Philip asked when they had agreed a price. 'Is your wife Russian or something?'

'Oh, no, nothing like that. She's from Lincoln. A yellow-belly, as they say. No, we just liked the sound of it, that's all. Actually, it was a compromise. My wife wanted Sasha and I wanted Kate so we put the two together and got Sashka.'

Afterwards, outside, the man showed Philip how to find reverse and how to raise the roof so that one could stand up without bumping one's head on the ceiling.

'It sleeps five. Two in the double bed, two in the bunk beds and one in the front – there's a cushion that fits between the passenger's and driver's seats. It's all in the manual, though. Ring me if you don't understand anything.'

'Right, thanks, I will,' said Philip, climbing into the driver's seat, thinking that this was absurd. In a minute he would wake up and find himself deadheading roses in the garden or stacking old newspapers ready to take to the tip. Middle-aged bank managers didn't buy camper vans from men they met in a shop. Or did they?

Una came out and stood on the step.

'It's got a little wardrobe with hangers,' she said. 'And a reading lamp. It's got everything. Aren't you going to go in, Mum?'

Helen looked at Philip as though he might sprout wings. It was so unlike him. That's what had taken her aback. Not that he had bought a purple camper van but the way in which he had done it – just like that, on the spur of the moment, without months of cautious deliberation. It was so out of character. No, that was not strictly true, she reflected. It was unlike him now but not as he had been when she had first met him. He had been spontaneous then. A man who took risks. Otherwise, she would not be alive. They would not be married.

She squeezed his hand, ducked her head and went inside. It was good to know he could still surprise her.

Later, that night, when he had got into bed and she was sitting on the edge of it, she said: 'I might bump into him, you know. He could still be in Bristol.'

'Who?'

'Him, of course.'

'Oh, him.'

'I was thinking about it today. How in my line of business . . . well, I could show him round a house and not even know it was him.'

'Would you recognise him?'

'I don't know. Maybe. It depends. Some people change more than others.'

Me, for example, thought Philip. You thought I had changed. That I had become a different person, a person incapable of doing something rash, plunging into the unknown. I saw it in your eyes when we were looking at the van.

'I'm sorry. I know you don't like talking about it.'

'Well, it's hardly surprising, is it?'

'No, I don't suppose it is,' said Helen dreamily, pulling at her fingers one by one. It was amazing how things turned out, she thought. How just one decision could change everything. That night, for instance, she had been scared, yes, but she had not done it because she was scared. That was what she found difficult to explain, what she had never admitted to Philip. She had done it because she was curious, because she wanted to find out what it was like, because her virginity had become a sore that had started to itch, that was driving her mad, that she wanted to lose. It sounded ridiculous. How could one do something like that out of curiosity? And yet she knew that she had. Of course, there had been other contributory factors. The fear. The drinks Vic had given her. The week she had spent alone in a strange city, knowing no one, her money running out. But the main factor had been simply the desire to find out. That was all.

Beside her, lying on his back, staring at the ceiling with his hands clasped under his head, Philip planned journeys in the purple van. They could go to the Edinburgh festival. Spend a long weekend in Wales. Maybe go even further. Abroad perhaps. He had always wanted to go to Istanbul. Travel wasn't just for the young, he thought.

13 ∫

Una went to see Sinead who was busy as always but who made room for her on the sofa, told her to make herself a cup of tea or coffee if she preferred, there was a bit left, there, in that red tin.

Above them, on the skylight, a slow drizzle fell, sticking dead leaves to the glass. Autumn had started.

'What are you making? Who is it?' asked Una as Sinead pinched out a nostril on the nose of the clay bust she was working on.

'My mother,' said Sinead, pummelling a piece of clay between her hands. 'When she was pregnant, someone once said a child would be the making of her. And they were right, weren't they? Because here I am, making her.' And she laughed sarcastically.

Una did not join in, aware that the laughter was a mask, a fan, a way of distracting attention. The product of an unlikely marriage between an Irish heiress and an American college drop-out of Polish descent, Sinead had never seen her father and had been abandoned by her mother when she was two. Her parents had met at a ball where her mother was a guest and her father a waiter. He had dropped chicken aspic on her lap. 'They should have known then,' said Sinead. 'It started with a mess and it went on that way. One long bloody mess!'

Her parents married six months after the ball and separated within the year when Sinead's father went out one day to buy a paper and did not return. Sinead's mother, who was three months' pregnant, was prescribed anti-depressants by her doctor and had been taking them ever since, often in hospital. She had already slashed her wrists three times.

Sinead had been brought up by a great-aunt, a retired Latin teacher, who watched the sun rise every morning and made pancakes for breakfast. Her father, meanwhile, had returned to the States where he now ran a successful road haulage business.

Una and Sinead had made friends on their first day at primary school thanks to their soft toys – a black rabbit and pink teddy respectively. The animals had made friends first, then their owners.

'What's it for?' asked Una, pouring the tea into white porcelain cups. Sinead followed William Morris' dictum that everything in one's house should be either useful or, in one's own opinion, beautiful. As a result, she had furnished her flat extremely sparsely, preferring to do without rather than buy something ugly.

Sinead looked up, then realised that Una was referring to the clay bust.

'A competition run by the Henry Moore Foundation,' she said. 'The first prize is a year's bursary and, at the end of it, a one-man show at Leeds City Art Gallery.'

Una looked for some milk in the fridge, failed to find any, and added a spoonful of sugar to the tea instead.

The rain was heavier now, the noise of the drops falling on the skylight audible above their voices. Una lay back on the sofa and watched Sinead's fingers move – moulding, pushing, pressing, squeezing.

'How long does it take to do a nostril?' she asked.

'Hours. Minutes. I don't know,' said Sinead. 'It all depends. Sometimes it will come right straightaway, other times you will spend hours and only be half satisfied at the end of it.'

'But how do you know when it does come right? When it is right? How do you know that?'

Sinead looked up, puzzled.

'You just do. You can see it. It looks right.'

Una put down her cup and waited for Sinead to ask about Rob. When she didn't, Una said: 'I thought I might get a job abroad doing voluntary work. In a refugee camp maybe.'

'Why?'

'Why? Well, to help, of course. To do something worthwhile, to feel I was doing something useful, something that . . .'

'They need doctors. Engineers, nurses, plumbers, carpenters – people with skills. Not English graduates looking for a bit of excitement, trying to get over the boyfriend they've just lost.'

Una flushed. Sometimes Sinead could be too honest. Brutal almost. There was no need to be quite so blunt.

'There's need here too, you know,' continued Sinead. 'You don't need to go halfway round the world to find it. Just look around you. Catch a bus to St Paul's or Easton. Walk around. Keep your eyes open. You'd be much more useful here. It might not be as interesting or stand out so much on the CV but you'd be doing far more good.'

Una stood up and dumped her cup in the sink. Why was it that her peers all talked to her as if they were ten years older, she wondered irritably? And she wished, not for the first time, that her parents were a little less ordinary, a little less safe – that they had done something or been somewhere that would give her a little more cachet.

'When do you have to finish it? When's the deadline?' she asked, sitting down again, fidgeting with the blue throw that covered the sofa.

'The end of November.'

'Two and a half months.'

'Yes, and it will take me that long.'

'But it looks almost finished. What else have you got to do?'

'Come back in four weeks and you'll see,' said Sinead. 'Actually, I've hardly started. It's going to be a real rush to get it done.'

'Will you have time to go out ever? To take the evening off?'

'Probably. Why?'

'I just thought we could go to see a film some time,' said Una, trying not to sound lonely. That morning, she had realised that apart from her parents and Martin and Teresa, Sinead was the only person she knew in Bristol. All her other old schoolfriends had moved away.

'Yes,' said Sinead. 'I think I could run to that. Not every week, mind. But every now and again. That would be fine.'

She wiped her hands briskly on one of the rags lying on

her work table. Then she covered the bust with plastic sheeting.

'Come on,' she said. 'Let's catch a train to Weston-Super-Mare.'

It rained all the way but began to clear while they were eating fish and chips in a café. There were lace doilies in the lavatory and pink nylon frills round a box of tissues. They could have tea or coffee with their meal, the waitress informed them, or a soft drink if they preferred. Sinead asked what the soft drinks were and was told 'Milk or water'. For some reason, this made them giggle. The picture on the wall, of a white, palm-fringed beach, also made them giggle. So did the hand-written, badly spelt note on their table informing patrons that the number of slices of bread served with full meals had been regretfully reduced from three to two because of increased competition. They were, in fact, ready to laugh at anything, gleeful at being somewhere new, at the sense of having escaped.

After they had finished their meal and bought half a pound of chocolate fudge in a cone-shaped bag, they walked along the beach. It was dry now, the sun struggling to break through.

'Race you to that rock,' shouted Sinead suddenly, pointing to a large lump of concrete with rusty spikes sticking out of it.

'But that's not fair,' protested Una as Sinead shot off, her hair tumbling free, sand flying up behind her.

But her complaint was lost in the wind. Friends, thought Una, smiling to herself. It was good to have friends. And she wondered why she had been worrying so much lately. Life was not an exam. There was no pass rate. No grades. She should just live, she thought. Just live. And she raced after Sinead, her lungs filling with air, her feet pounding the wet sand, running to meet the brightening sky.

14

But the worry came back the next day, like toothache, temporarily calmed, but now stronger than ever, nagging, insistent.

In the mornings, she snatched at her dreams, puzzling them out, ferreting them up from the black hole of sleep. She looked at herself in mirrors and shop windows as if there might be an answer there, staring back, glaringly obvious. Her life lay on her like a gum boil or hair shirt – sore, scratchy, impossible to forget.

What frightened her most was the multitude of choice. She could do this or that or that or that. But if she did this she could not do that. She could not design gardens and edit magazines at the same time. She was dazzled, bewildered, scared, aware that she could make the wrong choice. It was a bit like one of those mazes in children's comics. 'Help Baby Rabbit find the quickest way to his burrow,' they said. But which was the quickest? That one looked it. But was it? Roads could be deceptive, could bend round and round, take one back in the direction one had come from. It was easy in the comics. One could cheat – trace the way back from the end. But one could not do that in life. One had to guess – to risk choosing the wrong road.

'Get real,' she told herself. 'Don't be so precious. You're looking for a job, not a life. A job is not a life. It's what you do in order to live. Although not necessarily,' she added, thinking of Sinead. 'Some people live to work.' And she saw Sinead's hands, pressing, squeezing, teasing the clay into shape, the frown of concentration as she appraised the results. The problem was that she was neither one nor the other, she thought. She was not like Sinead but neither was she like the girl in the bread shop round the corner, eyes on the clock, mind on the weekend, the time when she would go clubbing with her mates. She was pure mermaid, lured by both land and sea, at home in neither.

She went to the Job Centre and made an appointment to see a careers counsellor. The counsellor was younger than she had expected with fair, bobbed hair and very clean, manicured nails. They talked about what opportunities were available and what Una liked and did not like doing and the counsellor recommended some books with titles like *Finding The End Of The Rainbow*. Una duly took the books out of the library and sent off a letter inquiring about graduate entrance to the diplomatic service – one of the careers suggested by the counsellor. An application form arrived a week later with large blank sections headed 'Use this space to tell us anything more about yourself which you feel may be relevant to your application'. Una put the form in the top left-hand drawer of her desk.

Advertising, she thought, watching the television one night, laughing at an advert for a new cheese spread. Or publishing maybe, she thought the next day, reading a piece in the paper about book fairs. Or teaching. That was a possibility. She had thought about that before.

She considered all these possible careers and discussed them with Martin and Teresa. And discussed them again. And again. But she didn't choose any of them. The truth was, she could not move. Like a nervous diver teetering on the edge of a springboard, she was paralysed.

After a while, she gave up fighting against this paralysis. She stopped reading the job sections in the papers. She cancelled her second appointment with the careers counsellor. She tore up the diplomatic service application form. Instead, she went on long walks, looking around as Sinead had suggested, waiting for inspiration. As she walked, she thought of Rob, two hundred miles away in Hastings. What was he doing now? What was he learning? Was the sky grey there too?

15

Una was forced to move when her parents announced that they were going to Europe for three months in the purple camper van. Helen told her one morning at breakfast after Philip had gone to the camping superstore to buy a spare bulb for the reading light. He went there most days now, it seemed, wandering up and down the aisles with an empty trolley, talking to the assistants about valves and safety locks.

'We thought we'd go to France first, then into Italy, over by ferry to Greece and from there to Bulgaria and Turkey.'

Una stared.

'The money's just come through, you see. We thought it would be a way of celebrating, of marking the end of Dad's career in the bank.'

'But what about your job?'

'Oh, they've been very understanding. They've given me a year's sabbatical. Said I can go back earlier if I want to.'

Una smiled bleakly. It was too much to bear. She should, by rights, be somewhere exotic now – Ladakh or Paraguay – dusty, travelworn, mosquito-bitten, drinking cold tea in the shade while she wrote up her travel journal. Instead, here she was in England in October, jobless, boyfriendless, looking for clues in the shape of the clouds. Meanwhile, her parents, middle-aged, settled, who had seemed quite content to spend their weekends ironing tea-towels and mowing the lawn until her father had gone mad and left his job, meanwhile they were proposing to trundle round Europe in a contraption that looked like Chitty Chitty Bang Bang's great-grandfather.

'That's OK,' she said. 'I'll be all right on my own. When are you going?'

Helen stretched out to take a piece of toast from the toaster, cut it in two, then wiped her knife carefully on the side of her plate.

'The thing is,' she said, 'Dad's arranged for someone to come and stay in the house while we're away. Someone from work, from the American parent company. He's being sent here on secondment for three months. He wants to bring his family – his wife and children.'

Una smiled again – it was quite an effort this time – and poured herself another cup of tea.

'Well, at least they won't have any problems finding a babysitter,' she said, imagining herself eating hash browns while spooning mashed banana into a baby's mouth.

Helen dipped her knife in the butter and spread her toast slowly and methodically.

'They've got three children, Una.'

'Yes? Well? It's OK. I said it's OK. I don't mind sharing.'

Helen put her knife down and picked up the Marmite jar.

Slowly her meaning dawned on Una.

'You mean there won't be room? They'll want all the bedrooms?'

'Yes.'

Una swallowed.

'But it's all right. There's no need to worry. I've spoken to Martin and Teresa. They say you're welcome to stay there for as long as you like. They say it'd be no trouble. That they'd be pleased to have you.'

Una drew her chair back.

'I'm not a parcel, you know, to be wrapped up and sent from one place to the next.'

She glared at her mother then stormed out of the room.

Helen sighed and spread her toast with Marmite. She had told Philip that Una would be too proud to live as Martin's lodger. But he had merely shrugged his shoulders. 'Fine,' he had said. 'Let her find somewhere of her own if that's what she wants. She'll soon find hot water doesn't grow on trees.' She had said something then about mixed metaphors but Philip had merely waved his hands dismissively and gone on with writing one of his lists. It seemed he had to write a list before doing anything these days. She would probably find one for making love soon, Sellotaped to the headboard. 'Ten thirty – undress and chat. Ten forty – start foreplay. Ten fifty – prepare to enter.'

She giggled at the thought then became serious again as she heard the muffled sound of Una crying upstairs. Really, it was quite extraordinary how Philip had changed since leaving the bank. A few months ago he had become hysterical because Una had walked home alone in the dark. Now he was proposing to go off and leave her for three months, apparently not minding where she lived or what she did. She would have to talk to him.

Injured pride made Una act with speed. She found a bedsit in the small ads of the *Post*. Owned by a Nigerian who had come to Britain as a penniless refugee in the sixties and now owned seventy properties, it was not in the most salubrious area of Bristol. Access was through a disused garage yard up an iron staircase. There was bad condensation and a healthy population of earwigs. But the aspect was open and the walls freshly painted. The carpet was not purple. Or orange. So Una took it, paying for the deposit with the money she had been going to use for her trip round the world, a gift from her grandfather, her father's father, who had died before she was born, who had left the money in trust, both for her and Martin.

She went to the Job Centre again and looked at the white cards on the wall advertising local vacancies, something she had not done before, thinking them beneath her. One, in particular, caught her attention. 'Can you listen?' the card said. 'Do you know how to change a baby's nappy?'

'Well, yes,' thought Una, reading on. 'I can do both actually.'

The card went on to say that it was looking for a junior care assistant to work in a refuge for women who had been abused, either physically, sexually or emotionally, by their husbands or partners. Una wrote down the reference number on the top right-hand corner of the card and queued at a counter where she was handed another card with more details about the job including a phone number.

She dialled the number in the phone box round the corner, using one of the phone cards her father had bought in case she ever found herself alone somewhere, late at night, without any money or transport home. A woman answered and said she needed to speak to Bridget, could she hang on, Bridget was on the fourth floor, there had just been a bit of a row.

Una waited one minute, then two, then three, watching the value of the card tumble on the screen in front of her. Finally, another voice came on, breathless but not, Una noticed, apologetic. Una explained that she was calling about the job vacancy. The voice asked how old she was, whether she was married, if she had any children, where she had seen the advert. Her answers all appeared to be highly unsatisfactory judging by the silence at the other end and Una fully expected the voice to say that she was sorry but they were looking for someone older, someone a bit more mature, a bit more experienced. To her surprise, however, the voice invited her for an interview the following day in a city centre department store café.

'We don't do interviews here because of the security,' said the voice. 'We have to be careful.'

The voice went on to ask if ten o'clock would be convenient, she would be wearing a purple cardigan, was quite small with short, dark hair.

Una said yes, ten o'clock would be fine, she was quite tall herself with reddish hair, sort of auburn really.

She wore a skirt to the interview but not a jacket, thinking a suit would be too smart. Bridget, she guessed, would be wearing trousers. And she was right. She was.

When they had bought their drinks and found somewhere quiet to sit, Bridget talked about the job. It was impossible to sum up in one sentence, she said. She would be a dogsbody really. Cleaning floors, answering the phone, child-minding, helping the women to fill in forms, accompanying them to interviews with solicitors and housing officials, offering them emotional support, listening, sleeping over . . .

'That's important, that is,' she said, stirring three sugars into her coffee. 'There are only four of us – myself, my deputy Jan, Kate – she's a senior care assistant – and then the junior care assistant – that's the post that's vacant. We take it in turns to sleep over. Someone has to be there twenty-four hours a day.'

'In case anyone tries to break in, you mean? One of the husbands or partners?' asked Una.

'That does happen occasionally,' admitted Bridget. 'But more often than not it's the women themselves. They're used to having their own homes, their own kitchens. It's hard to share with eleven other women. Sometimes, inevitably, there are disagreements. Like yesterday when you phoned,' she explained. 'We've got two kitchens, each with their own oven. Yesterday, two women wanted to use the oven in one of the kitchens. One said she'd got there first, the other that she had. It started quite amicably but soon came to blows. That's the sort of thing that can happen. Little incidents like that.'

Una asked how many women there were and was told the centre could accommodate up to twelve women and thirty children.

'We run a nursery in the mornings so that the women with young children can do a bit of shopping on their own or get their hair cut or whatever. It's mainly staffed by volunteers but sometimes we have to staff it ourselves.'

Bridget asked why she was interested in the job, did she want to become a social worker or something and Una said no, not exactly, she was not sure what she wanted to do long term but this seemed something useful, a valuable way of spending her time.

'The most important thing, the thing I have to keep reminding the volunteers, is not to put pressure on the women,' said Bridget quickly. 'We're not there to tell the women to leave their partners. We're there to offer them a refuge, a place where they can collect themselves and their thoughts, decide what they want to do. If they decide to go back, then that's fine. That's their decision. It's not our job to criticise them, to make them feel weak, to try to bully them into changing their minds. Some of the volunteers . . . they come barging in, most with perfectly good intentions, they think they're going to rescue all these poor women from their cruel, vicious partners, and they do more harm than good.'

She took a gulp of her coffee and looked Una directly in the eye.

'You see, a woman won't leave an abusive partner until she's ready to, until she's decided to herself. It can be very hard not to interfere, to watch a woman leave knowing that she'll be back in two or three months' time vowing that she's never going back, not this time, and then watch her leave again once the bruises have faded, the pain been forgotten. But it's the only way. The only way that works.'

Una nodded, trying to look serious and responsible, the kind of person one would want to employ.

'You haven't asked about the money,' said Bridget abruptly. 'Aren't you interested in earning anything?'

Una blushed and said yes, she was just getting round to it, and what would she be earning? Bridget told her. It was not very much. Not even a fifth of what her friend Rachel was earning in advertising but it would do, thought Una. She would have to live frugally – buy a bike like Rob. No, not like Rob. Just a bike. Forget Rob.

'That's fine. It's about what I was expecting,' she lied.

Bridget asked her to fill in a short form giving brief biographical details and the names and addresses of two referees and said they needed someone to start as soon as possible, would that be all right?

'I can start tomorrow if you want,' said Una eagerly. Too eagerly, she thought afterwards. She had sounded like a puppy with a new ball.

When she had completed the form, Bridget folded it in two and stowed it in her handbag, snapping it shut with a firmness that signalled the interview was over.

'I'll let you know next week,' she said, shaking Una's hand. 'I'm interviewing two more candidates this afternoon and one tomorrow.'

Downstairs, on the ground floor, Una tried out perfume in the beauty hall. The word 'candidate' had made her feel despondent. She was up against three, if not more, competitors, no doubt all with more experience and skills. And, as usual, she had sounded naïve and gauche. A spoilt, middle-class graduate at a bit of a loose end. That's what Bridget would be thinking. Perhaps at this very minute.

She did not tell her parents about the interview. Nor did she tell them about the flat. She wanted to present them with a fait accompli. She wanted to go in when they were sitting at the kitchen table, conferring over lists or routes, and say: 'There. That's what I'm doing. That's where I'm living. OK?' She wanted to see the surprise on their faces, the astonishment that she should have managed all this on her own.

But when she did, when, to her own surprise, she received a letter from Bridget saying she was pleased to offer her a job as junior care assistant starting the following Monday, they seemed pleased but not surprised.

'Oh, good. I'm glad you've found something,' said her mother.

'I didn't know you were interested in social work,' said her father.

Una retreated to her room to start packing her books. It was silly to feel hurt, she told herself. They were not just her parents. They were people in their own right with their own lives to lead. Even so, when she came down later to make herself a hot drink and heard her parents talking in the sitting room, she could not resist pausing on the stairs to eavesdrop on what they were saying – to find out what they thought of her news.

'I thought we could spend Christmas in Istanbul,' she heard her father say. 'What do you think? Do you think we'll be there by then?'

'I don't know. It depends on how much time we spend in Greece. I know it's quite far down but I would like to go to Athens. I've always wanted to go there,' said her mother.

Una returned slowly to her room, the drink forgotten. They could show a little more interest, she thought. They had become so wrapped up in themselves lately, so engrossed with their precious trip.

In fact, unknown to her, her parents had spent the previous hour discussing ways of keeping an eye on her in their absence.

'I'd feel happier if she was still with Rob,' said her mother. 'He was so responsible, so mature. I don't know what went wrong there. I know he let her down badly over the travelling and everything but I'd have thought she'd have forgiven him. I did think of ringing up his mother.'

'No, you can't do that,' said her father quickly. 'We mustn't interfere.'

'I know, I know. It's just it all seems so silly. I know she still likes him and I'm sure . . . well . . . he always seemed absolutely besotted with her. But you're right. They have to live their own lives. Make their own mistakes.'

'They haven't asked, you know,' said Philip later. 'Neither Una or Martin. They've never asked why I left, what happened, or anything.'

Helen reached out and put a hand on his knee.

'No, well, that's children for you,' she said.

16

Una threw herself into work with the zeal of the converted. Anxious to give her life meaning and shape – to find the answers to the questions – she made it her God. Those women, those poor, miserable oppressed women, she would rescue them, she thought. She would give them new hope, open their eyes, make their lives richer, bigger, fuller.

Bridget was pleased she showed so much enthusiasm but urged restraint, reminding her that the women in the refuge were emotionally vulnerable, that they were open to pressure, that they might take on more than they could cope with. Una nodded at this advice but did not follow it, allowing her enthusiasm to continue unchecked.

Rob was still there, lodged like a piece of grit but sometimes, occasionally for a whole day, she managed not to think of him, to see a newspaper without wondering what he was doing.

Sometimes, usually on a Friday or Saturday night, when she could hear the shrieks of teenagers queuing up outside the nearby nightclub, she imagined herself catching a train to Hastings, finding out where Rob was living, hammering on the door – the tearful, emotional reunion that would follow. But pride – pride and obstinacy and the fear of rejection – prevented her from ringing Rob's mother to ask for his address. He knew where she was, she told herself. If he wanted to contact her, he could.

Then, one night, cycling home in the rain, she was stopped by the police. She was labouring up a hill, her cheeks glowing with effort, when a police car slowed in front of her, the driver waving her off the road.

'Where are your lights?' asked the policeman, climbing out of his car.

Una looked down at her bike then up at the sky, surprised to see how dark it was.

'I haven't got any,' she admitted – honestly at least, thought the policeman.

He took her name and address, shielding his notepad from the rain with his jacket, and ordered her to take the bike to her local police station within the next fortnight, with both front and back lights correctly fitted.

'Can I ride it now? Just for tonight?' she asked.

'No,' he snapped, still smarting from the row he had had that morning with his wife.

And so she walked home, her shoes squelching with each step, arriving cold, tired, and wet. Never mind, she comforted herself. I'll have a hot bath. Eat something nice and easy. Go to bed early. There was a letter in her pigeonhole which she read after she had changed into dry clothes. It was from her mother. There was a postcard from the Rodin museum in Paris and a blue airmail paper letter. 'How are the Coopers getting on?' she wrote. 'Are they looking after the garden?' Una realised guiltily that she had not been calling round at her parents' house once a week as she had promised. The letter went on to describe the sights they had seen in Paris; the *fruits de mer* they had eaten at a restaurant near the Gare du Nord, the lobster caught fresh that morning, the long, lazy mornings spent sitting near the window in cafés, stirring sugar into coffee, watching people walk by.

Una folded the letter and put it in the pocket of her trousers, resolving to phone Martin and Teresa later that night, to offer to babysit so that they could go out – something else she had promised her mother she would do. There was no food in the flat, not even a tin of baked beans and so she ate toast, sitting huddled in front of the fire, the Rodin card propped above her on the mantelpiece, trying not to think of her mother's cooking, the winter puddings she made, plum crumble with mixed spice and real custard. She would feel better after a bath, she told herself. A long, hot bath. That would do the trick. But the pilot light had blown out and she could not relight it, throwing away match after match, giving up in the end, jumping into bed, only to discover that it was wet, that the roof was leaking, that there was a large damp patch directly beneath her pillow. She jumped out and dragged the bed away from the leak, flinging a towel on top of the damp patch, too tired to change the sheets.

She said Rob's name then. Tired, hungry, cold, miserable, she cried out loud.

'Rob! Why don't you ring? Please ring. Oh, Rob, Rob!'

17

Una met Germaine the next day. She was in one of the kitchens cleaning a grill pan when the doorbell rang.

'Can you go?' called Jan, the only other member of staff in the house.

Una peeled off the green rubber gloves she was wearing and went downstairs.

A small woman with short dark hair stood on the doorstep holding two children – one in her arms, the other by the hand. She was wearing a yellow V-neck jumper frayed at the cuffs, a black skirt, green knee-highs, and most noticeable of all, pink fluffy slippers. One eye was almost invisible, hidden by a puffy mass of green and black bruises, and her lip was cut, striped with dried blood.

'Have you got a room? Is there space for us?' the woman asked urgently.

Una stared, mesmerised by the bruises. The child in the woman's arms whimpered. She was shivering. So was the woman. None of them wore coats despite the bitter north-east wind.

'Yes, yes. Come in. Quickly! You must be freezing.'

'There's a taxi outside,' said the woman, pointing to the road beyond the high hedge that surrounded the front garden. 'I haven't paid for it. I've only got a pound in my purse.'

Una showed the woman into the ground floor sitting room then went back outside to pay the taxi driver. She was surprised when he told her the fare.

'Where on earth have you come from?'

'Gloucester,' he said.

Back in the sitting room, she said: 'I hear you've come from Gloucester.'

'Yes,' said the woman. 'He knows where the refuge is in Gloucester so I can't go there any more. He'd only go and beat the door down.'

Una nodded, strangely elated. This was her first 'new arrival', the first woman to turn up unannounced at the refuge since she had started to work there.

'How did you know how to find us?' she asked.

'I've been before,' said the woman in a deadpan voice. 'Earlier this year. About May.'

She noticed Una looking at her pink fluffy slippers and said: 'I'd only come out to get some milk. He dropped us off outside the Co-op while he went to park the car and place a bet. I asked this girl stacking shelves to let us out the back. I thought she wasn't going to at first but then she did. We ran all the way to the taxi rank. I was scared stiff he was going to come after us. I kept praying Len would be on the counter at the bookies and would keep him talking.'

Una tried to remember what she had been told on the two-day course she had attended on how to support abused adults. The most important thing you can do is to listen. That's what they had said. Just listen.

'Would you like something to drink? Have you had lunch?' she asked.

The woman said she wasn't hungry but would love a cup of tea. The children would probably like something to eat though. They'd had breakfast but nothing since.

'What are they called?' asked Una.

'He's Carl,' said the woman, pointing to the older child, 'and she's Jade.'

At the sound of his name, the boy began to pull at his mother's skirt.

'Where's my train? I want my train. I want to get my train.'

The woman pushed his hand away with unnecessary force.

'Shut up about your train! It's not here!'

Una introduced herself, stepping forward to shake the woman's hand. It was very cold, she noticed, small and cold like a fledgling fallen from the nest.

'I'm Germaine,' said the woman. 'Germaine Black. Good name when I'm like this.'

Una frowned then gave a quick smile as she realised the joke.

She made tea and jam sandwiches in the staff kitchen, filling two beakers with squash and opening a new packet of chocolate biscuits.

'Here you are,' she said, setting the tray down on the table by the window. The boy made a dive for the biscuits, helping himself to two, ignoring the sandwiches.

'Have you got a lid?' said Germaine, pointing at the cups. 'Only Jade will spill it otherwise.'

Una fetched a lid, making lists in her head as she went. She was as bad as her father, she thought, seeing them suddenly sitting in a café as her mother had described, the day stretching ahead like a beach early in the morning, untouched, sea-washed, whispering secrets.

When she came back, the boy was helping himself to a third biscuit. Germaine and Jade were still huddled in a chair, motionless, like puppets waiting for their strings to be pulled.

'Is she still in a cot?' asked Una, debating which room to give them. There were two rooms free. The one at the front was bigger but didn't have such a nice view as the smaller room at the back.

'Yes,' said Germaine. Then added: 'Where is everyone? Last time I was here it was like Piccadilly Circus. You couldn't hear yourself speak for kids screaming.'

'They're all at school,' said Una. 'Or at least most of them. I think the rest of them have gone down to the park to feed the ducks. And three of the women haven't got any children so I suppose that makes it a bit quieter.'

'Lucky them!' said Germaine, hoisting her daughter further up her lap.

'There are some toys next door. No, I don't think that's a good idea,' said Una, as the boy began to drag chairs over the floor.

'Carl! You heard what the lady said. Stop it!'

'There's a big yellow digger, I think. Go and see what it's doing. Just round there,' said Una, pointing at the nursery next door.

Carl stared at her defiantly for a moment then released his grasp on the chair he was holding and went into the nursery.

'Just like his Dad,' said Germaine. 'When he can't get what he wants, his first reaction is to smack you one.'

'Is that who . . . is that how . . . your eye . . . is that how it happened?' asked Una, curious to know and yet anxious not to seem curious.

Germaine tore a small piece off one of the jam sandwiches and inserted it in her daughter's mouth. Then she licked her fingers fastidiously. She had gone for a drink with a friend, she said, and bumped into a bloke, someone she'd known at school. They hadn't seen one another for years.

'I didn't know but there was this other bloke in the pub, a friend of Paul's. He saw us and last night he met up with Paul and told him a cock-and-bull story, that I'd been with this man, that . . . you know . . . we had a thing going . . .'

Una noticed that she kept moving her hands, clasping and unclasping them, twisting her skirt, round and round and round as though wringing wet sheets. She realised that her hands were hurt too, that the green marks she had taken for veins were bruises.

Paul had come in late, she said. She had already gone to bed and was half-asleep.

'He came upstairs and locked the door and then he grabbed hold of my feet and pulled me off the bed. Then he just went at me, kicking me, punching me, pulling my hair. He was shouting and shouting at me to tell him what we'd done. I said we hadn't done nothing, that we'd just talked, that I'd only seen him the once. But that just made him worse. He screamed at me that I was lying, that he knew I was lying. "Don't lie. Just tell me the truth. Tell me what you did." He kept on saying that – "Tell me what you did, tell me what you did" – and all the time he was punching me, mainly on the head because he knows it doesn't show up there. He woke up Carl and Jade, and they were both crying and screaming, and so in the end I said we had done it, I said we'd done it one afternoon while the kids was at me Mum's, that we'd gone round to this B and B place where he'd taken a room. I thought it might make him stop, that it was what he wanted to hear and it was, it must have been, because he just gave me one more wallop and then he laid off, told me to go and sort the kids out, to stop them screaming or else the neighbours would be complaining again, ringing up the council.'

She was so matter-of-fact, marvelled Una. So calm and detached, almost, no, yes, almost as though she was proud.

'I'm not going back,' she said, shaking her head violently as though Una had suggested that she should. 'Not this time. I'm not. No matter what he says or what promises he makes. I know he won't keep them. Last time he even said he'd see a doctor, that he knew he had a problem, that there were times when he just lost it, when he knew he was out of control. But he never did. He never does. He'll always be like it.'

Carl came back into the room wearing a pretend doctor's coat back to front and a stethoscope round his neck.

'Aah! Have you come to make mummy better?' said Germaine, holding out her arms.

But Carl pointed the stethoscope at her and made machine gun noises.

'Bang! Bang, bang! Bang, bang, bang!'

Germaine raised her eyebrows then winced.

'Ouch! I keep forgetting I can't do that,' she said.

We'll need photos, thought Una. Photos of the bruises. But we can do that later when the children have gone to bed. She led Germaine upstairs, introduced her to Jan who remembered her from May, then showed her the two rooms. Germaine chose the larger one at the front.

'You need all the space you can get. It can get very claustro-phobic. That's what I found last time,' she said.

Una nodded, ticking items off in her head. Nappies, towels, wash things, a change of clothes.

'Do you want to me call a doctor to have a look at your eye?' she asked. 'We can ask her to come here if you want. You won't have to go to the surgery.'

'No, it's OK. I can see all right. It's just badly swollen. It'll be OK once the swelling goes down.'

There were noises downstairs as the other residents began to drift in. Una introduced Germaine to one or two and was surprised at the way her manner changed, becoming notice-ably more cowed and wary, like that of a new recruit in a gang.

'How old is Carl by the way?' she asked, worried suddenly that she had misjudged his age.

'Just four. He's not at school yet,' said Germaine, reading her thoughts.

Good, thought Una. That was one fewer thing to worry about. She unlocked the airing cupboard and took out sheets and blankets. Bridget came back from court and demanded to know why someone had left a bottle of cleaning fluid on the floor in the front kitchen, the top off, just waiting for someone's child to come and drink it. Una explained and introduced her to Germaine who immediately said that Jade needed changing, she would take her to the bathroom.

'You'll need a doctor to see that eye,' said Bridget firmly. 'Come downstairs, will you, when you've changed your little girl, and we'll sort out the paperwork. I'll be in the office. You know where it is.'

Una waited for Germaine to contradict her but she didn't, just nodded, and said yes, OK, perhaps it was as well to be safe.

She opened the window in the bedroom to let in some fresh air. It was a bright afternoon, the first for many days, the sky cold cobalt, hard and clear as tapped glass. Someone was flying a model aeroplane, she saw, over there, on the playing field behind the allotments. She watched as it rose and fell behind the rooftops, wheeling and diving like a huge red bird, playing hide and seek with the few low clouds.

This was it, she thought. What she'd been looking for. The cause, the answer. She saw herself finding Germaine a flat, helping her choose curtains, babysitting while she went to evening classes, celebrating her first wage packet.

Then she turned to make the bed, yesterday's tears a word she had forgotten, a language she no longer spoke, not now, now that she was this new person, this new competent, worldly adult.

18

'Do you think they're all right?' asked Helen, deciding that the tall man in the expensive overcoat who had just sat down opposite the woman in grey was her lover, not her husband.

'Who?' asked Philip, not looking up, calculating mileage in his head. If they travelled on the back roads instead of the motorway, it would take them a day longer to reach Lyons and they were already three days behind schedule. On the other hand, the back roads would take them close to that village he had been reading about the night before, the one with six roads leading in to it and only four, so the story went, leading out. Besides, what did it matter if they were three days late? It didn't mean anything, not now, not when he couldn't even remember whether it was Tuesday or Wednesday.

'The children, of course. Una and Martin,' said Helen.

'They'll be fine,' said Philip, folding up the map, deciding to take the back roads. After all, that was what one was supposed to do when one was travelling – get lost, have adventures, experience the unknown.

'Do you think Una will be managing? That she'll be coping with the job? It sounded as though it might be very demanding – emotionally, I mean. You know how intense she is. I worry that she'll get too involved, that she'll take it all personally. Do you think she'll be all right?'

'I don't know. Probably. Besides, even if she isn't, we decided it was time she learnt how to sort out her own problems, didn't we, that it would be a good idea if we went away, for her as well as for us, that she was going nowhere and wouldn't, unless she had to.'

That was all very well, thought Helen. But it didn't stop her worrying. She decided to phone Una that night, even though it was only Thursday, not Sunday, the day on which they had agreed to phone once a week.

The door opened again and a man wearing a beret came in carrying two buckets full of tomatoes. He put them down in front of the bar and ordered a coffee with what appeared to be whisky.

'Do you think there's a market on today? There's an awful lot of activity compared to yesterday,' said Helen, looking out at the street beyond the table where the woman in grey and her lover sat. They were eating croissants, she saw, dunking them in bowls of fragrant hot chocolate, steam rising, slow and melancholy, fading into their faces.

'Let's have another coffee,' she said, tugging childishly at Philip's sleeve. 'And a croissant. Let's have a croissant each. I know we said we wouldn't. Not every day. But I just feel like one today.'

Philip touched the hand on his sleeve and squeezed it, delighting in her pleasure, the joy she took, had always taken, in small things – clean sheets, a walk in autumn, the smell of the garden after it had rained in spring.

Yes, he said, after he had ordered the coffee and the croissants. Yes, there probably was a market. There were far more people walking around outside than there had been the day before. And many of them looked as though they came from the country, as though they'd come in to sell the week's eggs or vegetables and buy meat and fish in exchange.

She loved him, she thought. Loved the way he made her feel special, like a new thing, found, wrapped in cotton wool and laid in a tin, a child's treasure. She had worried he would grow bitter, that he would resent the sacrifices he had made, blame her for what had happened. But he hadn't. He had been unhappy. She knew that. Had chafed at his job like a young horse, newly bridled. But he had never taken it out on her. And she loved him for this. Loved him more and more.

Their croissants arrived and they ate them, dunking them as the couple by the window had dunked theirs. They were talking now, she saw, their heads low and conspiratorial, almost touching, like trees arched across a road.

She thought of the evening it had happened as she had thought of it so many times since leaving England, as though being in a strange country allowed her to do so. It had not been like they said, how everyone had imagined. The man had been kind. When he found out who she was, the mistake she had made, he had been shocked. He had offered to give her money to stay in a hotel and pay for her ticket home. He had wanted to leave immediately, to take her with him, to find her somewhere safe to stay. It was she who had insisted, who had said she wanted to do it, who had persuaded him, forced him almost. And when she had, when they were lying there, side by side, naked, he had touched her so gently, been so full of quiet wonder, so careful. No one could have hoped for a better first lover. She had always thought that, only of course she had never been able to say so. She wondered where he was now. What he was doing. What he had done all these years. Whether he ever thought of her.

The couple by the window left and shortly afterwards Philip suggested that they should leave too. There was a market, they discovered. It was in the square where the old men had played boules the previous afternoon, gathering like crows as the effects of their *côtes de porc* wore off, almost all wearing starched white shirts and grey trousers. It was the kind of market peculiar to small French or Italian regional towns, as much a social occasion as an opportunity to shop. Everywhere there were groups of people talking, plastic carrier bags full of knobbly shapes spilling out at their feet. There was a fish van, a cheese van, and a woman selling chrysanthemums, probably the last of the year, only four or five bunches, tied with yellow string, spread out on an upturned cardboard box. Helen went to buy salami at one of the *charcuterie* stalls while Philip lingered among the smaller stallholders. An old man cut an onion in two and offered him a slice, insisting that he tried it, expounding its virtues. He bit into it, surprised at how sweet it was, rolling the taste round, while the man smiled, pleased at his surprise. He bought ten of the onions and sat down on one of the benches at the side of the boules ground, near where Helen was queuing. Did she realise, he wondered, looking up at the sky, streaked with the white trail of an aeroplane's flight? Did she realise how much it had hurt him to lose his job, the job he loved, that he had always wanted to do, that fitted him so well? He did not blame her. No, he had never done that. But he wondered if she knew. Before leaving England, he had read a newspaper story about a woman reunited with her daughter thirty-five years after she had given her up for adoption. 'There was a big hole in the centre of my life,' the story quoted the woman as saying. 'There was a loss . . . I was incomplete. Now I'm whole again.' He had known exactly how that woman had felt because that was how he felt – incomplete, as though something was missing. He looked up again at the sky, tracing the trail with his eye as it fell away, the sharp, clear line becoming ragged at the edges, fainter, fainter, then just the merest hint of white. He could ask again, he thought. They might have changed the rules. They might allow it now.

He would not have remembered that town if it had not been for this. Sitting on a bench, an idea dawning.

19

Rob felt someone touch his arm. It was Mandy, one of the girls he shared a house with.

'Come on, let's dance,' she said, catching hold of the banisters to keep her balance.

Rob looked past her into the gloom of the sitting room where a few figures were gyrating sadly to music. They had moved the sofa so that there would be room to dance and it stood in the hallway now, taking up most of the space, a red moquette three-seater with an unsightly stain on the middle cushion.

He explained that he had been about to fetch a drink from the kitchen.

'Do you want one?' he asked, trying to make up for turning her down.

She shook her head and slumped on to the sofa, hurt now as well as drunk.

Martin and Simon were by the door in the kitchen talking records. Chris and Adam and Jessica sat round the table discussing a newspaper story about a widow who wanted to use the frozen sperm of her dead husband to conceive.

'I mean he didn't give his permission. That's the point,' said Chris. 'Once you start allowing women to use sperm without the man's permission, well . . . they'll be having children all over the place . . . turning up at your door in the middle of the night demanding maintenance . . .'

'But they were married!' exploded Jessica. 'They wanted children. They'd discussed it. Everyone knew they wanted them. She's not making it up. Besides, when you get married, you're supposed to share all your worldly goods, aren't you, body and all? And if a man's sperm isn't part of his body or worldly goods, then I don't know what is.'

Rob found a plastic cup among the debris next to the sink, poured out the liquid at the bottom and opened a can of one of the least offensive brands of beer left. Some wag had stuck cigarette butts in the mouth of the pumpkin mask that had decorated the table earlier. There were chips floating in the remains of the mulled wine, a soggy mass of kitchen roll stuffed in an empty baked potato, and smears of what looked like peanut butter on top of the fridge. The floor was sticky with dropped food, mainly kidney beans, squashed to a pulp by the heavy duty footwear favoured by most of the guests. Rob wrinkled his nose with distaste, feeling staid and middle-aged. A year ago, he wouldn't have noticed the mess. Now he found it offensive. He was getting too old for parties like this, he thought.

The back door burst open and Samantha, his host, ran in from the garden, shrieking and waving sparklers.

'All right?' she said and thrust one of the sparklers into Rob's hands before dancing off into the hallway.

Rob slipped out the open door into the garden. There was a couple kissing on the patio and beyond them, huddled round the fire they had lit earlier, four figures including Beth, one of his other house mates. She called out, inviting him to join them but he shook his head and walked on, hoping they would think he was drunk. There was a bag full of last year's leaves lying on its side in the middle of the path. Rob sat down on it, feeling his head clear in the cool night air. The couple who had been kissing on the patio went into the greenhouse and shut the door behind them. There was a crash as they knocked something over. The group round the fire giggled then started to discuss whether first-born children were invariably conservative and younger siblings more disposed to take risks.

Rob watched them – the heads bent earnestly in discussion, the fire flaring up from time to time, lighting the faces. What about only children, he wanted to ask? What about only children born to parents that met because of a message in a bottle, thrown idly into the sea one day out of boredom and frustration and a half-remembered dream? What were they like, he wanted to ask? What was their destiny?

Instead, he walked out of the back gate to paddle in the sea three streets away. 'Come on,' she had cried, that New Year's Day almost three years ago on a Cornish beach. And she had torn off her boots and socks and run down the sand to the foam's edge, the wet slap of sea against bare skin. 'But it's freezing!' he had shouted, the wind snatching the words from his mouth. 'So?' she had retorted. 'You won't remember the cold tomorrow but you'll remember paddling with me on New Year's Day. You'll remember that. You'll remember that for ever.' And she had run in then, splashing, not flinching, arms outstretched as if greeting an old friend. 'Crazy girl. Crazy, crazy girl,' he had thought and bent down to take off his boots.

There were plenty more fish in the sea, he thought, bending down now, taking his boots off again. Only they were not her. There was something so unmistakable about her. She was so much herself, so irredeemably, unforgettably Una. Other people could quite easily be other people, he thought. If they cut their hair, changed their clothes, altered their accent slightly, they could be Mary instead of Beryl, Roger instead of Graham. But not Una. She was pure essence, bottled, intrinsic. There was no confusing her. And yet there was no placing her either. No setting her down, labelled, defined, done. She danced on the edge of his understanding like a teasing mermaid, within reach and yet never in reach. Never held firm.

He stepped into the water, holding out his arms as he remembered her doing. Her hair now. What a thing of glory that was, like an avenue of trees in autumn. A thing of shade and light, of hidden secret depths. How he had loved to watch her brush it. He had loved to hear her talk too. Sometimes, at college, when he was very tired, he had lain on her bed, in that room at the top of the house with the blue blind she had painted herself, and said, 'Talk to me.' And she had talked, sitting next to him on the bed, tracing the outline of his mouth with her fingers, telling him about her day, what she had seen and heard, the chance remark made by a friend that had changed her mood like a tide turning.

No, it was no good. It was nothing like it had been that first day in January. The sea had been wild then, the waves foaming round their legs. It was calm now, unpleasantly still. He waded back to the shore. Damn! What was that? He had trodden on something sharp. He stood on one leg, almost overbalancing, aware of how comic he must look – a man paddling in the sea at two in the morning, wondering whether his foot was bleeding.

Later, lying in bed, the cut on his foot smarting from the antiseptic lotion he had applied, he tried to remember how it had started, unravelling the months like a ball of string, looking for the knot. He had told her about the job. Had done it badly. That was it. And then he had not phoned and then, when he had, she had not answered. And then he had gone round and she had not been there or had but had not come to the door and then, yes, he had gone round and waited. Waited and waited until it was cold and dark and his heart hard. I won't phone her now, he had vowed. I won't make the first move. Not now.

It was all so silly, he thought. Somehow or other it had happened and now, here they were, like warring countries that had forgotten why they were at war but were reluctant to stop, too proud to make the first move.

Thinking these thoughts, remembering her hair, his body tight with lust and loneliness and the hard, dried-on residue of pride, he fell asleep and dreamt bad dreams.

20

A figure jumped up as Una cycled into the yard, startling her, making the bike wobble.

'It's me! Martin!'

Una dismounted, peering disbelievingly through the gloom.

'Martin! What on earth are you doing here?'

'Can I stay the night? Is that OK? I don't mind sleeping on the floor.'

'Well . . . yes, of course. Of course it's all right. But what . . . I mean, why . . .?'

'I'll tell you inside. I'm freezing. I've been waiting more than an hour. I thought you'd never come.'

She pulled off her gloves and padlocked her bike, cursing the lack of light, wincing as her bare fingers touched cold metal.

'There's going to be a frost,' she said, looking up at the first sharp stars pricking the dark.

'Dad would be suggesting thicker jumpers,' said Martin.

Una laughed. It had become a family joke that Philip waited as long as possible before agreeing it was cold enough to switch on the central heating. In reality, he usually turned it on some time in November but Una and Martin teased him by pretending that each year he waited longer and longer until one year when he had switched it on in January and turned it off a week later, claiming spring had arrived.

Inside, she rushed about, drawing curtains and plumping cushions, scooping yesterday's knickers off the floor and throwing them into the purple plastic box that served as her dirty linen basket. What had happened? Why had he come? Where were Teresa and Matty?

'Tea or coffee? Or there's hot chocolate if you prefer only you'd have to have it with water because there's hardly any milk left . . . unless you want to nip out and get some.'

'Tea please. With just the one teabag,' he replied.

That was another family joke. That Philip made tea with three teabags a person. He, for his part, claimed Martin merely waved a teabag near a cup. 'Hot water with milk,' he said whenever Martin made a pot. 'Gnats' piss.'

'Is this what you read now?' asked Martin, looking at the books piled next to her bed. He read out some of the titles – *Post-Trauma Stress and Critical Incident Debriefing, Transactional Analysis in the Workplace, Demystifying Child Abuse.*

Una scowled, embarrassed he should know of her attempts to develop her counselling skills. Martin had always mocked her efforts at self-improvement, dismissing them as phases. 'Una's Bible phase,' he had said when she had read the Psalms at night before going to bed. And later, when she had become vegetarian and had handed out anti-vivisection leaflets in the city centre on Saturday mornings, he had told their parents she was going through the nut crumble years, and not to worry, she would grow out of it, everyone did.

She handed him his tea and sat down on the floor on a bean bag – there was only one chair and Martin was sitting in it, his shoes unlaced, his legs stretched out as if he had just dropped in to discuss Christmas presents.

'So?' she said. 'Go on. Tell me.'

'Teresa's thrown me out.'

'What!'

'Teresa's thrown me out.'

'What do you mean?'

She couldn't have thrown him out. They were the happiest couple she knew – the ideal she aspired to. They were in love, they were her brother and her brother's wife, they were going to live together for ever.

'She's suggested we have a trial separation, that we live on our own for a few months, just to give us time to think.'

'To think about what?'

They had not said anything, neither of them, had not even hinted, and she had seen them for tea only two weeks ago.

'To think about us, where we're going. As a couple, I mean. Whether we . . . well, whether we still want to be together, I suppose.'

'But why . . . what's happened . . . I thought . . . I mean, you get on so well.' She petered out feebly, realising they had seemed offhand with one another that time they had come round for tea and before that, when she had had dinner at their house, how she had found Teresa working late at night on her own.

'You mean like you and Rob?'

She flushed. There was no need to bring Rob into it, she thought. This was about him and Teresa, not her and Rob.

'I'm sorry. It's just one always thinks other people get on well. It's so difficult to know what happens when the door's shut.'

'Is there someone else? Have you . . . ?'

'No, it's not that.'

'Teresa then?'

'No, no.'

'Well, what is it, then? What's happened?'

He sighed and drew his legs up.

'I don't know. I mean I do and I don't. There are several things. One is that Teresa's not sure she loves me enough to want to spend the rest of her life with me. Also, we seem to be arguing the whole time. And also, well . . .'

He looked down. Una waited, not saying anything, listening as she had learnt to do.

'I don't know if Teresa has said anything . . .'

She waited again.

He stood up suddenly, put his cup down and walked over to the fire.

'Teresa thinks I've got a drink problem. She wants me to get treatment and I won't. I don't need to. There isn't a problem. I enjoy a drink after work . . . it helps me unwind . . . but she thinks I need to, that I can't survive without one. But then today . . . well, I went through a red light on the way home and was stopped and breathalysed by the police. They said I was over the limit . . .'

'Martin!'

He wheeled round to face her.

'Only just! Even the police said I was only just. There was a wine-and-cheese party after lunch. A leaving do. I just had more than I thought. That's all. I wasn't drunk or anything.'

He sat down again, his shoulders hunched defensively.

Una stared. He could not have surprised her more if he had said he was becoming a monk. Her brother an alcoholic! It was just not possible.

'What are you going to do?' she asked quietly.

'Oh, I don't know,' he said bitterly. 'All the usual things, I suppose. Find some crummy flat somewhere. Take Matty to the zoo in the rain. Stew in self-pity.'

She rose and went to comfort him, feeling him crumple as she took him in her arms. This was her big brother, she thought, her brother who had been too old to play Ludo with her, who had an answer for everything, who was nicknamed 'No, but . . .' by their father, this was him now, crying, sobs shaking his body.

They ate curried mince left over from the night before with oven chips and frozen peas. For pudding they had fried bananas with long-life cream.

'How do you open it?' he said afterwards, drying up, pointing at the cutlery drawer.

'Sorry. The handle's fallen off. They're all falling off. Like this. Look.'

She opened the drawer underneath then prised open the cutlery drawer. It was amazing what one got used to, she thought, looking round the flat, seeing it with a stranger's eyes. That window, for example, the one that seemed to regard its frame as a second cousin twice removed. She had meant to do something about it. To complain to the landlord or buy a draught excluder. Instead, she had stuffed it with newspaper and forgotten about it.

The phone rang, surprising them both.

'What if it's Teresa?' said Una hastily. 'Do you want her to know you're here? What shall I say?'

'No. I mean yes. I don't mind. Tell her if she asks.'

But it was Helen, not Teresa, phoning to remind Una that it was Matty's birthday on Saturday, she wouldn't forget, would she? Una mouthed 'Mum' across the room at Martin, who scissored his arms violently, indicating he did not want to talk to her.

Yes, she was fine. So were Martin and Teresa. Absolutely fine, lied Una. They were thinking of taking Matty to the zoo for her birthday to see the penguins being fed.

'But I thought she was having a little party,' said Helen.

'Oh she is, she is, she still is. I think they're going to the zoo on Sunday or maybe the week after. You know, she's drawing people with fingers now,' she babbled. 'Great big fat sausages. And she's very particular about there being five. She's doing feet as well. Enormous flat things like flippers.'

Helen asked about Una's work and Una told her about Germaine and the children and her plans to find them a flat near by. There was one vacant in the same block, she said. She was going to ask the landlord if he took people on benefit. But what about them, she asked? Where were they? Were they still in France? And Helen said yes, near Lyons – they'd spent the previous night in a wonderful village with six roads leading into it but only four out.

'How come? That doesn't make sense.'

'I don't know. But there were. We counted them. It was driving your father mad. I thought he was going to suggest we stayed there another night just so he could work it out.'

Una talked about Sinead and the clay bust she was making and Helen asked if she had a cold only her voice sounded funny, different somehow.

'I fell asleep by the fire. That's all. I was asleep when you phoned,' said Una.

Helen said was she sure the fire was working properly, they could be ever so dangerous and did she know you could buy carbon monoxide detectors.

'What was all that about?' asked Martin when she had put the receiver down.

'Just the fire. She's worried it's going to poison me.'

'I must say it's not particularly effective. You're either too hot or too cold.'

Una was about to say that if he didn't like it he could always go back to his nice warm house but decided not to, instead making up a bed on the floor from the chair cushion, the bean bag, squashed as flat as it would go, and a spare pillow. She divided the blankets equally and gave Martin a jumper to wear over his pyjamas.

Later, when Martin was asleep, snoring softly, she got up and tiptoed to the window, opening it slightly in case her mother was right and there was something wrong with the fire. The moon was an odd shape, she saw. It was sitting in a lace shawl of cloud – greenish, see-through, like a blown duck's egg held up to the light. She turned back to face the room, noticing how Martin was curled up, each arm grasping the opposite shoulder, his feet protruding over the end of the bean bag.

He had always been different from the rest of the family, she reflected, climbing back into bed. It was not just that he looked different, that he was silver compared to their gold, his eyes green instead of brown or hazel, his hair black instead of their auburn, his skin white – clean sheet, peeled apple white without so much as a single freckle. He was different in other ways as well. Clever, very clever, impatient, cynical. He was also moody, given to depression whereas they, basically, were disposed to be happy. Yes, she knew her father had been unhappy. But that was because of his job, because of what he was doing. It was not his nature whereas unhappiness ran in Martin like a river through a land, swift, deep-flowing, difficult to divert. Was Teresa right, she wondered? Was he really drinking too much?

Her thoughts began to snag, to catch on sleep, running up ladders of doubt. She had thought her father would work at the bank until he retired. She had thought her parents would live in their house, in the family house, until they died or became too ill or old to look after themselves. And she had thought Martin and Teresa were the perfect modern couple, that they would stay together for ever. Now her father had left his job, her parents had left home, and Martin had left Teresa.

Thinking this, of how her world had turned upside, she drifted off to sleep and dreamt of a jumbled world in which people spread sacks on a still, unmoving sea.

'What are you doing? Where have the waves gone?' she asked, peering down into the green, glassy depths.

'They're there. Look. Over there,' said the people, pointing to the shore.

And she looked and saw that they were right. The land was moving – green fields rolling up to meet the sky as once the sea had done.

'What's happened? Tell me. Somebody tell me,' she cried.

But the people appeared not to hear, singing as they spread the sacks, red and gold and purple, covering up the green. She started to run, to catch at their clothes, to force them to look at her. And as she did, she realised they were not people. She had been mistaken. They had no faces – no eyes or nose or mouth. Their skin was white, smooth and white as peeled eggs. She screamed, covering her eyes, fighting to reach the land that had become sea. She would never understand now. Never.

21

Germaine sat in her room watching Jade sleep. Opposite her, Sellotaped to the wall, was a picture she had cut out from one of the Sunday supplements. It showed a round wooden table piled high with bread. There were round loaves and long loaves, plaits and brioches, buns and muffins. Behind the table was a kitchen dresser stacked with blue-and-white plates and beyond this a door, half open, leading to a cottage garden through which the sun streamed. It was the only thing in the room that was hers, she thought, the only thing apart from the clothes she had arrived in and the pink fluffy slippers and they had been a joke anyhow, picked up by Paul in an odds-and-ends bin at one of the local shops.

She had liked cooking, especially baking. They had always had an old-fashioned tea on Sundays. Scones, trifle, egg-and-cress sandwiches and at least two cakes. Mum had come, and her brother if he was not doing anything, and sometimes Paul's mum as well. Dawn, her friend, had sold her cakes at the car-boot sales she went to in the summer. They sold like hot cakes, she always said afterwards, laughing at her own joke.

There were no cake tins in the kitchens here. Nor any wooden spoons. She had mentioned this to Bridget who had said she was always buying wooden spoons, she didn't know where they went but yes, she would buy some next time she was at the cash and carry. She had not said anything about buying cake tins.

She hated the kitchens here. She hated the thin, battered saucepans, the chipped charity mugs, the other women looking on, sniffing, hinting that she was using too many rings on the cooker, spending too long, taking over the place. They had their tea to cook as well, didn't she know, they said, opening a can of sweetcorn for the fourth day running. There was a new white geranium on the windowsill in her kitchen at home, a cork noticeboard with coloured drawing pins, the red salt and pepper pots they'd been given as wedding presents standing sentinel on the table.

She hated the bathrooms too. How there was always scum on the side of the bath, always hair blocking the plug holes, always someone wanting to come in, banging on the door, shouting at her to hurry up. Last night it had been ten o'clock before she had been able to wash. She had been only a quarter of an hour and during that time three people had knocked on the door. Three people! She hit the bed with her fist, so violently that the soft toy someone had given Jade, a white bird with red wings, flew up into the air and landed on the floor.

She took out a cigarette, her last one, and lit it. What was she supposed to do? She could go for walks, yes, but where? It was getting cold now. Besides, Carl couldn't walk far. She wasn't going to sit in the library like those old men one saw – coughing, wheezing, pretending to read the papers. She was only twenty-one. She had her whole life before her. And here she was sitting in a room in borrowed clothes staring at a piece of paper torn out from a magazine. She could join a playgroup. Sit at the side with the mums while Carl hit other children with a dumper truck. But what was the point when she didn't know how long she was going to be here? Besides, how could she make friends? She could hardly invite them back to her place for coffee. 'Come up to my room. Yes, I know it's not big. That there are no comfortable chairs. No Aga. No flowers from the garden. But look at that picture. Yes, that one on the wall. Dream that you're there, sitting by the table, that the bread is warm, fresh, soft to the touch, that soon I will cut you a slice and spread it with butter and we will eat and drink and talk about our men.'

Someone banged on the door and she stubbed out the cigarette quickly. Jade was starting to get asthma. She had told the doctor she didn't smoke near her, had promised Una she wouldn't.

'He's said yes, he's said yes,' said Una, flinging open the door.

Germaine scowled.

'Ssssh! She's sleeping.'

Una glanced at the cot where Jade lay face down, her bottom stuck up in the air. Then she danced into the room and seized Germaine's hands.

'He's said you can have the flat. That he'll take you. Even though you are on benefit. I've got the key. We can go and see it. Now, if you want.'

'I'm not going before she wakes up,' said Germaine sourly. 'She was up twice in the night. If she doesn't sleep now, she'll be foul.'

She'd been smoking again, thought Una, looking round the room, catching sight of the bread picture, wondering why she'd cut it out.

'Where's Carl?' she asked.

'Downstairs in the nursery. Playing with the sand.'

'I'll make some tea, shall I? While we wait?'

'If you want.'

They sat on the bed together and talked of what Germaine would be able to do once she had a place of her own. Or rather Una talked and Germaine listened.

'You haven't drunk your tea,' said Una when Jade finally stirred, her face hot and red from where it had been pressed against the sheet.

'No. Sorry. I didn't feel like it. I've gone off it recently.'

The flat was smaller and shabbier than Una had imagined, shabbier even than hers. The sitting room was predominantly brown with beige curtains and a mushroom-coloured sofa. There were yellow tobacco stains on the walls.

'We can repaint it,' she said, trying not to show her disappointment. 'It will look better then. That always makes a big difference.'

The kitchen was at one end of the sitting room, more of a corridor than a room in its own right, not wide enough for two people to stand side by side.

'You'll be able to see the children when you're cooking. That's nice. They like to be near you, don't they? All children do.'

The red floor tiles were sticky with dirt, pockmarked with holes through which were visible earlier, older coverings –

grey lino, something blue and below that, floorboards, painted green.

They went into the bedrooms, one of which was only just big enough to take a single bed. Germaine looked round, seeing with a stab of homesickness the children's room at home – the basket full of soft toys, the alphabet mural, the picture of Babar the elephant in a hot air balloon. They'd been meaning to decorate it. They'd even bought the paint and the stencils. Paul wouldn't be able to do it on his own. He was no good at decorating.

'You'd have to have Jade in with you. Either that or let the children have the big room. That might be the best way round. There's quite a large airing cupboard, see? And the outlook is open. It's nice not to have a house directly opposite, isn't it?'

She'd never be able to go out, thought Germaine. Jade was only one. It would be twelve years, twelve years at least before she'd be able to go out for the evening. Una had said she would babysit but she wouldn't be here for ever. She'd marry, move away, buy a house of her own. What sort of life would it be for the children, growing up without a garden? And Carl was riding his tricycle so well. They'd talked about buying him a bike for Christmas. She'd never see her mum either. It was too far to come every week. Not without a car. Besides, it was damp. Damp and dark and miserable and it didn't matter what Una said, it would still look miserable even when it had been repainted because that was what it was, a miserable little flat.

'It's OK, isn't it?' said Una. 'I mean I know it's not palatial but . . . well . . .'

'Beggars can't be choosers,' said Germaine, finishing the sentence for her.

'Something like that. By the way, what's that? That toy Carl keeps on talking to?'

'It's a train. Your friend Sinead made it for him after we visited her. It came in the post this morning. He hasn't put it down since.'

'How nice of her. Can I see? Carl, can I have a look at your new train?'

Carl shook his head and ran off, kicking the sofa as he went past.

Una felt put out that Sinead had thought to replace the train

Carl was always talking about. She should have done that, she thought. She should have thought of it.

Outside, walking back to the bus stop, Germaine caught sight of herself in a shop window. Christ, what a mess she looked. Her hair needed cutting. It had gone all straggly and thin. And she had put on weight through sitting around so much. No man would look twice at her now. And only five years before they'd been fighting over her. No wonder Carl had kicked the sofa. She felt like kicking something herself. Anything would do. A door. A wall. Or that woman there. That slim woman with the blonde bobbed hair who was smiling at her husband. She felt like kicking her. Hard. Where it hurt.

22 ∫

Una bought fish and chips and ate them standing up in the shop, watching couples walk by in the dark, trying not to notice their joined hands.

There was nothing unique about her position, she told herself. Hundreds of couples split up every day. And all of them coped. They found ways of managing. Just as she was managing now, she added, trying not to be too hard on herself.

Afterwards, cycling home, she decided to visit Sinead. She would thank her for the train she had made for Carl, find out if she had finished the bust of her mother.

Sinead had clay on her hands when she came to the door and a smear on her right cheek, dried on, starting to crack.

'Don't you ever stop?' asked Una.

Sinead laughed.

'I don't stop because I don't start. I'm always doing it – even when I'm not doing it, if you see what I mean. In fact, often that's the most important bit – getting it right in my head.'

There was a smell of onions in the flat, also of baking. Two lamps were lit. One, on the table next to Sinead's bed, gave out a soft pinkish glow, the other, on her work table, a stronger, brighter light. The curtains were drawn but not fully. Una could see the street lamps across the road and beyond them the shapeless dark of the Downs and the black, starless night, land and sky in one skin.

'There's soup if you're hungry and fresh bread. Leek and potato. Over there in that red saucepan.'

'No thanks. I've just eaten.'

She hung up her coat on the hooks Sinead had made in

a blacksmith's forge in Devon. One had a kink in it like a swan's neck bent suddenly under water. This was the one she always chose.

Una approached the work table where the bust of Sinead's mother stood, shining in the light of the lamp like a field new-ploughed, sliced earth, slabs of brown. She looked at it for a few moments then sat down, stretched out a hand, hesitated, looked across the room at where Sinead stood near the window, then lightly, very lightly, touched a clay cheek. No, it was cold. Cold and slightly damp. The wrong colour as well. And yet one could fancy that there was blood there, the soft give of flesh, of warm skin. She looked at the nose, at the nostrils, the small delicate ears, the eyes, large but narrowed slightly, the mouth, lips parted, the teeth just visible, the lower jaw jutting slightly forward. There were lines under the eyes and also round the mouth but not many. It was the face of a woman in her prime. A woman with a sense of humour, smiling or just about to, her mouth moving open. Someone had just said something. It was funny but she didn't agree with it. That's why her eyes were slightly narrowed, the forehead puckered in the middle. She was halfway between a frown and a smile. Una looked across the room again then quickly back at the face. There was so much expression there, so much movement, so much life. Every grain worked.

'Is it how she is or how you'd like her to be?' she asked finally.

Sinead turned round, relieved. She hated those first few minutes, could never bear to watch someone looking at her work.

'Neither,' she said, walking across the room to join Una. 'It's how she could have been.'

Una picked up a piece of clay and rolled it into a pellet between two fingertips, squashing it flat, then starting again.

'Do you think it wouldn't have happened if she hadn't met him? That she'd have been OK?'

Sinead also picked up a piece of clay.

'It wasn't just him. Her mother died a month before he left and then there was me. Apparently, I didn't sleep very much. Or feed or anything. There were no health visitors or community midwives then, not like there are now. Her doctor gave her a prescription for some anti-depressant tablets and told her to come back when she'd run out. And so she did. She thought they would make her better, that if she kept on taking them she would wake up one morning and not want to cry. And when this didn't happen, when she still wanted to cry, she took more, and then more and more until one night she took so many she didn't wake up in the morning. The only reason they found her was because I'd posted some of my toys through the letterbox. The woman living in the flat opposite saw them when she went out to the shops in the morning. They were still there when she went out in the afternoon to post a letter and then she heard me crying. When she banged on the door and couldn't get an answer, she called the police. That's when they found her. I was thirsty apparently. That's why I was crying. I'd climbed on to a chair and found some biscuits on the table but I hadn't had anything to drink.'

She paused, grinding the clay between the palms of her hands.

'But no, in answer to your question, it wouldn't have happened. If she hadn't met him, she'd have gone back to Ireland and married a banker or lawyer and kept horses. In the summer, she'd have opened the garden to the public for charity. That's how it could have been, how it would have been.'

Una shivered.

'It's scary, isn't it, to think we could meet someone tomorrow, do something, just one thing, that would change our lives, change them for ever?'

Sinead regarded her steadily.

'It's scary but also exciting. I like it. It gives an edge to things.'

She looked down at the table then up again.

'Have you heard from Rob?'

Una stopped rolling the clay with her fingertips – suddenly – so that the pellet fell between them, landing on the table and rolling on to the floor.

'No. I told you. We're not seeing one another. Why does everyone keep asking? What do I have to do? Wear a banner saying, "No, we haven't got back together"?'

She bent to pick up the clay pellet, glad of the chance to

hide her face, to force back the tears that had sprung to her eyes.

Sinead sat down at the table.

'I suppose I ask because I rarely saw you without him,' she said slowly. 'And . . . well . . . because you seemed so right together. You seemed to fit him and him you, like pieces in a puzzle.'

Inextricably bound, thought Una. That's what he had said one New Year's Day, lying on the beach on the wet sand. That they were inextricably bound.

Sinead sprinkled water on to the clay bust of her mother then started to cover it with plastic.

'How's Germaine?' she asked, not looking up.

'Fine. Fine,' said Una, pleased to change the subject. 'We went to see the flat today. The one I told you about, in the same block as mine.'

'And?'

'Well, it's a bit grotty but I think it'll be all right when it's been repainted.'

'So she hasn't changed her mind then, about leaving her husband?'

'No, why? Why should she?' asked Una, sounding surprised.

'No reason. It's just I thought most of the women went back to their partners in the end. That's what you said, didn't you? That very few left for good. And it must be very difficult for her with none of her own things.'

'Yes. Yes, I suppose it must,' said Una, feeling unaccountably needled.

Sinead finished covering the bust, tidied away her tools and swept the table.

'Tea, coffee or hot milk and brandy?' she offered.

'What about the sloe gin? Is it ready?' asked Una, remembering how, on a previous visit, she'd found Sinead pricking sloes with a wool needle, her hands purple with juice.

Sinead shook her head.

'I'll have the milk and brandy then, with a bit of honey as well, please.'

She sat down and laid her head on the table, the smell of dried clay in her nostrils.

'By the way, I almost forgot,' she said, lifting her head suddenly. 'You remember Julie at school? The one who burnt her eyebrows once on a Bunsen burner and made such a fuss about it?'

'I think so,' said Sinead, frowning, measuring milk into a saucepan.

'Well, I bumped into her a little while ago and she said she was getting married. She said she'd send me an invitation. I didn't think she would but she did. It came yesterday.'

Sinead twisted a spoonful of honey round and round so that it didn't drip.

'Are you going to go?'

'I don't know. Maybe. Probably not.'

They drank the milk and brandy sitting cross-legged on the floor in front of the fire, talking about other people at school – Susie who'd met someone on a kibbutz and gone to live in Israel, Matt who was serving an eighteen-month prison sentence after stealing from his employer, and Katya, Katya who'd made everyone laugh with her impersonations, who was the best netball player the school had ever had, who'd drowned that summer swimming in a reservoir while staying with her grandparents in Yorkshire.

'You can stay the night, you know,' said Sinead when they finally stopped talking and realised it was nearly midnight. 'I can take the cushions off the sofa and make up a bed.'

So Una phoned Martin to let him know she would not be coming back that night and helped Sinead make up a bed on the floor.

'You're so tidy,' she said, coming back into the living room after cleaning her teeth. 'You even wring out your flannel.'

'Yes,' agreed Sinead, smiling. 'I have to be. I have to have space for the chaos inside.'

Una undressed in front of the fire, quickly pulling on the leggings and sweatshirts Sinead had put out for her.

'It's freezing. Even worse than my flat,' she complained, drawing the blankets up to her chin.

'You should see me when it's really cold,' laughed Sinead. 'I even wear a balaclava. I've often wondered what someone would think if they knocked on the door in the middle of the night. They'd probably think I was a burglar.'

She turned out the lights and they lay in silence for a while, listening to the roar of the wind in the trees outside.

Then Sinead spoke suddenly, startling Una.

'My father phoned yesterday.'

'What?'

'He's coming over. He wants to spend Christmas here.'

Una peered through the darkness, trying to make out the expression on Sinead's face, waiting for her to say something else. But when she finally spoke, it was not about her father.

'I used to think about you at Christmas,' she said.

'Oh?'

'Yes, I used to imagine you opening your stocking on your parents' bed, passing round chocolate money, wrapping paper piled high all around you. And later I would imagine you sitting down at lunch, reading out jokes from crackers while your father carved and someone put on a record of Christmas carols.'

Una stared guiltily at the dark shape a few feet away that was Sinead's face. She had never invited Sinead to spend Christmas with her family, had never thought she might be lonely.

'My great-aunt didn't believe in Christmas,' said Sinead simply. 'I bought her a present once, a scarf I think, but she told me not to and so the next year I didn't.'

Una reached out in the dark until she found Sinead's hand.

'I'm sorry,' she said, squeezing the hand tightly. 'I never knew. I'm sorry. I'm so sorry.'

23

Afterwards, when she had finished paddling, she had run along the beach, her long hair streaming behind her. She was always running, Rob thought. Not because she had to, because she was late, but because she liked to, because she liked the feeling of speed, of cold air against her face.

That was how they had first met. He had turned a corner and she had run straight into him, almost knocking him over.

'Are you OK? I'm sorry. I didn't see you. Oh my God, your nose! Here, look, I've got a tissue in my bag.'

And he had said he was OK, it was only a nose-bleed and why was she in such a hurry anyway, where was she going.

'Nowhere. Nowhere in particular. I was just making sure it still worked. My body . . . you know . . . that the legs still went round. Things have a habit of going rusty.'

And he had laughed and said did she want to make sure her digestive system still worked because if she did he would treat her to a coffee, over there in that bookshop, there was a café at the back, they did a good date-and-walnut slice as well.

On that day though, on that cold grey first day of the year, he had run after her, calling her name – 'Una, Una, Una . . .' – enjoying the sound it made, the way it pushed his mouth out and then in, like a rhythm, a beat in a song. And then he had caught up with her and taken her hand and they had run side by side, on and on and on, until finally they had collapsed on the wet sand, panting, exhausted, drunk with the joy of motion. Her face had been covered with hair, he remembered. He had had to move it from her lips in order to kiss her. They had felt one another's heartbeat, lifting jumpers and shirts, shivering as the other's cold hand touched warm skin. Afterwards, they had talked of the things they liked. It was a game they played. One of many. Lying down, looking up, he said something and then she said something and then he said something again.

'Listening to the rain in a tent.' 'The first apples in autumn.' 'The smell of fir cones burning on a fire, the sound of the ash falling.' 'That's two things. You're only allowed one thing at a time.' 'No, it's one thing. They go together. They're inextricably linked.' 'OK. All right. Just this once. A field of long grass blowing in a breeze.' 'Roasted chestnuts.' 'Rockets when they explode, especially the blue and the gold ones.' 'You.' 'And you.' 'That's one thing too. Two things inextricably bound.' 'Yes, I think you're right.' 'I am. I know I am.'

24

Una woke up with a crick in her neck and the start of a cold sore on her bottom lip. It was late, she saw, struggling to a sitting position and looking at the clock.

'Why didn't you wake me?' she asked.

'You didn't ask me to,' said Sinead, not looking up from the table where she was already at work, head bent, hair pinned back.

Una stumbled into the bathroom. She felt unaccountably irritable as though a dream lingered in her mind like the taste of something bad. There was no need for her to feel guilty about Sinead and Christmas, she reasoned, remembering the previous night's conversation. She had been a child. Children were selfish. They had to be. It was a basic survival instinct. She turned on the hot water tap and held the fingers of her right hand underneath it, realising after a minute or so that the water was not going to get warm.

Other people had children to dress and feed, and long journeys to make, she told herself crossly, hunting for a lost sock. And they managed. They arrived at work on time, with their hair brushed and shoes polished, some even with sandwiches made the night before. She would just have to get up earlier, be better organised.

Outside, it was raw and cold with a nasty creeping dampness. A car braked violently as a pedestrian stepped out into the road without looking. The driver sounded his horn and the pedestrian made a V-sign back at him.

It was that sort of morning, thought Una, mounting her bike and pedalling slowly away. A Monday morning on a Wednesday.

'Chip pan fire last night,' Jan explained with customary brevity when she finally arrived. 'Alarms didn't go off. Nothing wrong with the batteries either. New resident, by the way. Vivien. Put her on the second floor in number six.'

Germaine's door was closed so she knocked. There was no answer but she might not have heard, someone was playing some loud music two doors down. She knocked again. Still no answer. Una banged on the door.

'Germaine. Germaine. Are you there?'

She tried the handle. It was not locked. She knocked one last time and then opened the door. It was empty. The room was empty. The clothes, the toys, the wash things, the new purple toothbrush they'd bought yesterday for Carl after seeing the flat – they'd all gone. Someone had taken the sheets and blankets off the beds and left them in neat piles in the cot – sheets in one pile, blankets in another, pillow cases in another. The window was slightly open, the sound of cars on the wet road beyond the garden just audible. She looked on the table and the window-sill. But there was nothing. No letter, no message, not even a few words hastily scribbled.

She ran downstairs, taking the steps two at a time, jumping the last four. She found Bridget in the office.

'Germaine's gone. She's left. She's taken all her things. I've just been into her room and it's empty. There's nothing there.'

Bridget sighed. It had been a long night. First the chip pan fire, then Germaine, and then, when she had finally gone to bed and was just drifting off to sleep, the arrival of Vivien. She had spent two hours with Germaine telling her that if she wanted to go back she should, it was up to her, she shouldn't feel guilty.

'I know. She left about half an hour ago. She wanted to say goodbye to you but the taxi was waiting . . .'

'What happened? Did he come? Her husband? Did he persuade her to go back?'

'Nothing happened. She said she wanted to try again. That's all.'

'But we went to see a flat yesterday. She said she wanted to take it. It's all arranged.'

'She said to say thank you,' said Bridget patiently. 'She was very sorry to miss you. She made the driver wait at first but then he said he'd have to charge waiting time so she decided to go.'

'But she said she was never going back. That's what she said. That she wasn't going to give him any more chances. She said nothing would make her change her mind. Not this time.'

Bridget fiddled with her pen, clicking it on and off. Through the window she could see Jan raking dead leaves in the garden. That meant the fire alarm man must have left. She wondered what he had said.

'Yes . . . well . . . people change their minds, don't they? When they realise what it will be like living somewhere new, bringing up children on their own, making friends all over again . . . often they decide that going back is the lesser of two evils. And who are we to say that it isn't?'

She glanced at her watch.

'Una . . . look, I know you cared about Germaine and put a lot of effort into helping her but she's gone now. She wanted to go and she's gone and that's all there is to it. Meanwhile, there are other women here, women who haven't gone back or not yet and there are also things to be done. Like the stairs,' she added, drawing the job rota towards her. 'You were down to do the stairs this morning. And it's already gone ten.'

Something must have happened, thought Una. She wouldn't have just gone. She must have heard from him, spoken to him on the phone or something. She would have said otherwise.

Back in Germaine's room she took down the picture of bread, folded it small and put it in her shirt pocket. She found the pink fluffy slippers under the bed, pushed back towards the wall. She took those too, putting them in a plastic carrier bag and tying the ends.

None of them cared, she thought, switching on the Hoover and banging it angrily against the stairs. Not Bridget, not Jan, not even Kate. Not like her. She'd show them.

25

Una pressed her face against the cold glass of the window. It was a fine clear day, the branches of the almost-bare trees stretched like black fingers against the thin blue of the sky. 'Nice to see the sun again anyhow,' the man in the newsagent's had commented as she handed him the money for two tubes of Smarties. 'Yes,' she had agreed, catching sight of a schoolgirl shoplifting, wondering if he had seen too.

'You can drop me here,' she said, as the taxi driver turned into the road in which Germaine lived. 'Here will do fine.'

She paid the driver and looked at the piece of paper on which she had written the address. Number twenty-three. That was where Germaine lived. And she was standing outside number four. So she needed to cross the road and walk a bit further up. She looked around appraisingly. It was a council estate but, judging from the different styles of front door, many of the houses were now owned privately. She passed a small parade of shops – a hairdresser's, a general store, a newsagent's and, rather oddly, sandwiched in the middle, a shop selling deep-sea diving equipment. Further on, a thin woman in a headscarf and red tracksuit was sweeping the pavement, banging the brush against the kerb with angry, stabbing motions. She glanced up suspiciously, the suspicion giving way to a knowing leer as if she knew the purpose of Una's visit.

The garden outside number twenty-three was well kept if rather bare, a toy wheelbarrow half-full of scummy water the only sign that the inhabitants included children. Una knocked on the door, registering the almost-instant twitch of the right-hand neighbour's curtains. There was no answer. It occurred to her that Germaine might be out – a possibility she had not anticipated. She knocked again.

'Oh, it's you!'

Germaine stood in the open doorway. She was wearing a pink short-sleeved T-shirt under a pair of men's work dungarees. There was yellow paint in her eyebrows.

'I was on top of the ladder,' she said. 'I thought you were the postman. It's Jade's birthday today.'

'I came to check you were all right. I wanted to make sure,' said Una. 'Here,' she added, handing over the bag containing the Smarties. 'I bought some sweets for the children.'

Germaine relaxed slightly.

'They're not here actually. My mum's got them for the morning so that I can paint their bedroom.'

She opened the door wider.

'Come in anyhow. I'll make you a cup of tea.'

Una followed Germaine through a narrow hallway into a small but cheerful kitchen. For some reason it reminded her of the magazine picture Germaine had Sellotaped to her wall. Had it reminded her too? Was that why she had cut it out?

'I'll just wash my hands. Sit down. Put your coat somewhere.'

'You've had your hair cut.'

'Yes. Paul drove me to the hairdresser's himself. Said I looked a fright,' said Germaine, laughing at the admission. She filled the kettle at the sink and set out cups and saucers on a tray.

'Would you like some cake? Jam sponge or date-and-walnut?'

'Date-and-walnut, please,' said Una, looking round surreptitiously. She had expected the house to be squalid – had envisaged dirty milk bottles, a sagging sofa covered in dog hairs, yesterday's take-away wrappings sticking out of the bin and Germaine, pale and haggard, opening the door, flinging her arms round her, saying it had all been a mistake, she wanted to come back. Instead, the washing machine was whirring quietly in a corner, the breakfast things were drying on the draining board and on the table, weighed down by a red salt cellar, there was a shopping list in Germaine's neat, round handwriting – 'tea bags, mince, spaghetti'.

Germaine handed Una a cup of tea and a slice of cake on a blue-and-white plate.

'I had some earlier,' she said, explaining why she had not cut herself a slice too.

They sat facing one another, each cradling a cup.

'I brought . . .'

'I did try . . .'

They stopped and laughed.

'Go on. After you,' said Germaine.

'I was just going to say that I'd brought you your slippers. I found them under the bed.'

She took the pink fluffy slippers out of the carrier bag and put them on the table. 'Also, I thought you might want this,' she added, handing Germaine the magazine picture of bread.

Germaine smoothed it flat with her fingertips.

'I left the slippers on purpose,' she said. 'I never did like them. But I'll keep this. It will be . . . well, something to remember it by.'

So she was not coming back. She was going to stay, to try again, just as Bridget had said. Una put her cup down and looked up, noticing a collection of thimbles on a narrow shelf on the wall. There was one from Hastings, she saw, struggling to make out the gold lettering. Yes. 'Greetings from Hastings'. That's what it said.

The silence began to feel uncomfortable, heavier by the minute like a suitcase at the end of a journey. She cast about frantically for something to say.

'What colour are you painting their room?' she asked.

'Yellow. I wanted something nice and cheerful. Would you like to see it?'

Una said yes, she would, and followed Germaine back into the hallway, up the stairs and into a room with three and a half yellow walls and half a white one.

'It's lovely. Lovely and bright,' she said.

'Do you like it? Oh, good. I'm glad you like it,' said Germaine and became quite chatty all of a sudden, pointing out where she was going to do a stencil of ducks and how she was going to rearrange the furniture.

A door banged downstairs.

'That'll be Paul. He said he might be back for lunch.'

'Look, I'd better be going. I didn't mean to stay this long.'

They went downstairs, Germaine first, Una following.

'This is Una. She was very good to me in Bristol.'

The man standing by the fridge, turned, looked her up and down, then, after what appeared to be a brief internal struggle, stepped forward and shook hands. He was smaller than she had expected – sandy-haired and balding, with a gap in his bottom teeth. His expression was hostile but he said nothing, just nodded curtly. She put on her coat.

'I'll see you out,' said Germaine, picking up her carrier bag.

At the door, as she turned to say goodbye, Germaine touched her gently on the arm.

'I'm pregnant,' she said, so quietly that Una was not sure she had heard correctly.

But then she repeated it.

'I'm pregnant. I couldn't face it on my own. Besides, he's good with the kids. He's never lifted a finger to them . . .'

There was a noise behind her in the hallway as Paul came out of the kitchen.

'Goodbye then,' she called, raising her voice. 'Thanks for dropping in. See you. Bye.'

The door closed. Una walked down the path and back up the road. At the top, she turned left and then right again, walking just to walk, so as not to think.

When she was walked out, she sat down on a bench and then, like a tap turned on full, the thoughts came. She had been silly to go. Silly and naïve and presumptuous. She did not know Germaine. She had thought she did but today, sitting in her kitchen, she had realised how little they had talked and then, how it had always been about material things – forms, flats, grants, clothes for the children. She had never – this was incredible, almost unbelievable but she forced herself to acknowledge it – she had never, not even once, asked Germaine how she felt. It was as if she had forgotten Germaine was a person rather than a cause. That she had friends, routines, shops where she was known by name. That she might be lonely, homesick. Sinead had said something, about how Germaine might be missing her own things, but she had not listened. She had been thoughtless, thoughtless and selfish.

Walking back, finding the bus station, buying her ticket, it was as if she had developed a cataract in the space of an hour. The world was dimmer, duller, filmed with grey. 'I'm Una Dart, Una Dart, Una, Una, Una . . .' she said, over and over again.

But the words, like all words repeated, rang back hollow and meaningless. She was back where she had started. Looking for answers.

26

Helen stood on the deck and watched Brindisi slip slowly away. They were off again, on the move, and she was happy once more, soothed by the motion like a child rocked to sleep.

There were only three other people outside – a man with binoculars and a young couple, clearly newly met, ringed by desire like Saturn. The others had been driven inside by the cold and the lure of the pastries on sale – Greek delicacies, puff pastry whirls dripping in honey and nuts, nothing like the functional wrapped objects on sale in British ferries. Philip was down there with them, calming his stomach with brandy and his nerves with maps, planning the route they would take when they docked. She would have to go in soon too – it really was cold – but for now, for a little bit longer, she wanted to watch Italy go, to see, with her own eyes, the gap open up between sea and land.

If they could see her now – Paul, Linda and all the others at the office – what would they think? Her hands were chapped, her nails ragged, her hair longer than it had been for years. She had lost weight as well, her face regaining something of the shape it had had when she was younger. That morning, brushing her teeth, her hair loose on her shoulders, she had glanced at the mirror and been so surprised she had dropped her toothbrush. She looked like she had done. Not the same but similar, an older version. If he saw her now, would he recognise her? Would he want to recognise her? These were the questions she asked herself, that asked themselves, bobbing incessantly to the surface of her mind.

It was odd how it kept coming back. How, as each day passed, as she travelled further and further, she came closer, remembered more. She had been standing at the window wondering if it was too early to go to bed. She had been thirsty, she remembered, but had not wanted to fetch a glass of water, had not even known where to fetch one from. There had been a knock at the door and, without waiting for a reply, Vic had opened it.

'Someone to see you. I'll show him up,' he had said and disappeared, leaving her puzzled, frightened, expecting her father.

But it had not been her father.

'Sorry . . . I don't know you . . . do I?'

'No, you don't.'

They had stood there, staring at one another.

'Only Vic . . . he said . . . he said there was someone to see me . . . someone I knew.'

As she said this, she realised Vic had not said this, that he had not said anything about the person knowing her.

'I'm sorry . . . I must . . . I must have knocked at the wrong door.'

And he had begun to back away, to turn to leave the room. The sound of laughter had stopped him – the sound of laughter outside so raucous and so loud it must have been heard by half the street. He had stopped and she, still standing by the window, had looked out and seen the woman who had laughed, standing in the light of a street lamp, one arm round it, the other round the neck of a man. It had only been a glance but it had been enough to tell her everything. The woman was a prostitute. She was in a brothel and he, the man standing there, looking so embarrassed, had come for sex.

'I see . . . I mean . . . I think I know . . . my God . . . oh my God.'

She had put a hand up to her head, taken a step forward, faltered, and half sat, half fallen on the bed. He had rushed forward then stopped, fearful she would misunderstand.

Unable to speak, she had flung out a hand, clutched at his and pulled at it, dragging him down. She would be all right in a minute. If she kept very still and concentrated on her breathing, in, out, in, out, that's right, nice and steady, there, that was better. She lifted her head. Immediately, the room began to whirl. She lowered her head again, supporting it in the palm of her left hand.

'Do you want me to go? I'll go. I should never have come anyhow.'

She clutched his hand more tightly. He couldn't go. She couldn't let him go. Not on his own. She had to go with him.

Gradually, the spinning stopped. She raised her head again, slowly this time, and smiled. He hesitated, then smiled back

'I'm sorry. I just went dizzy, that's all. I have to keep very still and quiet and then it goes. It used to happen quite a lot.'

'Are you sure you don't want me to fetch anyone? You look terribly pale.'

'No, I'm fine. I'll be OK in a minute. I've just gone a bit shivery. It's always like that. I go very hot and then very cold.'

'Here. Put this on.'

And he had taken off his jacket and helped her into it. It was a tweed jacket, checked green with scuffed leather buttons, and it smelt of leaves and wood smoke and rich earth, crumbly to the touch. She had hugged it to her, her arms lost in the sleeves, although he was not tall for a man, not much taller than her but broad, the bulge of his shoulders visible beneath his shirt.

'Who are you?' he said gently. 'What are you doing here?'

She might have asked the same of him and what he was doing visiting a brothel when he was married – she had already seen the ring – but she did not. Instead she told him what had happened.

'But why didn't you go back? When your friend wasn't there, why didn't you go home?'

'Because I thought she would be back the next day. It's the right address. The woman in the flat opposite knows her. I thought she'd gone away for a long weekend. And then when she didn't come back the next day I thought that surely she'd be back the day after.'

Also, she had been too proud. She had not wanted to admit defeat. In her note, she had said she was leaving home for good. She had planned to write them a letter after a week or so, saying that she had found work and somewhere to live. She did not want her mother to worry.

'And did you tell him this? That man . . . what did you say he was called?'

'Vic.'

'Yes, Vic. Did you tell him this?'

'Yes, I told him everything.'

'But that's terrible . . . terrible! The nasty low lying little . . .'
And he half rose as if to confront Vic immediately.

'Maybe he thought I understood. He did say I would have to
work. But I thought he meant get a job. I'd told him about the
secretarial course, you see.'

'You can come back to my house,' said the man with sudden
determination. 'Either that or stay at a hotel. I'll give you the
money. And the money for your train fare. You do still want to
go back?'

And she had nodded, resigned now to the future her parents
had planned for her – a few years in a 'little' job, followed
by marriage and motherhood. One could not go wrong in
Cheltenham. There were so many nice boys. It was just a
question of choosing which one. That was what her mother
had said to Mrs Snape in the fishmongers, not realising she
had come in instead of waiting outside on the pavement. And
Mrs Snape had nodded and said the haddock was nice, fresh in
that morning, and how much was she wanting.

Remembering this and the way Mrs Snape had slapped the
fish on the scales, wet and cold, the tail sticking up over one
side, she had taken off the man's tweed jacket and hung it on
the back of the chair next to the bed.

'What are you doing?' said the man. 'I didn't mean . . . you
don't understand . . . I don't want you to . . . to . . . to do
anything. I want to give you the money. Please.'

But she had continued to unbutton her blouse and then had
taken that off too and placed it on top of the jacket.

'I do understand. I want to,' she had said, unhooking her
bra.

'But you can't . . . you mustn't. I don't want to. I don't want
you to.'

But he had looked, had looked despite himself, and wanted
to touch. She had seen it in his eyes. She lifted one of his hands
and drew it towards her. He let her but then pulled away as
if scalded. She drew it back again, this time holding it down,
pressing it against her breast.

He shivered and looked away, as if willing himself to stand
up. Then his other hand came down, felt for the other breast,
found it and held it.

'They're so beautiful . . . so beautiful.'

He was still looking away as if he didn't trust himself to see.

She stretched out her hands, placed them on his shoulders and ran them down the length of his arms, feeling the rise and fall of his muscles.

He turned and met her eyes then and she was surprised, frightened almost, by the pain in them, the hunger, reined in, but only just.

'I don't want to if you don't want to.'

'I do want to. I want you to make love to me. I want us to make love. There.'

She blushed, embarrassed.

He swallowed, bit his lip, his hands still touching her breasts, feeling their weight, their soft heavy roundness.

'I haven't . . . I know maybe you'll think I'm just saying this but I'm not . . . I haven't . . . I haven't been here before. Or anywhere like it.'

'Nor have I,' she said, unbuttoning his shirt now, breathing in his smell, touching his skin with her lips.

And then, suddenly, like something snapped, he rolled over, pulling her with him. Five minutes later when Vic looked in through a peephole they were both naked, tangled like string. He smiled sardonically. They were all the same, he thought. Even the ones from Cheltenham that spoke posh. When it came down to it, women were just like worms. If you showed them an open mouth, they wriggled.

Inside, back on the bed, the man said: 'Are you sure? You're sure you want to? We can still stop.' Of course, he might not have meant this. If she had said no, he might have been unable to stop himself, or been able to but not wanted to, gone on anyway, not caring. But she felt sure, both then and now, that he had meant it. And anyway, she had said yes.

27

'Bride or groom?'

Una looked puzzled.

'Bride or groom?' the usher repeated, waving his Order of Service booklet like a man at an auction.

'Sorry, Julie, I mean "bride".'

The usher, a tall gangly youth in top hat and tails who looked as though he had not quite got the hang of his arms, handed Una a booklet and directed her to a seat. She thought about telling him that his shirt was hanging out from his trousers like a third tail but decided not to. He would not thank her.

She had decided to come to Julie's wedding after all. It was something to do, an excuse to buy a new dress and besides, it might be fun, and she needed that badly. Bridget had reprimanded her for the way she had behaved with Germaine. She had become too involved, she had said, had put pressure on Germaine to leave her husband instead of allowing her to make up her own mind.

'She was pregnant,' Una had replied, stung into telling what she had resolved not to tell. 'That's why she went back. Not because she wanted to but because she was pregnant. I went to see her in Gloucester. She told me.'

'I know,' Bridget said coldly. 'I bought her the pregnancy testing kit. I helped her do the test.'

That had hurt. Hurt more than anything else. That Germaine had chosen to confide in Bridget rather than her. She had thought they were friends, that she was helping Germaine. Now she felt she had been a nuisance, an interfering busybody.

There was a sudden roar from the organ as the organist's feet slipped on the pedals. A baby two rows in front began to cry until his mother plugged his mouth with a dummy. 'Rod for her own back, that is,' commented a woman behind Una, none too quietly.

Una looked around. It was a Catholic church, white-walled, with a particularly gory depiction of the crucifixion behind the altar and enough gold candlesticks to go round half the congregation. The stained-glass windows were modern, predominantly red and blue, three on the right-hand side and two on the left, the one in the middle just plain glass, as though the authorities had run out of money or patience. The bridegroom's family must be Catholic, she thought. She could not remember Julie being Catholic at school but then, of course, she might not have asked.

'Excuse me.'

Una stood up to let a couple pass – a man, thin, apologetic, the dark collar of his suit jacket already flecked with dandruff, and a plump woman, presumably his wife, wearing navy with a large matching hat. Safe, thought Una, noticing the woman look askance at her dress, a short A-line dress in green devoré velvet. Navy was safe, safe and boring. She had bought the dress at a supermarket along with a small wholemeal loaf, two cans of soup and a tub of low fat sandwich spread. She had liked the colour and the feel of the material. 'All the rage, that is,' an assistant had said, seeing her hold up the dress in front of a mirror. 'Devoré velvet, that's what it's called.' She had tried it on and liked it even more. It was like running water – it changed colour as it moved. And so she had bought it, glad she had found something she could afford because she was finding it hard to manage now that the bills had started to arrive. The gas bill, phone bill, electricity bill and that week, to her horror, the council tax bill, something she had not allowed for at all, had not even thought she would be eligible to pay.

There was a rustle of interest at the back of the church and Una, turning, catching herself on her neighbour's hat, caught a glimpse of something white. A woman across the aisle in a purple cloche hat rose expectantly but the organist continued to play Bach until, exasperated, the bride's mother prodded him in the ribs and he switched, mid-chord, to Mendelssohn's bridal march.

Una turned and smiled as Julie approached because that was what one did at weddings. One looked at the dress and said how beautiful it was and privately resolved not to make the same mistake at one's own wedding. The dress was white, she saw, with net sleeves and neck, not cream or ivory as was increasingly the fashion. The skirt flared out from beneath the bust rather than the waist, making Julie look larger than she was and causing the more cynical members of the congregation to wonder whether she was in a certain way. Una noticed that one could see the freckles on Julie's arms through the net sleeves and was reminded of a spotted dick pudding, undercooked. There were two bridesmaids in pale mint and a pageboy in a floral waistcoat who ran to his mother's side after the first hymn and refused to go back despite threats from his father. Twenty minutes later, Julie and Chris were pronounced man and wife.

The reception was in the church hall which could be reached without going outside. 'Very convenient,' said the woman in navy to her husband as they queued to pass through the vestry. A woman in fuchsia pink crepe said at least it had kept dry, that was as much as one could hope for in November, and someone else said, yes, there had been snow at her wedding, but then it had been January, one always got the worst weather then.

There were seven others at Una's table, three couples and another single girl on her left called – rather appropriately, Una soon realised – Violet. They all introduced themselves and passed round the bread and butter.

'I'm starving,' said one of the boys, grabbing a bread roll. 'Cheryl made me miss breakfast. Said I had to have my hair cut instead.'

The others, who, with the exception of Violet, all seemed to know one another, laughed. 'Well, it was a good excuse,' said his neighbour, presumably Cheryl. 'I said he couldn't sit next to me if he didn't.' And she put up a hand and rumpled his cropped locks.

'What do you do?' asked Vanessa, the girl on Una's right.

'I . . . I . . . I work in a refuge for battered women.'

'Really! How interesting.'

She leant sideways slightly so that the waitress could put down her asparagus soup.

'Where do you find them? The women, I mean?'

'We don't find them. They come to us. Some of them know where we are, others are sent to us by the police or social services or the Samaritans even.'

'Oh,' said Vanessa. 'Oh, I see.'

Clearly, this was the extent of her interest because she spent the rest of the meal talking to her boyfriend. Una tried talking to Violet but found her painfully shy and so pretended she was listening to Vanessa, smiling as she swallowed cold buffet – beef and turkey and salmon, all mixed up in a tasteless mulch. After the buffet, there was raspberry pavlova, chocolate gâteau, or cheese and biscuits. Una had the pavlova and then, for something to do, tried the gâteau. The couples were talking about holidays now, swapping experiences of Greece.

'Oh, but you must go to Crete,' cried Cheryl. 'There's a mountain gorge you can walk through right down to the sea. We had the best holiday we've ever had there.'

'Are you going anywhere nice next year?' asked Violet suddenly, taking Una by surprise.

'I don't know. I haven't thought about it yet. How about you?'

Violet said she was going camping in Normandy with the girl guides. She was a Brown Owl, she explained.

'I think Julie's going to Minorca for her honeymoon,' she went on, her tongue clearly loosened by the half glass of white wine she had drunk.

'Their house is ever so nice. Have you seen it? They even got to choose their own kitchen. And the carpets and curtains. I'd like to have a house like that when I've got enough money.'

Una said no, she had not seen it, suddenly acutely conscious of how little she earned. The day before, she had bought white economy toilet tissue instead of the luxury tissue which came in a choice of shades – peach, magnolia or powder blue. It was two pounds cheaper, she had realised, a whole two pounds cheaper. But then it felt cheap just as her dress, she thought, looking round, seeing the silk and linen outfits worn by the other girls, looked cheap.

After the toasts and speeches, Julie came up to their table and thanked them all for coming.

'Julie, you look wonderful. Absolutely wonderful,' gushed Vanessa.

'I wouldn't have chosen that style for myself,' she said, when Julie had left. 'But it looks nice on her,' she added quickly.

Gradually, people stood up and moved around. The brides-maids and several of the other younger children started to play chase, tripping over handbags and treading on people's toes, ignoring the admonitions of their mothers to 'Be careful, mind, it will all end in tears'. The older women, their flushed cheeks clashing with the lime greens and mauves of their suits, slipped off their shoes under the table and talked of their weddings, how they would do things differently if they were getting married now. Several of the men disappeared into another room to watch the end of a football match on television. There had been a fire in the Channel tunnel, said one, coming back soon afterwards. Only a freight train but there had been eight injured even so. At the French end, it was. Had they heard? The couples on Una's table began to talk of what they would do if they won the National Lottery.

'I wouldn't tell anyone,' said Vanessa. 'I'd go into work the next day as though nothing had happened. I wouldn't want anyone to know until I'd decided what I was going to do.'

'You wouldn't be able to. You'd give it away,' said her boyfriend.

'I wouldn't,' she retorted.

No one asked Una what she would do or even tried to include her in the conversation. Looking down, she saw there was a red wine stain shaped like a heart on the white paper tablecloth. Next to it was a splodge of the asparagus soup. The string quartet, contracted to play for two hours with three ten-minute breaks, arrived late, blaming traffic jams caused by a warehouse auction of pine furniture just outside the town. Outside, it started to rain.

Una made for the door where she was caught in the confusion of people leaving and entering the dance floor.

'Lost your boyfriend?' said a man with a large stomach. She shook her head, suddenly tearful.

'Give me a dance. That'll soon make him come back.'

She shook her head again but then glimpsed Violet looking

around frantically, perhaps for her, and so allowed him to lead her on to the floor.

He told her his name was Duncan, that he was a pet food salesman from Selby and a cousin, well, second cousin really, of Julie's. She nodded, conscious of his stomach quivering between them like an indignant chaperone, the pickled onion stench of his breath. One of his braces slipped and he put up a hand to adjust it, replacing the hand lower down, nearer her bottom. She excused herself when the dance ended, saying there was someone she must talk to, an old school friend, someone she had not seen for years.

'Bet you ten pounds I get a date with one of them,' he said, pointing first in Una's direction and then at Violet, still looking lost.

'You must be joking. Fat slob like you! They wouldn't touch you with a barge pole,' said his brother.

Una slipped unseen into the church. It was gloomy inside, the lights all turned off, the candlesticks stiff and silent like sentries. She sat down near the front and sighed.

'Nothing quite like a wedding, is there, to make you feel lonely?'

She spun round, startled. There was someone else in the church, a man, sitting halfway back, leaning against a pillar. He stood up and walked down the aisle.

'Bride or groom?' he asked, sitting down again in the pew in front of her.

'Bride. I was at school with Julie.'

'Groom,' he replied. 'I was at teacher training college with Chris.'

'Oh,' she said, unable to think of anything else to say.

'I like your dress,' he added.

'Thank you. I thought maybe it wasn't quite right earlier. Not formal enough.'

'No, it's lovely. The nicest dress here.'

She could not make out his features but he was dark, she could see that much, his hair thick and wavy, almost down to his shoulders.

'I'm Geoff, by the way. Geoff Smart.'

'I'm Una. Una Dart. We rhyme.'

They laughed and shook hands. Outside, the sky slipped suddenly from grey to black like a page turned, leaving them in near darkness.

Back in the church hall, the women shrieked as one of the young men climbed on to a table and did the can-can. He was dragged off protesting by his girlfriend. Apart from those on the dance floor, the guests had now separated almost exclusively into two groups – the men on one side, the women on another.

'Woman next to me at work. Only twenty-six she is and she's already had a hysterectomy. "You ought to be careful," I told her. "You might change your mind. You might want them later on." But she swore she didn't want children. Not ever,' said the woman in fuchsia pink to the woman in navy.

On the dance floor, Violet allowed the Selby pet food salesman to press her closer. Men weren't so bad really, she thought, turning her face sideways so she didn't have to smell his breath. They were a bit like a cold shower. One got used to them.

'Have you ever been greyhound racing?' he asked, both hands on her bottom.

'No.'

'You should go. It's brilliant fun. I'm going tomorrow. Would you like to come?'

She hesitated, then accepted, wondering what her mother would say when she announced she wouldn't be going to church, she was going out.

'Who with?' she heard her mother ask, her voice shrill with alarm.

'Just someone. Someone I met yesterday at the wedding. You don't know them,' she imagined herself saying.

The Selby salesman smirked lasciviously and gave a thumbs-up sign to his brother. He had just won his bet.

28

'That man. What's wrong with his eye? Why does it look like that?' asked the boy at the next table, playing with the sugar spoon.

'I don't know. He must have hurt it. Don't point. It's rude,' cried his mother.

They were French which is why Philip understood them. A man and a woman and their son, possibly adopted, judging from their age and looks, the parents so dark, the boy so fair. He wore navy, knee-length shorts with turn-ups and a red Guernsey sweater, a pillarbox red, no hint of orange.

'Did he get shot? Did someone shoot him?' asked the boy hopefully.

'I don't know. Maybe,' said his mother.

The boy pointed the spoon at the occupants of the other tables and made machine-gun noises.

'Don't do that. François, stop it!' said the mother, conscious that the main news story the day before had been about a man running amok with a gun in Canada, killing twelve people at a petrol station.

Luckily, the boy's ice cream arrived at that moment, three scoops – chocolate, strawberry and pistachio – a triangular biscuit perched jauntily at the top like a sailor's cap. Children were more sophisticated on the continent, reflected Philip. Most six-year-old boys in England probably didn't even know what a pistachio was.

He was sitting outside at a café they had found by accident on their first day in Athens. It was in a small square, three streets away from any traffic, an antiquarian bookshop at one end, a

Greek orthodox church at the other, round and white, its bell tower protruding like a nipple into the cloudless blue of the sky. He was facing the church now, a gentle breeze rippling the green-and-white striped awning above him, his face warm in the sun. The square had the lazy, intimate feel of a family at home on their own, not expecting guests, their feet up on chairs. There were two tourist shops selling souvenirs, a shoe shop and an expensive-looking cake shop with pink muslin in the window and a replica urn, overflowing with sugared almonds. In the middle was a circular fountain, not running, and a few pigeons searching half-heartedly for crumbs. A woman stood outside one of the tourist shops looking at postcards and two more women stood talking outside the cake shop, the sound of their voices carrying to where Philip sat. Apart from them and the occupants of the café – a large group of young people, probably students, an elderly man reading a paper, the French family, and Philip himself – the square was empty.

Philip looked at his watch and wondered if Helen was enjoying herself. She had gone on a guided coach trip to Delphi. He had intended to go too but had cried off at the last minute on the grounds that he was tired. Besides, one could do too much sight-seeing, he had added. They had already seen the main sights – the Parthenon, Acropolis, and Lykavetos Hill. And she had said he didn't really like *being* in a place, did he – that once he had arrived, he wanted to be off again, on to the next place. And he had said wasn't that true of everyone and it was well known that it was better to travel than to arrive. And she had said maybe and remembered standing outside on the ferry from Brindisi, the taste of salt on her lips.

'I think he's a policeman,' said the boy, finishing his ice cream and reverting to his examination of Philip. 'He caught a robber and the robber shot him. Does it still work, do you think? Can he still see out of it?'

'That's enough. Stop it,' said the father, intervening for the first time. The woman glanced at Philip and smiled nervously, clearly hoping he didn't speak French. Philip's coffee finally arrived, the waiter apologising for the delay, or at least that was what Philip assumed, his Greek amounting to no more than a few guidebook phrases. He helped himself to sugar and stirred it in slowly, then, turning sideways slightly so that the French boy would not be able to see, he reached up and touched his left eye. He still called it his eye even though it no longer had any of the properties one associated with an eye. It was a husk really, a river run dry, dead fish in cracked mud.

'You won't know it's not there. Not after a while,' the eye specialist had said in hospital. 'You'll be able to see just as well. Well, almost as well.'

'Try telling that to the air force. They think I'm blind. That I should be learning Braille. That I'm mad even to think I could still pilot a plane.' That's what Philip had wanted to say. Something sharp. Something that would make the surgeon step back, that would force him to see him, really see him, see him as a man, not just muscle and tissue. But he hadn't because he was lying down at the time, dressed only in his pants, a white sheet drawn up to his neck – a state that was not conducive to an open exchange of views.

He had repeated what the specialist had said two months later when he had returned to base for what his senior officer described as an 'informal discussion' about his future.

The officer had smiled patiently in the way that staff at nursing homes smiled when an inmate demanded to know why lunch was late at nine in the morning.

'But apart from anything else, what would happen if you got something in the eye? A bit of dirt or an eyelash, say? If that had happened before, you'd have still been able to see out of the other eye but now . . . well . . . you know what I mean, Philip, it's just not viable.'

Philip had pointed out that he had been flying for five years and had not yet once got anything in his eyes but the officer had continued to smile, as if he were a difficult child that needed to be humoured because it was long past his bedtime, he was just tired really. He had repeated the word 'viable' several times in the conversation that followed and Philip, listening to him, watching him tap his desk with a silver ballpoint pen, had wondered if he knew that the word was derived from the Latin word *vita* meaning life. He was not viable, not capable of normal development and growth, like a foetus ripped from its mother's womb, soft, unformed, the cord still dangling. That was what they thought.

His appeal against the decision not to allow him to take up his old duties had been heard in June at Brize Norton. They had listened carefully, three old men sitting in a row, their backs to the window, forcing him to look into the sun, to squint, the brightness a taunt.

Afterwards, walking him back to the car that was to take him to the station, the oldest of the men, an air marshal, had talked about the sky, how he had met a man in the pub the night before who claimed to have seen the northern lights, the aurora borealis.

'Like a curtain opening suddenly. That's what he said it looked like. But I don't think he did see it really. I don't think you can see it as far south as this. Besides, he's a notorious drunk.'

To which Philip had replied that the man could have been right, they had been seen as far south as Bristol and not by a drunk.

They reached the car and the air marshal clapped him on the back and said he was a good chap, shocking bad luck he'd had, but not to worry, they'd see him all right.

'By the way,' he added, lowering his voice, 'how's your wife?'

Because, of course, they all knew he had a wife now. It had been in all the papers or at least all the tabloids. Page seven lead in the *Daily Express*. 'Knife attack victim marries rescuer'. And underneath, in a different typeface and a corny reference to his surname, 'The true "dart" of love. The RAF pilot who lost the sight in one eye while rescuing a girl from a frenzied knife attack is to marry – the girl he saved!'

'Fine,' said Philip, seeing his wife as he had left her that morning – tired after another sleepless night, suffering from heartburn, her ankles and wrists badly swollen, but still happy, still grateful, horribly grateful.

Good chap, the air marshal had repeated, and said they would be in touch, he would be hearing from them. And four days later he did. A piece of stiff white paper folded in three informed him that his appeal had been overturned. The paper was thick, good quality. They didn't stint on stationery. Not on those sort of letters. To be fair, they had offered him another job. Had said they would retrain him as an engineer or air traffic controller.

But he had turned down the offer. It was flying or nothing. If he couldn't be a pilot, then he didn't want to go anywhere near an airfield. Not ever. He had regretted this decision six months later but had been too proud to go back. A year later, when he still had no job, he had made tentative inquiries but had been told, less tentatively, that the offer had been withdrawn. Too much time had elapsed.

A sudden noise of chairs being dragged back, the metal of the chairs harsh, rasping against the flagstones like a wrong note on the violin, interrupted his thoughts. He turned. The French family was leaving, the woman urging the man to leave a bigger tip, asking why he had to be so mean always. As Philip watched, the boy began to run, his arms outstretched, tilting from side to side, heading for the fountain. He was a plane, a fighter bomber, and the pigeons were the enemy. He smiled sadly. That was how it had started with him. Standing at the top of Shoscombe Hill when he was six. Standing still. Still and silent. Then suddenly, eyes fixed on a crow, a stone, an odd-shaped branch, starting to run, arms out straight, taut as stretched rubber, weaving, calling . . . flying!

29

Geoff Smart was thirty-five and had a flat with a balcony overlooking the Avon gorge. A woman called Mandy came once a week to do his washing and ironing and another woman called Doreen did his cleaning. He was not married.

His sitting room was red, a soft roof-tile red, the colour of Victorian dining rooms. There was a sofa, an S-shaped armchair, a coffee table in old pine, suitably 'distressed' but little else, no bookshelves, because he liked to have space. Space was important, he said. On the coffee table, arranged in date order, were copies of various highbrow publications including the *London Review of Books, Prospect, Granta,* and the *New Statesman.* He also subscribed to two men's magazines which ran articles on hormone problems and whether boxer shorts were still fashionable but Una did not discover this until later because he kept them in his bedroom, also in date order. He was very tidy.

His car was green, the colour of Una's old school gym skirt. It had a box of white, three-ply tissues in the glove compartment and a bag for rubbish, mainly sweet wrappings. He had a weakness for lemon barley sugar and red liquorice, the kind nicknamed 'shoelaces' by children. There was little in his kitchen cupboards apart from real coffee – French roast, ground for a cafetière – sugar, anchovy relish, and a superior brand of coarse-cut marmalade. His freezer on the other hand was full – chicken korma, breaded cod steaks, steak-and-kidney pie, winter casserole, and cauliflower gratin. 'It's cheaper than cooking,' he said, noticing the look on Una's face when she opened the freezer door one day, mistaking it for the fridge. 'When you take into account your time and the electricity, it's much cheaper.' She had nodded, unconvinced.

His fingernails were white and clean and looked as though they had been professionally manicured, as indeed they had, but again, Una did not discover this until later. All she discovered then, on that first meeting, sitting in the church, was that his name was Geoff Smart, that he taught media studies at the same college as Martin and that he found weddings depressing.

'You don't look like Martin,' he said. Then added: 'From what I can see of you.' For it was very dark now, their hands moving like bats, gone before they had come.

'No, I know. Everyone says that.'

'By the way, tell me to mind my own business, but has Martin split up from his wife or something?'

'Yes. Why?'

'Nothing . . . it's just that . . . well . . . I thought he had.'

'What do you mean?'

'Well, he's been looking . . . well, shabbier, I suppose. As if he no longer had anyone looking after him.'

Una, who had herself noticed Martin wearing the same shirt three days running, felt a rush of guilt. But then, she wasn't his wife, she reasoned. And besides, she had a full-time job as well.

To change the subject, she asked about his job, what 'media studies' meant. He explained at length. She noticed that – even then. How he liked to talk, preferably without interruption. 'Holding forth', her mother would have said.

'Were you a journalist then? Before you went into teaching?' she asked.

'Not exactly.'

He said he had been a disc jockey on a community radio station in Portsmouth and later an account executive for a public relations firm. He had worked on retail accounts mainly – shampoo, hair accessories, even a new type of cleaning cloth. Then he had decided he wanted a change of career and had done teacher training. He had taught at sixth-form colleges first, moving into higher education only the year before.

'How about you? What do you do?' he asked finally.

She told him, concentrating on the counselling rather than

the cleaning. She did not want him to think she was a glorified housemaid.

'Sounds a bit depressing,' he interrupted. 'But worthwhile,' he added. 'A very good cause.' And he went on to say how wrong it was, quite wrong, that such bodies should have to depend on voluntary help to survive, leaving Una feeling cheated because she had not finished what she had been going to say. Even so, when they rose to leave and he asked for her telephone number, she gave him it.

'I hear you met Geoff Smart at Julie's wedding,' said Martin three days later, helping them both to macaroni cheese.

'Yes,' said Una. She could feel him looking at her, waiting for her to say something else.

She finished shredding the lettuce and reached for the oil and vinegar. French dressing was one of the few culinary accomplishments she had mastered.

'He runs our union. Our branch, I mean. That's why I know him,' said Martin.

That would explain his way of talking, thought Una. His tendency to . . . well . . . rant, she supposed, confident of being listened to. That and being a lecturer. Teachers did tend to be like that – a bit pompous and conceited, especially the men. Martin was unusual in that respect.

'By the way, I've found a flat,' he said afterwards when they were washing up, Una washing, Martin drying, because she didn't trust him to clean the cutlery properly.

'Where? Why didn't you say?'

'I am saying,' he said, returning a knife to the bowl with pointed display.

It was not a flat really, he said, but a room in a shared house. It was cheaper that way. But the room was large and light and there was central heating. Besides, it might be quite fun to be with other people and they were all professionals, two men and a woman. It was in Redland, he added, quite close to Matty and Teresa.

'That's good. You'll be able to see a lot of Matty then,' said Una. Although she reflected that he could hardly see any more of her. He had been seeing her every day after work which was much more than he had done before, as Teresa had observed dryly.

There was a programme on television that she wanted to watch, the second part of a six-part adaptation of Jane Austen's novel *Mansfield Park*. And so, after finishing the washing up, she fetched the duvet from her bed and curled up on the bean bag. Martin sat at the table marking essays. He had been offered two hours a week lecturing at the university. It was not much but it was a start. He was keen to leave the college. There were too many people like . . . well, Geoff Smart, he supposed. Not that he had anything against the fellow even if he was a bit of a philanderer. But he was hardly academic, more of an entertainer.

After half an hour he stood up and put on his jacket.

'Just going to get some more matches,' he said, quickly pocketing the box of matches by the cooker. 'I might call in to see Sol afterwards,' he added. Sol was a colleague who lived near by.

'OK,' said Una, not turning round. Unlike him, she was not intuitive, not for a woman, although becoming more so.

Outside, walking quickly to the bus stop, Martin wondered if he should tell Una that he and Teresa were seeing a marriage guidance counsellor. No. Not yet, he decided. It might raise her hopes. She might blurt something out to their mother. He would keep it a secret. It was best that way. Lots of things were.

30

Geoff bought bottled beer at the bar, the necks speared with lime, salted at the rim. There were no tables free and so they stood near the windows overlooking the water. Una felt nervous. It had been better in the church in the dark. She could have said anything then. Now she felt awkward and self-conscious. It was their first date.

The film was called *Breaking the Waves*, Geoff said. It was set in Scotland in the seventies and was about a young girl who married a man from the oil rigs. He wouldn't say any more in case he spoilt the story. He spoke as though he had already seen it although he hadn't, as Una found out later. He added that it had won the Grand Prix at the 1996 Cannes film festival. The director was Lars von Trier. Una nodded knowledgeably as though the name was familiar.

'I like your top,' he said.

She blushed.

'You should always wear green. It goes with your hair. Brings it out. You look like one of Rossetti's women.'

She blushed again.

There was a sex scene ten minutes into the film – naked, tender, violent sex. Bare flesh on a bed. Grappling. Touching. A kiss. And then another kiss. Una felt uncomfortable, not because of what she was seeing but because of who she was seeing it with – a man, a stranger almost, Geoff, not Rob. Had he done this too, she wondered? Had he sat in a cinema with a girl, a girl he barely knew, and watched people make love on screen? And had he thought of her then? Had he felt that he was betraying her as she did now, looking down, away, glad of the dark.

Geoff drove her home. She had intended to catch a bus but he insisted, opening the door, offering her a mint, putting on some music. When they drew up outside the yard that led to her flat, he thanked her but did not invite himself in, instead asking if she would like to have brunch together on Saturday. There was a wonderful place near the old market which did fresh bagels. She said yes.

The bagels were indeed wonderful, still warm from the oven, butter melting on them instantly. They drank coffee and tea and read the newspapers, giggling at the tabloids, the story of a man called Wardle who had paid ten thousand pounds at auction to buy the title Lord of Wardle and had then found out that he was adopted, that his real name was Parkes.

'I have to do some Christmas shopping,' he said when he had finished a second pot of coffee and said no, he did not want a third. 'Would you like to come too? There's a shop I'd like to show you. A hat shop.'

The streets were already crowded even though it was still comparatively early. A man was selling roast chestnuts by the fountain at Narrow Quay and they bought a bag, cracking the shells open with their teeth, eating them before they were cool enough, burning their lips. Further on, a man in a kilt was playing the bagpipes. 'Why's he wearing a dress? Men don't wear dresses,' asked a little girl. 'They do in Scotland,' said her mother. 'Is this Scotland then?' asked the girl. And the mother laughed.

The noise and the lights and good-humoured bustle of the crowds began to make Una feel festive. She bought a pair of gloves for Martin and a book on Middle Eastern cookery for her mother. Geoff bought himself a shirt, blue, a limpid sea-blue turquoise.

In the indoor shopping centre a small queue had formed outside Santa's log cabin. Una stopped to admire the reindeer and was told it was for adults too, not just children. She looked at Geoff.

'Shall we?'

'Yes. Go on. I've never been to a Santa's Grotto. My mother thought it was a waste of money.'

'Mine too,' said Una, feeling closer because of this admission, wanting to know more.

They went in one at a time, first Una, then Geoff, emerging hot and breathless, laughing at their childishness.

'What have you got?' asked Una, tugging at the ribbon tying her own present.

'I don't know . . . wait . . . yes . . . a key ring. A key ring with a mini torch.'

Una also had a key ring only hers had a small phial attached, presumably to hold perfume.

'Or you could put whisky in it for emergencies,' suggested Geoff.

'Every day then,' said Una.

'It's not that bad, is it? Your job?'

'No. No, of course not,' said Una, but without conviction, hearing this herself.

'The shop's up there. The one I told you about. On the fourth floor.'

They took the lift up, pressing their faces against the glass walls, admiring the Christmas decorations.

'Look. There you are. Try it on. Isn't it wonderful?'

He held up a hat – floppy, velvet, dark green like his car – the inside lined with silk. Una submitted to his hands, allowing him to pull the hat down at the back and up at the front, to tilt it sideways.

'There. What do you think? Do you like it?'

'Yes. It's lovely but . . .'

She looked around. The hats were all hand-made, a note in pink ink informing customers that hats could be made to order, that orders taken now would be ready by Christmas. There were no price tags to be seen.

'But what?'

She lowered her voice, annoyed he should press her.

'They're probably very expensive. I don't . . . I don't earn very much.'

'That's OK. It's already paid for. I just wanted to make sure it fitted. It's so disappointing to have to take things back. Come on.'

And he was ushering her out of the shop, waving goodbye to the assistant, saying no, they didn't want it wrapped.

'But when did you buy it?'

'Yesterday. It was in the window. I couldn't resist it.'

'Thank you. Thank you very much.'

And she put up her hands to feel the velvet, the soft deep richness of it, catching sight of her reflection as she did so, smiling back.

They bought blueberry muffins and prawn salad in the food hall at Marks and Spencer and caught a bus back to Geoff's flat, sitting at the top, their bags on their knees, the cold of the salad creeping through Una's jeans.

'It's fantastic,' she said, opening the French doors and going out on to the balcony. 'You can see for miles.'

'Yes, it is rather spectacular,' he agreed, coming out too, handing her a glass of white wine.

'It's best in the spring. You can see the sun set over the gorge. We'll have a meal outside then, even if we do have to wear hats and gloves.'

And she smiled and said that would be nice, not offended at the assumption that they would still be seeing one another in the spring, pleased rather.

They met next five days later. Geoff had tickets to a preview at a Bath art gallery. He didn't usually go although they always sent him tickets but this time it was someone he liked, he said. He already had one of her paintings, that small one in the hallway. Una was impressed although she did not say so. Nor did she say she had not noticed the picture he was referring to.

Just outside Bristol, slowing down as they approached a roundabout, they passed a hitchhiker holding a large cardboard sign on which was written 'Bath'. He was young, about nineteen or twenty, with curly red hair and a pale face that looked cold and pinched, as if he had been standing there some time. As they passed, his eyes met Una's and she smiled, confident Geoff would stop because they were going to Bath too, it would be no trouble. They continued to slow down but not fast enough, not as if they meant to stop. Una turned and saw that the hitchhiker had picked up his bag and was running towards them. She glanced at Geoff. He was looking straight ahead, indicating right, moving out. They were on the roundabout now, turning off, gathering speed.

'I thought you were going to stop. That boy back there. He was going to Bath.'

'I don't give lifts to hitchhikers,' he said. 'You never know who they are. It's not worth the risk.'

She opened her mouth to say something but then stopped, put out by the cold set of his jaw. She felt foolish. Foolish and hurt. The boy would think she had been mocking him when she had smiled. He would be cursing her now. But then Geoff smiled and asked if she was hungry because he was and what did she think about going for a crêpe afterwards. And soon the hurt was gone. Geoff was right, she thought. One never knew. The boy might have had a knife.

'I'll introduce you to Cassandra. What a crush! It's not normally this crowded.' And Geoff waved at someone the other side of the room.

Una giggled nervously, hemmed in by a large man in a yellow waistcoat. There was a sweet, heavy smell of expensive perfume and warm skin. Somebody handed her a glass of champagne. Somebody else offered her a canapé.

'Geoff, darling, so glad we could entice you over!' purred a woman in turquoise slub silk, placing a hand on Geoff's arm and appraising Una at the same time.

'Cassandra! I was just looking for you. How are you?' He kissed the woman on both cheeks and introduced her to Una and the woman said lovely, super, so glad she could come, wasn't that Eric who had just come in, yes it was, she absolutely had to speak to him, catch up later, toodle-oo.

'She's the owner,' explained Geoff, deftly steering a path through the crowd, pulling Una in his wake. 'Eric's one of her best customers. Retired businessman. Multi-millionaire, apparently. I'm not sure what he made his money in. Cassandra's talking to him now.'

He nodded in the direction of the door where the woman in turquoise was talking to a neat little man with very pink cheeks. Una nodded, dazzled.

'You look lovely,' said Geoff, leaning over and whispering in her ear. 'The prettiest girl here.'

She knew he was just saying this, just trying to be nice,

because he had not seen half the girls yet and anyhow there were some very beautiful ones among those they had seen, girls with long blonde hair falling like waterfalls down their backs, their shoulders like rocks in the sea, bare, beckoning. But she was still flattered. Someone handed her another canapé and she took one. A demure-looking waitress tapped her on the arm and said would she like some more champagne, madam. She glanced at her glass, was surprised to see it was almost empty already and held it out to be refilled. Geoff waved at someone else and a man stood on her toe, apologising profusely.

'Nina! There's Nina. So she did come after all. I must go and say hello,' said Geoff suddenly, waving frantically. 'She's the artist,' he added. 'The one who did the painting in the hallway. I won't be long.'

He moved away and was quickly sucked up by the crowd, leaving Una alone, squeezed tight between a table and three middle-aged couples.

'And how are your two?' she heard one woman say. 'Fine,' said another. 'Monica's just got another job. Something in TV. Not sure what exactly but it sounds very glamorous. And Max is still in Bahrain. He was over last month for a training course so we saw him for a weekend which was nice. Unfortunately, he's not coming over for Christmas this year because Tara – that's his girlfriend – says she can't stand all the travelling so they're going to Dubai instead. But we can't complain. The money's excellent and they've said that if he goes on doing as well as he is doing, they'll make him a partner next year. How about yours? What's Georgina up to? Wasn't she going to go to Switzerland or something?'

A roar of laughter from the other side of the room drowned the first woman's reply. Una stood on tiptoe to see where Geoff was but found her view blocked by two men arguing about the impact of the recent budget on the property market. No one was looking at the paintings, she saw. In fact, most people had their backs to them. Clearly, it was a social event rather than a cultural one.

The man who had stood on her toe earlier approached her and she looked round desperately. There were some leaflets on the table and she grabbed one, using it as an excuse to turn her back. It was about Nina, the artist whose work formed the majority of the paintings on exhibit. The daughter of a French consular official and an Hungarian dancer, she had been orphaned at the age of three and brought to London by one of her mother's lovers. There was some more biographical detail and then a description of Nina's work. She was not interested in colour, said the writer, but in tone and texture, in harmony between forms, a total balance. The leaflet ended with the words 'Influences? None.'

Intrigued, Una looked round again. One of the middle-aged women had moved apart to talk to someone else, creating a small chink in the bodies arrayed against her. She squeezed through. There. She studied the paintings carefully. The leaflet had been right. Nina was clearly not a colourist. The paintings were sombre – bowls and bottles and fruit in muted shades of green and brown and grey. For some reason, she was reminded of pickled eggs.

'What are the red stickers for?' she asked, turning to find Geoff at her elbow.

'It means it's been bought,' he said.

'But how come so many have been sold already? I thought this was a preview.'

'It is but if Cassandra thinks you might be interested in buying, she rings you up and invites you in before the preview even. She phoned me up last week.'

'And did you come?'

'No, I haven't any wall space left.'

'Oh. I see.'

She was beginning to feel faint from the heat and lack of air. Geoff disappeared again, promising he'd only be a minute but he absolutely had to speak to Humphrey, he hadn't seen him in ages. Una leant against the wall, suddenly revolted. In her mind, she saw the hitchhiker again, the appeal in his eyes, the glimpse of him running, glad, grateful. Rob would have hated all this, she thought. The chatter. The pretence. The backs to the paintings. He was a member of the Royal Academy. As a student, he had hitchhiked to London at least twice a year to see an exhibition, his lunch in his bag, cheese and Marmite sandwiches and an apple, too poor to buy anything in the café.

The voices around her began to swirl into one like colours on a spinning top. Yes, marvellous news . . . such a disappointment . . . still, credit where credit was due . . . not to be trusted . . . but she always was like that, ever since she was a small child . . . and this time, I meant it . . .

She struggled upright and looked for a way out. Then, seeing none, or at least none she could reach, she stopped struggling and suddenly, like a switch pressed, gave herself up to the atmosphere. It was fun, Rob was a spoilsport, yes, she would have some more champagne. This time, when the man who had stood on her toe approached her, she did not turn away but smiled, flirting outrageously. And later, driving back with Geoff, it was she who suggested coffee at his place.

31 ∫

Helen walked unseeing among the ruins at Delphi. There were guided tours but she had shunned them, pausing only to buy a small bottle of lemonade, unpleasantly warm. She wanted to be on her own – to wander freely in the past, her thoughts in tune with her feet. She was remembering.

After making love they had left the brothel, stealing softly down the stairs, pausing outside the room where Vic and another man were playing cards, hearing one of them turn on the radio to catch the football results. The door was half open and they crept past, one at a time, fearful they would be seen.

Three streets away Helen realised she had forgotten her handbag. She had remembered her overnight bag but had left her handbag hanging on the hook at the back of the door.

'I'll have to go back. It's got my purse in and everything.'

'You can't,' said the man. 'Besides, I thought you said you didn't have any money.'

'I don't. But it's got my cards in. My library cards, my blood donor card . . . everything.'

'You can't go back. Not now. It would be dangerous,' said the man and took her by the wrist.

At that point, perhaps hearing their raised voices, a policeman on his beat approached them. 'Evening,' he said, looking them up and down. The man let go of her wrist.

'Everything all right, Miss?' asked the policeman.

'Yes. Yes, thank you,' said Helen, seeing in his eyes that he was wondering if she was a prostitute, that he was thinking she didn't look like one but that one couldn't tell, not these days.

'Sorry,' he said after the policeman had left. 'I didn't mean to hurt you. I just didn't want you to do anything stupid.'

'That's OK,' she said, rubbing her wrist, suddenly regretting what she had done, realising she didn't even know his name.

'I'll have to leave a message at Barbara's,' she said.

'Your friend?'

She nodded.

'But she's not there. You said she wasn't there.'

'Yes, but I need to let her know I'm going home tomorrow. Otherwise she'll worry. She'll get home and find all the other notes I've pushed through the letterbox and she'll wonder where I am.'

They caught a taxi to Barbara's flat, sitting in the back, well apart, the earlier intimacy between them ruptured.

There was a light on in the flat. Although maybe it wasn't Barbara's flat, maybe she'd miscounted the windows. She climbed the stairs hurriedly, almost running, desperate for a face she knew.

'Helen! Thank God! I've been so worried. When I got home and found all those notes, I didn't know what to do.'

Helen threw herself into Barbara's arms, crying with relief.

'There. It's OK. I'm here now. It's OK. It's all OK,' said Barbara, rocking her like a baby, wondering who the man was.

'Come on. I'll make you a nice hot cup of tea, then you can tell me all about it. I was on holiday in Devon. That's why I wasn't here.'

Helen dried her eyes and glanced at the man, standing slightly apart, ill at ease.

'Do you want . . . do you need . . . your train fare . . . shall I . . . ?' he said.

'It's OK. I'll borrow some money from Barbara.'

'Right. OK. I'll . . . um . . . well . . . thanks. Well . . . bye then.'

He hovered uncertainly as if wondering how to take his leave, whether to shake her hand or kiss her. But in the end, he did neither. Just turned and walked slowly down the stairs.

'Who was he?' whispered Barbara loudly when she thought he was out of earshot.

'Just someone I met. He offered to lend me the money for my fare back. I'll tell you all about him.'

But she didn't. Nor did she tell Barbara about Vic. She told her about the row she had had with her father, how he had banned her from going out for a month after she had come back late from a dance. How she had left home the next day when her mother was at a Women's Institute produce fair, leaving a note saying she was going for good. She had not thought Barbara would be away, she said, had taken what she thought was plenty of money, had not realised how expensive bed and breakfast accommodation was.

'You must have got here just after I left,' interrupted Barbara, offering her another piece of Devon toffee and turning up the fire. 'I only left at two o'clock on Saturday.'

On the Wednesday, continued Helen, realising how fast her money was going down, she had not eaten lunch or gone to the cinema in the afternoon as she had done on the Monday and Tuesday. On the Thursday, she had bought only a cup of tea and a doughnut in the evening, eating as much as possible at breakfast. And that morning, sitting on her bed after breakfast, counting up her money, she had realised she did not even have enough money to pay for that night's accommodation.

'You poor thing! You must have been desperate,' said Barbara.

Yes, said Helen. But she did not say how desperate. How, when a strange man came up to her at lunchtime in the pub where she had gone to get away from the wind, she had not moved away as she would have done normally but had allowed him to buy her a drink. And another. And another. And possibly more. She had lost count. And how she had ended up telling him everything, how she had run away from home, how she had been going to stay with a friend until she found a job and somewhere to live, how the friend was not there, how she had run out of money.

Helen did not tell Barbara any of this or about how the man had said that was OK, he had a room going free in his house, she could have it if she liked only she'd have to work, he couldn't keep her. And how she had accepted the offer, thinking that his eyes were a bit funny, stary, as if they weren't focusing properly, and then telling herself not to be so silly, beggars couldn't be choosers, and following him out of the pub. And how he had led her to a house and showed her a room on the third floor and left her there. And how she had stood at the window, watching dusk fall, wondering what her parents would be having for tea, what they had said when they found her note, until she heard a knock on the door.

Instead, she pretended her handbag had been stolen while she was looking at a shop window. The man who had accompanied her to Barbara's had tried to catch the thief, she said. He had run after them – there were two of them, only young, sixteen or thereabouts – but they had got away. The man had come back for her then, she said. Had bought her a port and orange to steady her nerves and offered to lend her the money for a room that night and her fare home the following day. As she spoke, she marvelled at how simple it was to lie, how easily the words came.

'What was he called? What does he do?' asked Barbara suspiciously.

'I don't know. He didn't say.'

'But what were you going to do before you met him? Before your handbag was stolen? Where were you going to sleep?'

'I don't know. I couldn't have gone home even if I'd wanted to because I didn't have enough money for the train ticket. I didn't even have enough to send a telegram.'

'You poor thing. You poor, poor thing,' said Barbara, leaning across and clasping her by the ankles. 'And all this just because I wasn't here. If it had been any other week, I would have been. I haven't been away all summer. I was going to go to Norfolk in July but then, as you know, Dad died and I had to cancel it. After that, I decided not to take a holiday until next year but this friend, the one I went with, her aunt runs a small hotel. She let us stay for free as it was out of season.'

'It's OK. It's not your fault,' said Helen, seeing the room in the brothel, the man's hands, hair on his knuckles, black, tufted, like an animal, the smell afterwards – a smell she had not known before but did now, smelling it on herself still, wondering if Barbara could too.

'But if only you'd known. If only you'd had my number at work. They could have told you I was away, that I'd be back today.'

'I couldn't remember where you worked,' said Helen lamely, realising it had not even occurred to her to contact Barbara's workplace.

And then Barbara said was she hungry because if she was she could make her a cheese-and-pickle sandwich or bacon and eggs perhaps, she had gone straight out to the shops after getting back. And when Helen said yes, she was a bit peckish, she bustled about, making a fresh pot of tea, fetching sheets and blankets from the airing cupboard, making up a bed for Helen while the tea brewed. And all the while, she talked, asking Helen what she was going to do now, did she want to stay in Bristol and find a job or was she going to go home, it was up to her, she'd lend her some money either way but if she did want to go home then maybe she could wait until Sunday because that way she could introduce her to Jimmy, her fiancé, they were having lunch together the following day and later, in the evening, meeting up with some friends for a drink. And Helen said she probably would go home after all but there was no hurry, she could send her parents a telegram in the morning to let them know she was all right, and she'd like to meet Jimmy, like to very much. And while she talked and tucked in the sheets and said just one round of sandwiches would be fine, thanks, she nursed her lost virginity like a dog licking a wound, unable to leave it alone.

Later, lying in bed, her brushed hair spread about her on the cold, clean pillowcase, she remembered that her address book had been in the handbag as well as her purse. It had her name and address in the front. And she wondered if Vic would open it and see this and if he did, whether he would try to find her, drive to Cheltenham and ring on the doorbell, demand to see her. He had looked like the kind of person who might do something like that. And as she thought this, she remembered his eyes, the odd stary look they had had, and she shivered and turned on to her front, pressing her face into the pillow, trying to block them out. What had she done, she thought? What had she done?

32

She had almost died in hospital. The wound was not serious in itself – the knife had missed her vital organs – but she had lost a lot of blood and the doctor on duty, young, tired, and in a hurry because he was already forty minutes late for a date with his girlfriend, had misread her blood group and given her a transfusion of the wrong type of blood. The result was catastrophic. Her body had gone into shock, an infection had set in and she had developed a searing temperature, high enough to give her brain damage.

When her mother, tracked down by the police after Barbara reported her missing, arrived at hospital on the Monday afternoon, the registrar informed her that her daughter had not yet regained consciousness. Her condition was poor. Poor but stable, he added quickly, anxious she should not start to cry. He did not like to see women cry, still less to comfort them. He did not tell her about the transfusion or that the doctor in question had been suspended and would later be sacked, his career ruined.

'What happened?' asked her mother, nervous because she was not used to asking questions. Maurice, her husband, Helen's father, he usually saw to that. She noticed that a begonia on the window-sill needed attention. Also, that the windows needed cleaning.

'She was stabbed. A man went to help her and was hurt too. Stabbed in the eye. Several people saw the attacker running off so the police have got a fairly good description but they haven't arrested anyone yet. At least, not as far as I know. They don't always tell us immediately.'

*   *   *

In fact, the police had already arrested Vic but not for the knife attack. They had pulled over a car for speeding and found Vic inside on the back seat with enough heroin to supply a whole street. It was only later that a sharp-eyed constable, anxious for promotion, had spotted that the man in custody for drug dealing bore a remarkable resemblance to the poster of the man being sought in connection with a knife attack. He had duly reported his suspicions and, in return, although this was never explicitly stated, received the promotion he was seeking.

At least they hadn't cut her hair. That was her mother's first thought when she saw her. When she had been an angel in the school nativity play, all the other mothers had commented on how beautiful her hair was. How thick it was. How wavy. And such a lovely colour too. Really golden.

'Helen, it's Mother. Helen?'

She bent over the bed as if to kiss her but then merely patted her gently on the hand.

'Father sends his love. He would have come only he had too much work today. He says he'll try to come later in the week. Janet's made you some fairy cakes. I told her not to, that there wouldn't be time, but she insisted. They were still warm when I left. And I've brought you some black grapes. Seedless ones. You prefer black grapes, don't you?'

She turned to ask the nurse where she should put the grapes but saw that the nurse had left. For a moment, she panicked. In her mind, she saw herself running out of the room, jumping into a taxi, catching the next train back to Cheltenham. She had never wanted children. It had been Maurice who had wanted them, who had insisted on trying again for a boy. She had hated the sticky fingers, the toys on the floor, the endless clearing up. It was always she who had to pick up the pieces – to get up in the night when they were crying, change the sheets when they'd been sick. When he came home – later, she suspected, than was necessary – it was always calm, the children bathed and in their pyjamas, a meal in the oven, the plates warming. It was all very well for him to hug them then and call them Daddy's little darlings, he hadn't had to put up with them all day. And now here he was doing it again. Leaving it all to her.

She should have been at a meeting now. A meeting to decide how they were going to decorate the church for Christmas. It would have started now, the biscuits passed round, greetings exchanged. Oh, she knew it wasn't work. Not real work. But whose fault was that? She would have worked. She would have given anything to work instead of sing Humpty Dumpty.

The nurse came back into the room with a vase for the flowers she had bought and she said yes, she would like a cup of tea if it wasn't too much trouble, and sat down and got out her knitting. She had always done what had to be done.

She had regained consciousness on the Tuesday morning and watched her mother knit three rows in wool the colour of pink seaside rock.

The police interviewed her on the Wednesday after first politely asking her mother to leave the room. She told them everything, right down to the black hairs on the man's knuckles, everything except that it was her not him who had wanted to make love. They assumed she had been, if not raped, at least intimidated, too terrified to protest. Later that same day they went to the address she had given them but found it empty, stripped bare. The landlord, when they questioned him, said he did not know someone called Vic, that the house had not been let for some time. The neighbours acted dumb.

She told her mother what she asked but she did not ask much, afraid to tax her still fragile health or perhaps just afraid of what the answers might be. Barbara visited three times, bringing more flowers as well as magazines and a book of crosswords. Her father sent a card saying he would come the following week, he would take a day off work. She slept a lot. When she was not sleeping, she ate the purple grapes, sucking the flesh out first, then eating the skin, watching her mother knit. She knitted cardigans, at least three a day, sometimes more. The cardigans were for babies in India although sometimes Helen wondered if they were ever used for this purpose. She envisaged them instead being used as hats or mats, a trophy, something to barter with. Her mother, she sensed, did not care what they were used for or by whom. They were something to do. A respectable way of passing the time. Pink then blue then pink again. Just those two colours. She bought the wool in bulk.

On the Friday her mother went home, unable to hide her relief, already picturing the scene on Sunday after church, the crowd of well-wishers gathering around her. 'And how is Helen?' 'So glad to hear she's regained consciousness.' 'Do send her our best wishes.'

'I'll have to go otherwise your father will run out of clean shirts. I'll come back next week. Either on the Monday or the Tuesday. All right?' And she had nodded, looking forward to being alone.

But when she woke up on Saturday, she had felt lonely, had missed her mother's knitting, the shape of the cardigans marking the growth of the day. The nurse knocked on her door at ten o'clock. There was someone with her. A man.

'This is Philip. He's the one I told you about – the one that saved your life.'

She struggled into a more upright position.

'Well, I'll leave you to chat. Don't tire one another out,' the nurse said brightly.

'You look better,' he said when the nurse had shut the door.

She smiled, wondering when he had seen her, embarrassed to think of people looking at her and her not knowing.

'I saw you on Sunday,' he said, as if reading her thoughts. 'You looked pretty awful then. They were very worried about you.'

'What happened to your eye?'

'He stabbed it.'

'He?'

'The man. Whoever he was. The one that stabbed you too.'

'Is it . . . is it going to be all right?'

'No.' He tapped the bandage covering his left eye then cheerfully, too cheerfully, added: 'There's nothing there now. Just the socket. They're waiting for it to heal up and then they're going to fit me with a false one.'

She stared in appalled horror.

'You mean you . . . you . . . you're blind. Because of me . . . because you helped me.'

'Not blind,' he said, pointing to his other eye. 'This one still works. It's not quite so good at judging distances but apart from that, I hardly miss the other one now. Well, only every now and again.'

She covered both her own eyes with her hands.

'I'm sorry. I'm so sorry. Oh, my God! What have I done? What have I done?'

The man looked desperately around the room as if the curtains might provide inspiration. He stepped forward, laid an awkward hand on her shoulder.

'It's OK. Don't cry. It's not your fault.'

'But it is. It is,' she sobbed, mopping her face with the top of the sheet.

And she told him why. Not all then but gradually, day by day, not hiding anything except what she had hidden from the police – the moment when she had unbuttoned her blouse, had said she wanted to, had taken his hand, pressed it against her breast. Somehow, she could not admit that this had happened, that she had behaved like that, not even to herself, not then.

They were two months in hospital and in that time they shared grapes, shortbread, Jane Austen, Henry James and the Song of Solomon – the last three borrowed from the sparsely stocked shelves of the hospital library.

Afterwards, looking back, she decided that that was when she fell in love with him – listening to him read the Song of Solomon, the window open, dusk falling, the warm of his voice mingling with the cool of the air:

'I am the rose of Sharon and the lily of the valleys. As the lily among thorns, so is my love among the daughters.

As the apple tree among the trees of the wood, so is my beloved among the sons. I sat down under his shadow with great delight and his fruit was sweet to my taste.

He brought me to the banqueting house and his banner over me was love.

Stay me with flagons, comfort me with apples: for I am sick of love.'

* * *

She thought nothing when she missed a period. Or when she missed a second one. One often missed periods following a traumatic incident. She had read about it somewhere. It never occurred to her that she was pregnant.

33

The alarm on Geoff's bedside radio bleeped again. Geoff groaned, rolled over and switched it off.

'I'll have to get up,' he said.

Una stretched out an arm and felt for his body.

'I want to stay here all day. To have tea and toast, make love, sleep, start all over again.'

Geoff took hold of her arm and raised it to his mouth.

'Umm! Attractive proposition.'

He let the arm fall.

'But unfortunately not possible. Not today.'

And he jumped out of bed.

'Why not?' asked Una, opening her eyes, sitting up, hurt by his summary rejection.

'We could ring work . . . say we were ill or something.'

'I've got a meeting with the principal. First thing. About the new contracts. I've got to report back to the union on what he says.'

She watched him pull on his briefs – black with a red logo on the right-hand side. When he bent over, a small roll appeared on his stomach. It was like fat on pork – white and blubbery. She lay back again. She felt bad-tempered suddenly, her tongue furred up, her hair lank.

'Do you want a coffee?'

'No. Not yet.'

She did not like coffee first thing in the morning. She had told him this. Told him several times. But he did not seem to remember. Or maybe he did not hear in the first place. She tugged at the curtain behind the bed. It was another dull day – grey, still, like something dead. It had been like this for days.

'Here you are.'

She struggled upright again. Geoff handed her a cup of coffee.

'But I said . . .'

'Don't put it down on the wood, will you, because it will mark.'

And he was gone again, whistling tunelessly, the radio on loud in the bathroom, an MP explaining why he had resigned the day before, another man dead in Northern Ireland. She glanced at the clock. She would be late for work. But it didn't matter. She had been wrong to attach so much importance to work. It was not work that mattered. It was people. Relationships. She began to drink the cup of coffee she did not want.

Geoff came back in again smelling of aftershave. She watched him choose his clothes – his new blue shirt, a yellow tie, cream chinos from his trouser press. Her father had had a trouser press too, she remembered, only he had never used it. He had given it away last year or perhaps the year before to a man collecting junk for charity. She wondered where her parents were now, whether they were still in Greece or had crossed the border into Bulgaria. They wanted to spend Christmas in Istanbul. That's what her mother had said in her last letter.

Geoff was brushing his hair now, stooping slightly so that he could see himself in the mirror. As she watched, she saw him smile, not at her, but at himself, his reflection. She looked away, embarrassed. She had thought only women smiled at themselves in the mirror.

He planted a moist kiss on her forehead and she shrank back, recoiling from the smell of mouthwash. He suffered from slight halitosis, hence the mints in his car, she had realised, the chewing gum in his jacket pockets.

Alone in the flat, she put on his dressing gown and wandered into the kitchen. There was a note for Doreen propped up against the bread bin asking her to clean the fridge and the bathroom. A postscript added that the airing cupboard needed reorganising if she had time. And he was running short of bleach. Also food, said Una to herself, discovering there was no bread, only crispbread.

She took one and put on the kettle to make a pot of tea. She knew there were teabags because she had bought them herself the day before. And milk and chops and new potatoes, the latter expensive because they were out of season, imported from France. He had said she didn't need to cook, that they could eat out and she had said she didn't mind, that it was nice to eat in sometimes, to be all cosy, just the two of them. Afterwards, she had realised that it was he who minded, that he did not like to use his kitchen, was distressed at the sight of spilt fat on his oven. He had washed up immediately after the meal, unable to rest until everything had been put away again, the taps polished, the teatowels hung up to dry.

Going downstairs, she passed an elderly woman struggling to regain her breath on the first floor landing. There were two shopping bags at her feet, both full even though it was barely half past nine. They exchanged smiles and Una went on, then stopped and turned, looking over the stairwell at where the woman still stood, one hand grasping the banister like a claw.

'Would you like some help?' she called. 'Would you like some help with your bags?'

'Sorry?'

The woman looked down at her, puzzled. Una climbed back up.

'I said would you like some help with your bags. Are they heavy?'

'Yes, they are actually. Potatoes and onions. I'd run out of both,' she explained.

She wore a fake fur coat or perhaps a real one. Una could not tell. Her cheeks were ghostly with powder, crossed with lines like a mad-ploughed field, her bloodshot eyes marooned in green eyeshadow. She smelt of dried roses, pink petals pressed in a book of poems, forgotten about, then found much later, their colour sapped.

'They should put a lift in,' said Una, picking up the bags, one in each hand.

'Yes,' agreed the woman without a trace of self-pity. 'So I keep telling them. But the other residents don't want to because it would mean higher management costs. They say it's my choice. That I should go and live in a bungalow if I don't want to walk up stairs. Far more sensible for someone my age. That's what they said at the last committee meeting.'

She followed Una up the stairs.

'I said I had never been sensible and didn't intend to start now. That shut them up.'

Una paused, waiting for her to catch up, taken aback by the woman's forthright tone.

'Which floor are you on?'

'Right at the top. Would you like to come in for a coffee? I've bought biscuits as well as potatoes. Chocolate bourbon,' said the woman, stopping again to catch her breath.

So she lived opposite Geoff, thought Una, saying no, she couldn't stop, she was already late for work as it was. At the top, she put down the bags and said goodbye.

'I like the view. That's why I stay. It would kill me to live in a bungalow,' said the old woman.

And as she turned and put the key in her lock, wondering if the girl had heard, she was already halfway downstairs again; how fast the young moved.

'I'd like you to meet Una. Una, this is Pete. He heads up media studies at the college,' said Geoff.

Una shook hands with a dark, shambly-limbed man with an uncut beard. Someone else clapped Geoff on the back and cried: 'Good speech. Well done.'

'Divide and rule,' said another. 'That's what they want. That's what they always want. Bastards! I bet they're not proposing to come in during the summer holidays to catch up on their paperwork.'

Una was asked what she would like to drink. Then asked again, this time by someone different. Three drinks turned up on the bar in front of her – two pints and a half pint. She picked up the pint, made reckless by the atmosphere, the smell of men wanting to smack someone now, hard.

The emergency union meeting had lasted two and a half hours. Geoff had spoken first. Then there had been questions or, more often, comments – long, rambling asides on the need to stick together, to stand or fall as one. The tone of these comments had become more heated as the evening wore on, each speaker trying to outdo the previous one in their opposition to the proposals put forward by the college principal.

Una was not sure exactly what these proposals were. As far as she could make out, they were to do with the employment contracts held by the lecturers. The principal wanted to change them so that new staff would have different working conditions. No one had explained exactly what the new working conditions were but they were less favourable than those currently enjoyed. That much Una had understood.

'What I don't understand,' she said now – nervously, quietly so that only Geoff could hear – 'is why it affects you? I mean, your contracts aren't going to be changed, are they?'

Geoff wiped a smear of foam from his top lip and set his glass down as though he needed both hands free to be able to answer properly.

'It affects them and so it affects us. Put simply, their problem is our problem. That's how I see it. That we're all responsible for one another. You for me, me for you, both of us for the little old lady down the road who can't get out to the shops any more. We've got to help one another, the strong supporting the weak, the rich the poor, the clever the not-so-clever. It's the only way forward. Besides, it would soon become our problem. If we let this through and lecturers at other colleges also let it through, then as soon as any of us changed jobs, we'd have to sign the new contracts.'

'So what are you going to do?'

Geoff said something Una couldn't quite catch about ballot papers, a change in the rules, an attempt by the government to make it more difficult for people to strike.

'You're going on strike!' said Una.

'Up to the members, of course. But, judging by their reaction tonight, yes, I'd say we are.'

Someone tapped Geoff on the arm. Someone else shouted his name.

'Geoff! Over here! We need you.'

He turned to see who was calling then turned back to face Una, running a hand down her left arm.

'I won't be long. Don't let anyone else whisk you away. Tell them you're mine. All mine.'

Una smiled foolishly into her drink. The rich the poor, the strong the weak . . . yes, he was right. People had to help one another, to look after those less fortunate than themselves. She felt a warm glow as she surveyed the scene in front of her – the ceiling festooned with streamers and underneath it, some standing, some sitting, some lolling against walls, men and women, laughing, talking, sharing. Looking round, she felt suddenly that she had arrived, that the unknown destination towards which she had been travelling had been reached. She was there. In it, at it, with it.

Later, after the landlord had protested that he really had to close or he'd lose his licence, the police had already been down once that week, they stumbled out into the empty street, singing, swaying, their warm breath white puffs in the cold night, like dandelion seeds, unblown. There was Jane and Liz and Norman and Tim and someone else whose name Una couldn't remember and next to him, Melissa or was it Fenella, she wasn't sure, but it didn't matter, nothing mattered except that they were together, all of them together.

One by one the others left but she and Geoff kept on singing. They sang all the way back to his flat and all the way up the stairs, stumbling, giggling, clutching for a firm hold in the dark. At the top, the door opposite Geoff's flat opened and a light went on. 'It's gone midnight,' a voice informed them crisply. Una blinked, dazzled by the glare. It was the woman she had helped that morning, she saw. She was wearing slippers now and a long quilted dressing gown, turquoise with green swirls. Geoff said nothing although Una felt his arm tighten. The woman looked them up and down, not appearing to recognise Una, then sniffed dismissively and closed her door.

Geoff aimed a key at his lock, missed, tried again, was successful.

'There,' he said, shutting the door behind them, grasping Una by her bottom, squeezing her against him.

'Silly old bat.'

34

'But why? Why?' asked Bridget, seeing the letter she had posted that morning saying she would not be home for Christmas, she and Matthew had decided to stay in Bristol, it would be their first Christmas together. She looked Una straight in the eye.

'Why?' she asked again, unable to keep the anger out of her voice. She had put Una down for the Boxing Day duty. Now she would have to find someone to replace her. She couldn't ask Jan because she had volunteered to do Christmas Day. And Kate was going home to Edinburgh to see her brother, back in the UK for the first time in four years. It would be unfair to ask her. Damn Una!

'I . . . I . . . I just felt I wasn't doing anything worthwhile,' said Una apologetically.

She had known it wouldn't be easy telling Bridget she wanted to hand in her notice. That morning Geoff had suggested she should give up her job in order to help him with the strike and she had said yes, still flushed with the camaraderie of that night in the pub. He had said he would pay her what she had been earning until she either found a new job or became eligible for benefit. As they talked, she had heard the sober tones of a BBC newscaster announcing ugly clashes on a picket line in Leeds, questions asked in the House of Commons, stones thrown. She had told herself it wouldn't be like that, that this was a small local dispute unlikely to arouse public interest let alone sympathy. But she had been unable to prevent herself feeling excited, newly important.

'What do you mean? What do you mean "worthwhile"?' asked Bridget. 'What do you think these women would do if we weren't here? Where would they go? Most of them have got no money. And they couldn't go to friends or relatives because then their partners would know where to find them. We're the only place they can go.'

'I know, I know. I'm not saying *you're* not doing something worthwhile, that the *refuge* isn't worthwhile. I'm saying I felt *I* wasn't doing anything worthwhile.'

'Because you weren't running the show? Is that what you mean? Because Germaine Black went back to her husband instead of moving into the flat you found for her? Because, when you said you wanted to do something worthwhile, to help other people, you didn't mean you wanted to clean floors? Is that it?'

'No, no, that's not it . . .' started Una.

But Bridget was in full flood now, her anger increased by the sight of someone's child playing in the back garden, no coat in sight and frost still on the ground. Christ alive! Didn't the mother have any sense?

'It's not a production line, you know – helping people. You don't see instant results. I told you that. You can't force people into change. You have to wait for them to come to it themselves. And that can be very frustrating. Frustrating and demoralising. But that doesn't mean we're wasting our time. We're not.'

'I know *we* are not wasting our time. That *you're* not, *Kate* isn't, *Jan* isn't,' said Una, determined to have her say. 'The thing is, I felt *I* was. That's all. Maybe I'm just not suited to this sort of job. Maybe I haven't got the right character . . .'

'Oh, don't give me that crap,' said Bridget, suddenly tired and fed up, tired of the constant struggle to secure adequate funding, to find suitable volunteers, to listen to women saying they weren't going back, not this time, never again, as though she believed them.

'So what are you going to do then?' she asked, her voice small, deflated. 'Have you got any plans?'

Una explained that the lecturers at the further education college had voted to go on strike about proposed changes to their working practices. Her partner was the branch secretary, she said. He had asked her to help out. There would be a lot to do – organising a picket line, liaising with national officials, keeping the local media informed.

'Beats hoovering, I suppose. Much more glamorous,' said Bridget.

'It's not like that,' said Una, stung into self-defence. And she repeated what she had heard Geoff say in the pub about everyone being responsible for everyone else.

'Yes, yes, yes,' groaned Bridget. She had heard it all before, had said it herself too, not so long ago, although longer than she cared to remember.

She saved her most pointed remark for the last.

'I'm disappointed. That's all. Disappointed in you.'

And she watched Una's face crumple. It had worked. But then it always did.

Walking away, Una told herself that Bridget had no right to say she was disappointed with her. She was not a schoolgirl to be ticked off for cheating in a spelling test. She was a woman, a grown woman, and she was going to help run a strike. And yes, it did beat hoovering.

And she stepped out boldly, the word 'disappointed' still needling her, a poisoned arrow tip lodged firm.

35

Rob parked at the bottom of the road so that he could not be seen from the house. The car was green – lime green, dirty lolly green – bought with a loan from the bank despite his mother's objections.

'I need one for work,' he had explained. 'Otherwise I won't get any good stories. Just the car boot sales and weddings.'

'If you need one for work they should provide one. I don't see why you have to go running up debts just to do your job.'

'Besides, it will be useful for getting there and back as well. The trains don't run all that often. And I'll be working late some days. I can't take your car all the time.'

She had said nothing to this, reasoning that it was his life after all, one only learnt by one's mistakes.

And so he had bought the Vauxhall Chevette that somebody's friend's wife's son was selling – fourteen years old, with a clutch that was going, a faulty starter motor, and bodywork that even the previous owner admitted was poor. And he loved it.

He had decided to see Una, moved at last to action by the sight of a red salt dough angel. He had been decorating the Christmas tree while his mother made mince pies. Neither of them liked mince pies but she always made them on the pretext of having something seasonal to offer visitors. Rob suspected she also made them because his father had liked them. It was a way of remembering him, of telling him he wasn't forgotten.

He had fetched the boxes from the loft, cut the string tying the lids, and slowly, gently, so as not to break anything, taken out the decorations, rediscovering them fondly as he did every year – the yellow cardboard star he had made at nursery, the red salt dough angel he had made at school, the imprint of his five-year-old finger still visible on the tip of a wing, and oldest of all, the pink felt stocking his mother had made when she was a girl, her blue embroidered initials lurching crazily to one side. And as he looked at them, deciding which to put up and which to put by, he remembered that the year before he and Una had decorated the tree together, squabbling over how to do it, whether there was too much red or not enough gold, fighting over the angel. Afterwards, when it was done, they had turned off all the other lights, taken the cushions from the sofa and lain down on the floor, looking up into the branches, peaceful in the knowledge that his mother was out for the evening.

He would go and see Una, he decided. It was all so silly. So childish and futile. This could go on for ever. Someone had to make the first move. Why shouldn't it be him? And so, after he had finished decorating the tree, he had gone to a florist's and bought a miniature tree, tiny, less than a foot high. He had spent the rest of the afternoon writing messages – about her hair, how he loved it, the way it changed colour when it moved, gold then brown then red. About the hill overlooking Bath – their hill – that walk on the beach on New Year's Day, her mouth, the day they had met. He had folded the messages small, wrapped them in tissue paper and tied them to the tree with red thread from his mother's sewing box. It was a love tree.

And now, sitting in the car at the end of her road, he lifted the tree from the floor in front of the passenger seat and checked to see that none of the messages had fallen off. No. They were all there. He opened the door and got out, holding the tree inside his jacket so that it did not get bashed. There were lights on in the house, he saw. Lights everywhere.

'Yes?'

A woman stood at the door, a woman he had never seen before, with orange hair in two plaits and round, surprised-looking eyes.

'Is Una in?' he asked, thinking that the woman might be a friend, a relative perhaps, come to stay for Christmas, someone he had never seen before.

'Una? No, there's no Una here,' said the woman in what Rob

recognised as a Californian accent. Then, in a rush, she added:
'Oh, Una! You mean the Dart girl? The daughter?'

Rob nodded.

'Yes. Una Dart. Have they moved house?'

'No. We're just renting from them. My husband, he works for
the same company as Philip. As Philip used to, I mean. The parent
company. He's here on secondment.'

'Where are Mr and Mrs Dart then?' asked Rob, noticing a
tangle of toys in the hallway, a large teddy propped up in a
tractor.

'I don't know exactly. Probably in Turkey. They did say they
wanted to spend Christmas in Istanbul.'

'Turkey! What are they doing in Turkey?'

'Haven't you heard? How long is it since you last saw them?'
asked the woman.

'Six months. I've been away. I've only just got back.'

'Oh well, that explains it,' said the woman, reassured. 'Philip
took early redundancy and they bought a mobile home. All over
Europe they've been. France, Italy, Greece. That was the last time
they sent us a postcard. From Athens.'

'Did Una go with them?'

'No, no, she's still in Bristol. She comes round every now and
again to make sure we're all right.'

'You don't happen to have an address for her, do you? Only
. . . well . . . I wanted to wish her happy Christmas.'

The woman said she didn't. She had an address for the brother,
Malcolm, no, Martin. Or she could give Una a message the next
time she called.

'No, it's OK. I'll wait. Do you know when Mr and Mrs Dart
are getting back?'

The woman said sorry but no, she didn't know the exact
date.

'We're leaving on January the fifteenth. Staying overnight
with a college friend of mine in London and then flying out from
Heathrow on the sixteenth. So I suppose any time after that.'

Rob nodded, dispirited. Back in the car, he put the tree on the
floor once more and leant his head against the steering wheel.
He had planned the whole day. He knew he shouldn't have,
that he was laying himself open to disappointment but he had

done, even so. They would have lunch in a pub – one with good food and real ale, not far from the Cheddar Gorge. Afterwards, they would walk along the Mendips Way. Not far because it was cold, bitter cold, with a searing east wind and besides it would be almost dark by four, the shortest day of the year. When they got home they would light a fire, apple wood with fir cones. He had put the wood aside last night, made sure it was dry. They would toast muffins, burning them as they always did but not minding, scraping the burnt off, spreading the butter thick. Later, when they had drunk two or perhaps three pots of tea and exchanged stories of the last six months – fragments of memory, like broken glass picked up from the floor, not fitting together – they would roast chestnuts in the embers.

But she was here, he thought. She was in Bristol. She hadn't gone to Thailand or Hong Kong. There was that at least. Comforted, he drove home, wondering what she was doing at that very moment, whether she had decorated a Christmas tree and, if so, whether she had thought of him.

36

Someone had whistled. Yes, there it was again. Two notes – sharp, urgent, and yet low at the same time. Philip rose, moving the bedclothes gently so as not to disturb Helen and tiptoed to the window. The shutters were closed but not locked, pulled to against the chill of the dawn. He opened them slowly, the peeling paint coming away in his hands like charred skin, a small flake lodging under his right thumbnail.

Istanbul lay before him, splendid in the pink of the rising sun, its skyline a glorious architectural cacophony. He caught his breath, remembering that it was Christmas Day, that he was here, in Istanbul, the Paris of the East, the old capital of the civilised world, Byzantium. He stepped out on to the narrow balcony, pulling the shutters to behind him, and looked down into the street. A man was standing with his back to him, looking up at a first floor window at the house opposite. A girl was leaning out of the window, a long black plait hanging over one shoulder. She was holding something, dangling it at the end of a long, graceful arm. Suddenly, with a whirl, she flung it up into the air where it fluttered, helpless, then floated down to the ground. It was a letter. The man ran and snatched it up and thrust it in his jacket. For a moment, the girl stayed at the window, smiling down. Then, quickly, she was gone, the man walking away, the street silent again. Philip watched the closed window, fascinated, wondering if the girl would reappear.

But she did not and so after a while he looked away, up towards the east where the sun had broken free of the last sticky threads of night and was resting, gathering its strength before the long, daily climb. Back in England, children were

opening stockings, he thought. Wives and mothers and grand-
mothers were fretting over turkeys, trying to get ahead with
the sprouts, exhorting children to put used wrapping paper in
the bag provided or something would get broken. And outside,
fathers were getting out the car, grumbling, struggling with the
cap of the de-icer, wondering if there would be any chance of
slipping out for a quick pint.

There had been a plane in his stocking one year. Only a
cheap thing, a balsa wood kit, easily snapped. He had made
it immediately, sitting cross-legged on his bed, his six-year-old
fingers clumsy with glue and rubber bands. But it had flown. He
still remembered that, the shock when, having stretched out his
arm, pointed the nose of the plane at the opposite side of the
room, and flicked with his wrist, the plane flew. Soon after that
he had taken out a library book on planes and begun to scour
the sky by day as well as night. 'Look where you're going!'
his mother had cried. 'One of these days you're going to walk
straight into a lamp post.'

There had been other planes after that. Model ones. He had
made them dutifully, following the instructions, careful not to
let the paint drip. Afterwards he had put them away on a shelf
in his bedroom, out of sight. It was the flight he liked, the motion,
the clean cleaving of air. The thing itself was just metal. No more
than that.

Underneath, a boy cycled past, rearing up on one wheel,
showing off. Further up the street, a door opened suddenly.
There was the sound of a woman's voice, shrill, angry, then
something black flung into the road. The door banged shut
and the cat, for that was what it was, he saw, picked itself up
haughtily, looked around and crossed to the other side of the
road where it sat down in the sun.

They had been five days in Istanbul. During this time they
had visited the Blue Mosque, Topkapi Palace, the Hippodrome
and the Cistern Basilica. They had climbed the city walls, eaten
skewered mussels and grilled lamb intestines at a street stall near
the British consulate, haggled over the price of a massage at the
Turkish baths in Suterazi Sokak, taken a two-hour cruise up the
Bosphorus, watched belly-dancing in a nightclub, drunk tea in
the tea garden near the Old Book Bazaar, and wandered for

hours in the Egyptian Bazaar where they had sampled dried mulberries and seen a young boy being fitted for his white circumcision suit. They had eaten at random, struggling to make themselves understood, pointing at the food on neighbouring tables – lentil soup, fresh pizza, stuffed green peppers, roast ground lamb with spices and onions.

A shutter clattered open at the house next door and a head-scarfed woman leant out with a rug which she proceeded to beat with a stick. Two small boys emerged round the corner kicking a tin can. A dog barked. Philip heard a sound in the room behind him and peered through the shutters. Helen had woken up, he saw, her hands clasped, her arms raised high above her head, yawning. He opened the shutters and went back into the room, causing Helen to squint at the rush of light.

'Happy Christmas,' he said, climbing back into bed.

'Happy Christmas. Ooh, your feet are freezing!'

'Yours aren't,' he said, wrapping himself round her, breathing in her warm, slept-in smell.

She hugged him back, looking out at the bleached blue sky.

'We did it. We're in Istanbul,' she said.

'I know. I know.'

They laughed and hugged again.

'Wait,' she said, leaning sideways, feeling under the bed. 'Here you are.'

She handed him a small package wrapped in dark blue paper decorated with silver cresent moons.

'Happy Christmas, darling.'

He unwrapped it, puzzled by the shape and feel.

It was a pair of flying goggles, Second World War by the look of them, still in remarkably good condition.

'Where on earth did you find these?'

'In that antique shop near Lyons. Do they fit? Try them on.'

'I will, I will, wait a moment though.'

He jumped out of bed and rummaged in the top shelf of the wardrobe.

'Here you are. Happy Christmas to you too.'

'When did you buy this?'

'Not telling. Go on. Open it.'

She did so, trying not to tear the paper, a thrift impressed on her by her mother and now passed on to Una and Martin.

'It's beautiful. Really beautiful.'

She held it up so that she could see the pattern better. It was a scarf, lapis lazuli blue, embroidered with gold.

'What are they doing?' she asked, looking more closely at the embroidered figures.

'I don't know. Dancing. That's what I thought anyway. Do you like it? Try it on.'

'I will. I will. You try yours on too.'

They both donned their respective presents then turned to face one another.

Helen giggled.

'You do look funny.'

'You don't. You look beautiful,' he said, leaning over and kissing her.

She lay down, her head on his chest, listening to the beat of his heart. He stroked her hair.

'What are we going to do today?'

'The Sancta Sophia, I thought,' said Philip. 'I don't want to leave without seeing that.'

'As long as we don't spend all day there. I don't think I can admire many more mosaics or prayer niches.'

'It closes at four so we can't stay late even if we wanted to. Besides, I thought you were the one who enjoyed sightseeing.'

'Well, you can have too much of a good thing,' she said, nuzzling him, sliding her fingers round his arm, feeling the skin change from rough to smooth.

They dressed slowly, enjoying the luxury of their private bathroom. For breakfast, they ate *simit* – toasted circular rolls covered with sesame seeds – and tea in the café opposite the small mosque near their hotel. It was warm, hot enough to sit outside although they chose to sit inside, smiling at the café owner who recognised them now.

'About fourteen centigrade, I should think,' said Philip, taking off his jumper, signalling to the waiter carrying a tea-laden tray.

They entered Sancta Sophia the way recommended by their guide book, on the side by Sultanahmet, through what was once the Forum of Augustus, walking slowly, one step at a time, their eyes adjusting slowly to the dark.

'It's incredible,' said Helen. Above them, the main dome soared like the sky seen lying down in a field – a huge naked expanse of blue.

'The Emperor Justinian thought so too,' said Philip, consulting the guide book. 'Apparently, when he first saw it, he said: "Glory to God that I have been judged worthy of such a work. Oh Solomon! I have outdone you!"'

Helen nodded, moving off towards the centre of the dome beneath which a young boy stood, clapping his hands, laughing at the echo. Philip followed, reading about breccia columns, the Ottoman chandeliers and the famous mosaics, covered with plaster when the Turks took Constantinople in 1453.

'Who's that?' asked Helen, pointing at a mosaic portrait at the end of the south gallery.

Philip consulted his book again. 'The Empress Zoe, I think. Yes. When it was first put in, she was married to someone called Romanus. Then he died and she married someone called Michael so she had Romanus' picture taken out and Michael's put in. But then Michael died as well so she had his portrait taken out to make way for one of her next husband, Constantine.'

He closed the book and took her hand and they walked back towards the Imperial Door near which a huddle of people had gathered round one of the columns. As they approached, a woman broke free, shrieking and holding up a finger.

'What are they doing? What's she saying?' asked Helen.

They watched, standing apart a little, anxious not to give offence.

'They're putting their finger in something,' she whispered.

'Oh, I know, I read about it, wait a minute . . .' said Philip, fumbling to find the Istanbul section.

'Yes. Here we are. It's a weeping column. You're supposed to stick your finger in the hole and make a wish. If your finger's damp when you take it out, your wish comes true.'

'Shall we try it? Come on. Let's,' said Helen mischievously, smiling at the woman in front of her in the queue.

She inserted her right index finger, wishing quickly, silently, withdrawing it slowly.

'Did it work? Is it damp?' asked Philip, looking over her shoulder.

'Not telling. Go on. You do it too.'

She walked off, feeling dizzy suddenly, looking for somewhere to sit down.

Philip found her outside, leaning against a wall.

'Are you OK?'

'Yes. I just went a bit dizzy. That's all. Did you make a wish?'

'Yes.'

'Come on. I'm hungry. Let's have something to eat.'

They ate at a cookshop in the Grand Bazaar, flaky pastries stuffed with cheese and chopped parsley, followed by dried figs from a stall nearby. Afterwards, they wandered among the little back streets and bought going-home presents – a chunky bangle for Una, a brass letter-opener for Martin made in Swordmakers' Street, engraved with his initials.

At six they returned to their hotel room and showered, Helen first, then Philip, lying down afterwards on the bed, listening to the day turn.

'I think we should do something special on our last night here,' said Helen drowsily.

'We are,' said Philip. 'I've already planned it.'

'What? Where are we going?'

She sat up, suddenly wide awake.

'It's a surprise.'

They caught a dolmus to Sand Gate near the old harbour of Kontascalion and had dinner in one of the city's best seafood restaurants. Afterwards they caught a night ferry to Uskudar where they drank coffee and brandy overlooking the Bosphorus, the tiny fishing boats bobbing on the waves beneath them, lit up by the searchlights of passing ferries.

'I want . . . I think . . . I want to fly again,' said Philip when he had finished his third brandy. 'When we get home, I'm going to join a flying club. There are plenty near Bristol. They won't mind that I've only got the use of one eye. At least I'm pretty sure they won't. I'd have to take a refresher course but it probably wouldn't take long. A few months or so. I've been thinking about it. It would be . . . well, you know how much I loved it.'

'Good,' said Helen, leaning across the table, putting a hand on his. 'Good. I'm glad.'

They stayed like that, hand on hand, until a waiter approached and removed their empty glasses.

'Was that what you wished for? Today, in Sancta Sophia? To fly again?'

'Yes,' he said, grinning foolishly.

He did not ask what she had wished for and she did not tell him.

37

Helen had wished to see him again. Holding her finger in the hole, she had prayed that they would meet – not for long, not to be friends – but so that she could find out who he was, what he did, his name even. She wanted to let him know that he had a son, a granddaughter too, black-haired, white-skinned, green-eyed, the image of her grandfather, or at least as she remembered him, standing there, at the top of the stairs outside Barbara's flat, wondering what to say.

The case had taken a long time to come to court, delayed by wrangling about what charges should or could, be brought. In the end, much to Philip's satisfaction, the police had decided that it could, realistically, charge Vic with Helen's attempted murder, and had done so. She herself had not much cared what they charged him with, wanting it only to be over, for Vic to be locked up, safe, behind bars.

Martin had been two months old when the trial started, still breast feeding. She had had to take him to court, handing him over to Barbara or Philip when it was her turn to give evidence. Barbara had proved a stalwart friend. She had agreed to say nothing to the police about the man who had accompanied Helen to her flat that night, had asked no questions, not then or afterwards, understanding she did not wish to talk about him. Helen had been dismayed when, eighteen months after the trial, she had announced that she was emigrating to Australia, and distraught when, three months later, Jimmy, by then her husband, had written from Adelaide to say she had died suddenly of a brain tumour.

The police had tried to persuade her to change her story, to say that the man had been violent, that she had struggled, had been hit even. But she had remained intransigent. This was the father of her child, she thought. She was not going to slander him, not even to increase the chances of a conviction.

'It will look odd,' said the chief inspector leading the case. Later, in the same interview, he leant across his desk – oak, she remembered, with a photo of a black labrador in a cheap gilt frame – and said: 'Why didn't you leave? Why didn't you just walk out when you discovered the mistake you'd made?'

'I was scared,' she said. This was true. She had been frightened. Then she reminded him of how much she had had to drink, of how unused to alcohol she was at the time.

'I was not myself. I was not thinking properly,' she said, knowing she could not say she had enjoyed it because he would be shocked. Women were not supposed to enjoy it, not nice ones, especially not virgins.

'So you didn't put up a struggle? You didn't try to fight him off?'

'He didn't hurt me. He was gentle,' said Helen, knowing this was not what he wanted to hear.

At the trial, Vic argued that she knew he was a pimp, that she had gone back to the brothel willingly, had given no sign of alarm when he had shown a strange man into her room. Later, when he had looked in through a peephole, they had been at it like rabbits, he said. If she was a virgin, then he was a Dutchman, he said, and a pink-eyed, blue-haired one at that, he added, causing someone to snigger in the public gallery.

She had taken advantage of him, he claimed. Had used him to bring her a client and then run off without giving him his share of her earnings. When he had followed her that night after seeing her come out of a pub, he had had no thoughts of revenge – had merely asked her for the money he was owed. But she had spat at him, he said, had made offensive remarks about his virility. That was why he had pulled out a knife, he said. There had been no premeditation.

The prosecutor insisted that Helen had received no money. She had left her handbag behind in the house, he said. That was how Vic had known how to find her. Barbara's address was the only Bristol one in her address book. The defendant must have lain in wait outside the flats and followed Helen to the pub. When she had decided to go home early instead of accompanying the others in her group to a late night film, he had seized his chance. He had probably been high on drugs at the time, he said. And he mentioned the heroin that had been found on Vic at the time of his arrest.

'Did the man force you to have sexual intercourse with him?' asked the counsel for the defence.

'He did not hurt me,' said Helen, searching the faces in the public gallery. Was he there? Had he read about the trial in the papers? He had not come forward despite several appeals by the police. Did that mean he was not from Bristol, that he lived somewhere else, perhaps a long way off. He had had a slight accent, she remembered, but only very slight and she was not good at accents, could barely tell a Scottish one apart from an Irish.

The barrister said he had not asked whether the man had hurt her. Had he forced her to have intercourse, he repeated.

'He did not tie me up, if that's what you mean, or hold a gun to me or a knife or anything like that,' said Helen, straining her ears, hearing the distant wail of a baby, possibly Martin.

No, that was not what he meant, said the barrister. What he meant was could she have said no? If she had wanted to, could she have stopped him?

'Yes. No. I mean, I'm not sure. He was not violent. It was not like that. He tried not to hurt me,' said Helen, gripping the edge of the witness box. She was sure it was Martin crying. Her breasts started to leak milk as they always did when she heard him crying. She could feel the milk seeping through her blouse. Soon, a damp patch would emerge on her cardigan.

Could she have stopped him? Yes or no?

'I don't know,' said Helen, her bottom lip starting to tremble.

Had she tried to stop him?

'No, I didn't. I didn't think to. I was . . . it was . . . it all happened so fast.'

'And did you enjoy it?'

A shocked murmur ran though the court. The counsel for the prosecution stood up to protest.

'I . . . I . . . I don't know what you mean,' said Helen. Martin was screaming now, the milk flooding from her breasts. She would have to go to him. She had to.

'Did you enjoy the act of sexual intercourse?'

'I . . . I . . . I can't . . . it . . . it . . . please . . . I'm going to . . .'

And then she fainted, as she had known she was going to, the public gallery in uproar, women saying that it was a disgrace, a young girl like her, of course she hadn't enjoyed it, how could he even suggest such a thing.

The judge adjourned the court for an hour, after which the trial proceeded more or less smoothly, with the jury acquitting Vic of attempted murder but convicting him on the lesser charges of grievous bodily harm to both Helen and Philip. He was sentenced to five years for these convictions and twenty for supplying heroin, a charge he had been convicted of earlier, the sentences to run concurrently. In the event, he served only two years, dying of an overdose after a fellow inmate's girlfriend smuggled in what turned out to be seriously contaminated cocaine.

She had not been surprised when her father disowned her. They had never got on, her father openly favouring her younger sister, Janet, even sending her to a private fee-paying school instead of the grammar school she had attended. She had disgraced the family name, he wrote in the terse style he employed for his reports – he was a government schools' inspector. They could no longer hold up their heads in town. And as for her sister, well, they had had to take her out of school because of the jibes from the other girls. She was being tutored at home now at great additional expense. The word 'expense' had been underlined three times.

She had been hurt, though, that her mother had not made a stand, had not tried to contact her secretly behind her father's back. Afterwards, years later, an old school friend who had moved to Durham and heard nothing of what had happened, revealed that her letters to Helen in Cheltenham had been returned with the words 'Not known at this address' scrawled across the envelope in her mother's handwriting. She had cried then, cried for hours, wondering how a mother could be so hard.

She had gone to her mother's funeral, though, three years after the trial, a note from Janet having informed her of the date and time and place. She had arrived late, wearing dark glasses and a headscarf, and stood at the back.

'What did she die of? I didn't hear,' she whispered to her neighbour, a woman she did not recognise.

'A heart attack according to the doctors, grief according to the family,' said the woman. 'You heard about the elder daughter?'

'Yes,' said Helen. Yes, she had heard about that.

'Not a word from her since. Not a single card or letter. Not even when she was taken into hospital although the family let her know, said she wasn't expected to live.'

Bastard, thought Helen, as her father passed, supported by Janet. Lying bastard! But she said nothing, following the cortège at a distance, not going into the graveyard, not wishing a confrontation. Afterwards, when the other mourners had left, she laid snowdrops at the grave, small and humble among the bouquets already there, red and yellow hothouse blooms, crackly with florists' ribbon.

Her father had lived much longer, dying only ten years ago, another note from Janet informing her of the fact. There had been no mention of the funeral though and she had not asked, guessing that her father had told Janet not to tell her. Now, for all she knew, Janet was dead too. There had been no word since.

38

'Looks like snow,' said Tim cheerfully, spreading his hands wide over the glowing coals of the brazier.

Una looked up, dropping her clipboard, fumbling to pick it up again with gloved fingers, clumsy with cold. A woman in a hand-knitted hat and scarf, the wool cheap and nylon, the bright blue colour too harsh for her skin, stopped and talked for at least five minutes, both signing the petition and taking a leaflet. But she was the kind of woman who would talk to anyone, reflected Una, the kind of person who would freely relate her life history to a fellow passenger on a bus, who would walk into a bank and tell the cashier what her daughter had given her for Christmas – pink slipper socks, those socks with rubber bits on the bottom to stop you from slipping, never had any before but I must say they're cosy, I even wear them in bed.

A few grimy flakes of snow fell then stopped. Una caught one in the palm of her hand, watching it melt against the green leather. The gloves had been a Christmas present from Geoff, designed to co-ordinate with the green hat. They had caught snowflakes, she remembered, she and Rob, leaning out of the window in the house she had shared in her final year at university, stretching out their hands, glorying in the slow, silent fall of white. They had examined them under a magnifying glass, trying to see if it was true that every flake was different. Afterwards, they had turned the magnifying glass on themselves, on their eyes and ears and skin, giggling at their enlarged tummy buttons, the furry follicles of hair.

'I love every scrap of you,' Rob had murmured. 'Every freckle, every wrinkle, every mole.'

'I don't have any moles,' she had protested.

'Well, I would if you did,' he had replied, 'even if you were covered with them, spotted like a ladybird.'

Later, they had gone sledging, queuing up in the toy shop to buy a sledge, screaming with excitement as they sped down the hill in the park, leaning back, their legs out straight in front of them, wanting to go faster and faster and faster, for it never to stop, that clean, frightening, wonderful rush of air. It had been dark when they had left, their clothes wet and heavy, a cut on Una's cheek where they had leant too heavily to one side and been flung off, Una landing face down on a stone. She reached up now to feel the place where the cut had been. There was still a faint silvery thread of scar, invisible probably to the naked eye but not under a magnifying glass, she thought, remembering his words: 'I love every scrap of you'.

Half an hour passed. She collected three more signatures – her least productive period so far. Two non-union lecturers left the college and one went in, accepting the leaflet thrust at him. Tim fetched coffee in polystyrene cups from the bakery on the corner, forgetting, like Geoff, that she preferred tea. She drank it anyway, reflecting that at least it was hot. Liz called by on her way to pick up her daughter from school. She had seen Jane, she said. She was looking for somewhere to park. She wouldn't be long.

'Park? I didn't know she'd gone in the car. No wonder she's taken so long,' said Tim resentfully.

'Well, it is Thursday. Supermarkets are always busy on Thursdays,' said Una.

'It's not Thursday, is it? I thought it was Wednesday. It's Wednesday today.'

'It's not. It's Thursday. Look!'

And she pointed at a copy of that day's evening paper someone had left folded in the cardboard box next to the brazier.

Tim said in that case he had a dentist appointment, he was sorry but he'd have to go, he was having a new crown fitted.

Una took up his station behind the brazier. She had to keep the fire going, she reasoned. Besides, it was dangerous to leave it unattended. Someone might bump into it and knock it over.

An elderly woman signed the petition then a young woman

pushing a pram. Women were the most sympathetic, she had discovered, although there was a certain type, usually in their fifties or sixties, who felt strikes were unacceptable under any circumstances.

She was surprised therefore when a young man in a leather jacket stopped.

'Are you from the college? Is this the picket line?'

She said yes it was, picking up her clipboard, an explanation pat on her lips.

'Is Geoff Smart around?'

Una explained that Geoff was at a meeting in Swindon but would be back by four. The man looked put out.

'We're from MTV,' he said, pointing down the road to where two other men, presumably his camera crew, were unloading something from the back of a van.

'Only we were hoping to get some footage for tonight,' he said doubtfully. 'What about his deputy? Liz Spencer, isn't it? Is she about?'

Una said no, Liz was fetching her daughter from school and then going straight home.

'She's a single parent, you see,' she explained, looking anxiously up and down the street to see if Jane was coming.

The man looked at her more closely.

'Did you say you worked at the college?'

'No. I'm Geoff's girlfriend.'

'I thought you didn't look old enough to be a lecturer. Are you one of his students then?'

'No, I've just left my job. I'm helping out while I look for another.'

The man turned to speak to his colleagues who were struggling towards them, their feet slipping on the damp pavement. He looked at his watch.

'Do you mind if we take some footage now that we're here? Only we need the union side. We've already talked to the principal. We would have let you know we were coming but the news editor only decided at the last minute that he wanted to run the story. I'm Dann Hopkins, by the way. Dann with two "n"s.'

Una stuttered that she didn't know, she didn't have anything to do with the college really, she was just Geoff's girlfriend, it would be better if they waited until Jane got back, she was one of the lecturers, she wouldn't be long, they could do an interview with her.

'If we could just take a few shots of you handing out leaflets. Could you come out from behind the fire? Yes, that's fine. Is that a petition you've got there?' he asked, not appearing to have heard what she had just said.

Una allowed herself to be led into the view of the camera, flattered despite herself, aware that a small crowd had gathered, eager to see themselves on TV. There were usually more on picket duty, she gabbled – at least four – only Tim had an appointment at the dentist's, Fran was off sick with a chest infection, and Jane had had to nip to the shops to buy food for some guests that were arriving that night.

'Is there a banner or placard anywhere? Yes, that will do. Now, if you could just hold that and then hand out some of your leaflets. That's grand. Grand.'

Una did as instructed.

'Now, Una, if you could just tell me what the strike is about?'

Una glanced nervously at the cameramen.

'Are they still filming?' she whispered. 'Only I said, I'm not really the right person to ask. I'm just Geoff's girlfriend.'

That didn't matter, said Dann in a normal voice. They would be talking to Geoff as well. Now if she could just explain, in her own words, what the strike was about.

Reassured, Una gave a somewhat halting explanation.

'What is so wrong about the changes in working practices put forward by the principal?'

She began to explain then stuttered to an abrupt halt, realising how little she knew about what exactly had been proposed.

'I'm sorry. I really don't know enough about it . . .'

'And yet you're willing to stand out here in the freezing cold in their support?'

'I'm just helping Geoff. I don't know all the ins and outs of why they're on strike. He hasn't . . . we . . . he's been very busy. We haven't talked about it that much. The reasons behind the strike, I mean . . .'

Dann signalled to the crew that the interview was over. That was fine, he said, absolutely fine, they'd have to rush or they wouldn't get back in time to process the film, could she ask Geoff to ring the studio as soon as he got back.

Jane arrived shortly afterwards.

'Everything all right? Where's Tim?'

Una explained about the dentist appointment.

'MTV have just been. I told them I wasn't a lecturer or anything but they filmed me anyway. They're going to do a phone interview with Geoff when he gets back from Swindon.'

Jane clapped her hands with delight. It was just what they needed, she said. There had been plenty of coverage in the local papers but nothing on TV so far.

'When are they going to show it?'

'Tonight, I think. They said they'd already done an interview with the principal.'

Norman arrived ten minutes later but showed little interest in the news about MTV. He still had not worked out the answer to five across in the *Guardian* crossword – one chap upset without love from a woman, first letter 'n'.

'Naomi!' he said suddenly. 'Of course. That's it.'

And he took the crossword out of his anorak pocket and filled in the answer.

They packed up early, the snow coming down in earnest, the flakes small and hard, gritty against their skin. Una left a message for Geoff at the Quaker Meeting House where they had turned one room into their strike headquarters then cycled home. There was a letter from her mother on the door mat, describing Istanbul and saying they hoped to be back by the twenty-seventh. Una read it in front of the fire, savouring the descriptions of their walks in the bazaars, the Street of the Mat Makers aromatic with the scent of nuts and spices and fruit, the breathtaking beauty of the Sancta Sophia.

She had spent a wretched Christmas herself, waking up alone on Christmas Day with no stocking to open, the flat cold and cheerless, the previous day's washing-up eyeing her reproachfully across the room. Lunch, at Teresa and Martin's house, had been a strained affair. Even Matty had seemed off-colour, whining throughout the meal, throwing a tantrum when she ran out of presents to open and finally pounding Martin with

her tiny fists with what Teresa said was rage at his apparent
desertion. And Geoff, who was staying with friends in Exmoor,
an arrangement that he would have broken, he said, if it had
been possible, had not phoned as he had promised, ringing on
Boxing Day afternoon instead, clearly hungover.

Una unhooked her new Matisse calendar from the noticeboard
near the door. The twenty-seventh was in just over two weeks'
time, she saw, a Monday. She would have to go round and
see the Coopers, she realised, make arrangements about the
key. She glanced at the clock and saw that it was almost five
forty-five, the time for MTV's main news programme. Forty-
eight lecturers were on strike in a dispute about proposed new
working practices, said the newscaster, moving on seamlessly
from a report about an arson attack. A brief interview with the
principal followed but Una did not hear what he said, suddenly
anxious, wondering if Geoff had seen the note, thinking she
should have said no, had refused to let them film her. Then
she heard Geoff's voice, distorted by a bad line but audible,
persuasive, ringing out in defence of everyone's right to a good
education. It was OK. He had seen the note. It was all OK. But
no, there she was, looking cold and forlorn, the green hat too
low over her forehead, the newscaster saying that unfortunately
Geoff Smart had not managed to explain what the strike was
about to his girlfriend, Una Dart, the only person on the picket
line that afternoon. The camera moved in close and she heard
her voice, horribly young and gauche, saying she had just left her
job, that she was helping out while she looked round for another,
she didn't know much about the strike really, they had not talked
about it, Geoff had been so busy. There were normally more on
picket duty, the newscaster continued crisply – a snigger barely
contained – but apparently the others had been called away that
afternoon, one to the dentist's, another to the shops. Then the
picture switched abruptly to one of Clifton Suspension Bridge,
the newscaster describing how new higher railings were to be
erected to prevent suicide attempts.

Una turned the television off and almost immediately the
phone rang. It was Geoff.

'Have you just seen what I have?' he asked, his voice acid.

'Yes, I'm sorry . . .'

'Sorry!' he exploded. 'You made us look idiots. Why did you say all that about not knowing what the strike was about, about us not talking about it? You know just as well as anyone else why we're on strike.'

'But I don't . . . I mean, I thought I did but then when he started asking me questions I realised that I didn't, not really, not enough to be able to argue your case.'

'Why didn't you tell the reporter to speak to someone else then?'

'But I did. I did. I told him Jane would be back soon . . .'

'And all that stuff about Jane being at the shops and Tim at the dentist? Did you really have to tell him that? Couldn't you see it would sound bad?'

'I was just chatting,' she said lamely, taken aback by the violence of his attack. 'I was just explaining why I was there on my own. I didn't know he was going to use it.'

'And why did you have to say you'd left your job? What had that got to do with anything?'

'I didn't say it off my own bat. He asked me. He asked me if I was one of your students. Besides, what's wrong with saying I've just left my job?'

'What's wrong is that it makes you look like an airhead. A silly, feckless, irresponsible airhead and, by association, us too.'

She had done her best, she said, angry now. It wasn't her fault no one else had been there. If he wanted to get at someone, he should get at them. At Jane and Tim and all the others who were always skiving off.

'Don't worry, I will!' he shouted. 'As from tomorrow, I'm doubling the rota. There are going to be eight people on that picket line and I mean eight people. I'm not taking any more excuses. People will just have to rearrange their dentist appointments.'

There was no need to shout, she said, to which he replied that he was not shouting and that he would see her tomorrow, goodbye.

And he rang off abruptly, leaving her holding the receiver, crying, smarting at the word 'airhead'. Was he right? Was that how she had come across? Or was that how he saw her? As a bit of fluff, a pretty young thing, a bimbo with more bust than brain?

39 ∫

Una picked her way through the rubbish bins left out the previous night and still waiting to be emptied. Beside the bins, in piles of varying height and tidiness, was the Christmas detritus too large or awkward to fit inside. Empty wine crates, cardboard boxes that had housed children's presents – self-assembly plastic wheelbarrows, toy vacuum cleaners, miniature kitchens complete with pop-up toaster – and, most melancholy of all, Christmas trees in their last throes of death, brown, up-ended, some even hacked in two.

There was still some snow on the pavement – grey and smudged, like mascara left over from the day before. She walked slowly, out of character, thinking that a new year had begun and she had made no plans, no hopes. Her life was passing her by like a ship on the horizon. They had become separated. She did not know how or why or when, she just knew that it had happened, that she must clamber back on board, quickly, before it slipped out of sight, disappeared into the silver, limitless distance that was the future. 'The ways we miss our lives are life.' That was what someone had said. And that was what was happening, she thought, as she climbed the steps, rang the bell.

Sinead looked surprised when she opened the door.

'I wasn't expecting you. Why aren't you at work?'

Una explained that she had left the refuge, was looking for another job, helping out Geoff with the strike while she looked.

There were pictures of wolves on the table – magazine pictures, postcards, books from the library and even a giant poster, one corner torn, showing a wolf howling, its head thrown back, the taut grey of the throat exposed.

'What's all this for?' said Una, picking up the poster, holding it at arm's length to see it better.

'My next commission,' said Sinead, glancing privately at her watch, wondering how long Una would stay, she had wanted to come up with a sketch that morning.

'A wolf? I didn't know you did animals.'

'I do anything as long as I'm paid for it.'

Una laughed.

'You know what I mean. Although, you're right. I prefer people.'

She filled the kettle at the sink.

'Tea? Not too strong?'

'Yes,' said Una, glad someone had remembered. 'I found a white hair this morning,' she added, leafing through the wolf pictures. Don't cry wolf – that's what Martin had said to her one afternoon in the summer holidays when, aged about five or six, she had fallen over in the park and made a disproportionate fuss. She had not known what he meant, she remembered. When they got home, she had hurried upstairs and climbed on the stool to look in the bathroom mirror, peering for incipient signs of fur or fangs or glittering, predatory eyes.

'So?' said Sinead. 'I find one nearly every morning.'

'Yes, but your hair is black. That's supposed to go white early. Mine is auburn.'

'I wouldn't worry,' said Sinead with mock compassion. 'You probably won't find another for ten years. By that time, they'll have invented something to stop hair going white.'

'Oh, I'm not going to dye it. I'm going to age gracefully.'

'That's what everyone says until they start to age,' observed Sinead tartly.

She handed Una her tea and clunked mugs.

'Happy New Year! And may it be one of fresh growth – of opportunities seized and turning points turned.'

'What's that supposed to imply?'

'It's not supposed to imply anything,' said Sinead. 'What's got into you this morning? Why are you so prickly?'

Una said nothing. How could she explain that she had woken assailed by doubt, needing the comfort of arms, the sound of the words 'I love you', the knowledge that she was desired?

'Who wants a wolf anyway?' she asked, fingering the wolf poster.

'My father.'

'Your father! But I thought he said he couldn't come after all, that one of his lorries had gone out of control and killed three people, that he would have to leave it till Easter.'

'He did. But then he changed his mind. It turned out only one person had been killed and she was on the road not the pavement as everyone had said at first and so he decided he could come after all.'

'When? How long did he stay? What did you do?'

'He was very big,' said Sinead, choosing to answer a question that had not been asked. 'Much bigger than I'd expected, with enormous hands – great long, flat fingers, like something by Michelangelo. Brown hair going white. But gracefully, ever so gracefully,' she added with a smirk.

'He arrived at Heathrow the day before Christmas Eve and we spent the night in London at a hotel. The next morning, we walked up Bond Street and he told me to choose what I liked from the shops. From all of them. Every single one. Whatever I fancied.'

'And did you?' asked Una, unable to imagine Sinead as a reckless consumer.

'No. I did choose a brooch, though. See?'

And she leant across the table, pulling her jersey away from her chest so that Una could see the brooch pinned on the left-hand side.

'It's beautiful. What is it?' asked Una, admiring what appeared to be silver embossed with gold, shaped like a capital 'Z' melting into a 'C'.

'I don't know. It wasn't expensive or at least not compared to most of the other things in the shop. It's by someone who's just graduated from art school. The first piece of her work they had sold. I was pleased when they told us that. To think that I was supporting . . . well . . . someone like me, I suppose.'

'And did you come down here?'

'Yes, we hired a car in the afternoon and drove down and I made up a bed for him on the floor, just like I did for you that time. He didn't even complain about the cold.'

'And what was he like? Was he how you thought he'd be?'

'No . . . I mean I don't know, I'm not sure what I did think.
I think I thought he'd be . . . well, you know, how Americans
are supposed to be – brash, loud, a bit pushy. But he wasn't.
He was quiet if anything. Urbane, well read, the kind of person
who picks up literary allusions, who knows what obscure words
like "agon" and "enchiridion" mean.'

'What?'

'They were in this book I was reading last night. I had to look
them up in a dictionary.'

'And it was OK? It wasn't too awkward? What did you do on
Christmas Day?'

'I cooked him Christmas lunch. Not a turkey. I thought that
would be a bit silly between just the two of us so we had a chicken
instead. But a nice one, free range, and I did all the trimmings
– bacon rolls, sprouts with chestnuts, roast potatoes, cranberry
sauce. Afterwards, we went for a walk on the Downs and in
the evening we drove over the suspension bridge and went for
a drink in a village pub with suitably quaint locals and beams. On
Boxing Day, we just mooched around in the morning and in the
afternoon we went to the pantomime. I didn't think we'd be able
to get tickets but we phoned up and got a cancellation – five rows
back in the stalls. It was the first pantomime he'd been to.'

'And what about your mother? Did he . . . did he . . . did he
go and see her?'

'Yes,' said Sinead, her voice tightening. 'He drove over the day
after Boxing Day. I think he stayed the night there but I'm not
sure. His flight back wasn't until the day after – in the afternoon
– so he could have done. He would have had time. But I don't
know. I didn't ask.'

'And did he . . . did he say anything about why he left? Did
you talk about it?'

Sinead looked Una full in the eyes, then stood up abruptly and
walked over to the window. A man in a wheelchair was waiting
to cross the road, she saw. There was a newspaper in his lap, a
red-and-green striped shopping bag in the tray beneath his seat.
She watched as a car slowed to let him cross. How could he be
so cheerful, she thought, as he smiled and waved his thanks at
the car driver.

'He . . . I think he . . .'

She turned and walked back to the table.

'I think he panicked,' she said, flicking open the cover of one of the library books. 'He was twenty-one. That's a year younger than I am now. He'd come to England for a year off while he thought about what he wanted to do – whether he wanted to go back to college. He was studying philosophy, you know. I never knew that. Anyhow, suddenly, he found himself married, expecting a child, and living the other side of the world from his friends and family. He said he didn't mean to leave, that he didn't plan it or anything. He said he just went out one morning to buy a paper – which is what my mother has always said, so at least they agree on something. There was a woman in front of him at the newsagent's buying some magazines. When she went to pay, she dropped the magazines and one of them fell open at a picture of the Grand Canyon. He said he picked the magazines up and as he did, he saw this picture and was immediately seized – paralysed, that was how he put it – by this terrible panic. That he hadn't meant to marry, hadn't meant to have a child, hadn't meant to live in England, hadn't meant to do any of the things he was doing, and that now he would die without seeing the Grand Canyon, that he would never see it, not unless he left.'

She paused, imagining that moment, that moment that was to prove so critical, the moment when her father stooped, saw the picture, was hit by a wave of nostalgia or regret or fear or all of them, all mixed up together, a huge complex breaker of emotion sweeping him up, taking him with it, changing his life and the lives of his wife and unborn child, for ever.

'Of course,' she added, toying with the book cover again. 'The ironic thing is – he still hasn't seen the Grand Canyon. Still, I suppose that was just symbolic.'

She stood up again, this time walking over to the kitchen area where she topped up their mugs.

'That's all he said. What I've told you. I didn't ask anything else. About why he didn't write or ring or come over to see me. I didn't ask him any of that because . . . well, we've got the rest of our lives to talk. I don't need to know all the answers now. Besides, I'm not even sure I want to know the answers. Not now. I did once. When I was younger, about fourteen or fifteen, I wanted to desperately, as if, somehow, knowing the answers would change everything, change it back to how it had been or could have been. But now . . . well . . . I think he went and that's that. Knowing why he did this or that won't change anything. And anyhow, even if I did want to know, I'm not sure that he could tell me. He would say something, of course, give me some sort of explanation but I'm not sure it would be the real one. I'm not sure he knows the real one himself. What I mean is that sometimes we do things and then, later, we look back and wonder why we did them and we don't know. We just did them. Sometimes I think that's a good enough answer – to say we did something because we did it.'

She walked back to the window where she stood sideways, the line of her chin like a leafless tree in winter, black branch against a blue sky, each twig distinct. She was beautiful, thought Una, wondering about her ancestors – Irish landowners, Polish intellectuals, Catholic and establishment, Jewish and émigré. And here she was now, their descendant, living in a Bristol attic, planning wolf sculptures. How strange it all was – how things turned out, where people ended up.

As she looked at her, wishing she would not bundle her hair up like that, pulled back, scrunched in, grips jabbed in any old how, she felt her own hair.

'Do you think I should have my hair cut?' she asked.

Sinead turned, frowning.

'No. Why?'

'I thought maybe it makes me look a bit young – like a schoolgirl.'

'Why are you so worried about your hair all of a sudden? Has someone said something? It's Geoff, isn't it?'

'No,' said Una, flushing. 'No, he hasn't said anything. No, I just thought that maybe I should do something with it instead of letting it hang there like . . . like . . . well, like . . .'

'Like something out of a fairy tale,' interrupted Sinead. 'You must be joking! Have it cut? Most women would kill for hair like yours. In the bit of the *Odyssey* we studied for Greek GCSE there was this character called Nausicaa. I can't remember much about her except that she had this fantastic hair. She was called the "golden-tressed one". And, you know, whenever I read that, I always used to think of you.'

She walked back to the table and stood behind Una, taking hold of her hair with one hand and pulling it through the other, like a needle through thread.

'Rob always loved your hair,' she said, leaning forward. 'He said something about it once. When we'd all gone out together. That day in the Cotswolds. I think it was then. How he thought of it as something alive.'

Una tugged free and stood up.

'Which reminds me,' said Sinead, speaking hurriedly now to pre-empt Una. 'I almost forgot. I thought you might be interested. Look!'

She walked over to the desk she had rescued from a skip four doors down the previous summer. It had had one leg missing which she had replaced herself, matching the wood, asking advice first from a cabinet maker, a friend she worked for occasionally.

'I don't normally buy it but I just happened to and I saw his name. See?'

She handed Una a piece of newspaper. It was an article about the strike, Una saw, and at the top, under the headline, it said 'by Rob Perry'. Rob had written it. Rob. He was back.

'There's a quote in there from Geoff so presumably Rob must have spoken to him,' said Sinead, walking over to the sink and washing up their mugs with unnecessary clatter.

Una sat down and read the article. When she had finished she read it again. It was a short piece, long by the standards of a tabloid newspaper, but short by the standards of anyone interested in what it was about. Even so, it told Una more about the strike in five minutes than she had been told in eight weeks by anyone else. It told both sides of the story, elegantly and succinctly. But, more than that, it put the story in context, in the context of the changes happening nationally in higher and further education, and the political and social reasons for these changes. And Rob had written it. Rob. He was a journalist. He was working, doing what he wanted to do, what he had left her to do.

Had he spoken to Geoff on the phone, she wondered? Or had

they met? And if they had met, what had he thought of Geoff? Had he liked him?

'Do you mind if I keep it?' she asked as Sinead came back towards her, drying her hands on a tea towel. 'Only we try to keep all the cuttings. I haven't seen this one which means we might have missed it.'

'Of course not,' said Sinead, looking away tactfully as Una folded the article small and tucked it in her back jeans pocket.

Una stood up, fetched her coat from the hook with a kink in it and put it on, leaning forward to do up the zip.

Sinead twisted the teatowel tightly then watched it spin free.

'I might . . . I might be going to the States.'

Una straightened up, the zip still undone.

'What? To see your father?'

'He's got a flat in New York. There's no one there at the moment. He says I can live in it rent free for a year.'

'But what about your work?'

'What about it? I can work there just as easily as here.'

'But what about the bursary from the Henry Moore Foundation? The show at Leeds City Art Gallery?'

'There were seven-hundred-and-eighty-three entrants to the competition this year,' said Sinead, speaking slowly and patiently as if dictating to a copy typist. 'Some of them were just as good, if not better than me. Besides, even if I did win, I still wouldn't be able to live off the bursary. It would cover my rent and buy me the odd pizza. That's all.'

'But what would you do in New York? You wouldn't be able to claim benefit out there, would you?'

'I don't know what I'd do. Something. Anything. It's not like here,' said Sinead, frowning, moving towards the door, anxious to be alone again with the wolf pictures. 'It's only an idea. I won't be going next week or even next month. I don't find out the results of the competition until March.'

Walking downstairs, Una thought about what Sinead had said, imagining her waitressing in some crummy downtown diner, a white paper cap on her head, too tired at night to sculpt. But no, she thought. Sinead would not fall into that trap. She was too tough. Too determined. A survivor.

Outside, she felt for the bulge of paper in her back jeans

pocket. It was OK. It was still there. Reassured, she started to walk, striding out, the shape of the day ahead hardening in her mind. It occurred to her that Rob might have seen her on TV the night before. If he had, what had he thought? Had he thought her silly? A feckless, irresponsible airhead? No, no, remember, he loved every scrap of her, every scrap. Especially her hair, she added. What was it Sinead had said? That he thought of it as something alive. Yes, that was it. Something alive.

Thinking this, repeating his words, she tugged at the band holding her hair in a ponytail. Then she began to run, jumping over the rubbish which lay in her way so that the refuse collectors, turning the corner, met this sight – a girl running, her coat flapping open, her long hair streaming behind her, playing leapfrog with the bin bags. A gold streak.

40

It was Saturday night and Rob had nothing to do. No party, no darts match, no cheerful chat in a pub followed by takeaway curry and coffee in someone's flat. A fellow reporter had suggested meeting up for a drink but then his girlfriend, a dental nurse in Chester, had announced she was coming to stay for the weekend and the idea had been dropped.

He surveyed the contents of the room where he was sitting on a cushion, his back against a radiator, socks drying on either side of his head. The black-and-white TV, a present from his mother, in one corner. The bed, disguised as a sofa with the use of three cushions and an ethnic throw from a charity shop. The plant he had bought the week before in a burst of homemaking enthusiasm. Likewise a cork noticeboard and a print by Picasso of a couple staring moodily into the distance, the background turquoise blue, the woman's top bright orange, two empty glasses in the foreground. And on the table, in the middle, in place of a vase or a candlestick or a fruit bowl, none of which he owned, a book with a marbled cover, designed as a photo album but now holding his newspaper cuttings – his first story, his first front page lead, his first theatre review.

On his first day, Ewen, the grubby, short-necked news editor with an estranged partner and three-year-old son in Newcastle, had said: 'Normally, you'd be doing weddings and jumble sales for a month followed by the housing sub-committee if you were lucky. As it is, I'm so short-staffed, I'm throwing you in at the deep end. You'll either sink or swim.'

And, with that, he had handed Rob a piece of paper on which

was written the name and phone number of a car mechanic convicted of driving while disqualified after riding a bike powered by a garden strimmer engine.

'Three hundred words by ten-thirty. We've got a picture,' he said and walked off, leaving Rob biting his nails, reaching for the phone, wondering how to write 'strimmer' in shorthand.

Since then, he had swum, and with no arm bands either, at least not according to his colleagues. In just five weeks he had had two front page leads, one page three lead and four page five leads plus innumerable 'shorts' and picture stories.

He had felt huge elation when he had seen his first by-line, and even more so the day he had written his first front page lead – Friday, the third of January, the date etched on his mind. He had phoned up his mother, bought a 'heat and eat' chicken korma supper and treated himself to a half bottle of Baron de la Tour, *Appellation Fitou contrôlée*. But then, on Thursday, only six days later, when he switched off the ten o'clock news in the evening, he could not remember what he had written that day. And the day after, on the Friday, writing a story about a disagreement between the city council and a housing association about a joint housing project, he realised that he was telling the story, not how it was – a mild difference of opinion about how the project should be run – but how the news editor wanted it – a bitter row that was threatening to scupper the entire project. The story duly made the page five lead and later Ewen, on his way to smoke a cigarette outside in the relative calm of three o'clock, lobbed a 'well done' in his direction, a remark which caused astonishment among those sitting near by.

'My God, did you hear that? Ewen's paid someone a compliment. Quick, has anyone got a tape recorder? Quick!' they joked as Ewen barged past the payphone and the drinks machine, both out of order. Rob meanwhile, the conversation he had had that morning with the housing association chairman still running through his mind, remembering his offer to drop in any time, any time at all, he'd be pleased to show him round, felt dirty, grey scum on his tongue.

Seeing the album, thinking of this incident, he rose, walked over to the table and opened the book. 'Hotel arson.' 'Youngsters' panto joy.' 'Council jobs fear as £12m cutback looms.' 'Murder riddle hopes.' 'Four held in police drug raids.' 'Strike looms on binmen's pay.' The headlines mocked him like a chant in a school playground, a row of jeering faces daring him to jump the vast expanse of muddy water that lay before him or face the ignominy of walking round it.

It seemed to him suddenly that he had made a terrible mistake, that he had confused 'doing' with 'being'. To be, fully to be – to love and be loved, laugh, cry, hope, sorrow – that was to live. To see new life rush out, slippy with blood, between the legs of the woman you loved. To stand in a churchyard on a soft, still afternoon while they buried your father and someone behind you said: 'Who's that? Over there? That woman in the big hat? Is that one of Joan's daughters?' That was to live. 'Doing', meanwhile, 'doing' was merely 'doing'. Pebbles in a desert, a path that led nowhere, a roomful of gold to a man dying of thirst.

On an impulse, he snapped the album shut, went out to his car and drove round to Una's house even though he knew she would not be there, could not be there because it was still only January the eleventh, four days before the American family was due to leave.

Kit Cooper, freshly emerged from the bath, her hair damp, her skin smelling of the aromatherapy oil she had added to the water to dissolve the tension of the day – vainly, it turned out – saw Rob ten minutes later as she parted the curtains on the landing to see whether it was snowing again.

'Dan, look, there's that boy, the one I told you about, quick . . . !'

Her husband, irritable because he had had to forgo watching an important rugby match on TV that afternoon to take the kids to the park, came out from their bedroom, half undressed.

'Look, see, I told you there was something odd about him, didn't I?'

They both watched as Rob walked up and down the road outside, occasionally glancing up at the window of the room where their youngest child slept, his limbs flung wide like a stopped windmill, his favourite soft toy, a spotted black-and-white dog, squashed under his head.

'I thought you said he was a friend of Una's.'

'That's what he said. It doesn't mean he is. After all, he didn't want me to give her a message or anything. And he didn't take the brother's phone number or address.'

Dan, chilly in just his shirt and underpants, shifted impatiently from one foot to another.

'He probably just wanted to see if she was back. Maybe he's an old boyfriend or something,' he said, keen to be in bed, glancing at his wrist where his watch would have been if he had not removed it ten minutes earlier.

'I don't know, I don't feel happy,' said Kit, drawing her bathrobe more tightly across her chest. 'You think we should call the police?'

'What and tell them there's a man walking outside in the street. Don't be silly. He's not *doing* anything. He'll probably go home in a minute. Look, see, I told you.'

They watched as Rob climbed back into his car, switched on the engine and drove off, pulling in on the main road to let an ambulance pass, checking to see that his seatbelt was fastened. There had been a light on in her old bedroom, a dim one, probably a night light to ward off ghouls and ghosties.

> 'Three little ghosties
> Sat on three posties
> Eating buttered toasties
> Greasing their fisties
> Up to their wristies
> Weren't they BEASTIES!'

He had sung that when he was small, sitting on his own post at the bottom of the garden, eating his own buttered toast. He smiled at the recollection, remembering his mother's admonitions not to wipe his greasy hands on his shorts because she was not washing any more clothes, not today.

The phone was ringing when he got back, the sound clearly audible in the quiet, middle-class street where he was renting a first-floor flat.

It was his mother, phoning to warn him that temperatures were forecast to drop to minus five that night, he had checked that his taps weren't dripping, hadn't he, only he didn't want his pipes to freeze.

He assured her that he had – a lie. He had not even noticed it was particularly cold.

'What's the matter? You sound breathless.'

He explained that he had been out, that he had run up the stairs to pick up the phone.

There was a pause while she waited, hoping he would say where he had been. When he said nothing, she went on: 'I saw Una on TV the other night. The day before yesterday. Something to do with a strike at a college. I couldn't quite work out what she had to do with it. I only caught the end of it.'

'Oh?' he said, controlling his voice, careful not to give anything away.

She paused again, then said he was welcome to come over for Sunday lunch if he wanted. Rob stood in the hallway looking at the phone, feeling guilty, thinking that his mother was probably lonely, that he should take her out for a meal perhaps. He found a tap dripping in the bathroom, turned it off and opened a can of beer, conscious of how absurd this was, that he, a young man of twenty-two, should be sitting at home on a Saturday night, the time still only half past ten.

There was plenty to do, of course, out there in the city that lay beyond his two Yale-locked glass doors. Films, plays, bars, discos, bowling alleys, concerts, debates, stand-up comedy in smoke-filled basements – everything that a modern, cosmopolitan city had to offer in the late twentieth century. But it was no fun without someone else, without someone to talk to and share it with. And not just someone, he added silently, pouring the beer into a glass. It was no fun without Una.

He walked through into the living room and saw the album lying there, on the table where he had left it, like an insult. He picked it up and banged it down again, two stories floating free, landing wrong side up on the floor, adverts for loft conversions and a golf roadshow. This, this, for the sound of her laugh, her joyful rush, that mouth. To exchange this for that! He pushed the album under the bed where it could not be seen.

It was the little things he missed most. Sitting down after a day apart exchanging moments – the row he had witnessed between two ramblers in his mother's tea garden, hurling abuse between mouthfuls of scone, the hour she had spent with Matty in the park, 'Push me higher, higher, make my feet touch the clouds'. Reading out bits from the Sunday papers to one another. Cooking a meal and arguing good-humouredly about the best way to cut an onion. Waking up together – drinking tea in bed.

God – how he missed her!

41

Philip looked in the *Yellow Pages* on their third day back. Fencing services, fibre glass, fire alarms, floor cleaning, florists, flying. There it was. Flying. He scanned the adverts. 'Learn to Fly at Bristol, gift vouchers available, friendly one-to-one tuition, pleasure flights and trial lessons, resident examiner . . .' There was certainly no shortage of flying schools.

He picked up the phone, his palms sweating, then put it down again hurriedly, hearing a noise at the door, thinking it was Helen, back already from the supermarket. No, it was just the post. An Oxford University Press 'Special Sale Catalogue' addressed to Martin and what appeared to be a bank statement for Helen. He put both on the table in the kitchen and went back to the phone.

Just do it, they can only say no, he told himself as he hesitated, heart pounding. Only? Yes, only. But only can be all, the one and only, unique, incomparable. Just do it. Go on. Do it.

He gripped the receiver and punched in the number, watching the digits appear on the screen in front of him.

The first one sounded doubtful. 'I don't think so, I'd have to ask, of course, but I'm pretty sure the answer would be no . . . you say you've got no sight at all in the one eye . . . yes, I see . . . if I could just take your name and number?'

The second gave him more hope. 'Possibly. It's not something we've ever come across before – at least, not to my knowledge. When did you say you last flew? And you were in the RAF for how long? I'll have to check it out. Let me get back to you . . . You'd rather ring me? Fine. OK. Ring me tomorrow then. At about three. The name's Neil. Neil Hooper.'

Helen came in just as he was putting the phone down, her arms stretched taut by the weight of two carrier bags.

'Was that for me, darling?' she asked, not stopping, walking straight through to the kitchen.

He wiped his palms on his trousers. They had not said no. They had not laughed at him, had not sniggered out loud at the idea.

'No, it was the bank. I was just checking a few figures. Finding out the balance in our account.'

She came back into the hallway.

'Only I phoned work earlier to speak to Paul. To discuss when I would go back. I thought it might be him. He was out when I called.'

He fiddled with the notepad next to the phone, not looking at her, conscious his face might give something away.

'Are there any more bags to bring in?'

'Yes. Lots. I've had to stock up on everything.'

'Right . . . well . . . I'll go and get them.'

Helen then went back into the kitchen to unpack the shopping. It had been kind of Una to buy enough food to last them a few days. She had even put a bottle of white wine to chill in the fridge. Then there had been the bowl of hyacinths in the sitting room, fragrant with blue promise, the vase of white freesias in their bedroom, clean sheets on the bed, fresh towels laid out in the bathroom. She had been extremely thoughtful, uncharacteristically so. Or maybe not, she thought, as she lined up tins of tomato in her dried goods cupboard. Maybe she had changed. Certainly a lot seemed to have happened while they were away. Martin and Teresa, for a start. That had been a shock. Although not totally unexpected. She had sensed a tension in their relationship before they left. She knew Martin was not entirely happy in his work, that he wanted a job that would give him more research time. But there was something else as well, something they had not discussed. Eight months ago, he had asked why only her name appeared on his birth certificate. She had said Philip had been away on business when she had registered the birth, that they had never got round to adding his name at a later stage. At the time, he had appeared to accept the explanation, but now she wondered if he had, remembering the look he had given her when he had told her of his separation from Teresa, as if to say 'You know. You know why.'

She sighed, folded the empty carrier bags, and filled the kettle at the sink. Then there was Una. She had been dismayed to learn she had given up her job, that Geoff, a man fourteen years her senior, was paying her to help him run a strike. It was an arrangement she thought highly undesirable, dangerous even, but of course she could not say this, could say nothing, not to either of them, to Una or Martin. She had to watch while they burnt their fingers, to wait, patient, bandages at the ready, praying they would see the flames before it was too late.

Philip came in and dumped two bags on the floor.

'Tea or coffee?' she asked.

'Tea,' he said. 'The weather doesn't seem right for coffee.'

'Yes,' she agreed, looking out of the window at the low belly of cloud hanging over the garden. 'I'd forgotten how depressing January can be. So grey.'

They put the rest of the shopping away, bumping into one another, reaching for the same things, awkward in this old-new domestic territory.

'What would you like for dinner tonight?' she asked, pouring out the tea. 'I thought maybe stew. It's the kind of day for one.'

He said yes, that would be lovely, maybe he would light a fire, later, in the afternoon, it was the kind of day for that too. They talked of other things then – the need to order more logs, Una's decision not to move back in with them, whether they should invite Teresa and Martin both for lunch on Sunday or separately, one for lunch and one for tea.

'I'm going to see Jane later this morning – you know, my friend from the talking newspaper,' said Helen, standing up, taking their mugs to the sink. 'She phoned yesterday, said they'd had a real struggle getting the newspaper out while I've been away. I must say it was quite flattering. It's nice to know one is missed.'

She held up a glass to the light, checking for smears. The Coopers had broken remarkably little, she thought, especially considering they had three young children. Just a few plates and a serving dish, one she had never liked anyway, a wedding present from Philip's father. She was glad she would no longer feel obliged to use it. She put the glass to drain and plunged her cloth into another. After seeing Jane, she would go round to the office, she decided. It would be nice to catch up on all the gossip, to show off her tan before it faded. She would ask Paul if she could have another two weeks off. That would give her time to sort things out – to have her hair cut, get her clothes in order, put the house back together. Then there were those Italian classes she had been meaning to join. The woman at the university had said it was probably too late to join the course running now, that it was already halfway through. But there was another course starting in March, she said, one aimed at beginners, there were still two places left if she was interested. She pulled out the plug and turned on the cold tap, watching the dirty water drain. It had been good to go away. Since she had come back, she had felt excited. The world was new again, fresh-hatched, each day a surprise. She might learn Italian but then again, she might not. She might take up fencing, retrain as a teacher. Who knew what she would do? She felt capable of anything.

Philip watched her as she worked then slipped away upstairs to think, an impulse he had not lost, still, after all these years – the need to be up, high, away from the ground.

In the bedroom, he opened the window, letting in the cold, damp January air. Up there, up above all that grey, the sun was shining. He had not forgotten how that felt, breaking through from cloud to sunlight, the way it reminded him of Virginia Woolf's words: 'I meant to write about death, only life came breaking in as usual.'

What if they said no? What then?

42 ∫

He could be dead, of course. He could have had a heart attack, been killed in a multiple pile-up on the M4, stepped out from the kerb at the wrong moment, a lorry coming too fast, the driver hurrying home for his son's birthday. He could have contracted AIDS, been mugged and shot by robbers, lost his foothold while trekking in Nepal, falling eight hundred feet, no identity papers in his bag, giving the local police more work in one month than they had had in a year. He could simply have moved away. Bought a crofter's cottage in the Orkneys, a villa near the Costa del Sol, a chic apartment in Chelsea with a trompe l'oeil painting in the living room.

He could have done any of these. But this did not stop Helen from looking. His smell. That was one of the things she remembered most distinctly. The way his jacket had smelt of a garden in autumn – leaves, wood smoke, dug earth. And so, now, when the husband of the couple she was showing over a ground-floor two-bedroom flat in Clifton approached her with a query about the central heating boiler, she sniffed – discreetly, disguising it with a pretend cough. No, too much aftershave. He was not the kind of man who would have used aftershave. Besides, now that he was closer, she could see that his eyes were hazel, not green, his skin too sallow, not white as she remembered it, peeled apple white, the same as Martin's and Matty's. But his skin could have changed, she supposed. So much would have changed. His hair, or what remained of it, would be white or grey, his eyes bloodshot, his arms slacker, softer. This man's build was right, though, she thought, appraising his shoulders. Stocky, broad, not much taller than her, slightly top-heavy.

She answered the query about the boiler and assured the wife that yes, all the carpets and curtains were included in the price. The kitchen was new, she said, only six months old, hand-painted. They moved into the open-plan sitting room, chill with antique furniture and Afghan rugs and she pointed out the fireplace, Georgian, original, in regular use. That was honeysuckle that they could see on the patio, she said. It would be lovely in the summer when it was in bloom, sitting outside with a drink at dusk, that was when it would smell most intense. The couple nodded, moving closer to the French windows, picturing themselves relaxing after a hard day on the golf course, a bought pizza heating in the oven, fresh figs for dessert.

She was good at that – at helping people to imagine themselves as the owners of the property they were looking round, their pictures on the walls, their crockery on the dresser, a sepia photo of great-aunt Agnes in the alcove in the sitting room.

But that did not mean she could picture him, she told herself, as the couple thanked her, said goodbye, promised they would be in touch first thing in the morning although she knew they wouldn't. She could have made up the black hair and green eyes, wanted to believe that Martin looked like him, that they had the same eyebrows, the same temperament – bookish, gentle but moody too, given to introspection.

She phoned the office on her mobile to report the end of the appointment then took one last look round the flat. There was one thing she could do, she supposed. She could put an ad in a newspaper or magazine. Some even ran special columns. She had read one at the hairdresser's the other day. 'Where are they now?' it had been called. 'Contact missing relations, old school friends and long-lost but not forgotten loves – or be found yourself . . .' Underneath, there had been a list of people sought by mothers or school secretaries or simply friends who had lost touch, forgotten to copy the new address from the Christmas card and then thrown the card away, only remembering when they saw the dustbin lorry moving off up the road. 'Janet Greaves, was at Loreto Convent, Moss Side, Manchester, 1959–1964, Rachel Foster was wondering where you are now. Please contact Box No 563.' 'Roger Hughes, last heard of Catterick Army Garrison,

North Yorkshire, 1945, contact Patrick Lucas, 129 Cairns Crescent, Kutztown, PA, USA.' 'Charlotte Jane, born 15 May, 1964, Hounslow Hospital, Middlesex. Mother searching for you. Box No 391.'

But what could she say? How could you look for someone when you didn't even know their name? 'Who were you? We met in a brothel, Friday, September 26, 1969. I fainted. Contact Box No 293.' No, no it was ridiculous. Besides, he was not the sort of man who read 'Where are you now?' columns.

But she had to do something, had to, for Martin's sake as much as hers. How could she tell him who his father was if she didn't know herself?

43

Philip parked the car and got out. Above him a small plane circled, gleaming like the slice of a seagull's wing, white through blue. In front of him, gathering speed on the runway, was another plane, taking off now, lifting its wheels, tucking them neatly into its breast. Two young men in flying suits lounged nearby, leaning against a wall, laughing in the sun. He sniffed the air, tentatively at first, then more boldly, like a dog off the lead, feeling the hairs prick on the nape of his neck. It was twenty-eight years since he had stood on an airfield.

'Neil Hooper, please.'

The man in reception looked at the diary in front of him.

'Neil? He's giving a lesson at the moment. Did you have an appointment?'

'Yes.'

The man turned so that he could see out of the window.

'I think that's him now,' he said, jerking his head in the direction of the plane, still circling above the runway. 'He shouldn't be long. Do you want to wait?'

There were two chairs in the room, both sagging, and a generous supply of old flying magazines but Philip chose not to sit down. He needed to keep moving. He had phoned Neil as agreed at three o'clock but he had not been there. He had phoned again the following day and spoken but not received a definite answer. Neil had said he was pretty sure it would be OK, he'd have to take a medical, of course, if he wanted to fly solo but that shouldn't be a problem, it was only class three. He just needed to check with their insurance people. Why didn't he come out on Saturday and have a look round? He'd have spoken to them by then. Would eleven be all right? And Philip had said yes, he wasn't doing anything on Saturday morning, eleven would be fine, and had counted the hours until now, here, pacing up and down, glancing up at the sky, his armpits wet with fear.

The door swung open and a man came in, stamping his feet on the mat, shouting out something to someone outside.

'Mr Dart? Neil Hooper. Sorry to keep you waiting. First lesson was late. Birthday present. They're always the worst.'

He was about his age, thought Philip, or maybe younger, yes, probably younger, mid to late forties – tall, good-looking, close-shaven. Like an American tycoon in a black swivel chair. An advert for cigars.

They shook hands.

'Come on. Let's go to my office. We can sort everything out there.'

Philip followed him down a corridor, through a door outside, across a small yard and up three small steps into what looked like an old mobile home. Sort everything out? Surely that meant . . . no, no, don't jump to conclusions, he told himself, as someone somewhere turned on a radio, music exploding, then dying, a spent rocket, the volume knob turned down.

'The answer's yes,' said Neil, sitting down, offering Philip a cigarette, taking one himself.

'The insurance people say it's fine. They've had other cases before, apparently. One only the other day at Bournemouth Flying Club. Research scientist. Test tube blew up in his face. He'd just taken off his glasses to take a phone call and forgot to put them on again. Nasty!'

He leant forward, struck a match, lit his cigarette and inhaled deeply. As he'd said on the phone, he went on, Philip would have to take a medical if he wanted to get a Private Pilot Licence but that shouldn't be a problem unless he had any heart problems. Philip shook his head, digging his finger nails into his palms to bank the joy down. Yes, yes, yes! He'd also have to take some written multiple choice exams in subjects like air law and meteorology and be cleared to fly solo by his instructor. It would take about forty hours of flying, possibly a bit longer depending on the weather.

He'd remember this moment. Remember it for ever. The small

white plane circling in the blue sky. The young men lounging against the wall. Their laughter – suggesting that all was to come, that all would come. The blare of the radio. And now, here, sitting in a converted mobile home, cigarette smoke in his nostrils, his joy stopped up with a line of purple marks across his palm.

'We cannot cage the minute
Within its nets of gold.'

That's what Louis MacNeice had written. But we can, we can, thought Philip, clenching his fists tighter, sensing an idiotic smile break cover and run across his face. This minute was netted, every second of it, caught like a butterfly in rock, fossilised.

He'd been in the RAF as well, said Neil. Had taken voluntary redundancy the year before as part of the defence cuts in Germany. He hadn't really wanted to leave the RAF but his wife had wanted to come back to the UK and their son had been unhappy at boarding school so it had seemed the right thing to do. A former colleague had suggested he go into insurance. Had even given him the name and number of a firm in Weston-Super-Mare that employed several ex-RAF personnel. But he hadn't wanted to give up flying. That's why he'd taken this job even though the pay . . . well, it wasn't brilliant, put it that way, not compared to what he had been earning.

Philip nodded, catching sight of a black-and-white photo on the desk showing Neil taken twenty or perhaps thirty years ago, standing in front of a two-seater plane in what looked like the middle of the desert, his eyes scrunched tight against the glare of the sun. Next to it was another photo, also black and white, showing the face of a young woman in profile. His wife, Philip wondered? The person who had taken the photo of Neil in the desert? Or just a friend?

'That was my first wife,' said Neil, seeing the direction in which Philip was looking. 'She was killed in a crash in Wiltshire. Compton Abbas airfield. I don't know whether you know it. It's between Shaftesbury and Blandford.'

Philip shook his head, disconcerted by the starkness of such a revelation from a virtual stranger – and another man, to boot.

'It was her first flight after giving birth to our daughter. She struck the side of a valley as she was coming in to land. I don't know why. At the inquiry, they suggested she'd lost her ability to judge distances accurately. Implied that mothers with six-month-old babies had no right to be flying aeroplanes. But that wasn't it. She'd no more lost her ability to judge distances than I'd lost my legs. There was nothing wrong with the engine. At least, not that they could see . . . It was the engine that killed her. It was forced back into the cockpit on impact. The paramedics said she'd have died instantly.'

Philip nodded, looking, despite himself, for another photo, a photo of the second wife, the one who'd wanted to come back to the UK. But there wasn't one and he knew, without being told, that this one disliked flying.

'How did it happen, by the way?' asked Neil, changing the subject abruptly.

'What? My eye?' said Philip, fighting back the urge he always had when someone referred to it, to touch it, as if somehow it might have changed, become soft instead of hard, changeable instead of fixed, a lump of glass masquerading as the window to his soul.

'Yes, only they usually pull out all the stops to keep you flying if you're injured in service. Friend of mine. Injured his leg during an emergency parachute landing. Told me later it was the best thing that ever happened to him – in terms of work, that is. Said his career really took off after the accident.'

'Yes, well, it didn't happen while I was flying. I was stabbed by someone I'd never met before. A heroin addict. I saw him attack my . . . this . . . this girl and went to help. Then he turned on me.'

As he spoke, he watched Neil's face, looking for the flicker of recognition that would show that he knew, that he'd heard, because surely there still were some pilots out there that remembered, that told his story from time to time – 'One of the most promising young pilots the RAF has ever had . . . brilliant career in front of him . . . and all gone, just like that, just because he happened to be in a particular place at a particular time. Terrible waste. A tragedy really. Don't know what he's doing now. Never heard of him since although I did once hear someone say they thought he'd gone into the hotel trade.'

But there was nothing, not even the slightest lift of the eyebrows to suggest his story sounded familiar, something someone had mentioned once, perhaps in jest, confident it was the kind of thing that happened to other people.

'They did offer me other jobs. But they were all on the ground and, like you, I didn't want to give up flying.'

There was a moment's awkward silence as if, instead of bringing them closer, their separate revelations had created a distance, a chasm of past life which they would now have to cross before they could talk comfortably about other things, men's things, the rugby on Saturday, why Wales had played so badly.

Then suddenly Neil was standing up, stubbing out his cigarette, saying when did he want to start, he had a free slot on Wednesday if he was interested and ten minutes later, his deposit paid, a course of lessons booked, Philip was back in the car, whooping, thinking that he would remember this too – letting the joy out through the nets of gold.

44

Philip doused the bonfire in paraffin, struck a match and stood back as last year's leaves exploded into flame. If only one could get rid of other things so easily, he thought. Lost years, for instance. Wasted opportunities. Fearfulness. Because, standing here, feeling his cheeks grow warm with the heat from the fire, he recognised that it was this – fearfulness – that had been responsible for all those years as a sheep. He had pretended it was his eye, convinced both himself and others, but, in truth, his eye had had little to do with it. He could have left the bank, found another job, one that was more suited to his talents and temperament, but he hadn't because he was fearful, fearful of difficulty, struggle, risk. It had been safer to stay, more comfortable.

He poked the fire violently, dislodging a large branch that toppled sideways, narrowly missing his foot. Still, he had done it now. He had cast off his sheep's clothes. This was how he would live now. As a tiger. Every day his last.

Helen, who had just returned from lunch with Matty and Teresa, watched him from the kitchen window, wondering why it was that men liked fires so much. Did they satisfy some primeval instinct – to ward off danger, warm the family, cook the meat that had just been hunted? She smiled, remembering lunch, how Matty, playing with her toy kitchen, had brought her tea in yellow plastic cups, fennel with raspberry tarts.

Philip busied himself as she approached, picking up stray leaves and twigs as if to say that he wasn't just watching, wasn't glorying in the hungry lick of flame, that he was working really, honest.

'What did he say?'

He turned, his smile telling her the answer before he even spoke.

'They said yes.'

'Yes! Philip!'

She flung herself at him and they danced around the fire, arms clasped tightly about one another's necks, causing Mrs Chandler next door to pause on the landing on her way upstairs to clean the bathroom – to wonder if they had contracted something, out there, wherever they'd been, dysentery or malaria or one of those other foreign diseases, they'd been acting peculiar ever since they'd come back, it would be a pity if they had, they'd been such a nice couple before.

'I'm so happy! So happy, so happy, so happy!'

'I'll have to take a medical but he says that won't be a problem – at least not because of the eye.'

'When do you start?'

'Wednesday. He's going to teach me . . . well, you know, remind me of anything I may have forgotten. He used to be in the RAF as well. He took voluntary redundancy last year.'

Helen drew back suddenly, struck by a thought, a thought so glaringly obvious she was stunned it had not occurred to her before.

'What are you going to tell the children?'

He stared.

'You're supposed to be scared of flying, remember?'

'I'll just tell them I'm confronting my fear then. Challenging it head-on.'

Helen frowned doubtfully.

'Do you think they'll believe you?'

'Don't see why not. They'll just see it as another example of how odd I've become since leaving the bank. Besides, they've got enough of their own problems to worry about. How were Teresa and Matty, by the way?'

'All right. Matty's got a bit of a cold. Teresa says they're seeing a marriage guidance counsellor. Did you know?'

Philip shook his head. He and Martin had gone out for a drink together the night before but, as usual, had succeeded in exchanging the minimum amount of information in what passed as conversation. But then this was hardly surprising. When he looked at Martin, he felt like a traveller on a long-distance train, waking up suddenly in the middle of the night, recognising no landmarks, everything unfamiliar. It wasn't just that Martin looked different. He thought differently, felt differently, gestured differently. He even cupped his chin in his hands when he was thinking – something Philip never did, nor Helen. He knew how the mother duck felt in the *Ugly Duckling*, had had problems reading this story to Martin when he was a child. If he was honest, he was afraid of Martin. And he sensed that Martin knew this.

He poked the fire again, the flames now slower – fatter, sated. A solitary spark flew up and his hand rose automatically even though there was nothing to protect on that side, nothing vital anyway, the eyeball plucked, the socket scraped clean.

'You should go and see the doctor about it, you know,' said Helen.

'About what?'

But he knew what she meant.

The lids had started to sag, the lower one rolling out, the upper one sinking, giving him a garish, freakish appearance. No wonder that little boy in Athens had commented on it. It was enough to startle anyone. The other day, walking past a parade of shops, a girl in a pushchair had burst out crying as he approached. She could have been startled by a passing bus, bitten her tongue, been told no, she couldn't have any sweets, not now, but Philip was convinced it was the sight of his eye that had frightened her and had hurried past, turning his face the other way.

'They might be able to do something about it. Make it better fitting. Fill it out or something.'

'Maybe.'

'Do you want me to book you an appointment?'

'No, it's OK. I'll do it.'

He walked over to the garden bench, propped his stick against one side and picked up a bag lying on the seat.

'Look. What do you think?'

Helen peered inside the bag, then examined the label.

'Lovely. Where did you get them?

'At that new garden centre that's just opened. I called in on the way back. They'll be up by May. I thought it would be nice to have a bit of colour. We don't usually have much out by then.'

'Are they all blue?'

'Yes. There were some white and pink as well but I decided not to get them.'

'Do you want some help putting them in?'

'No, it's OK.'

The earth was soft, still damp from the rain the day before, breaking easily at the cut of his trowel. There. That was deep enough. He put his hand in the bag, drew out one of the bulbs and popped it in the hole, covering it with loose soil then patting the top firm. In five months, less probably, this small brown, papery-skinned runt of an object would be a flower, purplish blue, a sight to gladden the eyes. He began to dig another hole, then another and another and another until all the bulbs were planted, the sun low, night leaking over the horizon. He sat back on his heels, triumphant. There. All done. It was amazing what one could do when one did it.

45

'Are you nervous?' asked Neil.

'A bit,' admitted Philip. 'It's been a long time.'

'You'll be fine. Couple of hours and you'll feel like you've never stopped.'

He pushed open the door and Philip followed him across the Tarmac to where the planes stood, lined up in a row, tethered to concrete bollards like dogs outside a shop. It was Wednesday, Wednesday afternoon, the cloud high, the wind light to moderate, good weather for flying.

Philip had been worried when he had drawn the curtains that morning and seen the grey sky, the trees moving in next door's garden. But by ten o'clock the cloud had lifted and the wind dropped. By twelve the sun had come out. Now it was almost perfect.

'I'll just check the fuel,' said Neil, shouting to make himself heard above the noise of a helicopter taking off near by. 'You get in.'

Philip did as he was told, bunching up his knees, lowering his head. God, he had forgotten how small they were, how flimsy. It was a two-seater Cessna 152, space in the back for a couple of bags, coats maybe, a picnic lunch. Nothing else. He touched the control column, gingerly at first, like a child reaching out to stroke a strange cat, nervous in case it scratched. Then more strongly, gripping it now, his hands welded.

'Right. That's OK. Fuel almost full,' said Neil, climbing in beside him.

Philip shrank back into his seat, his hands falling away.

'You'll find not much has changed. Very little probably.'

Philip ran his eye over the controls. The altimeter. Compass. Throttle. Trimmer. Primer. Radios. Yes, it was all there. Some of it a bit bigger, some a bit smaller or a slightly different shape. But otherwise it was unchanged.

'If you could just fasten your belt, check your seat is locked and that the door is properly closed. I know a lot of this is going to be old hat for you but I have to run through it even so,' said Neil.

He went through a list of pre-start checks, thumbing off each item on the clipboard lying on his lap. Philip watched and listened, his skin prickling with recognition, every sense alert. It was like having a child, he thought, reading nursery rhymes again, the old words coming back, the hurt of rejection in the playground, bloodied knees, taunts from other children. 'Nah-nah, nah nah-nah!' Everything familiar, old and new at the same time.

'Right. I'm going to start the engine now. If you can put your headphones on then we'll be able to hear one another.'

He was still shouting even though the helicopter had long gone, as if trying to make himself heard above the noise of Philip's need, like rain drumming on the roof, so loud he could hardly hear himself think.

Philip watched giddily as Neil leant forward, turned the key, carried out the after-start checks, taxied to a holding point near the runway and then ran quickly through the engine power checks and pre-take-off checks.

There was a crackle from the radio then a babble of voices, first Neil's, then another man's, the words fast and furious, a foreign tongue. Philip struggled to understand, to separate the sounds like strung beads then put them back together again, a necklace of words.

'OK. We've been cleared by air traffic control.'

He pressed the primer, pushed the throttle in, adjusted his headphones.

'Here we go.'

They began to move, to edge away from the other planes, turn the corner, taxi gently down the taxiway. Philip looked down at his hands lying there uselessly in his lap like something chopped in two, a spring turned off at the source. He was like a bridegroom posing for his photo – uncertain how to hold them, whether to clasp them in front or behind or let them hang straight down, dangling by his side.

'I'll take us up and down today. Just until you get the feel for it again,' said Neil, not looking at him, as if reading his thoughts.

'Yes. Fine,' said Philip and gripped the edge of the seat. He had to hold something.

They began to gather speed, the green of the grass and the grey of the runway to mix and blur. Philip concentrated, listening, waiting, his body taut as a circus high wire. And then, suddenly, they were off, up, the nose rising sharply, the ground falling away, the horizon pure blue. His stomach leapt, that old familiar leap, sharp as a smell.

'Take you back, does it?'

'Yes. Just a bit,' said Philip and cleared his throat.

He looked out of the window, his hands slackening, the tension easing slightly. There. There it was again. The big picture. All England around him. And the light, the light on the land, he had forgotten that, how it looked when you were on top of it. One field lit up, another in darkness, as if God had got a new torch for Christmas, was trying it out. Everything soft. Soft and small. Woods like pubic hair. A brown fuzz.

'All right?'

Philip nodded, not trusting himself to speak. There was a sudden bump. Then another. Smaller this time.

'Just a bit of turbulence. There's always quite a lot over the city centre,' said Neil and pointed out Clifton suspension bridge, Bristol City football club, the new cinema multiplex.

'That's Filton airfield over there. See it?'

'Yes,' said Philip, his eye following the direction in which Neil was pointing.

Of course he could see it. Up here, he could see everything. He was whole again, unscarred. He had not thought of this. He had thought he would be flying, flying not seeing. He had forgotten that the two were one, one and the same, that to fly was to see. And now he was doing it, doing both, after all those years. God, what a fool he'd been.

He leant back, easy now, the tension gone.

'We're coming up over Thornbury. Do you want to take control now?'

'Yes. Yes please.'

He laughed at his own eagerness and Neil laughed too.

'Sorry. I know you've been itching to take over. But I had to take us up. Just this first time. Just until I know how you are.'

'It's OK. I understand.'

He leant forward.

'Just keep the big picture until we reach the Severn. Then we'll head east slightly, up towards Gloucester. I don't want to do too much this first time. I just want you to feel comfortable. To get the feel of it again.'

Philip grinned. He was flying, flying again, up there, up in the sky, poised, waiting, ready to swoop just for the hell of it, for the sight of the land rushing up to meet him, a pot of colour boiling over. Green, brown, grey, blue. It was better in summer. The colours brighter.

'OK. Raise the nose. Now lower it. Yaw to the left. Good. Now, trim it out, will you?'

Philip felt for the trimmer with his right hand, his left still on the control column, his eye on the horizon. There? No, not quite. It was still rising slightly. Yes, that was better.

'Good,' said Neil and Philip could hear the respect in his voice, the acknowledgement that he could still fly, still, after all these years, and he felt his heart swell fit to burst.

'Now, back again. This time, yaw to the right. Good. I can tell you don't really need me. That's Slimbridge Wildfowl Trust down there. I was there at the weekend with my son. He's into birds. Both kinds. Not planes, though. Thinks I'm mad. Motorised lawnmowers. That's what he calls these. What about you? Your son interested in flying?'

'No . . . he . . . he . . . you see . . . no, he's not really.'

'Might come to him later. When he thinks you've given up on him. Sometimes they don't want to do what you've done just because they think you want them to. Which I suppose you do. At least I do. Chip off the old block and all that. It's nice to think of things carrying on, being passed down the generations. Still, I can't talk. My dad was a butcher. So there you are. Turn us round again, will you? I told control we wouldn't be going much further than this.'

They swung back again, facing Wales, the sun in their eyes,

going down now, the horizon hazy, difficult to tell land from sky.

'How does it feel?'

'Good. Very good. I just wish I'd done it thirty years ago. That's all.'

'Still. You're doing it now, aren't you? That's the main thing. Like riding a bike, isn't it? You don't forget.'

Philip reached for the trimmer, felt for the right point, leant back again.

'You can do what you want now, if you like. Just as long as you tell me what you're going to do and you keep to this side of the Severn.'

And so Philip did what he wanted. Nothing fancy. No dives or rolls. No stalls. There was plenty of time for that. Just up and down and right and left, feeling his way, gently, touch by touch, like making love to a new woman. Finding out what worked. 'They're all different. All different and the same. It's finding out what's different that's important.' That's what his RAF instructor had told him.

'OK. Time's up. We'll have to start heading back. Do you know where we are? Or do you need directions?'

'Same way as we came?'

'That'll be fine. I'll just check with air traffic that there's no one else in the area.'

Philip pointed the nose south again, gripping the control column tightly, like a child on a park swing, reluctant to get off. He glanced across at Neil. No. No point asking. He'd only get him into trouble. Rules were rules. He ought to know that. Ought to know it better than anyone. All those years in the bank.

'OK. I have control,' said Neil.

He said it as a question rather than a command, waiting tactfully for Philip to sit back, to loosen his hold on the column.

'Can I follow you through?'

'Sure. Course you can.'

And so Philip held on, loosely, so that he didn't interfere with Neil's movements.

The radio crackled again.

'There's someone else coming in before us. Over there. See?'

Philip scanned the horizon, his eye sweeping across it like the beam of a lighthouse, a brush across a polished floor, searching for the telltale glint.

'No . . . I can't see it . . . oh yes, I've got it.'

'I'll hold back. Give them plenty of room.'

They began to circle, coming down slowly at the same time. Philip rejoiced secretly at the delay, not wanting it to end, savouring those last few minutes like the pages of a good book, feeling the thickness between finger and thumb.

The glint grew, took shape, became a plane, coming in now, slow and steady, that's the way, steady does it, and then the pause, always the pause, that fraction of a pause, as if taking stock, catching its breath, then down, down, down. Smooth, nice. A good landing.

'Right. Our turn,' said Neil and wheeled round for the approach.

Philip shut his eye, hearing the engine noise change as Neil pulled the throttle out. He could do this in his sleep. Had done almost, many a time coming back from a night flying exercise, the dawn just stretching, the sky like stirred dark cream.

Four hundred feet, three hundred, two hundred, one hundred. He opened his eye. Neil was concentrating, frowning, as if he were the pupil and Philip the teacher. They were crossing a main road now, approaching the runway. Philip glanced at the controls then back at the runway, tightened his fingers, not much, just enough to feel it properly. Fifty, forty, thirty-five, thirty. Twenty. Down. They were down. Bumping along. Braking hard. Hard but steady. Another good landing.

'Well done,' said Philip. Then laughed. 'Sorry. I keep forgetting.'

'Never mind. You'll be doing it next time. Just as soon as you've passed the medical. You got the list of doctors, didn't you?'

'Yes,' said Philip, taking his hands away suddenly as if burnt.

'It's OK. You'll be fine. I've told you. Plenty of people fly with only one eye. As long as you can still hear.'

They were approaching the other planes now, heading towards the space they had vacated an hour earlier.

'It's the devil's own game to park without bumping one of the others,' said Neil and swore softly as he came in too tight on the right-hand side.

The engine cut out. Neil took off his headphones. Philip did too.

'All right?'

'Yes, thanks. That was great. Fantastic.'

They sat there silently for a moment, each secret with their own thoughts. Then suddenly they were busy again, doing, Neil reaching back to pick up his clipboard, Philip leaning forward to tie up a shoelace.

'Right. Give me a ring won't you, as soon as you know about the medical. When did you say you'd booked it for? Monday, wasn't it?'

Philip nodded.

'Don't worry. You'll be up there on your own in a few months. Licence and all. Just you wait.'

Back in his car, driving into Bristol, Philip remembered the day he had told his parents he wanted to be a pilot. They had not objected, not openly anyhow, but had looked pained, his father in particular, his hopes of passing on the business dashed. Dart & Son, Commercial Insurance Brokers Ltd. A ripped dream.

'But why? Why?' they had asked.

'I don't know,' he had said, twisting his napkin round and round. They were finishing breakfast. Porridge. He had never liked it since.

He had tried to explain but it had come out all wrong. Like a bodged sum, the ink smeared. Illegible.

'I just do. That's why. Does there have to be a reason?' he had shouted in the end. And pushed back his chair, boorish, intractable.

Now though, now it would be different. He could answer them now, say that coming down, walking, driving, being on the earth rather than in the air was to know how the serpent must have felt when God said: 'Upon thy belly shalt thy go and dust shalt thou eat all the days of thy life.' They would have understood that. Surely they would. Surely.

46 ∫

Philip took a tie from his wardrobe and held it up against the shirt. The tie was yellow, the shirt blue. Sun and sky. The first, best colours.

'Surely you don't need to wear a tie,' said Helen, coming in from the bathroom. Her hair was damp from the shower, a smear of toothpaste on one cheek.

'No, maybe not.'

And he put the tie back, catching sight of himself in the mirror as he did so, feeling ridiculous. They weren't interested in the colour of his shirt, for Christ's sake, he told himself angrily. They were interested in his chest, the power of his lungs, the beat of his heart. Above all, in his eye. His one eye.

It was the day of the medical. The day. The day that would decide it all. And he couldn't decide which shirt to wear.

Helen had boiled him an egg for breakfast, setting the table prettily with a check tablecloth and a vase of daffodils coming out of bud. There was a smell of fresh coffee and toast, the hum of voices on the radio.

He sat down and opened his egg, cracking the shell with the back of his spoon. One, two, three. There. It came off easily, cleanly, as he liked it to do. Helen passed him the butter. Their hands met but not their eyes, her two and his one. These sought refuge in the morning papers.

They had given him a list of doctors in the Bristol area approved by the Civil Aviation Authority to conduct medicals. He had studied the list as if revising for an exam, poring over the names as if there was an answer, the right name, the one that would let him pass. Charles Ingham. Stephen Clifford. Geoffrey

Pattison. Joseph Stengel. He had chosen the latter because it sounded foreign. Because maybe a foreigner, an expatriate, someone who had suffered, who had felt lonely and homesick, would be more sympathetic, more willing to make allowances. Now he doubted the wisdom of his choice but it was too late to change. He had already made the appointment.

Helen cleared her throat.

'Have you read this?'

She showed him an article on page eight headlined 'Taking the sting out of bees and wasps'.

'No, not yet.'

He turned the pages to find the article in his copy of the paper. It was about a new desensitisation programme at Harrogate's district hospital for people allergic to bee and wasp stings. The programme involved injecting people with tiny amounts of wasp venom to build up their immune systems.

'There might be one here, mightn't there?' said Helen.

Philip shrugged.

'It's worth asking surely. This doctor, the one you're seeing this morning, maybe he'll know.'

'It's no problem, really, carrying the tablets around.'

'Yes, but you forget them.'

'I don't.'

'You do sometimes.'

'Very occasionally.'

He patted his pockets ostentatiously and got up to fetch the marmalade.

The hospital, like all hospitals, was confusing, with a multitude of signs that conflicted with the map he had been sent. Beyond reception, opposite the lifts, there was a sale of homemade cakes and knitted goods in aid of research into children's cancer. He bought a date-and-walnut cake to kill time, telling himself that he could give it to Una, she needed cheering up. Upstairs, there was another reception area. A woman sat reading in the waiting area, a man, perhaps her husband, dozing by her side. Beyond was a ward, some patients clearly visible, others screened by green flowered curtains. A male orderly walked past. Then another, his trouser legs too short.

Philip handed his appointment card to the woman at reception and watched her tick off his name on a list.

'If you'd like to take a seat,' she said in the slow, sing-song voice of those used to dealing with the physically and mentally infirm.

Philip sat down, fighting the desire to slouch, to shrink into himself like a prodded snail. The woman who was reading looked up then quickly down again. Ten minutes passed. Fifteen. Twenty. Philip noticed a piece of red tinsel left over from Christmas poking out from behind one of the radiators. One of the three doors opposite reception opened. A man came out.

'Mr Dart?'

Philip got up, feeling the woman stop her reading again and look up, wondering what exactly was wrong with him, how bad it was.

The man shut the door behind them and asked him to take a seat. He was small and dark, a neat bird of a man, his movements like the peck of a beak. He had Philip's notes, he said, so he knew about the eye. And he patted a fat brown envelope lying on the desk in front of him. It was a standard medical, he said, similar to those given for life insurance purposes. He would be checking Philip's hearing and lungs, his reflexes, blood pressure, and his eyesight, of course. Naturally, that was important.

'If you could stand up. I'd like to measure your height first. You might want to take your jacket off. It's a bit stuffy in here. The window won't open.'

Philip did as asked, drawing himself up to his full six-foot-two height, anxious not to lose so much as half an inch. Dr Stengel checked his weight next, then his blood pressure, then his lungs, asking him to blow into what looked like a plastic toilet roll.

'Now could you look at the sign on the wall opposite and read out the letters on the top line. And the second? And third? Fourth?'

Philip faltered, stopped, admitted that they were hazy now, he wasn't sure whether it was an 'h' or a 'b'. Dr Stengel nodded, wrote something down. Next he pointed to a poster above his desk.

'Can you tell me what colour the circle is?'

'Red.'

'And the triangle?'

'Green.'

'And the rectangle?' 'Square?' 'Star?'

'That's fine, fine,' he said and asked if he drank. How much a week? And what about exercise? Did he play any sport?

'Not as such,' admitted Philip. 'I do quite a bit of gardening and I like walking. But I don't go every weekend. Just every now and then. I used to play badminton but then the person I played with moved away so I stopped. I've been meaning to take it up again but I . . . I . . . I haven't yet.'

He trailed off, conscious that he sounded defensive, that he was making excuses.

Dr Stengel smiled.

'That's OK. You don't have to pound the squash courts four times a week. In fact, often the ones who do are the ones I worry about.'

He glanced down at his notes.

'Now. Your hearing,' he said and stood up. 'I'm going to tickle your ear and whisper a number at the same time. I want you to say the number out loud.'

Philip felt himself stiffen, sweat trickle down the inside of his armpit. It was a 'b'. He could see now. He was sure it was a 'b'. But it was too late. He had failed. He should have just guessed. Bluffed it. It was too late now.

'Five. Thirty-three. Nine. Twenty-six.'

Dr Stengel sat down again.

'And generally? You feel well, do you? No problems sleeping or anything? No persistent headaches?'

'No. Nothing like that. Yes, generally I feel well. As well as I've ever done.'

Why didn't he just cut the formalities and say he'd failed, thought Philip. That he was sorry but he couldn't pass him, not with his eye, he'd be a danger to others as well as himself. That he hated to disappoint but still, better safe than sorry. Eh? Eh?

'And your eye? Your good eye? That doesn't give you any discomfort?'

He looked down at the papers in front of him, rifled through them.

'You haven't . . . I think I'm right in saying that you haven't ever had a problem with it?'

'Yes. They said I might. That it might develop . . . what was the phrase . . . ?'

'Sympathetic ophthalmitis?'

'Yes. That's it. No, it's been fine. I thought it was starting to get inflamed once but it turned out to be just a bit of grit.'

Dr Stengel chewed the top of his pen then pointed it at Philip's left eye.

'You know, if you wanted, they could do something about that at the eye hospital.'

'Oh?'

'Yes. You should see your doctor. Ask for a referral. It's not a big operation or anything. They just insert a silicon ball to give the eye more volume then put in a better-fitting prosthesis. It's quite straightforward. One of my patients – someone I'm seeing about something completely different – had it done recently. Now you can't tell which eye is false – not unless you look closely.'

'Right. Thanks. I'll ask about it. I know . . . well . . . I know it's been getting worse,' he said, remembering the boy in Athens, the child in the pushchair who had burst out crying.

'And you're allergic to wasp and bee stings?' said Dr Stengel, looking down again, writing fast then glancing at his watch as if Philip had overrun his allotted time.

'Yes. That's what I've been told.'

'Carry anti-histamine tablets, do you?'

Philip brought them out from his pocket.

'Right. Fine.'

He began to stuff Philip's medical notes back into their brown envelope, cursing as one of the sides ripped open.

Was that it? Wasn't he going to send him for a chest x-ray, take some blood tests, check his cholesterol level, ask him to give a urine sample? Wasn't he going to monitor his pulse rate before and after exercise?

'Is that . . . is that it?'

'Yes. That's all. Told you it wasn't anything to get worked up about. Not the class three. The other medicals, the one for the Commercial Pilot's Licence, for example, that's a lot more stringent. But this one, no, you're fine, nothing to worry about.'

'You mean . . . you mean I've passed?'

'Just as long as you get your licence by October. It's my silver wedding anniversary on the fifteenth. I thought I'd treat my wife to a weekend in Paris. Private plane and all.'

Philip frowned then realised Dr Stengel was joking. He had passed. He could fly again. Fly! The relief was so intense that for a moment he thought he was going to cry or fling his arms round Dr Stengel's neck. Then the moment passed and he was in control again. Philip Dart. Retired bank employee. Married. Father of two. Or at least, to two.

Somehow, he found himself downstairs again opposite the lifts, having signed the necessary forms, written out a cheque for the required fee and shaken hands with Dr Stengel. The cake stall was still there although there were only two cakes left, a plain jam sponge and a fruit cake, slightly sunken in the middle. He bought them both as well as the last bag of scones and a knitted Easter bunny. A different woman served him, small, black-haired, Irish by the sound of her.

'Lovely day it's turned into,' said the woman, taking his money and counting out his change.

'Yes,' agreed Philip, looking round for a window through which to confirm her assertion but failing to see one.

'Blessed, we are.'

He took the change then, on second thoughts, handed it back to her.

'Oh yes, we're that all right. Blessed.'

And he walked out. Out of the hospital into the rest of the day which, as the woman had claimed, had turned out lovely, the sun shining, car windows wound down, spring in the air and everyone hopeful because of it, most of all him, Philip Dart, himself once more.

47 ∫

Una scanned the departure screen to see if Sinead's flight was listed. Yes, there it was. 'Flight BA 563 to New York, departs 12.35.' It had not been delayed. At least not yet. The flight before was going to Lilongwe, the flight before that to Qatar, and before that to Moscow.

She looked around, feeling suddenly small and insignificant, aware of all that was going on, out there, in all those other countries. Green paddy fields, silent like a picture, a tiny figure bent double, black, a speck of dirt on the clean green canvas. Wipe it clean. There. All green again. There were hundreds more where that came from. Thousands. The sweatshops in Taiwan, ten girls to a room, each dreaming of a better life, counting the days and the money, building hopes with each brush of their long black hair, in the evening when it was cool, not yet quite dark, when they would sit and talk, nurse their aching limbs, boast in this little scrap of the day that was theirs, half an hour at the most. Africa. The very name like a poem. A-fri-ca! Children playing in a road, their mothers comfortable in a porch behind, a blind woman muttering as she felt her way past, the tap-tap-tap of her stick drowned as the women burst into laughter, loud laughter, sweet laughter, a great warm bellyful. In Poland, a pregnant seventeen-year-old schoolgirl jumping from the bathroom window of her parents' ninth floor flat after being turned away for an abortion by five local hospitals. And in Geraardsbergen, a small Belgian town, a fight breaking out when a man tried to stop a friend drinking live fish during an annual festival.

The queue edged forward. Alongside, in the queue for Malaga, a suitcase fell off a trolley, narrowly missing a sleeping baby. A woman, thin, bad-tempered, wearing make-up that looked sticky to the touch, harangued her husband as he heaved the case back.

'I told you that was going to happen! Why did you put the big ones on top of the small ones? Anyone can see they're going to overbalance.'

A boy, about twelve, presumably their son, flushed red, conscious that everyone was looking on. Una counted the bags on their trolley. There were six, three large, two small, and a holdall.

'What are you thinking?' asked Sinead, pushing her own case, just the one, forwards along the floor with the flat of her foot.

'Nothing. Just how strange it all is. All these people. All going somewhere.'

All starting new lives, she added to herself. Ending old ones, casting them off like sheep wriggling free from the shears, frisky light.

'Look at that woman! Look!'

Una turned to see a tall, black woman sweep past. She wore a purple silk tunic over purple silk trousers. Her arms were ringed with gold, right up to the elbows, jangling as she moved. Her bearing was proud, haughty, her head held high. She looked like a princess. Probably was.

A row broke out at the front of their queue, a small swarthy man shouting, waving papers in the air. The check-in staff smiled unswervingly, their cool incensing the man, making him shout even louder. The couple behind Una and Sinead shook their heads disapprovingly.

'Always one, isn't there?' said the woman, speaking to no one in particular. 'Told you we should have got here earlier,' she added, speaking now to her husband. 'If he carries on like this, we won't have time to get that perfume Muriel wanted in duty free.' The man glanced at his watch, opened his mouth as if to point out they still had a good hour and a half then shut it abruptly.

Una and Sinead exchanged looks.

'Do you think you will stay there?' asked Una, the question leaving her lips before she was even aware she had thought it.

'I don't know. Maybe. It depends.'

'Was it because you didn't win the competition?'

Sinead had come second in the sculpture competition to win a year's bursary and a show at Leeds City Art Gallery, an achievement Una had heard of only because her mother had read about it in the local free newspaper.

'Not really. I probably wouldn't have gone if I had won, simply because I'd have been putting together work for the show. But I'm not going *because* I didn't win. It just felt right, as if something had clicked inside me.'

'What will you do though? How will you support yourself?'

'Keep my eyes open. Look. Listen. Glory in the unfamiliarity of it all,' said Sinead. 'I may get a job teaching. There's this place Dad knows about, a sort of college where kids go who've been chucked out of other schools and are in trouble with the police. Apparently they do a lot of art and pottery. Dad knows one of the teachers there. He says he can get me an interview if I'm interested.'

Una frowned, pained by how definite it all sounded. A flat. And now, almost certainly, a job.

'You will write though, won't you?' she said, trying to keep the hurt out of her voice, the indignation that Sinead should go, should leave her to face the future on her own.

'I'll send you a postcard every week,' promised Sinead. 'You can imagine me writing it sitting in a coffee bar somewhere, ordering bagels while I think of what to say.'

The queue edged forward again, the swarthy man's problem apparently resolved, his wife smiling, gathering up their children like shells on a beach, as if unsure whether to take them or not.

Sinead opened her rucksack and took out her ticket and passport. The rucksack was new. So were the red jeans, the purple and red plaid shirt, the black bomber jacket – all bought with the proceeds of the prize Sinead had been ashamed to win because it was the second prize, not the first, seeing this as failure. Her hair was loose too, a mass of dark curls, bouncy like heather on a moor, fragrant in the warmth of the sun.

The check-out woman took the ticket and passport, glancing at Sinead with professional speed, like a supervisor in factory production, checking the precise alignment of chocolates in a box. Only six months in the job and already bored, she privately categorised people under 'holiday', 'business' and 'other'. This girl was definitely 'other', she decided, although it was not immediately clear what sort of 'other'. Perhaps a student on an exchange programme or a nanny. Striking looks. Shame about the hands though. And she glanced smugly at her own well-manicured talons.

'Smoking or non-smoking?' she asked, glancing at her watch, her brief interest in Sinead extinguished.

'Non-smoking. I'd like a window seat please, if that's possible.' The woman smiled, nodded, and tapped at her keyboard.

'Just the one case?'

'Yes.'

The case was new too, the first she had owned. All her previous travelling had been of the rucksack variety, mostly in Greece, sleeping on rooftops, listening to the whine of mosquitoes and the blare of discos.

'There you are. Gate number 26. It should be boarding in about an hour.'

Sinead took her boarding pass and passport and put them back in her rucksack next to her sponge bag, diary, address book, camera, change of underwear and a small wooden box of which she was particularly fond, green, star-shaped, containing a sixpence dating from the year of her birth, a present from her mother.

'Where now?'

'Shall we go and have a drink?' Una suggested, anxious to delay the final goodbye.

They took the escalator upstairs and wandered among the shops until they found a café. There was a fast-food counter at the front selling coffee and croissants and a sitdown area inside, the tables divided into cosy cubicles like old-fashioned railway carriages.

'Have you got anything to read?' asked Una, catching sight of a bookshop opposite.

'Yes. One of Shusaku Endo's. Although I'm not sure it will last. I've been getting through it faster than I expected.'

'Right. I'll go and get you something to read. You get the

drinks. I'd like a tea and something to eat. Anything you think looks nice.'

Sinead started to protest but Una was already gone, a dismissive hand waving the protest away.

Una bought Margaret Atwood's latest novel and a collection of short stories by leading contemporary female writers. At the till, she also picked up copies of two national newspapers – one broadsheet, one tabloid – and three magazines, one literary, one satirical, and one on current affairs. Enough to keep Sinead going for several weeks, she decided, weighing the Atwood book in her hands, wishing she could afford to buy it for herself as well.

'Do you think they're quadruplets?' asked Sinead, nodding in the direction of a neighbouring table.

She had bought Danish pastries, Una saw. Great thick wodges of sticky stuff. Fresh orange juice as well as tea and coffee. She handed Sinead the books and magazines and sat down while Sinead exclaimed that she shouldn't have, leaning over to squeeze her hand, a gesture of affection for which Una was unprepared and took badly, tears springing to her eyes.

'Probably,' she said, blinking quickly.

There were four girls at the table, all of the same height, build, and age, all with the same straggly fair hair and beaky nose and all dressed identically in peach-pink tracksuits and yellow canvas shoes. A man, presumably their father, was attempting to keep control from one end of the table, looking harassed, like a football referee at a cup final match, waiting for the whistle that would signal his release.

They ate silently, suddenly awkward with one another like a couple on a blind date, each wishing the other one would say something, and yet dreading it too, feeling their self-control grow soft at the edges.

'Didn't you say they're voting today? About whether to go on with the strike or not?'

Una looked at her watch.

'Yes. Two o'clock,' she said. 'Geoff will know the results by the time I get back.'

'What will you do if they vote not to go on?'

'I don't know,' said Una, fiddling with her serviette, pleating it tightly.

'Get a job, I suppose.'

She scrunched the serviette into a ball with sudden violence and rammed it in an ash tray.

'You're so lucky. Knowing what you want to do, growing up knowing it, knowing it will always be there, part of you, like an extra arm or leg. You've never had to choose, to worry you were making the right choice, that you might wake up in twenty years' time and think "If only . . . if only I'd done that . . . or that . . . or that . . .".'

'There's always regret,' said Sinead. 'Even when you know what you want to do. You just want too much, to do too many things, be too many people. If you're not careful, you'll end up doing none of them.'

'I know, I know,' said Una, speaking more fiercely than she had intended, causing the father of the quadruplets to look up, his attention momentarily distracted from the argument about a spilt drink – a jam doughnut made soggy as a result.

'Besides,' went on Sinead, leaning forward on one elbow, toying with the spoon in the sugar bowl, 'I'm not sure you're right about being lucky. It's a gift but also a burden – a yoke you can't shake off.'

There was a crash as a waitress slipped on the spilt drink, two glasses of half-finished banana milkshake sliding off the tray she was carrying and smashing on the floor. The quadruplets giggled, four jam-smudged mouths moving as one.

Sinead put down the spoon and drained her coffee.

'Don't you have any idea?'

'No. Maybe I should just lower my standards, settle for something that's not too humdrum or badly paid. Maybe that's all people like me can expect – should expect. And yet, for some reason, I feel there *is* a job out there that I want, that's fitted for me and me for it, not like you and sculpture, not as well as that, but well enough to wait for, to want. I just don't know what it is, that's all. I keep thinking it will come to me, turn up like something lost, a mislaid glove but it doesn't, or at least, hasn't. Not yet.'

'It will, it will,' said Sinead, glancing at the departure screen above Una's head, noticing that the flight to Lilongwe was now boarding.

The waitress cleared their table, her overall still damp from where she had scrubbed at the spilt milkshake. Now she would smell of bananas the whole day. And she hated the things. Made her retch, they did. And she banged the cups down, irritable, her day now set in sourness.

'Has Geoff ever been to your flat?'

Una frowned, puzzled.

'No. Why?'

'I just wondered.'

'It's more comfortable at his. It's also a hell of a lot warmer.'

'What, you mean you can wash up without wearing an overcoat?'

'Something like that.'

They both laughed, their eyes meeting briefly, searching for the flare of recognition of what was happening inside, behind the pleating of the serviette and the toying with the spoon.

'I've got something for you. Here,' said Sinead, reaching into her rucksack, taking out a small package.

Una unwrapped it slowly, easing the Sellotape off the paper like a plaster off skin. Under the paper there was bubble wrap and under that, tissue paper, yellow, Easter bright. It was a figure, a model of Una, running, her hair flying out behind, one hand stretched forward as if reaching for something just out of her grasp. Una turned it round, examining it from all angles, marvelling at how Sinead had caught her, not just how she looked but how she was, her essence. Sinead watched anxiously.

'Why running?'

'Because you always are. Hasn't anyone ever told you that before?'

Yes, thought Una. One person, in particular. Rob. And she remembered the day she had run into him. Literally. Rib against rib. Almost winding herself in the process.

She leant over and hugged Sinead across the table, feeling her shrink back involuntarily, holding her all the stronger because of this, as if she could make up for all the hugs Sinead had missed as a child, growing up, alone, with a great-aunt who didn't believe in Christmas.

'Thank you. It's beautiful. Really beautiful. And so me. All of me, I mean. Not just me on one particular day in one particular mood.'

'Really? Do you think that?'

'Yes. I'll have to be careful who I show it to. It's worse than a diary. More revealing.'

'Good,' said Sinead. 'I'm glad that's how you see it. That's what I was trying to do. To show the inside as well as the outside, like a pomegranate cut in half, those red fleshy seeds revealed, the last thing you'd expect just looking at the skin.'

Una rewrapped the figure and placed it her bag.

'Come on. I'd better go. It's started boarding,' said Sinead, nodding in the direction of the departure screen.

There was a queue at security, an elderly woman having inadvertently emptied the contents of her handbag on to the floor while looking for her passport. The man who had been in front of them at check-in was helping retrieve her possessions, they saw. Handing up lipstick and mirror compacts while she said how sorry she was, she didn't know how it had happened.

'I'll ring you on Saturday, OK?'

Sinead was businesslike now, tunnel-visioned like a marathon runner, seeing only the next step forward, then the next and the next and the next.

Una nodded miserably, wanting Sinead to say it was a mistake, that she wasn't going after all. She stretched out her hand, reached forward, but Sinead had already turned away, was moving off, putting her rucksack on the conveyor belt, checking to see there was nothing metallic in her pockets. She collected her rucksack from the other end of the belt and walked forward to passport control. Una waited, craning her neck, waiting for her to turn round, to wave one last goodbye. She saw her take back her passport, stow it away again in the rucksack and then turn, briefly, not long enough to recognise Una in the crowd. She saw her raise her left hand, push it forward as if the air were a door, then swivel sharply on her heels and march off, disappearing almost instantly in the rush of bodies on the other side. Una watched, her eyes blurred, clutching for just one more glimpse, searching for red legs, red topped with black, that particular combination. But there was nothing. Just men in suits and a party of nuns in green. She waited five minutes, then ten, then fifteen. Finally, when it was clear Sinead was not going to come back, that she had gone, truly gone, she walked slowly away.

The coach journey back to Bristol was uneventful save for a hail storm just outside Reading and a traffic jam west of Swindon caused by a jack-knifed lorry. She arrived at five just as it started to rain, the pavement thick with bad temper. There was standing room only in her bus and so she stood, the sharp corner of a fellow passenger's briefcase jabbing her legs, water from a rolled-up umbrella dripping on to her back.

She bought an evening paper at the corner shop. Also bread, butter, rhubarb yoghurt, tinned herring roes, lettuce and chocolate. There was a circular from a health club in her mail box offering massage on Tuesday mornings at a fifteen-per-cent discount, a letter from her bank inviting her to 'Spring into Action' with a five-thousand-pound loan and a postcard from her friend Rachel, presumably on a skiing holiday judging from the Alpine scene on the front. She dumped the shopping on the table, lit the fire, and picked up the phone. There was no answer from Geoff at home so she tried the Quaker Meeting House even though it was almost six by now. Liz answered, her voice barely audible above what sounded like a party in full swing.

'It's Una. Is Geoff there?'

'Una! Hellooooo! It's Liz.'

She sounded drunk.

'Is Geoff still there?'

'Geoff? Geoff? Yes, Geoff's here.'

'Can I speak to him?' said Una, shouting to make herself heard.

There was a crash which Una interpreted as Liz dropping the receiver followed by the sound of someone giggling. Then the line went dead. Una dialled again. This time a male voice answered.

'I want to speak to Geoff,' she said, irritated now.

'Hold on. I'm not sure where he is. I think he's next door. Wait a moment.'

He put the receiver down, someone else picking it up again almost immediately and singing 'Auld Lang Syne'.

'Hello. Geoff Smart.'

'It's me. Una.'

'Una. There you are.'

'Well? How did the vote go?'

'We're going back. Only three against. One abstention. Every-one else in favour.'

He went on to say that this was not a climb-down, that they had gained a significant amount of ground as a result of the strike. For example, existing staff who applied for new jobs at the college would be allowed to keep their old contracts. He talked with the speed and fluency of one not used to interruption, as if he were conducting an interview on local radio, labouring to make his point understood. Una said 'yes' and 'I see' in all the right places, waiting for him to ask how she was, how it had gone. Surely he hadn't forgotten? She had told him about it last week. How there was no one else to see Sinead off. How she was her oldest friend. She had to go. He did understand, didn't he? If it had been anything else . . . And he had said yes, yes, of course he did, it didn't matter, they would manage without her, friends were more important.

'You wouldn't believe how busy it's been. The phone's been red hot. And then, just now, just when we'd decided it was time to crack open the beer, the phone went again and it was this chap from the BBC wanting me to take part in a documentary about the changing face of education. Due to be screened this summer, he said. They're filming in April. So that should be interesting, shouldn't it?'

Una said yes, it should, in a small, quiet voice. He had forgotten. She had wondered at the time if he was listening, really listening, listening to remember rather than just listening to keep her quiet so that afterwards, when she had finished, he could unzip her jeans, peel them off, fumble with the catch on her bra.

'Are you OK? Only you sound a bit subdued.'

'Fine. Just tired. That's all.'

'Why don't you come round? We're having a sort of end-of-strike bash. Drinks at the Magpie at seven followed by a meal at Jacaranda's at half eight.'

'Maybe. I'll see how I feel.'

'OK. I'll have to go. Pete needs to call his wife or something. Speak to you tomorrow.'

She put on her Billie Holiday tape and settled down in front of the fire with the paper she had bought. She knew all the reporters' by-lines now. Mike Byrne. Sarah Brindle. Hilary Long. Dave Spencer. Alan Westwood. And Rob Perry. There was normally at least one story with his by-line although not today, not by the look of it, nothing at all. She reached out and pulled down the scrapbook she was keeping of his stories. There had been two yesterday. One about hospital patients offered AIDS tests after their gynaecologist had died suddenly and been found to be HIV positive. Another about a promise from the city council to clear asbestos from a block of flats in a £1.5m decontamination programme. The day before, there had been a picture story about a promising young gymnast. The day before that a story on a new mobile children's library. With such scraps she was piecing together his life.

She lay back and closed her eyes. It was so strange to think he was here, in the same city, perhaps not very far away even, perhaps listening to music too, winding down after a hard day.

She thought of Sinead. It would be quiet now on the BA 563 flight to New York. The meal would have been served and eaten, the duty-free trolley wheeled up and down, earphones dispensed. People would be settling down, dozing, reading, watching the in-flight movie. What was she doing, up there, wherever she was, high above the Atlantic?

What had she meant, she wondered, when she had asked if Geoff had ever been to her flat? It had been an odd question to ask. Although maybe not so odd. Maybe a roundabout way of saying something else. Because, now that she thought of it, she was not sure that Geoff even knew where she lived. Of course, he knew roughly. The area. But the name of the street? The number? She was not sure he knew that. Not sure he had ever asked. And that was odd, or rather it was revealing. How could he not know, how could he not want to know if he . . . if he . . . if . . . She recalled his voice on the phone, the distracted tone, the shouting and laughter in the background.

She sat up and began to sing alongside Billie Holiday, softly at first, faltering, then louder, growing in confidence, belting it out now, singing as if her heart would burst, as if her heart were her voice, glorying in the melancholy.

She was jobless again. Looking for something to do. What now?

48 ʃ

The man inside the phone booth raised his voice.

'So what do you want me to do? What do you want me to do?'

He jerked his head as he spoke, punching the words home. Young, dreadlocked, with an enormous padded anorak reaching almost to his knees, he would have looked more in place talking on a mobile, standing in a doorway somewhere, one arm raised against the noise of the passing traffic.

Helen looked away, nervous, wanting it to be over and done with, to be back in her car, safe, anonymous, a middle-aged housewife with a part-time job, irreproachable. A figure emerged round the corner and she tensed, only relaxing when she saw it was no one she knew, a woman in tan tights and a flowered summer dress, unwashed grey hair tied back in a ponytail. She had chosen this area because it was the other side of the city from where she lived. Also, because it was an area in which Walker & Ward sold few houses. Even so, one of her colleagues might pass through, take a short cut on their way somewhere else, see her standing there on the pavement, waiting to use a public call box, wonder idly who she was calling, why she wasn't using her mobile.

The man's voice rose again in anger.

'So what? So fucking what? No, I'm telling you. That's it. Over. Done. Fin-it-o!'

He banged out of the booth, scowled at Helen and set off down the road at a run. She dived inside quickly, before she lost her nerve and rammed the one-pound coins into the pay slot. She had written the numbers down. All the national broadsheets plus the *Daily Mail* just in case. She did not think he would be a *Daily Mail* reader, hoped he wasn't, but his wife might take it, he might glance through it occasionally. It was worth a try.

'Yes. Hello. Yes. I'd like to place an ad in your personal column.'

A female voice told her to hold the line please, she was putting her through. There was a brief snatch of recorded music then another voice, male this time. She repeated her request and was again told to hold the line. This time there was no music, just a ringing tone interrupted by a bored-sounding woman.

Helen repeated her request and was asked when she would like the ad to run.

'Next week. From Monday to Saturday. The whole week.'

He might not see the paper on some days. He might be too busy. Of course, he might not see it at all but she was not going to think about that.

'And what do you want to say?'

Helen took a deep breath.

'We met in a Bristol brothel . . .'

'Bristol what?' asked the woman.

Helen blushed.

'Brothel.'

She spelt it out, trying to sound nonchalant as though it were 'bread' or 'broom'.

'Oh. Right.'

Helen went on.

'Friday, September the twenty-sixth, 1969. I fainted. Who were you?'

She paused.

'That's it.'

'I'll just read it back to you. "We met in a Bristol brothel, Friday, September the twenty-sixth, 1969. I fainted. Who were you?" Is that it? Is that right?'

There was a different tone in her voice. Disgust. Fear. Curiosity. Pity. Helen could hear her thinking 'A pro, eh? One of them.'

'How do you want to pay?'

'Credit card, please.'

She read out her number and the card expiry date, gave the woman her name.

'You want a box number, presumably?'

Helen panicked. Of course. The replies. She had forgotten about them.

'Yes. Sorry, I'd forgotten . . . how does it work?'

'We forward the replies to you,' said the woman, contempt now uppermost. 'If you could just give me your address.'

Helen complied, her voice small and apologetic, hating herself for sounding so, the unknown woman for judging her.

'Is that it? Is that everything?'

The woman said yes, it was, and gave her a reference number, distant now as if holding the receiver away, not wanting to be contaminated by the sound of Helen's voice.

'Any problems, give me a ring. The name's Sharon Priddy.'

Helen ticked the first number on her list. One down, four to go.

She met with the same reaction at the next paper and the next too, hardened by the fifth, meeting contempt with contempt. When she had finished, she folded the list of numbers into four, tucked it in her handbag and pressed the button to retrieve unused coins. It had cost her seven pounds and taken her twenty-three minutes.

Twenty-three minutes and twenty-eight years, she said to herself, walking away, imagining him opening the paper, reading the ad, reading it again, staring at it until his wife asked what was the matter, he looked like he'd seen a ghost and he said he had, or thought of saying this, instead merely folding up the paper, cutting out the ad later, secretly, hiding it in his wallet.

Would he reply immediately or would he wait? Would he dash off an answer or agonise over the right words? What would he say? What did she want him to say?

Inside the car she pulled down the sun visor to examine herself in the mirror. The face she saw looked healthy, still tanned by the Turkish sun, attractive but not spectacularly so, the hair still golden although duller than it had been once, more mousy – the face of an ordinary, middle-aged woman. This was the face everyone else saw. Her friends. Her children. Her husband. Particularly her husband. He thought she had been scared, drunk, not herself. Like the policeman, like her father, like everyone else, he was revolted, also excited, by the thought

of her having sex with a stranger. How could she tell him that
in that moment, in that act, she had been more true to herself
than she had ever been, before or since? No, no. Better to go
on as they were, separately together, sharing everything except
their loneliness. Maybe that was as much as one could expect.

49 ∫

'Excuse me . . . excuse me . . . do you know where the Italian beginners' class is?'

The figure she had addressed, a thin lanky man in a cheap suit, turned and eyed her wearily as if she were the tenth person to ask him this question.

'Up the stairs. Turn left. Go right to the bottom. Then turn left again. It's the third door on your right.'

Helen thanked him and made her way up the stairs, nervously registering the oil paintings crowded thickly on the walls, the ornate carving on the banisters.

There were twelve people in the room when she walked in, seven women and five men. One of the women, small and neat with black bobbed hair, glossy as a wet jackdaw, glanced up.

'Mrs Dart?'

Helen nodded.

'Good. We're all here then. Find yourself a seat.'

Helen slid unobtrusively on to the nearest chair while the jackdaw woman made her way to the front of the room and introduced herself. Her name was Maddalena Cox, she said, and she was going to be teaching them over the next twelve weeks. They would be using the BBC course *Buongiorno Italia* mostly, although they would dip in and out of other books. As stated on the information sheet they should all have received, the aim of the course was to enable them to use simple colloquial Italian in everyday situations, for example, ordering a meal, shopping, or asking directions. First, though, to break the ice and help people to get to know one another a bit, she'd like them all to stand up and say a little bit about themselves –

what their name was, what they did, and why they wanted to learn Italian.

'I'll start with myself,' she said, leaning back against her desk, the sleeves of her top, an angora wool crossover in grey blue, pushed up to reveal thin, girlish arms. 'I came to England fourteen years ago and met my husband in York Minster. We both wanted the last postcard of the famous Rose window.'

She paused.

'I got it.'

The woman next to Helen laughed.

'We were married two years later much to both our parents' relief – I think they were worried mainly about the phone bills – and came to Bristol five years ago when my husband got a job here in the history department. We have two children. Our son, Leonardo – Leo for short – is nine. Our daughter, Frederica – Freddy for short – is seven. I started teaching four years ago, mainly because I was worried I was starting to forget my Italian vocabulary. In my spare time, I make stained-glass hangings which I sell at craft markets. And, by the way, please call me Maddy. Maddalena is a bit of a mouthful, even for Italians.'

She paused again.

'That's enough about me. Let's hear about you. Mr Piper? Would you like to start?'

She nodded in the direction of one of the men sitting at the back of the room, a good-looking young man in a purple rugby shirt. He stood up confidently.

His story was similar to hers, he said. His girlfriend, Iria, was Italian and they were planning to spend their summer holiday with her family in Vicenza. Last time they had gone, she had had to translate everything for him. This time, he wanted to get by on his own. He was a copywriter, he added, and his name was Finn.

Two women followed. Then another of the men. Then a third woman. As she listened, Helen could feel herself shrinking into herself. They all sounded so much more exciting than her, she thought, so much more interesting and dynamic.

'Mrs Dart? How about you?'

Helen swallowed nervously and stood up.

'My name is Helen Dart and I'm married with two grown-up

children. My son is an English lecturer, specialising in etymology. He is married with a little girl, Matty, my first grandchild. My daughter, Una, has just left university and . . . well, she's not doing anything much at the moment. I think she knows what she doesn't want to do but not what she does want to do . . .'

Several of the other older women laughed sympathetically as if they had sons and daughters similarly afflicted.

'As for me, I work part-time at an estate agent's and help run a talking newspaper for the blind in my spare time. I want to learn Italian because . . . because, well, I suppose it was my husband who started it. He took early retirement last autumn and we spent about three months travelling around Europe in a camper van. Since we've come back, he's taken up flying which . . . which is something he's always wanted to do. And this made me start thinking about the things I've always wanted to do, one of which is to learn Italian. And I thought, well, I don't need to retire in order to do it. I can just do it. And so I am.'

She sat down, her heart thumping, eyes fixed on the table in front of her. And the other thing I've always wanted to do is find out who the father of my son is, she added silently. And I'm doing that too. Or at least trying to. And she glanced at her bag where the list of newspaper numbers lay, tucked between a book of second-class stamps and her council leisure card – a scrap of paper, potential dynamite.

It took ten minutes for her pulse to return to normal and by that time they had already started chapter one – how to ask for something.

'I'll just play you that scene again,' said Maddy, pressing the rewind button on her tape recorder. 'There. Did you hear how the owner of the bar said *"prego"* when the girl thanked him. *"Prego"* is a word you'll hear frequently in Italy. It means "that's all right" or "not at all" and it's the standard response to *"grazie"*, particularly from people serving in shops or restaurants. Now, let's listen to the next scene, recorded at the zoo in Stresa near Lake Maggiore.'

Helen raised her eyes from her book and looked furtively round the room. Three of the men were too young. Of the remaining two, one was too tall. The other . . . well, the other was about the right age and height. And the right build. And he was wearing a tweed jacket. She peered more closely, trying to decide whether his hair had been black or brown, his skin once white. As she did, he looked up and saw her staring at him. She turned hastily away.

She found the lesson fun and not as difficult as she had expected. Maddy was a good teacher, quick to spot if anyone looked confused.

'Right. That's all for today,' said Maddy, snapping her book closed. 'I'd like you to do the exercises at the end of this chapter before you come next week and also read through the next chapter. Are there any questions? No? Well, thank you all very much for coming and I look forward to seeing you next week.'

There was a scraping sound as people stood up and drew back their chairs. Helen bent down to put her books away.

'Excuse me?'

She straightened up, feeling someone touch her lightly on the arm.

It was the man in the tweed jacket.

'Your face . . . it looks familiar. Were you . . . did we . . . ?'

50

'Well, this is nice, isn't it? Sunday lunch *en famille*,' said Geoff, helping himself to parsnips.

'Do you know, I can't remember the last time I had a proper roast with all the trimmings,' he went on. '"Heat and serve" is about as far as I go in the culinary department.'

He made it sound as though they were indulging in some quaint rural tradition, thought Una, jabbing savagely at the potatoes with her fork.

'There should be a serving spoon somewhere, darling. Yes, there. Look!' said her mother.

Una glowered.

Geoff picked up his knife and fork and started to eat, apparently unaware that Philip, who had been carving, had not yet helped himself to vegetables.

'Umm! Delicious! What is it – pork?'

'No . . . er, lamb. Leg of lamb, actually. The stuffing's apricot,' said Helen.

Una raised her eyebrows. Surely he could tell the difference between pork and lamb. She waited for him to pass the gravy to her father then, when he did not, leant across him to pass it herself. She felt at once critical and protective towards him, her loyalties divided, sensing her parents' unspoken questions, their desire to know more about him, to find out what sort of a man he was, whether he was a fit partner for their daughter. This was the first time she had invited him to Sunday lunch and, so far, it was not going well. First, he had arrived late, a cause of much irritation to her mother who planned roast dinners with military precision, even writing out a timetable in advance. Then he had made an unflattering remark about her father's choice of wine. And now he had started to eat before everyone else.

'Philip's taken up flying,' said Helen brightly. 'Has Una told you? He's training to get a private pilot's licence.'

'No. Really! How interesting. No, she hasn't. She hasn't said anything.'

Una mumbled something, her mouth full. She was sure she had mentioned it. But she wasn't going to contradict him. Not now.

'Yes, he's already had quite a few lessons. Haven't you?' said Helen, turning to Philip.

'Fifty hours' worth,' he said. 'It will be my fifty-first tomorrow.'

'Fifty! I didn't know you'd had that many. You only started a few weeks ago.'

'Nine, actually,' he corrected her. 'Even so, I've been surprised myself at how quickly it's gone. It's because the weather's been so good. Some days I've fitted in two or three hours. That soon adds up.'

'Do you have to take exams?' asked Una.

Philip explained that there were three practical exams – the navigational flight test, the cross-country flight which involved landing at two other airfields, one at least fifty miles away, and finally the general flight test. If you passed that, you got your licence, he said.

'And when are you taking that? The general flight test?' asked Una.

'Well . . . actually . . . I'm . . . I'm . . . I'm taking it tomorrow.'

'Tomorrow!' exclaimed Helen. 'You're taking your final exam tomorrow? You never said!'

'No . . . well . . . I didn't want everyone to start getting anxious on my behalf.'

He leant across to touch Helen's hand but she withdrew it sharply, too hurt to be mollified.

'Anyhow, I have said now.'

'Only because Una asked,' said Helen.

'I was going to tell you. Of course I was,' he insisted, wondering if he would have done if it had not come out like this.

Geoff poured himself another glass of wine. That was his third, thought Helen. She hoped he wasn't intending to drive anywhere afterwards. At least not with her daughter in the car.

'I think it takes quite a few people that way,' said Geoff, leaning back expansively, his knife and fork splayed wide across his plate.

'What does?' said Una, irritated by the way he was resting one arm along the back of her chair.

'Retirement. I watched a programme about it not long ago. Apparently, it's quite normal to do something totally out of character at first. To take up some new hobby, something you've never shown any interest in before. It's supposed to be like an act of rebellion – a way of marking the transition. But apparently it soon passes. It's like a teenage craze. I wouldn't worry,' he said, turning towards Helen, 'he'll soon go back to digging the garden or doing the crossword or whatever he did before.'

'I'm not worrying,' she said tartly. 'And anyhow, it's not a craze. Philip's very serious about it.'

'Oh yes, I'm sure he is. Don't get me wrong. It's just that it can be a difficult time. The end of some things, the start of others. I know my mother went . . . well, to be frank, a bit peculiar for a while. Not that I'm suggesting you have,' he added, turning to his host.

'I'm glad to hear it,' said Philip.

'How do you mean "peculiar"?' asked Una.

'Well, as soon as she'd retired, she went and worked in a dogs' refuge – even though she didn't like dogs.'

'Dad didn't like flying,' mused Una, half-heartedly chasing a piece of meat around her plate with her fork then giving up. 'At least that's what he always said.'

Philip glanced at her, his face a deliberate blank. Did she suspect anything? Did she think his story – that he had taken up flying to confront one of his oldest fears – too outlandish to be true, even though it was true, in a way.

She grinned back.

'Don't you remember that time we drove all the way to Spain? Martin was always complaining that I took up more than half the back seat. He even measured it once, don't you remember, and drew a line down it in red felt tip. You were ever so angry when you found out. I think it was a company car.'

'Yes, I do remember something like that.'

No, it was OK. She didn't suspect anything. Otherwise, he'd have seen it on her face. She'd never been able to lie, never been able to hide anything, her heart always open, her feelings exposed, not like Martin. He'd been the secretive one, the one who had brooded, tight-lipped, sulking. She had shouted, slammed doors, thrown things even. But it had been short-lived. A brief flare of anger like the light from a falling star. Then she had been Una again. Their sunny girl, coming back from the park one day aged about seven, stripping off her tracksuit bottoms, wet from the slide, clambering on top of him where he sat, hot and stuffy among the Sunday papers. Her skin had been cold and damp, her breath fresh as dew, her hair wild – tangled gold.

'Daddy,' she had said, wrapping her arms tightly round his neck, forcing him to put down the paper. 'Daddy, you are the best daddy in the whole wide world.' Then she had run off, skipping into the kitchen to help Helen roll dough.

He looked round. Everyone had finished except for Una, who barely seemed to have started, who was pushing her food to one side of the plate now, putting down her knife and fork. What was the matter with her? She'd always had such a hearty appetite, had never been tiresome about food like the daughters of some of their friends. She'd always tried everything, even oysters, shutting her eyes, downing them in one, squealing at the sudden rush of sea in her mouth.

'More meat anyone?' he asked, picking up the carving knife and fork, remembering his father suddenly, lecturing him in the dining room, the curtains half-drawn against the glare of the sun, his bare legs sticking to the leather-backed chairs. 'No, not like that. It's not an axe. It's a knife. Gently! Here. Give it to me.' He had been clumsy on purpose, knowing that it distressed his father, that he took a pride in his carving, that he wanted to pass on his skill to his son. How obstinate he had been, refusing to accept this gift, to learn how to carve a joint of beef so that the slices fell away from the knife, curling up like pink leaves in autumn, see-through thin.

Geoff held out his plate.

'Just a little bit. It's sheer gluttony . . . I'm not hungry. But it's too good to refuse.'

Helen pursed her lips. She had been hoping to make shepherd's pie for supper the next day. Now, there wouldn't be enough. She turned to Una and noticed her plate.

'Aren't you hungry?'

'No. Sorry. Not very.'

She looked tired, thought Helen. Tired and washed-out, her hair dull, her skin blotchy and pale.

'Were you up late last night?'

'Yes. Sinead phoned. She woke me up.'

'Really? How is she? How's she getting on?'

'Fine. She's got a job at that college I was telling you about.'

'The one for school drop-outs?'

'Yes. Something like that. She's also working a couple of days at a cabinet maker's. You know she used to do that sometimes over here?'

'No.'

'No, well she did. I think she's quite good at it. She even made her own bed. Carved the headboard and everything.'

'And is she happy? Is she liking it?'

'I think so. It's hard to tell. She's never very communicative. But yes, she sounds happy.'

'Do give her my love, won't you, the next time you speak? I was always very fond of her.'

'Yes. OK.'

And Una began to collect up the empty plates, indicating she did not wish to talk about Sinead any more.

She stacked the plates on top of the dishwasher and wiped the gravy off her fingers with a piece of kitchen paper ripped from the roll hanging on the wall. Her mother was so well organised, she thought, seeing her own kitchen cupboards, a muddle of spilt flour and broken spaghetti. It never even occurred to her to buy kitchen paper.

'Can I take anything in?' she asked.

'Just the cream,' said her mother. 'Pour it into a jug, will you?'

Helen unhooked the oven gloves and took the lemon meringue pie out of the oven. She had spent all morning in the kitchen, determined that the roast potatoes would be crunchy, the meringue perfectly risen. Now she wished she hadn't made so much effort. He didn't deserve it. And she saw his arm again, lolling possessively along the back of Una's chair, as if she were just so much meat to be sucked and chewed.

'Pudding too!' exclaimed Geoff when she set the pie down on the table. 'What a treat!' And he beamed round the table, confident he was making a good impression because that was what girlfriends' mothers liked – compliments about their cooking. It had always worked before.

'What are you two going to do on this glorious afternoon?' asked Philip, sensing his wife's growing hostility, anxious to prevent any open outbreak.

Una glanced at Geoff. He had not said anything but she had assumed that they would spend the afternoon together, perhaps drive out to Clevedon and walk along the coast path, go back to his flat afterwards and make love. She did not want to do this. She did not particularly want to do anything. But she assumed that they would because he would expect it. And so she was surprised, surprised and also put out, when she heard him say that actually he had to work, it was a pity when it was such a lovely day but there it was, it couldn't be helped.

'I'm sorry,' he said, seeing the look on her face. 'I would have said earlier only I didn't know whether Liz would be able to find someone to look after Ellie.'

'Liz?'

'Yes. We're thinking about introducing a new course – something more vocational. Pete – you know, the head of our department – he's asked us to come up with a formal structure so that he can put it to the principal.'

'What are you going to do, darling?' asked her mother. 'Only Dad and I thought we might drive out to Westonbirt Arboretum if you'd like to come. It should be beautiful now – everything bursting into leaf . . .'

Una said thanks but she needed to rewrite her CV. There were a couple of jobs she wanted to apply for, she added, pushing back her chair and picking up the remains of the lemon meringue pie.

They drank coffee and tea in the sitting room, Geoff examining the pictures on the wall before sitting down, smiling secretly at himself. As if making a private joke about their lack of taste, thought Helen. No doubt he would regale his friends later.

Geoff left first, saying that Liz's ex-husband had agreed to look after their daughter Ellie only for two hours.

'I'll ring you later. OK?' he said, kissing Una lightly on her left cheek. She nodded, miserable now at the prospect of spending the afternoon on her own.

They walked back into the kitchen.

'Well, he seemed nice enough,' said Philip, trying to be jovial, looking from his wife to his daughter.

'Oh, don't start!' said Una wearily. And she turned and began to load the dishwasher. Her parents exchanged glances above her head but said nothing.

They cleared away the rest of the lunch in virtual silence, Helen washing, Philip drying, Una clearing the table. The sideboard had been reorganised, she found, when she went to put away the placemats. And she felt a lurch of dismay. She no longer belonged, no longer even knew where things went.

On impulse, she went upstairs and looked into her old room. Yes, it was as she'd thought. Everything had been changed round. The bed in a different position entirely.

'The Coopers did that,' said her mother, startling her, coming up right behind her. 'I can change it back if you like.'

'No. It's OK. Don't bother. There's no point,' said Una.

They walked downstairs again together and Una put on her coat.

'Thanks for the lunch. It was lovely. Really nice.'

'Don't you want Dad to run you back? It would only take him a minute.'

'No, I'd prefer to walk. I could do with the exercise. And it's good to see the sun again.'

Helen and Philip watched her walk slowly down the path.

'You didn't like him, did you?' said Philip.

'No, well, it's hardly surprising, is it?' said Helen with uncharacteristic venom. 'Look at her!'

'What do you mean?'

She turned to face him, her eyes blazing.

'She used to be so vital. Like one of those trick birthday candles. You know, the ones that relight themselves after you've blown them out. She was unquenchable. Now look at her. She's got about as much spark as a wet sponge. He's sucked all the life out of her, drained her dry.'

'We don't know that . . .' Philip started to protest.

'We jolly well do,' said Helen. 'If it's not him, then what is it? He's going out with her, isn't he?'

'Yes, but . . .'

'But nothing. He's not making her happy. That's all there is to it. Just look at her. Look at the way she's walking. So slow and heavy. She never used to walk. She used to run, to bounce, swing, skip, but walk, no, she never walked. Don't you remember that time we booked a holiday flat in Cornwall? How the people underneath us knocked on our door one morning to complain about the noise of her feet on the floorboards. "Can't you teach her to walk?" they asked. Don't you remember that? How you suggested that maybe they'd like to give her a few lessons if they thought it was so easy.'

'Yes,' said Philip, smiling at the memory. The smile faded as he watched Una walk away. Helen was right. She had changed, slipped away while they weren't looking, become different.

'Maybe she's just grown up. She's been through a lot these last six months. Splitting up with Rob, then us leaving, her first job, Martin and Teresa, then Geoff and the strike and everything.'

'I suppose so,' said Helen.

'It's OK. She'll bounce back. That's how she is. Us. The best and worst of us,' said Philip.

'Were you really going to tell me about your exam?'

'Of course I was. I didn't know myself until Friday.'

He glanced at her face and was surprised to see tears, or what looked like tears, glistening in the corner of her eyes.

'I'm sorry. I didn't mean to upset you.'

And he put an arm round her shoulder and drew her close.

Round the corner, out of sight, Una began to quicken her step, to walk a bit faster, then a bit more and a bit more. She had to shake out of this, she thought, this muddle of doubt and introspection. So what if she didn't have a job, if her best friend had emigrated, if Geoff didn't love her? So what? She was still alive, wasn't she, still able to see and hear, to rejoice in this sudden leap into spring, the forsythia all out, a brave splash of yellow? She broke into a run, darting out in front of a car, forcing the driver to brake suddenly, to press down on his horn. She waved, smiling an apology. Yes, it was good to run again.

51

'Three for you,' said Philip, coming in from the hallway and dumping a pile of letters on the table next to her plate.

Helen examined them. One was a clothing catalogue. The second a postcard from a former colleague on holiday in the Scilly Isles, the third a large brown envelope with a London postmark. She read the postcard, then opened the clothing catalogue, making sure that it covered the brown envelope, remarking that she needed a new swimming costume, her old one had gone all baggy at the front.

'It's funny how the forties-style swimsuit has come back into fashion. Look!' she said, pointing at a picture of a model sporting the kind of costume she remembered her mother wearing on a childhood holiday in Cornwall.

'What? Oh, yes. Yes. Still, they say everything comes back into fashion if you wait long enough. Look at flares. Even Una was wearing some yesterday and do you remember how she used to snigger at that picture of us on holiday in Norfolk where you're wearing those flowered flares. Do you remember?'

'Yes, I remember.'

She remembered the holiday in particular. It had been their first holiday together, the first they had been able to afford, their honeymoon they had called it. They had rented a cottage with a hammock in the garden, a babysitter down the road and Scrabble, backgammon and cribbage in a cupboard under the stairs. There was a tin of scones waiting for them when they arrived, the fire neatly laid. It had been May, the hedges thick with cow parsley, bluebells in the woods and Philip had been relaxed, more relaxed than she had ever known him. She had thought it was because they were on holiday, because he had finally got a job, finally come to terms with the loss of his eye. And then, one day, cycling along, the wind in their faces, the fields flat and straight all around them, he had remarked on the sky, how big it was here, all sky and earth and water, how it was like being in with God at the creation, rolling back the waters and calling the dry land earth.

He had not said it was like flying but she had known that was what he was thinking and had realised then, the seat of the bicycle hard between her thighs, the scent of wild garlic in her nostrils, how much it hurt him not to fly, how much it would always hurt him.

'Are you sure you don't want me to drive you in? I don't mind. Honestly. I haven't got anything planned for today.'

'No, really. I'd prefer it if you didn't come. I don't think I could bear it knowing you were watching. I think it's better if I go on my own.'

'But you will phone me, won't you? You will let me know immediately.'

'Yes,' promised Philip, starting to gather up their cereal bowls. 'Yes, I'll do that.'

'It's only a formality, isn't it? You said yourself how it had all come back, how little you'd forgotten.'

'That doesn't mean I'll pass. It's not just a test of how well I can fly. It's also a test of my ability to stay in control in an emergency. They ask you all sorts of questions. I might panic and say something silly. I don't know. I don't want to be complacent.'

He walked over to the sink.

'I think I'll do a bit of gardening before I go,' he said, looking out of the window. 'See how those bulbs I planted are coming on.'

'What time is the exam?'

'Half eleven. I'll leave at about half ten. I want to give myself plenty of time.'

She waited until he had changed into his gardening clothes, pretending to be absorbed in her catalogue, the new scoopnecked ribbed T-shirt in lapis, vanilla, parsley and tint of pink. Then, when the door had clicked firmly shut and he had wandered, whistling, over the lawn to the bottom of the garden, inspecting the magnolia on his way, she slid the brown envelope out from under the catalogue and ripped it open. It was as she had thought. The first of the replies. Five envelopes, all marked with one of the box numbers she had been assigned. She stood up and walked over to the window. It was OK. Philip was squatting at the far end, weeding. She returned to the table and opened the first envelope. It contained one piece of paper, A4, folded in three. She unfolded it. Someone had cut out letters from newspaper headlines to make a word. The same word covered the page. Cunt. That was the word. Over and over again. Lines and lines of it. She stared at it, shocked. Then, quickly, she refolded the paper and put it back in the envelope. The second envelope contained a two-page letter, typed, single-spaced, exhorting her to turn to God, to listen to her inner voice and be washed clean. It quoted extensively from the Bible, mainly passages concerning Jesus' forgiveness of sinners, Mary Magdalene in particular. The third was a sheet ripped from a spiral-bound notebook. 'I want to fuck you dry, tie you up, leave you, come back, do it again, you fucking whore!' Helen swallowed, then scrunched the paper into a ball, hearing the thump of her heart. The remaining two were both in this vein. All three were well written but then that was hardly surprising, she thought. After all, they were broadsheet readers. She put her hand back in the large brown envelope in case there was something else, something she had missed. Then she peered inside. No. Nothing. She stood up then, took the envelopes, the five small ones and the large brown one, and put them in the rubbish bin, pushing them deep down, under last night's potato and carrot peelings, this morning's teabags and coffee grains, deep deep down. Then she washed her hands, holding them under the cold water tap, feeling them turn numb. She had not expected this. She had expected to get no replies, to be sent a crisp note informing her that there had been no answers to her advert, perhaps she would like to run it again, they could offer her a reduced rate. But this. No. She had not expected this. She ought to have known better. Thinking about it now, she realised she should have expected it. An advert like that. It was ready-made for cranks and perverts.

Outside, in the garden, Philip flung a worm clear of the blade of his trowel. There was a robin now in the magnolia, he saw, eyeing him brightly, head on one side. Next door Mr Chandler had started up his lawnmower. He was renowned for his lawn, was even said by some to go across it on all fours, ruler in one hand, nail scissors in the other. Philip smiled. Spring had come as it always did, taking him by surprise, stealing in during the night, a rush of leaf and bud. He picked up a clod of earth and crumbled it between his fingers, feeling the rich moist stickiness. The bulbs he had planted were coming up, sharp spikes of green growth, sky-bent. He sat back on his heels and looked around. It never failed to delight. That was the surprising thing, he thought. Even though it came every year, it was always new. Years ago, hundreds of years ago, men had been talking and writing about spring. They still did today and would do, as long as men were men and earth, earth.

> 'Rise up, my love, my fair one, and come away.
> For, lo, the winter is past,
> The rain is over and gone;
> The flowers appear on the earth;
> The time of singing is come,
> And the voice of the turtle is heard in our land;
> The fig tree putteth forth her green figs,
> And the vines in blossom give forth their fragrance.
> Arise, my love, my fair one, and come away.'

He felt the sun warm on the back of his neck and the earth stirring gently all around him, stretching like a waking child, limbs still bound with sleep.

'Philip, Philip, it's quarter past. Do you want another drink before you go,' called Helen.

He plunged his hands one more time into the soil then stood up, recharged, ready to go now, wanting to be up there, up in the sky, in those deep blue arms. Turn this way. Yes. And that way. Yes. Back again. Whatever you say. A kite on strings.

'No. No thanks. I'd better hurry,' he said, gathering up his tools and walking back to the house.

He changed hurriedly, scrubbing his nails in the bathroom but failing to remove all the dirt, leaving it there, a living talisman.

'You will phone me, won't you? I'll be waiting. I won't go out, not even into the garden,' said Helen.

He jangled the car keys loudly in his pocket.

'Yes, yes,' he promised and kissed her lightly on the forehead – an abstracted, sexless kiss.

And then he was gone, accelerating with unnecessary speed to the end of the road, causing Mrs Chandler next door to tut-tut from the window of her spare bedroom and remark to herself that they'd never been the same, not since they'd come back from that trip, such a pity it was. And they'd still got that dreadful purple caravan thing. Such an eyesore. It made her feel ill just to look at it.

Helen washed up the breakfast dishes then walked round the house and opened all the windows wide, waving to Mr Chandler who had stopped to have a break, teabag tea in a cup, real bone china, and a biscuit, digestive probably. Mrs Chandler was not the kind of woman to experiment.

There was a patch of sunlight on their bed, round, like the mark left by a sleeping cat. She felt it, first with her fingers, then with her cheeks. First, there had been the disappointment about the man in the tweed jacket at her Italian class who, it turned out, had been a teacher at Una's junior school. And now this. There was nothing else for it. She would have to tell Martin. Have to tell him she didn't know who his father was. That she would never know. In her mind, she saw Philip shaking hands with his examiner, making a joke, laughing about something they had both heard on the radio that morning. It wasn't fair, she thought, smacking the pillows flat. His wish would come true, the wish he'd made in the Sancta Sophia. It was already true. He was flying. Doing what he'd always wanted to do. But her wish wouldn't come true. It couldn't. Not ever.

'It's Philip, isn't it?'
'Yes.'
'Bill Anstey.'
The two men shook hands.
'I've heard about you. Ex-RAF, aren't you?'

*　　*　　*

She'd clean the stairs. Wash down the paintwork. Brush the carpet. That would take her mind off it. Hard physical work.

'It's just like a driving test really. The aim is to make sure you're proficient in all the standard manoeuvres and can handle an emergency. When did you say you were in the RAF?'

Philip told him.

'No, that was before me. I just wondered. When I first saw you I thought I recognised you from somewhere.'

No, she wouldn't clean the stairs. She'd sort out her wardrobe instead. It was in a terrible state. Yesterday, she hadn't even been able to find a hanger for the blouses she'd ironed. She'd have to be ruthless, to make herself give away clothes she hadn't worn for more than a year. It was a good day for spring-cleaning. That would make her feel better.

'Are you ready?'

'Yes.'

'Come on, then. Let's go. There's no point hanging around. Not on a beautiful day like this.'

No, she couldn't face that. All those choices. Holding up her old short-sleeved polo shirt, once blue, now faded to a soft indigo violet, and deciding, probably for about the fourth time in the last ten years, that she couldn't bear to throw it away, not yet, and anyhow it was useful for painting, or would be, if she did any.

'If you could take us up north-east of the city. Up towards the Severn.'

Philip obeyed.

'I'd like you to circle now, yawing to the left, maintaining the same height.'

It was starting to cloud over now, the wind getting up. It was funny how quickly that could happen. Like a tide at sea. The water calm one minute then suddenly choppy, waves coming from all directions.

She needed to do something simple. Something simple and

straightforward. Something that didn't require any thought, that was mechanical, a matter of muscle. The windows. That's what she'd do. She'd clean the windows. And she went downstairs, put on a pair of rubber gloves and found a clean cloth.

'In a few minutes, when I say "now" I want you to demonstrate a stall and then recover from the stall on my command.'
'OK.'
Philip tightened his hands on the control column but only slightly. It was going well. So far, he hadn't put a foot wrong. Or a hand. Or an eye. The eye, he corrected himself.
'Now!'

That was better. Much better. She hadn't realised how dirty they'd become. In fact, now she thought of it, they probably hadn't been cleaned since before Christmas. Certainly, she hadn't cleaned them since coming back. And Mrs Cooper had probably had enough to do, what with three young children.

'What would you do if the engine stopped? . . . And if there was a fire? A fire in the engine? What about then? . . . And how about an electrical failure? What would you do then? . . . And if the radio failed? . . . And if you discovered you hadn't got enough fuel to reach the nearest airfield?'

She stood back to survey the results of her work in the kitchen. Yes. They were gleaming now. Not a smear or smudge in sight. Even Mrs Chandler wouldn't be able to fault them. She glanced at her watch. It would be almost over. Maybe it already was. He might be coming down now, at this very moment, pushing forwards on the controls, lowering the nose, feet ready on the pedals.

'Take us back now. Any way you like. I think we've covered enough ground. Or rather sky.'
And he laughed at his own joke.

She'd do the sitting room next. She didn't want to do the bedrooms in case the phone rang and she didn't hear it. Not

that that was likely. It had a loud ring. But even so. She didn't
want to chance it.

Philip undid his seat belt. Would he tell him here, now, sitting
on the airfield or wait until they were inside?
    'Right. We'll go inside. Debrief over a cup of coffee. That's
what I normally do.'

Helen dipped the cloth into the bucket, swished it around and
then squeezed it out. Good old-fashioned soap and water. There
was nothing like it. Certainly not those silly, spray-on products
most people used nowadays. Was that . . . it sounded like it . . .
yes it was, it was the phone! She scrambled off the chair she had
been standing on and ran into the hallway, fumbling with the
rubber gloves.
    'It's me.'
    'Well? Go on. Tell me.'
    'I've passed! Helen, I've passed! I've passed, I've passed!'
    'Yes! I knew it . . . I knew it . . . oh, Philip, that's wonder-
ful . . . that's fantastic . . . oh, I am pleased . . . oh, I'm so
pleased.'
    'I thought maybe Cornwall first. And then maybe Devon. It's
a long while since we've been there. All those high hedges.
And then, maybe, in the summer, in June maybe, we could
go to France. Brittany perhaps or Normandy. What do you
think?'
    'Yes, yes. I don't mind. Anywhere.'
    'I can't wait to fly you somewhere. I can't wait for you to
see what it's like. It's so different from being in a big plane. So
completely different.'
    'As long as I'm allowed to close my eyes when we take off. I
don't mind it when we're up there or even when we land. It's
just the take-off I find scary.'
    'I want you to get changed. I'm going to take you out to lunch.
Lawson's. I'll see if we can get a table there. OK? I won't be long.
I'm coming straight back.'
    Helen put down the receiver and slumped into the chair by
the side of the table. She had wanted him to pass. Of course she
had. She knew how important it was to him. And yet part

of her hadn't, she realised. She had wanted him to fail. To be down here with her. Earthbound. Heavy. Hurting.

The big picture. Half land, half sky. A balance. He had got it again. It had taken him a long time but he had found it now. He wouldn't lose it again, thought Philip.

52 ∫

She slept with him and woke with him. Even though she was not there, she was always there, like the Mary in John Clare's poem, filling his arms.

Was he mad, thought Rob? Should he go and see his doctor, explain that something was troubling him, a girl to be precise, his old girlfriend? Una was the name. He could not stop thinking of her.

He saw her in the morning, he saw her at night. He saw her in a laugh, a glimpse of long hair, the sight of someone running. He saw her everywhere.

He had tried to lead his mind elsewhere, to divert it like a river but it always came back, flooding the banks of his self-control, his sandbags of work and work and more work until they told him to go home, even Ewen the news editor, he would be no good to anyone if he carried on like this.

He had tried to blot her out, to fill his mind with other things, to leave it no time or space or energy with which to think of her but she always found a chink, a crack in the join, and burst through. She was there in the night when he woke sweating, the bedclothes too hot, the wail of a police siren lonely in the dark. She was there in the day admiring the blossom in his mother's garden, poking fun at the election leaflet dropped through his letterbox. She turned up at the most inopportune, unpredictable moments – when he was brushing his teeth, interviewing the Lord Mayor, searching for a cut toenail that had fallen on the floor. She was always with him.

Other people thought he was normal. That he thought of sex and sport and food and what was on telly that night. If they knew, if they could see inside, see how he clung to her like a bee to a flower, they would think he was obsessed, that he needed help. And maybe he did. Maybe he did. But he didn't want it. No. If he was frank, if he was honest, he didn't want to forget her. No, no. Even to say it, even to think it, was to cut and bleed. He didn't want to move on, to cast her off like yesterday's fashion. Better this sad, sorry, infected state than that raw nakedness.

Maybe he was mad. Probably he was. He didn't mind.

'Una.'

He said her name softly. Just to say it was to feel better.

His heart was a boomerang and she the starting point. There was nowhere else for it to go.

53 ∫

It was like a mother's lap or a slept-in bed, thought Philip. Warm, comfortable, familiar. An old tool worn smooth with handling. A park bench shiny with use, warm in the sun. Had flying always made him feel like this, he wondered? Whole, full, right – as if down there, down there on the ground, he was wrong, incomplete, a self-assembly toy with the instructions missing. Or was it only because it made up for the lack of an eye, because it allowed him to see what other people couldn't? If it had not been for the accident, would he have felt like this?

He shivered. It was cold up here, with only a shirt and underpants under his flying suit. He should have left his trousers and jumper on. He leant forward and switched on the heating.

'Why exactly did Dad decide to take up flying?' asked Una, digging her nail into the stem of a daisy and threading another stem through the hole.

Helen looked up from the book she was reading. It was Philip's first solo flight after obtaining his Private Pilot Licence and they had all come to watch. Afterwards they were going to picnic near Blagdon Lake and have an Easter egg hunt for Matty.

'I think it was leaving the bank. It made him see things in a different way. Gave him the time and space to sit back and look at his life. Decide what he wanted to do.'

'But why was he so frightened before? Had he had an accident or something? Had he been involved in a crash?'

Helen looked thoughtful.

'I think he'd set his mind against it. Decided that it wasn't for him. You know how obstinate he can be.'

*　　*　　*

He would just go up to Chepstow and back again, just so he could say he'd flown to Wales. He didn't want to keep them waiting too long. And he suddenly noticed Matty's wooden duck, lying on the floor in front of the passenger seat. She must have dropped it when she had climbed in to have a look at the controls. He hoped she wasn't missing it.

Helen glanced at her watch.

'Dad should be back soon. He said he'd only be about half an hour,' she said.

Una picked up the binoculars.

'And I'll huff and I'll puff and I'll blow your house down,' said Martin, putting on his best wolf voice as he read to Matty.

Teresa lay back on the red-and-green tartan rug and closed her eyes.

Only another five minutes or so now. Philip wondered if anyone was looking out for him with the binoculars. Una maybe. She had seemed more interested than Martin. But then she had always been the one who had played with cars, he remembered. The one who had said she wanted to be a train driver when she grew up. Martin had read. Read and done jigsaw puzzles and later, when he was allowed to, watched television.

He had been surprised when Helen, sitting in the cockpit beside him earlier, had said that she knew, that she had always known. Surprised and also slightly put out. Thinking about it now, he realised he had not wanted her to know. It had been his hurt. He had not wanted to share it. He had thought she would not understand it, feared that she would.

Helen wondered what Philip had been going to say when he had leaned over – before he had changed his mind and kissed her and said he loved her. He hadn't . . . no, surely not. She had never given him any hint of it, not like him, cycling in Norfolk, exclaiming about the sky, the size of it.

'There's one coming down now. It might be him,' said Una, standing up, walking forwards slightly to get a better view.

'No. Too big,' she said. 'Slightly different shape as well. There's another one behind it though. Just coming into view. Maybe that's him.'

What a day. Perfect it was. They'd be queuing all the way to the coast if it carried on like this, kids rowing in the back, are we there yet, Mum, bet I see the sea first. He was glad he wasn't down there with them. Not yet.

'That's him. That's Dad. He's coming down now,' said Una. Helen looked up expectantly. Martin continued to read. 'And he huffed and he puffed and he huffed and he puffed but the house of bricks did not fall down.'

Ouch! What was that? It felt as if someone had jabbed him in the thigh. Philip shifted uncomfortably in his seat. He was going all tingly. His legs, his arms, his neck, his face . . . it felt as if he was on fire . . . what on earth was it? He ripped open his flying suit. Something fell out, and rolled on to his lap. He looked down. It was a wasp. A wasp or a bee, still half asleep by the look of it. He'd been stung. He reached automatically for his anti-histamine tablets and then remembered. He hadn't got them. They were in his trousers. The trousers he had taken off so that he could put on his old flying suit.

'Does anyone else want a look?' asked Una, turning round to look at her family.
Helen squinted against the glare of the sun.
'No, it's OK, darling. You look.'
'No thanks,' murmured Teresa, not opening her eyes.
Martin, now starting the *Billy Goats Gruff*, shook his head.

The wasp – he thought it was a wasp – must have been in his flying suit. It must have climbed in while the suit was in the loft. They had suspected there might be a wasps' nest there. Helen had been going to ring the council pest control office. Very slowly, he shook the wasp off his lap on to the seat beside him, leant over, picked up Matty's duck and bashed it against the wasp, grinding it into the seat.

He was starting to feel funny, to come up in huge red swollen blotches. But it was OK. He could land in a few minutes. Surely he had that long. He would be all right once he had landed. They would take him to hospital, give him adrenaline and hydrocortisone. He would be OK. He glanced left and right. No. No one else about. He would have to do it without clearance from air traffic. There was no time. Besides, he was not sure he could manage that, to think about two things at once. He was starting to feel weak, his thoughts to stretch and slow. He pushed forward sharply on the control column and pulled back on the throttle. There was an angry crackle from air traffic as they asked him to make contact. What the hell did he think he was playing at? He did not reply.

'What's he doing? Why's he wobbling like that?'
   Helen looked up again.
   'What's the matter? What did you say?'
   'It's just Dad. He seems to be coming down funnily. He's tilting to one side,' said Una, not taking her eyes away from the binoculars.
   'He'll be OK. He's . . .' Helen bit her tongue. She had been about to say that he was an old hand, a fighter pilot, an experienced flier.
   'I think it often looks odd from the ground,' she added, just for something to say, not sure if this was true. 'He knows what he's doing.'
   Una frowned, not convinced.

It was OK. He was going to do it. Just two more minutes. That's all he needed. He felt dizzy. He had started to tremble. His whole body was shaking. In a moment he was going to faint. He could see it coming, coming to swallow him up like the black of a tunnel, to suck him into empty, dark nothingness. He felt unconnected, disassociated, his mind and body foreign, strangers speaking a different language.
   They would want to know what had happened, why he had crashed, because he was going to crash, he could see that now. He ought to say something. With an enormous effort, he forced

himself to open his mouth. His tongue felt heavy and slow, as if weighted down, coated with clay.

'Wa . . . wa . . . wassshp sh . . shtiiiing,' he said.

He ought to say goodbye to Helen and the children too. Just in case. They would be able to play back the tape. He was not sorry. He had done it. Lived as a tiger again, every moment sharp. He should tell them that. That was what he wanted to say.

But it was too late. He was going now, going. He was about to slump forward, the whole weight of his body against the controls. The nose would plunge down, the plane go into a dive. It would all be over in less than a minute. He could see what was going to happen, even as it happened, as air traffic alerted the airfield fire crew, called for an ambulance.

'No . . . no . . . Dad! Dad! Dad!'

Una began to run, screaming that he was going to crash, she had known it, seen something was wrong.

'What's the matter? Where's she going?'

Helen scrambled to her feet, dropping her book, letting it fall face down.

To her left, beyond the runway, the other side of the road to Gloucester, she saw a plane. It was coming down, nose first, heading straight towards the ground.

She put her hand to her mouth.

'Oh my God! No . . . no . . . please . . . no . . . no!'

Martin and Teresa jumped up. They too saw what she had seen.

Matty began to cry. Teresa took hold of her, turned her the other way, wrenched her head round, not letting her see, saying it was OK, it was OK, it was all OK.

Philip came round. It was only for a few seconds but it felt like an hour. In those seconds, he saw, as if from a long way away, as if he were another person, a spectator not the participant, that what he had thought would happen, was happening. He tried to right his body, to push it back, but nothing happened. Then he was going again, slipping away, the dark crowding in.

'Ti . . . ti . . . tigerr betterrrr,' he said.

His mouth fell slack.

Then, in the last of the light, summoning all his energy, squeezing the words out, he opened his mouth again.

'Hellllennn . . .'

Then he was gone, the plane rushing down, hurtling towards the ground, hitting it, smashing, cracked. Exploding in a great gasp of flame.

54

'Let me go, let me go!'

Una lashed out with her fists.

'I can't. It's not safe. It might explode again,' the man said, holding her firm.

'Please . . . my father . . . he's in there . . . it was his plane . . . please . . . please!'

She wrenched away, broke free, began to run towards the flames. But he caught her, grabbed hold of her wrist, pulled her back. She thrashed around, kicking and scratching and punching.

'You can't do anything. The fire crew are there. They'll get him out. It's OK. He'll be OK. They've called for an ambulance.'

She bit him, sinking her teeth deep in his arm, and he yelped with pain.

'You can't go!' he shouted. 'I'm telling you. You can't go. You'd only get hurt. They're doing all they can.'

Defeated, Una slumped to the ground.

'Dad . . . Dad . . . my Dad . . . that was my Dad . . . !' she sobbed, her whole body shaking.

The man sank to his knees and put a hand on her shoulder.

'They'll get him out. Don't worry. They know what they're doing.'

He lifted her and she let herself be lifted, limp in his hands, the fight all gone.

'Come on, now. There. There. It's OK. He'll be OK,' he said, the words coming out pat and easy, thinking 'He'll be lucky to come out of that alive, he'll need a miracle, he will. A miracle. That's what he'll need.'

55

'Careful . . . wait . . . his foot's stuck . . . don't pull!'

'I'm not.'

'There. It's free. Come on . . . quick . . . let's get him out of here!

They lifted Philip clear of the wreckage, smouldering now, the air acrid with the stench of burnt rubber.

'Nothing broken . . . at least nothing obvious . . . can you find a pulse?'

'No . . . nothing.'

They set to work, taking it in turns to give him mouth-to-mouth resuscitation.

Behind them, their colleagues continued to hose down the remains. One of the wings had snapped right off, the break raw and jagged, like a chicken bone wrenched in two. The cockpit, though, was strangely intact, the glass of one window not even smashed.

'Here's the ambulance . . . about bloody time!'

'Keep going! We've got to keep going . . . he might come back.'

The ambulance screeched to a halt beside them and the crew leapt out.

Beyond the runway, near the airport buildings, a small crowd had gathered, mainly staff but some passengers as well – three businessmen, a female research scientist due to address a conference in Paris the following day and a family of four bound for southern Spain, the children in shorts and white socks.

'I suppose all the flights will be delayed now while they clear the runway,' complained one of the businessmen, pulling out his mobile phone and punching in his home number to tell his wife he might not be home in time for tea after all.

Further away, on a layby, a woman in red sandals banged angrily on the roof of a car, chipping her nail varnish as she did so, speaking more irritably because of this.

'Come on, we'll be late. You know how Dad hates to be kept waiting!'

Her husband, who had climbed on to the roof to get a better view, got down reluctantly.

'An ambulance has arrived,' he said, opening the door to the driver's side. 'It looks like there was just the one person inside. Just the pilot. But I can't see properly. It's too far away.'

'It'll be on the telly tonight. You'll be able to see then,' said his wife, examining the chipped varnish.

'Yes, I suppose so,' said her husband.

And he started the engine and drove off.

56

'What happened?' asked the ambulance driver

'We don't know,' said one of the airfield fire crew. 'One minute he was coming in to land, everything perfectly normal, the next he'd gone into a dive. There was no mayday or anything. It was all over in minutes.'

'Heart attack, probably.'

'Yes. Either that or a stroke.'

'Who's that? What the hell do they think they're doing?'

They all watched as a small group broke free from the crowd of onlookers and began to walk towards them.

'It's John . . . John with the family by the looks of it . . . who's going to tell them?'

'I will,' said the senior paramedic, wiping his hands on the grass. He straightened up.

'Give them some space, will you?'

The others moved away, sheepish, curious.

Helen, Martin and Una walked arm in arm towards the ambulance, not looking at one another, not saying anything. There was no point running, thought Una. No point hurrying. He was dead. Dead as the sky was blue and the grass green. She would not be running again.

The man in front introduced them.

'This is Mrs Dart, the wife of the pilot, and his son and daughter.'

He too moved away.

'Can I see him please?' asked Helen.

The paramedic led them into the ambulance and drew back the sheet. Then he stood to one side.

His eye was empty, the left eye, the socket bare and gaping like a room cleared of furniture. There was a gash on his chin and another on his right cheek and some of his hair was singed. He looked blotchy as well, swollen, like the guy Una and Martin had made once and burnt on a bonfire at the bottom of the garden. It had failed to burn even when they had poked it with sticks, pushing it into the fire. Then, just when they had started to feel scared, to think it was mocking them, that it was somehow magic, it had burst into flames and toppled sideways, screaming, or at least so Una had imagined because she had run into the house and refused to come out, refused ever to make a guy again.

'Was he already dead when the plane crashed or did the crash kill him?' asked Helen.

'We don't know,' said the paramedic gently. 'We don't know that yet.'

'What about the rest of him? Is he . . . did he . . .'

'His hands were burnt and his knees as well. But not badly. His right foot was injured. You can look if you want.'

Martin looked away.

'No, it's OK. I just wondered.'

Helen stretched out a hand then let it fall.

'Do you think I could be alone with him for a moment?'

'Of course,' said the paramedic.

They all left the ambulance. First Martin, then the paramedic, then Una.

Alone, Helen stretched out a hand again and touched the empty, eyeless socket.

'I'm sorry,' she whispered, bending down and kissing it. 'I loved you, I did still love you,' she said, seeing the letters in the rubbish bin, the replies to her advertisement. 'It wasn't that I didn't love you any more . . . I just wanted to find out . . . to know who he was . . . that's all.'

Then the memories came rushing in, so strong and many they made her reel, and she put out a hand to steady herself. Philip saying it didn't matter when she told him she was pregnant, pregnant with another man's child; Philip dancing round the room after she had given birth to Una, crying for joy; Philip telling her he had found a job, he was going to work for a bank;

Philip coming first in the fathers' race at Martin's school; Philip running her a bath, massaging the back of her neck when she was tired; Philip buying the purple camper van; Philip in Istanbul on Christmas Day, saying he wanted to fly again, that was his wish; and most of all, oldest of all, Philip in hospital, reading to her, nursing her, wooing her with words.

'I am the rose of Sharon and the lily of the valleys. As the lily among thorns, so is my love among the daughters.

As the apple tree among the trees of the wood, so is my beloved among the sons. I sat down under his shadow with great delight and his fruit was sweet to my taste.

He brought me to the banqueting house and his banner over me was love.

Stay me with flagons, comfort me with apples: for I am sick of love.'

She bent down again, crying now, the tears falling fast and wet.

'I loved you . . . it was you I loved . . . you . . . you!'

57 ∫

Rob decided to make one more round of calls before buying some sandwiches. It had been a tedious morning. He was the only reporter on duty and there was nothing in the diary apart from a church flower festival and a children's Easter bonnet parade, neither of which, according to the news editor, required his presence. Instead, he had been left with a pile of press releases to knock into fillers, a task he despised. It wouldn't have been so bad if it had been raining but it was sunny, gloriously sunny, the blossom all out, windblown white and pink. He felt as if he was the only person working in Bristol.

He called the police first, hearing the same recorded message he had already listened to twice that morning. Then the fire service. Nothing doing again. Finally, the ambulance service.

'We had a call from a flying club near Bristol airport at eleven forty-five,' said the officer on duty.

Rob, who had been slumped sideways doodling on his notebook, jerked upright.

'Report that one of their planes had crashed off the runway. Only the pilot on board. That's all we know so far.'

Rob scribbled frantically.

'Why didn't the fire service know anything about this?' he asked.

'The airport have got their own fire crew,' explained the officer.

Rob thanked him and picked up the phone book to find the flying club's phone number.

Yes, there had been a crash, he was told. Yes, the pilot had been killed. No, they could not yet release his name. He was a man in his late fifties, that was all they could say. No, they did not yet know what had caused the crash. The Air Accident Investigation Board had been informed. It was up to them to establish the cause. They could not release any more details. Not yet.

Rob slammed down the receiver, left a message on the duty photographer's mobile phone, jammed his notebook in his jacket pocket and ran downstairs, both hunger and boredom forgotten. He was off, out, on the case, 'our man on the spot', Rob Perry. This was what he loved about journalism – the buzz, the excitement, never knowing what he would be doing from one moment to the next. He would get the front page splash tomorrow. It would be his fifth.

He spent more than three hours at the airport talking to whom-ever would talk to him – the businessman with the mobile phone; the family bound for southern Spain, the children grubby now, the girl's face sticky with tears and chocolate; other pilots at the club. The dead man had taken up flying only recently, said one. He had been a pleasant man, married, he thought, with grown-up children. Another, who gave his name as Alan, said the dead man had got his Private Pilot Licence only the week before. He had been at the club the day he passed. No, he didn't know him well. He'd only spoken to him once or twice. He was retired, he thought. He must have been. He'd been at the club nearly every other day during the last couple of months. Philip, he thought he was called. But he couldn't be sure. As he said, he hadn't known him well . . . Rob wasn't going to quote him, was he?

The woman kicked off her red sandals and padded across the room to switch on the television.

'A light aeroplane crashed this morning at Bristol airport kill-ing its pilot,' said the newscaster, glancing down at his notes.

'The plane, a two-seater Cessna 152 owned by the nearby Lulsgate Flying Club, was coming in to land at eleven forty when it plunged into a steep vertical dive crashing twenty yards west of the runway and exploding on impact.'

'Gary . . . quick . . . it's that crash . . . the one we saw this morning,' called the woman.

Her husband appeared at the door, a glass of whisky in his hand. He had always found his father-in-law trying.

'The pilot, the holder of a Private Pilot Licence, is said to be in his late fifties and married with grown-up children. The authorities have not yet released his name,' continued the newscaster. 'The crash caused long hold-ups at the airport with some flights delayed for up to four hours.'

There followed an interview with the mobile phone businessman, by then sounding extremely irate.

'Nice tie he's wearing, isn't it?' commented the woman, bending down to scratch her left calf. 'Look, it's got little Easter chicks all over it, isn't it sweet?'

'Humph!' grunted her husband, taking a good swig of the whisky.

If his father-in-law reminded him one more time that he had only four GCSEs including one in metalwork, he'd strangle him. He knew he would.

Rob found out the name of the pilot at half past seven that evening – Philip Dart. Immediately, he thought of Una's father, his stomach plunging into sudden horrified freefall. But no. No, it couldn't. It couldn't possibly be. Una's father was afraid of flying. There was no way it could be him. Besides, Dart was a common enough name. So was Philip. It was just a coincidence. Reassured, although still sick in the pit of his stomach, he went to the library, walking carefully, slowly, as though he had just come round from a general anaesthetic, did not yet trust his legs. He switched on the computer to see if there were any cuttings on a Philip Dart. No. It didn't look like it. There was a story about a Frank Dart, a local auctioneer and Rotary club chairman, also a story about a sixteen-year-old Ruth Dart, county netball player. He went over to the filing cabinets lined up in the centre of the room and opened the drawer marked 'Da – Em'. Not all the cuttings had been computerised yet. The older ones, the ones dating from before the 1970s, were still in paper form, yellowing bits of folded newspaper stuffed into brown envelopes, some so full they had split at the sides.

Daly . . . Damsell . . . Daniells . . . Dark . . . Darling . . . Dart

... here it was ... A.E. Dart, E.S. Dart and P. Dart. He checked to see if there was another P. Dart. No, just the one. He took the envelope over to the table by the window and shook out the contents. There were quite a few cuttings, all dating from more or less the same period by the look of them. He unfolded them, the paper stiff, creased only in the one place as if the envelope had not been opened since the stories had first been filed. He glanced at the headline on the top cutting – 'Stab hero loses eye' – then started to read. 'One of the RAF's most talented young fighter pilots may never fly again after a vicious knife attack.

'Philip Dart was stabbed in the eye when he rescued a young girl from a mystery attacker in Bristol last month.

'Now he's been told by doctors that he will never regain the use of his left eye and may lose the sight in his right eye as well.'

Rob frowned. It couldn't be the same Philip Dart. The pilots at the flying club had said the dead man had only just taken up flying. He looked at another cutting headlined 'Knife attack victim fights for life.'

'A young woman is today fighting for her life after a vicious knife attack in Bristol on Saturday night.

'The woman, who has not yet been identified, was stabbed in the chest and abdomen by an unknown attacker in Finch Street.

'She was rescued by RAF pilot Philip Dart who heard her screams for help. Mr Dart is also in hospital after receiving knife wounds to his left eye.'

Rob rifled through the remaining cuttings. One described the arrest of a certain Vic Hine in connection with the knife attack, others reported on the subsequent trial. He was about to put the cuttings away, convinced that the Philip Dart they featured was not the Philip Dart who had just been killed, when something caught his eye. It looked like a wedding report. Yes, it was. 'Stab victim marries rescuer – The girl who almost died after a vicious knife attack in Bristol in September has married the man who rescued her. Helen Summers and RAF pilot Philip Dart were married yesterday at St Mark's Church, Henleaze. The couple ...'

Rob smiled. So it had ended happily after all. He glanced at the picture. Then he looked more closely, his heart starting to pound. It couldn't be, it wasn't, it couldn't . . . but it was. The Helen in the picture was Una's mother. And if she was Una's mother then the man, the RAF pilot, was her father. Rob swallowed, seeing the future drop away like the edge of a cliff, the past roaring below, white and angry, greedy to have its say now, to smash dreams on rocks – all the usual modest human hopes lost in the mad churn of waves, no beach to gentle their rage, to draw it out into a soft, quiet lapping at the shore. Una. Where was Una? Had she heard? Did she know? Had she been there perhaps? Seen it with her own eyes? He read the cuttings again, all of them this time, line by line. Una's mother had run away from home, she had slept with a stranger in a brothel. The prosecution claimed that she had enjoyed it, that she knew what she was doing. 'They were at it like rabbits,' said the defendant. Una's father had been a pilot in the RAF. A fighter pilot. He had come to Bristol to see a friend after a week's training course in Wiltshire. He had been due to leave the following morning.

Rob pushed the cuttings away, fighting for air, for a hold, something firm, hard, reassuring, something that would make sense of this confusion, bring the day back to normal. Even if Una's father was the Philip Dart in the newspaper cuttings, even if he had been an RAF pilot, it didn't necessarily mean he was the pilot that had been killed, he told himself. No one at the flying club had said anything about the dead man being blind in one eye. And besides, they had said he was new to flying, that he had only just taken it up. It must have been someone else. Must have been. But if it wasn't someone else, if it was him, Una's father, dead now, still and cold, broken-boned, burnt-skinned, lying somewhere, in a room he didn't know, that didn't know him, he would have to tell Una. Have to tell her that her father had been an RAF fighter pilot, that he had lost his eye rescuing her mother from a drug-crazed knife attack, that her mother . . . her mother . . . that there had been a trial, a man jailed, lives seared. If he didn't tell her, she would read about it in the paper. Even if he didn't write about it, even if he pretended that he'd never found these cuttings, even if he took them home, ripped them into tiny pieces and burnt them, watching them shrivel into black with his very eyes, the story would still get out. Someone somewhere would remember, would put two and two together, would tell someone else. That was how it was with stories. They always got out in the end.

He picked up the phone. He would phone her. If it had been her father, she would know. He would be able to tell by her voice. He punched in the number. Waited. In the distance, there was the wail of an ambulance as another life turned over, flipped like a pancake by an aimless God.

'Hello. Hello? Who is it?'

Rob put the receiver down slowly, hearing her voice become more frantic and shrill – 'Hello . . . hello . . . is anyone there . . . hello . . .' – as if it might be someone ringing to say there had been a mistake, a terrible mistake, her father was not dead.

He ran out of the room, jumping the stairs, three at a time, fumbling with the lock on his car, the speed a drug, anaesthetising the pain. There might be other people there. Her mother. Martin. Relatives maybe. Friends. People who had heard, who had come to offer comfort. He hoped there wouldn't. He didn't want to talk, to explain, to accept a cup of tea and let it grow cold, wondering what to say. Una, his Una, laughing, talking, running Una, her father dead, cold and dead. Had she been there? Had she seen it happen? No . . . no . . . He switched on the radio and turned the volume up loud, shutting out the thoughts but hearing them still. Una's mother had had sex with a stranger after meeting a pimp in a pub. Afterwards, she had left the house . . . the brothel – even in his mind he found it hard to say the word, to associate it with Helen, Mrs Dart, Una's mother – but she had forgotten her handbag. The pimp had found out where her friend lived. Had followed her. Attacked her. She had almost died. Rob shook himself violently, causing the car to swerve, the driver behind to sound his horn. Seven hours earlier, he had been about to buy sandwiches for his lunch. He had been a different person then.

There was a light on upstairs, also one in the kitchen. Next door someone was calling a cat or dog. 'Jasper! Jasper! Jasper!' Further along, at the house with the swimming pool, the one you could see from Una's window, there were candle flares in the garden and the sound of voices and laughter. They were having a barbecue, the first of the year, asking about holidays and children and the health of mothers. It was like France, wasn't it, said one? She couldn't remember sitting out at night so early in the year. Her neighbour nodded agreement, complimenting herself silently on her red toenails.

Rob went to the back door and listened. There was the chink of glass then the sound of a drawer being opened and shut. He lifted his hand to knock on the door but, as he did, it opened. Una came out, wearing a green-checked apron, a bag of rubbish in her hand.

She lurched back, an arm flying up as if to defend herself.

'It's OK. It's me. Rob.'

The arm fell. She looked exhausted, her skin greyish yellow, her eyes shrivelled, the red of her mouth frayed like the end of a ribbon. He hung there, wanting to hug her but not knowing how, as if he had forgotten the right word, the months apart holding him back.

'I heard. I'm sorry. I'm so sorry, Una. I heard what happened.'

'Yes,' she said, her voice dull, not looking at him, as if now she knew who he was, she was not surprised, as if there could be no more surprises.

He held out his arms, then let them fall to his side, waiting for her to say something, to rage, rant, break down in great chest-heaving sobs – anything to bridge the silence.

'I . . . I . . .'

She did not move.

'I . . . I . . . I found these,' he said, holding out the envelope of cuttings. 'When they told me the name, I went to the library to see if we had any cuttings. I didn't know it was your father then. I thought it couldn't be.'

He paused. Still, she did not move, as if trapped, frozen, snared in that moment.

'They're about your father. About your mother too. About something that happened before you were born . . .'

He paused again, struggling to find a way that would prepare her, knowing there was no way. It was too much, too much for anyone. First the death of her father, then the death of her past or at least the past as she knew it.

'I . . . I didn't want you to find out from someone else. For someone to ring you up. Another reporter. It may be in the papers tomorrow. I don't know. I don't know what I'm going to do . . . what I should do. You'll understand what I mean when you read them. Here. Take them. I'm sorry. I feel terrible. I wish I didn't have to do this, that I hadn't ever read them. Please. Take them. I'm sorry. I'm so sorry, Una.'

He pressed the envelope into her hand, feeling the tears run down his face, turning away, ashamed, panicked. There was a burst of clapping from the garden with the candle flares then the sound of voices calling 'Speech, speech, speech!'

'It's his birthday. His sixtieth,' said Una. 'Dad would have been sixty too in a few more years. We would have held a party like them. Invited all his friends.'

Her voice was matter-of-fact, as if announcing that it was going to rain tomorrow, it had said so on the weather forecast.

He glimpsed the inside of the kitchen suddenly, the table full of tins and jars, rows of spice bottles laid out like counters in a game. Oregano, marjoram, thyme, paprika . . .

'I was cleaning out the cupboards,' she said.

She looked away.

'I had to do something.'

Then, in an instant, she was all brisk movement, opening the lid of the bin, dropping the rubbish inside.

He caught her hand.

'Una?'

'Yes?'

Now she too was crying, looking away, one foot already in the kitchen.

'I've written my phone number on the envelope. If you want me to do anything, absolutely anything, please tell me. Promise me that.'

Yes, she said. Yes, she would. And she thanked him and shut the door. Down the road, at the house with the party, they began to sing 'For he's a jolly good fellow.'

58

Helen woke early and listened to the silence. This was how it would be now, she thought. She would stretch out her arm in the morning and find just the sheet, empty, bare, white, like a shell washed clean by the sea.

He would not be bringing her a cup of tea today. Not today or tomorrow or any day. He would not be looking up from his paper at breakfast and saying 'Hey, have you seen this?' and reading her something he had found interesting or funny or moving. There would be no more talking now, no more dreaming, no more sitting outside together watching the swallows swoop as dusk fell. None of that. None of any of that. There was no more 'they'.

She dressed hurriedly, pulling on her painting clothes, the ones he had urged her to throw away, the ones he didn't like to see her wear, caring more about her appearance than she did. It was important that she did it now, quickly, while the grief was still sharp. If she waited, she would not do it. Besides, someone might try to stop her.

The picnic hamper was in the hallway, the beef casserole still in its flask, probably still warm. She would have to throw it away later, unwrap the cutlery, put the napkins back in their drawer. But all that could wait.

There had been a dew overnight, the grass wet, new cobwebs glistening in the rose bed. As she shut the door softly behind her, a magpie flew up with a great chatter and flash of wings. What did they say? One for sorrow, two for joy, three for a girl, four for a boy . . . She looked, as she always did, for a second. But none came.

She started with the tulips. They wouldn't come at first, the roots clinging on, like a child to a mother's breast. Next, she pulled up the daisies and grape hyacinth, scrabbling with bare hands in the soil he had made, soft and silky, black sugar, feeling the roots, the leaves, the stalks, the brush of petals against her skin. She piled the uprooted flowers on top of one another like corpses in a massacre. In a way, it was a massacre, she thought, seeing the holes multiply, her hands grow sticky with sap and blood. The delphiniums and hollyhocks, the tight new leaves just peeping out. The lupins. The violas and phlox. The sweet williams and night-scented stock, cornflowers and lilies, campanula and asters. She spared nothing, nothing that he had planted. If he could not live, they could not either. She could not bear to watch them grow. She did not want to smell them, to see their colours, the blues and purples he had loved best, the cheerful orange of the marigolds, the white of the stock, like young girls in moonlight, foolish and glad.

She left the roses because she had helped plant them. Also the clematis and the lilac and some of the larger shrubs. She poured the paraffin out freely then threw on a match, stepping back quickly as she had seen him do. There was a rush of flame then the crackle and spit of sap. She watched the green leaves shrivel, the yellow and red of the tulips blister and blacken. Behind her, she heard the door of the kitchen open and close but did not turn round. It was OK now. She had done it.

'Mum, what are you doing?' asked Una.

'I'm burning his plants,' she replied defiantly.

She continued to stare at the fire, the flames dying now, the paraffin all burnt, the plants too green to burn properly. Her hands were bleeding, Una noticed, her face smeared with blood and mud where she must have put up a hand to push back her hair.

'I know,' she said.

'What?'

'I know about Dad. That he was a pilot. How you met. The trial. Everything. Rob came round last night. He'd found the old newspaper cuttings. He brought them for me to read. He thinks it may be in the paper today.'

Helen lifted her hands and examined them. The nail on the

little finger of her right hand had ripped in two. She could feel it starting to hurt. She would have to go in, find plasters and cream, run the water till it was hot, soak them.

'Why didn't you say? Why didn't you tell us? We would have understood. Why did you make up all those stories?'

Helen let her hands fall, feeling her arms swing by her sides.

'You don't know everything,' she said slowly, turning to face Una.

'Martin . . . he's . . . he's . . . he's not your brother. He's . . . he's your half-brother.'

Una stared.

'You mean . . . you mean . . .'

'I mean the man I met in the brothel is his father,' said Helen.

Una swallowed hard.

'Now do you see? Do you see now? Do you understand?'

She took hold of Una by the shoulders and began to shake her.

'I don't know who he is. I don't know where he lives or what he does. I don't even know his name. Not even his name. Do you see now? How I couldn't tell Martin? Do you understand? Say you do . . . please say you do . . . do you . . . do you?'

She fell away sobbing. Una stared dumbstruck. This was her mother. Her calm, sensible mother. She stretched out a hand and touched her, tentatively at first, then more firmly, folding her in, drawing her close. And in that gesture, that one simple gesture, she grew up more in ten seconds than she had done in ten months. This was pain, she saw. Real pain. A raw wound – gaping, open. What she had been feeling, all that doubt and searching, that quest for meaning, for purposeful work, that was no more than the selfish, self-centred introspection of a spoilt child, a child who had never tasted loss or struggle or sorrow, whose definition of hardship was a pilot light blown out, no hot water for a bath. It would be different now, she saw. Everything would be different. She would be the mother and her mother the daughter, for a while at least.

'It's OK. I do understand. I do. Please, Mum . . . don't cry . . . it's all right. Come on. that's right. There. It's OK. I understand.'

Gradually Helen quietened.

'It wasn't like they said. It wasn't like they said in the papers. He didn't force me. He was gentle. So gentle. He didn't even want to. Not at first. It was me that wanted to. I could never tell anyone that. Never. And yet I wanted to. How I wanted to. I wanted to tell it like it was. Without explaining or apologising or trying to justify myself. I just wanted to tell it. Only there was no one I could tell it to.'

'You could tell me,' said Una, helping her mother walk back towards the house. 'Come on. I'll make you a cup of tea. You can tell me then.'

59

There was a student juggling in the garden outside, Una saw. He had mastered three balls but kept dropping the fourth. In the middle, on the grass, already brown even though it was still April, four girls ate popcorn from a striped cardboard box. How young they looked, she thought. How young and foolish. She found it hard to believe that only a year ago she had been a student too.

Geoff came in, his shirt the colour of rape in bloom.

'Don't!' he said, before she could say anything. 'I know. You need sunglasses. People have been telling me all morning.'

And he held out his arms to give and receive a kiss, frowning when she stayed where she was.

'Are you OK?'

'No,' she said. And she told him what had happened.

He expressed disbelief, shock, disbelief again.

'I didn't even know he had taken up flying.'

'Yes, you did. That time you came for Sunday lunch. We talked about it. He had an exam the next day.'

He was failing. He did not know it but he was failing the test. Soon, she would leave and she would not see him again. It would be over. She felt quite dispassionate.

He asked how it had happened, whether the engine had failed or her father had had a heart attack.

'We don't know. He just went into a dive as he was coming in to land. The plane exploded as it hit the ground. There was no way he could have survived.'

'You were there? You saw it happen?'

'We were all there.'

She explained about the picnic, how they had been going to have an Easter egg hunt, all of them, the whole family together.

He rubbed her right shoulder, briskly, as though to erase a stain, and said that must have been terrible, absolutely terrible. She could see he was imagining retelling the story to friends, enjoying the gasp of horror, the sympathy and respect for one involved in such a tragedy, even if only second-hand.

'Sit down. Go on. I'll get us a coffee.'

Una called out to say that she didn't want one but he was already gone, newly self-important, the partner of a girl who had watched her father die. She looked out on the garden again. The juggler was still there, still struggling to keep a fourth ball in the air, but the girls had gone, replaced by a couple, the boy lying down with his head in the girl's lap, the girl stroking his face.

Fragments of her time with Geoff lodged in her mind. He had driven past the hitchhiker, she remembered. Had called the old woman in the flat opposite a silly old bat when they had come back drunk from the pub. She remembered watching him dressing, how he had smiled at his reflection when he thought she wasn't looking. He had asked her not to put hot drinks down on the bedside table in case they marked the wood. She should have known. She should have known that first night when he looked at the hitchhiker and drove on. She had known. She had just pretended otherwise.

Geoff came back and she looked at him, seeing him as if for the first time, amazed she had lain naked next to him, had touched him, had wanted to. Had she been someone else then or was she someone else now? He had wet lips, she remembered. Blubbery.

She poured the coffee out of the window so that it splashed on to the stones below, the couple looking up in astonishment.

'I didn't want one. I don't particularly like coffee. I never have done,' she said.

Geoff looked put out but said nothing. It was the shock, he reasoned. It was only to be expected. She wouldn't be herself for a while. He would have to be patient.

He asked more questions, damning himself with each word he spoke. Had her father had a heart condition? How had her mother taken it? When would the Air Accident Investigation Board know what had happened? Una answered distractedly, watching the juggler.

'What are you doing?' he asked as she leant out of the window and began to clap.

'He did it. Four balls. He caught them all.'

'Oh, him.'

She could tell he thought it was inappropriate to clap someone for catching four balls the day after the death of one's father.

'Presumably, you won't want to go tonight, will you?'

They had been invited to a preview of a sculpture exhibition at the art gallery in Bath. She had been looking forward to going – to comparing the work with that of Sinead.

She shook her head.

'I'm staying at Mum's.'

He looked at his watch – not overtly, he tried to avoid doing that, but she caught the movement of his eye nevertheless.

'I've got a lecture. I'm already ten minutes late.'

She moved away from the window.

'I'll go.'

'Are you sure you're OK?'

But he did not offer to cancel his lecture, he did not say he was sorry her father had died even though it was not his fault, he did not try to hug her. She waited for him to save himself but he was already gathering his books and papers together.

She opened the door.

'Una, wait, where are you going? Wait!'

She ran down the stairs. It was at the flood now, the tide in her life. She had to grasp it, ride it. Otherwise, she would be lost. Crushed to silt on the shore. She ran faster. Faster and faster. She did not look back.

'You are joking, aren't you?' said the hairdresser, lifting her hair with both hands and letting it flop down. 'I know women who would kill for hair like this.'

'No,' said Una. 'I want it off. All off.'

'You haven't had a row with your father, have you? Or your boyfriend? Only if you have, don't you think you'd better wait until . . .'

'My father's dead.'

There. That had stopped her. Una sat up straighter, sensing her new power.

'How short do you want it?'

'Like that.'

She pointed to a picture in a magazine. The hairdresser began to cut.

When it was over, Una ran her hands through the stubble that was left.

'I'll take this,' she said, bending down and picking up a long golden hank from the floor.

'It will remind me of what I used to be.'

Una phoned Geoff that evening knowing, despite herself, that part of her still wanted him to pick up the phone, to say he was coming over, now, he didn't care what she said, he wanted to be with her. There was no answer.

She phoned directory inquiries to find out the number of the art gallery, hearing the murmur of other voices in the background – normal people with normal lives, giving out numbers for restaurants and cinemas. Cassandra answered.

'It's Una. Una Dart. I don't know whether you remember me. I came over a few months ago with Geoff Smart to see the Nina Bouchier exhibition.'

Cassandra began to wail, saying it was terrible, an absolute tragedy, Geoff had told her, he had phoned her that afternoon, said she wouldn't be coming . . .

'Is Geoff there? Has he arrived?'

'Yes. Just this minute. Would you like to talk to him?'

Una said yes, she would and heard the clunk of the receiver as Cassandra let it fall. He would be eating canapés soon, licking his fingers, explaining that a red sticker meant the exhibit in question had been sold, yes, he would have another glass of champagne, thank you.

'Hello? Una? Are you there? Una. Are you still there? Una?'

He had been laughing before he came on the phone. She could hear it in his voice like she could smell what he had eaten by the scent of his skin.

'Goodbye.'

'What? What do you mean? Una? Say something. Please. Una!'

She put the receiver down and felt her head with the palms of her hands. It was ticklish, prickly raw.

'There is a tide . . . which taken at the flood . . .'

There. She had done it now. She was on it, riding it. She would not be lost.

60

At night, Una dreamed of the flight. Not of the crash but the flight. The way the plane had risen, bold and straight, like the line made by a pen on a piece of paper, blue on white, reversed.

She had thought she would dream of the crash, had feared it, putting off going to bed that first night in case she saw it again – the wobble, the tilt sideways, first one way then the other, and then the dive, the sickening lurch in her stomach as she started to run, to scream, knowing she would never reach him, never be heard.

But instead she dreamed of the flight. The majesty of it, like a cathedral stolen into at dawn, silent, ghostly, the white stone chill against bare feet. She would fly. It was obvious. She would be a pilot. Like her father. Unlike him. Now that she knew, it was what she had always wanted to do.

The RAF careers officer said she needed two A levels and five GCSEs. It was a long selection process. She would have to have an interview in Bristol first. Her application would then be forwarded to the Ministry of Defence for approval. If this was granted, she would be sent to Cranwell, the RAF training centre in Lincolnshire. She would be tested in Maths, English, hand and eye co-ordination, judgement of time, speed and distance, memory, leadership, computer skills, fitness, general knowledge, airforce knowledge. At the end, she would be interviewed by four officers who would fire questions at her about anything and everything. There was a high failure rate. If she succeeded, she would be accepted on the six-month basic training course. After that, she would start to train in the trade she had chosen. Why didn't she come into the office? He could give her more information then. Una said yes, she would, and made an appointment for later that week.

'Why do you want to be a pilot?' asked the RAF officer, leaning back in his chair, flexing his hands. It had been a long day and he was finding it difficult to concentrate. That evening he and his wife, Jane, infertile due to a botched appendix operation when she was ten, would meet the child they had been invited to adopt, Thomas, aged two, an orphan.

Una was swift to reply, as if she had been lying in wait for this question, stalking it all afternoon.

'Do you believe flying is a vocation – you know, like being a painter or dancer?'

The officer looked taken aback as if she had asked whether he wore pyjamas in bed.

He leaned forward, his curiosity aroused.

'Yes, I do. I do. Very much so, in fact. Why?'

'Only that's how I feel. When I left university, I didn't know what I wanted to do. All I knew was what I didn't want to do. And yet I had this feeling, I don't know why, that there was something I wanted to do, something that was made for me, and that if I waited, I would find out what it was. And so that's what I've done. That's what I've done all year. Waited. And then, a little while ago . . .'

She paused, wondering how much to say, how much she wanted to say.

'Someone I knew took up flying. I went to see them fly one day and as soon as I saw the plane take off, I knew. It was like suddenly understanding long division. As soon as I knew, it was as if I'd always known. It felt so easy and right. So obvious.'

She paused.

'I suppose that sounds silly. Silly and romantic.'

'No,' said the officer slowly, taking notes.

Three weeks later, Una received a letter inviting her to attend the selection tests at Cranwell. Her application had been approved by the Ministry of Defence.

61

Una came downstairs to find her mother up, the marmalade already on the table, blueberry and lemon, a present from Rob. One of many.

'What's that?' she asked.

'Matty's duck,' said Helen, tugging at the string so that the duck waddled across the table, narrowly missing the teapot.

'They found it. These as well.'

She held up the goggles she had given Philip in Istanbul.

'Look, they're not even scratched.'

Una examined them. She had not told her mother about the letter, had not even said she wanted to be a pilot. She was thinking of a way, the right way, the way that would not hurt.

'They thought I might like to have them. They've sent a tape as well. What he said as he . . . before he . . . before he went down.'

Una took the bread out of the bin and cut two slices. Two crooked slices. She had never been able to cut bread straight. Her father had always complained about the waste – great heels of bread thrown away because they were four inches thicker on one side than the other.

'Anything else? In the post, I mean.'

'A bill from the pest control people. A postcard for you. That's all.'

Una met her mother's eyes.

'He might not have seen it,' she said. 'He might have been away at the time.'

It had been in all the papers. National as well as local. On the television too. Everyone knew. Bridget and Kate at the refuge, Julie, even Rachel in London. Mrs Chandler was no longer speaking to them. It was hard to believe he had not heard. If he wanted to, he would be able to find them easily. Dart was a common name but it was not that common. There were only twenty-seven Darts in the Bristol phone book. She had counted.

'If I just knew his name. Just his name. That would be something. Something to tell Martin.'

Una frowned, wanting to be able to say that it didn't matter, Martin didn't care, but knowing that it did matter, he did care.

She picked up the postcard. It was from Sinead – a brief lyrical account of eating mango on her balcony one Sunday morning, the juice dripping down on to the street below, a man shouting up, saying his shirt was stained. Her work was going well, she wrote. She had been offered the chance to exhibit in a gallery, quite a good one too. She had made a curry the night before. Chicken with red split lentils. There was a delicatessen near by that sold black olives in oil and herbs, fresh coriander, and pecorino cheese, both young and matured, as good as one could buy in Italy. She had discovered it by accident diving into a doorway one evening to shelter from the rain. The owner was Lebanese-French, with an Irish great grandfather. She was teaching him how to throw pots.

Una smiled and propped the card up against the blueberry marmalade. Sinead and the delicatessen man were lovers. That was her way of saying so. She had never been direct when it came to relationships, treating them as if they were fragile and insubstantial, a head of dandelion seeds, liable to be blown away by a movement too sudden, a word too loud.

'Come on.'

'Come on what?' asked Helen.

'Let's listen to the tape.'

She knelt on the rug in the sitting room, took out the tape already in the machine and inserted the tape handed to her by Helen. It was labelled on one side only – P. Dart, followed by a reference number.

There was a rush of noise, like air heard through the window of a moving car, a voice, his voice, both strange and familiar, like much-loved music rediscovered.

'He said your name. At the end. "Helen." Listen.'
Una rewound the tape and pressed the play button.
'Yes, yes, you're right,' said Helen slowly.
So he had been thinking of her. He had said her name, the last word he had said.
'Play it again.'
Una rewound the tape to the start.
'That sounded like "washing".'
'No, it's two words. Listen.'
Una pressed the stop button, rewound the tape again.
'Wash shing, fling, thing, no, there's a "t" in there. Of course, "sting". He's saying "wasp sting." The pathologist was right. He was stung by a wasp. He's telling us he was stung by a wasp.'
'What about the next bit?'
'Sounds like tie. Then something beginning with "g". Girl. Ger. Ga. The next word starts with "b". Bet something.'
'Tiger better!' shouted Helen, hearing it suddenly, how it would sound if it was slowed down, slurred, the last squeezings of speech from a thickening tongue.
Una played it again.
'Tiger better. Tiger better. Yes, I can hear it now.'
Helen frowned.
'What does he mean? Better than what?'
Una repeated the words, trying them out, like a baby faced with a new taste, uncertain whether to spit or swallow.
'Better than sheep,' she said suddenly, her face lighting up with recognition. 'That's what she said. That woman who was killed climbing a mountain. K2, I think. "Better to live one day as a tiger than a thousand years as a sheep." Only afterwards, when she'd been killed, everyone was saying it would have been better if she'd lived as a sheep because she had two children. Don't you remember? Dad cut out the story from the paper. It was on the noticeboard in the kitchen for ages.'
'Tiger better,' said Helen softly, as if speaking to herself. 'I suppose he was saying he knew he was going to die and didn't regret it because he'd lived as a tiger again after all those years as a sheep. Yes. That's right. I understand now.'
She rewound the tape and played it again, a smile hovering

just out of sight. Una relaxed. She would be better now. Thank God he had lived long enough to say her name.

'If you had to choose between living one day as a tiger and a thousand years as a sheep, which would you choose?' asked Una.

They were on the swings in the park, their movements synchronised, legs forward then back, forward, back, the way fathers taught their children.

'Both,' said Rob, grinning. 'One day as a tiger and then a thousand years as a sheep.'

'You can't choose both. One or the other. Which? Go on!'

'A sheep then. A thousand years as a sheep. Quantity rather than quality.'

'I'd be a tiger,' said Una, letting her head flop back so that all she could see was the sky, two blue arms waiting to hold her.

Rob laughed.

'You don't need to tell me that. You're pure tiger. Unadulterated. Unsweetened. Red in tooth and claw.'

'I'm not red in tooth and claw!' protested Una.

'Yes, you are. Look!'

He pointed to a purplish mark on his arm, shadowy, indistinct, like a shape glimpsed under water. Una had made it wielding a barbecue fork on the banks of the River Wye one May Bank Holiday.

'That was an accident,' she protested. 'I slipped.'

'Yes, well . . .'

'I did!'

She began to swing higher and faster. When she was small, her father had taken her to the park on Saturday mornings. They had gone to the newsagent's first and bought a paper and two threepenny mixes, one for Martin, one for her. The sweets came in a paper cone, pink on the inside, white on the outside. As soon as they arrived at the park, Martin would run off on his own towards the big slide or the climbing frame, scornful of their company. She always went on the swings first, the square ones with bars to stop you falling out.

'Come on,' he would say, lifting her up. 'Let's see if we can kick that cloud down. Let's catch a piece of sky to take home to Mummy.'

And she had believed him. As she rose higher and higher, toes outstretched, she had thought she really would touch the sky. When she stopped and got down, she would look at her shoes and be surprised to see there was no blue there, not even a scrap of white. Next time, she had thought, her belief undiminished. Next time I'll do it.

She closed her eyes, leaning back, stretching forward, toes pointed. Maybe this time. Maybe this time she would do it.

62

Una lifted the flaps of a cardboard box and peered inside. Christ, he hadn't wrapped anything up! How could he be so stupid when he was so clever.

'Martin!' she called. 'You can't leave these like this.'

He looked up from the corner where he was packing dried food in a plastic carrier – pasta, tomato purée, rice – the bag closed with a clothes peg to stop the contents spilling in the back of Helen's car.

'Why not? We're only going a mile down the road. I didn't wrap them when I came.'

Una sighed and began to take the crockery out of the box.

'Hey, what are you doing?'

'Teresa won't be very pleased if you turn up with a load of smashed plates. These were a wedding present, remember. A *joint* wedding present.'

Martin hesitated.

'OK. As long as you don't take too long. Matty's going to a party at three. I said I'd take her.'

He was going back, much to the relief of Helen and the delight of Matty. She'd made a special monster out of her new Lego to show him when he arrived.

Una packed quickly, humming in tune with the music playing low on the radio. Outside, it was raining again, April rain in May, over as soon as it had started. The window was open and she could hear a mother telling a child off, the child answering back, their voices drowned as a motorbike roared past. She used broadsheet pages for the plates, tabloid for the cups and saucers, wedging them tightly in case she had to brake sharply.

Halfway through the second paper, she came across their story, a 'follow-up' as Rob had told her it was called, the one based on the report from the Air Accident Investigation Board saying the crash was due to pilot action rather than mechanical failure. It was on page nine – the story had moved back gradually as the days passed, from page one to page three to page five and then a jump to page nine. The last story had been just three paragraphs long on page sixteen, a left-hand column squashed next to a review of an organ recital at St Mary Redcliffe. She read the story now, even though she had already read it, had cut out another copy and pasted it in her scrapbook along with all the other cuttings.

'Did you ever know?' she asked suddenly. 'Did you ever guess that Dad wasn't your father?'

Martin looked up, a box of garlic in one hand, a packet of dried yeast in the other. The carrier had started to split, Una noticed. She would have to put it inside another one.

'At a subliminal level, yes, I suppose I've known for a long time,' he said. 'And then, I don't know, about a year ago, I needed my birth certificate for something, some form I was filling in. I was looking at it and I suddenly noticed there was only one name on it – Mum's name. I didn't think much of it but when I mentioned it to Mum later she became quite defensive. That was when I really started to wonder. About all sorts of things. Why there were no photos of our grandparents on Mum's side. None. Why she never talked about them. Why, if Dad had really injured his eye in a firework accident, he was so relaxed on bonfire night. I mean, if my eye had been blown to bits by a rocket I wouldn't have gone near the damn things again. And yet he didn't seem to mind at all. Why I looked so different from the rest of you. Black hair instead of brown or auburn. Green eyes. Pale skin. When we were small, do you remember, people were always saying how different we looked, how they would never have guessed we were brother and sister?'

'Yes, I suppose so. I never thought anything of it at the time.'

'Neither did I. Not then. But later I did. And then there was Dad. I'm not blaming him, I'm not saying he did it consciously – I'm sure he didn't – but he treated me differently to you. It wasn't that he favoured you exactly – he didn't, at least not openly – but there was something, something in the way he looked at me sometimes, or spoke to me, that was different. Now, now that I know, I can see that he was scared of me. No, scared's not the right word. Wary, rather. Apprehensive. When you came home from school and said one of your poems had been chosen to go in the school magazine or that you'd been made captain of the hockey team, he could rejoice with you wholeheartedly. He knew where he was with you. He knew who you were, where you were from. With me, it was different. When I came home and said I'd come first in the inter-school chess league, he was pleased, yes. But he didn't . . . he couldn't feel that genuine paternal pride that comes from feeling that your child's success is your success. He couldn't share my success in the way that he could share yours. He didn't feel part of it. Also, it scared him. What else, he thought? What else has he inherited that we don't know about? And it didn't help that I was so different. I mean, it wasn't just that I looked different, I was different. We didn't like the same games, the same food, the same TV programmes, nothing. We had absolutely nothing in common, not even our shirt size.'

'Do you think he will get in touch?'

Martin shrugged his shoulders in the quick, dismissive way she had found so infuriating when they were younger.

'No. Probably not. He didn't then, during the trial. Why should he now? He doesn't even know I exist, remember. Anyhow, he's probably got children of his own. Grandchildren as well. As well as Matty, I mean. Why should he rake up the past?'

'But you want him to, don't you? You do want him to?'

'Yes and no. Yes because I want to know. I want to know who I am, where I'm from. At the moment, I feel incomplete, like a jigsaw with some of the pieces missing. No, because I might not want to know what there is to know. I mean, it was a brothel, after all. And, once you know something, you can't unknow it.'

He glanced at his watch.

'Come on. We'll have to get a move on. Didn't Mum say she wanted the car this afternoon?'

'Yes, but only at four. She's delivering the talking newspaper with Jane.'

She wrapped the last cup and saucer and sealed the box firmly with parcel tape. There were two boxes of crockery, one of saucepans and assorted kitchen utensils and two bags of food. In the bedroom there was a suitcase, a laundry bag, portable radio, two bin liners full of bedding and a box of odds and ends, a large framed photo of Matty sticking out of the top. They loaded the car in between showers, a double rainbow appearing as they finished.

Matty was waiting for them when they arrived, standing by the window on her plastic, 'Grow Tall' step, looking anxiously up the road. She pulled Martin inside.

'I've got something to show you, Daddy. A surprise. Come on.'

And she led him into the sitting room.

'Look! A monster. It's got three heads. One for you, one for Mummy and one for me. Which one do you want, Daddy?'

Martin pretended to give the question serious thought.

'I think I'll have that one,' he said, pointing to a yellow square with a black tube protruding from its top.

Matty looked disappointed.

'I need that one. That's so that I can breathe under water.'

'Oh, right. OK. I'll have another one.'

'Why don't you have this one, Daddy?' said Matty, pointing to the head sprouting two red roof tiles at right angles to its cheeks. 'You have big ears too.'

'Do I?' said Martin, feeling his ears, small by the standards of most adult males.

'Sort of big.'

'Oh, OK. I'll have that one then.'

Matty crouched, pulling Martin down with her.

'Look, it's got lots of windows. Can you see?'

'I can . . .'

'Do you like it? I made it for you. It's a surprise.'

'I think it's lovely. Thank you.'

Listening outside, watching them hug through the crack of the door, Una thought: 'If he could see this, he would want to get in touch. However many children he has or grandchildren. He wouldn't want to miss seeing this.'

63 ∫

Helen was on her knees in the garden when she heard the gate open. Damn, she thought! She had wanted to get these planted before she made supper. She sat back on her heels, screwing up her eyes to see. But the sun was low, streaming down the path. She could see only a shape, a man, stocky, small, coming towards her, pausing, coming on again. She put up a hand then struggled awkwardly to her feet.

But it was only the window cleaner, come to collect his money, saying what a lovely evening it was, glorious, it would go on all summer like this if he had his way. She paid him, nursing her disappointment as she counted out change, pressing it down, stemming the flow like blood from a cut finger.

One day it would be him, she told herself, glancing down at her feet where the flowers she had been going to plant lay waiting in plastic trays. Pansies. On special offer at the garden centre. Philip would have been horrified. But one had to start somewhere. For it was June now, a picture of hay meadows near Lechlade on the calendar in the kitchen. She had survived the funeral and the inquest and had gone back to work. In the mornings she no longer cried when she stretched out her arm and found bare space.

She moved the plants into the shade and washed her hands in the kitchen, watching the soil, the soft brown soil Philip had made, mix with the water and drain away. One day she would hear the gate and look up and it would be him, she told herself as she took an onion from the vegetable basket and began to slice it thinly. He would tell her his name. Michael. Michael Donovan. Say that his father had been Irish, hence the name and the accent. Add that he had taught English, linguistics mainly, the development of the English language. His father had never forgiven him.

She took a frying pan and poured in oil, waiting for it to heat before she added the onion. He would explain that he had been away, three months in New Zealand. That was why he had not come before. He had not known.

She stirred the onion and wiped her eyes with the back of her hand, imagining him here, Martin's father, standing talking to her, evening coming in through the open window. He would say what had happened that day, that Friday afternoon in September 1969. How his wife could not have children. How they had stopped making love, stopped talking, stopped sharing anything. How that day he had gone for a walk, had walked and walked, not looking where he was going, just walking, wondering where it would end, how long they could go on like they were doing – not talking, not sleeping together, not even eating at the same time. How he had sat down somewhere, he didn't know where, and Vic had sat down next to him, taken him by the arm and led him to her room. He had not asked where they were going, he said. He had just followed. He was not trying to make excuses. He was just saying that at that moment, that particular moment, he would probably have gone anywhere with anyone. When Vic had opened the door and showed him in, he had been as surprised as her. He had not, it had not . . . not been how they said in the papers. Had it? Had it?

She imagined him looking up at this point, his expression pleading, imploring, as if he doubted his memory of what had happened that day, had begun to think he had made it up. And she saw herself consoling him, touching him lightly on the shoulder, breathing in his smell, that smell she remembered – leaves, wood smoke, dug earth – saying no, he was right, it had not been like they had said.

She opened the fridge, took out the steak mince she had bought that morning at the butcher's and added it to the onion, turning up the heat, browning it quickly.

She would ask him to write it all down, everything – his name, age, job, everything he had told her, in case she forgot, in case she thought she had dreamed it. Afterwards, when he had finished, when she had taken the paper and folded it in four, tucking it into her shirt pocket, she would ask him into the sitting room. She would find the album with photos of Martin and hand it to him, open at the front page, at the picture of a baby, asleep in his cot, one tiny fist poking out from the blanket.

'That is our son. Martin,' she would say. 'I called him Martin.'

There would be a long silence and finally he would look down, would start turning the pages. She would leave him and when she came back he would have reached the last page, the one showing Martin holding Matty, and would be staring at it, his chin cupped in his left hand, a posture that seemed familiar, that would make her frown, wondering where she had seen it before. And then she would smile. Of course. She had seen it in Martin. She knew why now.

Thinking this, picturing the scene, Helen wiped her eyes again, the tears real now.

64 ♪

'Hurry up,' Rob urged.

Una fumbled with the straps on her shoes.

'You still haven't told me where we're going,' she complained, irritable at being woken so early, at being told to get dressed quickly, there was something they had to do.

'Ssssh! You'll wake Mum. Besides, I said. It's a surprise. You'll find out when we get there.'

She pulled on a jumper and struggled into her jacket, her arms stiff and clumsy. Rob opened the door. As they went out, she glanced at the clock on the wall above the cooker. Half past five! Damn him. It had better be good.

There had been a dew overnight, the grass still wet, shimmering in the pale first light of the sun. He drove towards Bath, turning off soon afterwards on to a narrow lane, the verges steep with cow parsley, fragrant with wild garlic and dogrose. She wound down the window and breathed in deeply. There. That was better. She had woken up now, shaken off the last sticky trails of sleep.

'When did you say your course started?' he asked abruptly.

'September.'

She had passed the selection tests, had been accepted as a trainee RAF pilot. In September she would leave Bristol to start her training.

'But I'll come back often. I'll have to. There are no hills there. I won't be able to stand it. Anyhow, that still gives us two whole months.'

He turned left then right, the car climbing steeply. Suddenly, she knew where they were going. They were going to their hill, the one overlooking Bath, her favourite place. They had not been back there yet, had not even mentioned it as if both sensed that it was too soon, their wounds too fresh, too lightly healed.

'Are we . . . we are, aren't we . . . we're going to . . . ?'

He stretched out a hand and stopped her mouth gently.

'Don't,' he said. 'Don't guess. I want it to be a surprise.'

But she was right. He parked where they had always parked, next to the barn at the end of the lane, and switched off the engine.

'Come on.'

'Come on where?'

'You know.'

And he took hold of her hand.

The wood was alive with birdsong, dappled with light and shade, the rinse and run of colour – the sharp bright green of the leaves, the dark green of the moss and ivy, the greys and browns and silvers of the bark. Una could smell the warm earth, steamy with growth, the sweet decaying odour of old leaves rotting, the dead feeding the new, the new reaching out, stretching up to touch the sky, long and lovely, a rush of green.

They came out into the open, the bright blue like a slap, forcing them to stop and blink, to give their eyes time to adjust. For the sun was up in earnest now, rising fast, pushing down the last purplish black shadows that still lingered in the west.

Una could make out a shape in front of them, something new, something that had not been there before.

'What is it?'

'Go and see.'

It was a tree, six foot high, its roots wrapped in black plastic, a hole already dug, fencing erected to protect it from animals, one side left open.

She stared.

'You said it needed a tree. That that was all it needed. A tree to give some shade.'

Yes. She remembered now. She remembered saying that.

'Come on. It's your tree. You've got to plant it.'

He took a knife from his pocket and cut the roots free from their black plastic cladding. She felt the leaves. They were soft, floppy, newly sprung, like silk.

'But the farmer . . . what if . . . ?'

'He said yes. He even helped me put up the fencing.'

He opened the sack lying next to the tree and took out a spade and trowel, also a hammer, wire clippers, staples, a mallet.

'So that's what you were doing yesterday afternoon.'

'Yes. That's why I left the tools here. I didn't want you to see them in the car. I didn't want you to guess.'

He lifted the tree upright and squeezed through the opening in the fence.

'Come on.'

She followed him and knelt by the hole, grasping the slim trunk just above the roots, steadying it to make sure it was balanced.

'What is it?'

'A beech. Because of the look of the leaves. Especially in sunlight. Besides, it's mainly beech in the wood.'

She placed the roots in the hole and pulled at the earth piled high on both sides, first with her hands, then with the trowel, and finally, standing up, with the spade.

She stamped the earth down.

'There. Is that firm enough?'

'I don't know. Let me see.'

He let go of the crown and felt the earth with his feet.

'Yes. I think so. I've brought a stake anyhow to stop it getting bashed about.'

He fetched the stake and sunk it into the grass near the base of the tree, using the mallet to drive it down deep.

'There. All done.'

He stepped back and flung the mallet on the ground, drawing Una close.

'Thank you,' she said and lifted her mouth to his.

They stood there, arm in arm on top of the hill, watching the young branches finger the air.

There was no answer, thought Una suddenly. There was only looking and striving. And one had to look, to keep on looking, even though one knew one would not find. Rob was not the answer even though she loved him. Nor was flying even though she loved that too or would do. This, possibly, was the beginning of the answer, this joy, this being alive and feeling alive, feeling it all around her, rejoicing in the light, the land, the throb of the earth. But it was only the beginning.

She broke free from Rob and began to run down the hill to where the green met the gold and beyond that, the blue, the blue rushing forward to meet her, rising up, gathering her in.

'Una! Where are you going? Una!' shouted Rob.

She called out something but her words were caught and blurred by the breeze.

But he thought, he was sure, he would almost swear she had said: 'Touch the sky!'